MURDER
ON A
SCOTTISH
ISLAND

BOOKS BY LYDIA TRAVERS

THE SCOTTISH LADIES' DETECTIVE AGENCY SERIES

The Scottish Ladies' Detective Agency

Murder in the Scottish Hills

Mystery in the Highlands

Death in a Scottish Castle

LADY POPPY PROUDFOOT SERIES

Death at the Highland Loch

MURDER ON A SCOTTISH ISLAND

LYDIA TRAVERS

Bookouture

Published by Bookouture in 2025

An imprint of Storyfire Ltd.
Carmelite House
50 Victoria Embankment
London EC4Y 0DZ

www.bookouture.com

The authorised representative in the EEA is Hachette Ireland
8 Castlecourt Centre
Dublin 15 D15 XTP3
Ireland
(email: info@hbgi.ie)

ISBN: 978-1-83618-465-2
eBook ISBN: 978-1-83618-464-5

To Julie
Partner in crime and brilliant writing buddy

ONE

August 1924

'Looking forward to seeing you soon, Catriona.' Poppy put the telephone receiver down on the side table and turned to her lady's maid.

'We need to start packing, Elspeth,' she said, uncrossing her shapely legs and rising from the chair in the hall of her Edinburgh house. As she did so, she caught a glimpse of herself in the gilt-framed mirror. Glossy chestnut bob, hazel eyes with a hint of gold-brown and a determined chin; the latter was essential when dealing with Inspector MacKenzie of the Edinburgh Detective Branch. 'An old friend has invited me to stay on the Isle of Skye,' she went on. 'We leave tomorrow.'

'Skye, is it, my lady?' Elspeth gave a small, disapproving sniff as she made her way towards the wide staircase. 'You'll be needing sensible, warm clothes, I expect. It will surely be a wee bit nippy in the evenings that far north. I've heard they are little more than barbarians there,' she went on, 'although I suppose the Inner Hebrides must be more civilised than the Outer Hebrides.'

Poppy sent her maid a quelling look. Elspeth was middle-aged, some three inches taller than Poppy's five feet two, with a thin face and grey curls pinned close to her head – and she was a force to be reckoned with. Lesser women, not to mention lesser men, had been known to quail before a stare from Elspeth's eagle eyes, or a word from her sharp tongue.

But Poppy's look was wasted on Elspeth, who didn't appear at all abashed. Poppy laughed. 'You are being ridiculous, as you will soon find out for yourself. Skye is to the west, which is warmer than here in the east. Besides, Inspector MacKenzie is from the Outer Islands and you surely don't think he is a barbarian?'

Elspeth turned, her foot on the bottom step, to look back at her employer. 'He's a police officer, my lady, so he cannot be a gentleman. But I'll say no more on that point, as it's not my place to do so.'

Poppy had met the police inspector in June when two murders had taken place on the Balfour estate in Culross where she had been staying with her lady's maid. Poppy, with a little help from Major Lewis, her eager-to-please four-year-old black Labrador, had assisted Inspector MacKenzie in bringing the murderer to justice.

She thought of the American director, and his leading man and lady – the handsome Eddie Peavey and the brash blonde bombshell Beth Cornett – all fellow guests at that midsummer party at Balfour House, and sighed. Despite the cocktail parties taking Edinburgh by storm, Poppy's life had seemed rather dull since then. Perhaps it was something to do with the delectable Inspector MacKenzie not being at any of them...

'Perhaps a new case will fall into my lap while we're on Skye,' she said.

Elspeth shuddered. 'We must hope not, your ladyship.'

Poppy disagreed, but she said to her maid, 'Come into the

library before you pack and you can help me choose where we will break our journey for a night.'

Poppy strode jauntily into the book-lined room, Elspeth following. Major, stretched out on the rug, opened one chocolate-brown eye, looked at them, and closed it again. Poppy crossed to one of the shelves, took down her old school atlas and flipped through the pages.

She rested her finger on an island off the west coast of Scotland. 'There is Skye.'

'I've heard it's very bonnie,' Elspeth conceded, thawing a little.

'I believe it is.' Poppy paused for a moment as she recalled her tall, thin, whiskery-chinned geography teacher at Edinburgh Ladies' College. Of the seventy-nine islands that make up the Inner Hebrides, the woman had informed the young ladies, only thirty-five are inhabited, and of these Skye is the largest. It is also exceptionally beautiful, Poppy could hear the woman add, a rapturous expression on her face, with its rising mountains, cascading waterfalls and flaming sunsets.

'We will stay in Portree, the capital of the island,' Poppy went on, 'at the hotel my friend owns, *Eilean a' Cheò*.'

Poppy's grandfather, like Catriona's, had later in life been a civil servant in India, and their respective wives had gone with them. Poppy's mother, missing her own mother, had taken young Poppy to stay with her parents for two months. Catriona's mother had done the same with her wee girl, and the two six-year-olds had formed a lasting friendship. This was the first time Poppy had visited the Skye hotel now owned by her dear friend Catriona and her husband Rory.

'Catriona tells me it's Gaelic for Isle of the Mist,' Poppy added, 'which is also the Gaelic name for Skye.'

Elspeth peered at the map and frowned. 'There are a lot of mountains between here and there, my lady.'

'We won't be climbing them on foot,' Poppy pointed out. 'Fergusson will drive us in the Bentley.' She examined the map again. 'It looks as though we will take the road from Edinburgh to Inverness, then to Kyle of Lochalsh and finally the boat over the sea to Skye.'

She broke into song, her alto almost hitting the high notes.

> *'Speed, bonnie boat, like a bird on the WIN-N-*
> *NG,*
> *Onward! the sailors cry...*

'Very nice, your ladyship,' Elspeth said quickly, before Poppy could finish the chorus.

Poppy saw the pained look on her maid's face. 'Yes, Elspeth, I know a lady doesn't suddenly hit the vocals, but you must admit there's something about "The Skye Boat Song".'

She bent her glossy chestnut bob back to the map. 'What do you say to our breaking our journey at...' She tapped on the map. 'Plockton? I've heard it's a charming village on the shore of Loch Carron, known as the Jewel of the Highlands.'

'Plockton may be charming,' Elspeth began disparagingly, 'but—' She caught sight of Poppy's expression and gave a resigned sigh. 'Shall I inform the butler of our departure, tell Fergusson to prepare the car, and reserve rooms in an hotel in Plockton, my lady?'

'Thank you, Elspeth. Oh, and don't forget to pack my sketchbook, will you?'

Elspeth turned and left the room, softly humming "The Skye Boat Song".

Poppy smiled.

'My lady,' Inspector MacKenzie said, lifting his cap as he reached her. A breeze stirred his dark curls.

Poppy's heart gave a small but unmistakeable leap as she looked up at him. There was something quite delightful about this man with his seductive Hebridean accent. As to his uniform – the high collar, the well-buttoned-up jacket hugging his athletic frame – it was rather like the inspector himself, she thought. It would be fun to unbutton him, in the metaphorical sense, of course...

Her Labrador was making his presence felt by nudging the policeman's leg. Inspector MacKenzie smiled and bent down to stroke the dog behind one ear.

'Inspector MacKenzie.' Poppy had not seen him since Lady Balfour's midsummer party in June. 'What a pleasant surprise.'

He straightened and replaced his cap. 'I heard you were leaving for Skye this morning, your ladyship.'

This was another surprise. 'How on earth did you know that?'

One dark eyebrow rose. 'I am an officer of the law, my lady. We have our methods.'

Poppy frowned. 'But I don't see how my movements can be of any interest to you.'

'You never can tell, your ladyship.'

'I don't believe I've committed any sort of crime recently...' She tapped her foot. Fergusson was still holding the car door for her, and Elspeth hovered, waiting for Poppy to take her seat.

'Have you come for any particular reason, or simply to wish me an enjoyable holiday?' Poppy asked.

Inspector MacKenzie fixed her with his dark gaze. 'I have come to ask you to make a concerted effort to keep out of trouble while you are away, my lady.'

Under her bright blue beret set at exactly the requisite angle, Poppy opened her hazel eyes wide. 'I will do my best, Inspector, but I really can't promise.'

.   .   .

The Bentley left Edinburgh, crossed the Forth and into the wooded valleys of Fife and Perthshire.

They stopped for coffee at the village of Blair Atholl and admired Blair Castle, the home of the Duke of Atholl, the only person in the United Kingdom allowed to raise a private army to act as his personal bodyguard. What fun to march with the Atholl Highlanders, she thought, remembering the writer H.G. Wells's description of the Great War as 'the war to end war'. It was comforting to think there would never be another world conflict.

Then, leaving the village and castle behind, the Bentley climbed the high mountain Pass of Drumochter with a splendid view of the snow-capped mountains beyond. They sped through the majestic Cairngorms, bustling Aviemore, the vast ancient Caledonian Forest of Scots pine, and some six hours after leaving Edinburgh, they finally skirted the sombre battle-field at Culloden Moor.

They were coasting into Inverness when the Bentley spluttered and juddered, steam billowing from under its sleek bonnet.

Fergusson drew the car safely to the side of the road, where it came to a halt. 'There seems to be a problem, my lady. I will see what it is.' The chauffeur pulled on the hand brake and hopped out. He folded back the bonnet and with his gloved hands wafted the steam away.

Elspeth fidgeted in the front passenger seat, as Fergusson's head with its peaked cap disappeared under the bonnet. 'I do hope it isn't anything serious, your ladyship,' she said.

'I'm sure we all do,' Poppy told her maid. 'Any idea what the trouble is, Fergusson?' she called to him.

He withdrew his head. 'The engine has overheated, my lady, and the radiator is leaking. I can't say I'm surprised, with all these hills we've been going up and down. It looks like she may need a new radiator.'

'Oh dear, that does sound serious...'

'Not too disastrous, my lady, but it does mean the Bentley will need to go into a garage for repair.'

Elspeth tutted. 'We will have to spend tonight here in Inverness.'

'Not at all.' Poppy reached for the car door to climb out, and Fergusson hastened to open it for her. 'Do your best for the Bentley, Fergusson, and get the garage and any accommodation you may need to send me the bill. Elspeth and I will take the train, and you can follow on when the car is ready.'

'The *train*, my lady!' Elspeth looked in horror at Poppy's red coat, her blue dress with its three layers of pleats showing underneath. Her gaze travelled down to Poppy's blue T-bar shoes. 'But you are not dressed for public transport!'

'Nonsense.' Poppy stepped out of the car and accepted the fur stole which Elspeth grimly handed to her. 'A lady is always prepared.' Or was that a Girl Guide? No matter, Poppy thought, the principle held.

Besides, she was stiff from the journey and looking forward to stretching her legs. She rearranged her blue beret, smoothed her gloves and took her beaded bag from Elspeth.

'It is lucky I packed your overnight bag for the night in Plockton,' Elspeth muttered, turning to lift the small case from the back of the car.

'Not luck, Elspeth,' Poppy said with a smile, 'but the foresight of an *exceptional* lady's maid.' Ignoring the caustic look Elspeth sent her, she clipped the leash onto Major's collar and followed the sign towards the railway station. 'We will enjoy the scenery from the train window of the ladies' compartment,' she called back to her maid, who was collecting her own overnight bag. 'But first, we have time for a decent lunch in the station buffet.'

The echoed words, '*Station buffet*,' came bitterly towards Poppy from behind.

. . .

As the train pulled out of Inverness railway station, Poppy removed her blue kid gloves and settled back in the first-class carriage, prepared to enjoy the magnificent views the four-hour journey had to offer. Major curled up on the floor between the two women with his head resting on Poppy's foot, and was soon snoring. Elspeth held on her lap the small valise containing Poppy's inlaid walnut jewellery case and stared stonily out of the window.

Station after station passed by, fertile land at first, then changing to magnificent mountains, their tops wreathed in mist, and wide tracts of forest.

'Isn't nature wonderful?' sighed Poppy.

Elspeth chose not to reply.

Up and down the railway line went, until they were climbing so steeply that Poppy pitied the fireman shovelling hard in the hot cab to maintain steam. She looked at the guide-book, resting open on her red-coated lap.

'We're on the four-mile climb to Raven Rock,' she read aloud from her *Burrow's Guide to the Scottish Highlands*. 'A high cliff where the ravens hold their annual ball.'

Almost immediately Elspeth drew in a sharp breath, as if it would help the train squeeze through the narrow pass between the rocks. Within minutes they were speeding down again, the clackety-clack of the wheels on the track growing faster, towards the shores of another loch shining like a jewel in the late after-noon sun.

They were halfway through their journey when they slowly approached the signal box at Achnasheen. A signalman stood waiting by the side of the track.

'I wonder what's happening?' Poppy let down the leather strap to open the window and put her head out.

'My lady, come back in!' Elspeth called anxiously from her seat. 'You will get clarts all over your face!'

'It's only soot, Elspeth. It'll wash off.'

As the train drew close, the fireman leaned out of the cab, a satchel-like token in his hand. On his outstretched arm the signalman caught up the loop of the oncoming satchel and with his other hand passed his own token to the fireman, and they were off again at speed.

'Elspeth, isn't this *thrilling?*' Poppy tugged at the window strap to close it and pushed the brass knob through one of the holes in the leather to secure it. 'I think we will travel by train more often in the future.'

'I'm sure Fergusson will be pleased to hear that news,' Elspeth muttered.

Mountain after mountain rose in the distance. The sparkling lochs with shores of sand and pebble seemed only a few feet from their window. The vista gave way to clear burns bubbling over stony beds as the water meandered through grass-land dotted with sheep. Once again, the engine began to struggle as they travelled uphill.

'This must be Luib Summit,' Poppy said, consulting her guidebook to the Highlands. 'It's the highest point of the line with eight miles of hard climbing.'

Overhead the buzzards hung; then, past the summit, the train gathered speed as it descended. It dashed along for some miles, until the line began to rise again.

'Achnashellach.' Poppy read the platform sign as they steamed into the station. 'Burrow's Guide says that thirty years ago this was the site of an incident.'

'What sort of an incident would that be, your ladyship?' Elspeth asked warily.

'Well, we're at the top of a steep incline. The engine was detached to do some shunting. The rest of the train, which had a broken rear brake, rolled back down towards Achnasheen. Fortunately it slowed when it reached the uphill gradient—'

'That's a mercy.'

'And then it started rolling forward again.'

Elspeth's jaw dropped.

'Unfortunately,' Poppy continued, 'the engine had been sent back to pick up the coaches, but by this time it was dark and it crashed into the rest of the train travelling towards the engine. Eight passengers were injured, but thankfully there were no deaths.'

Elspeth smoothed the wool of her navy-blue lady's maid coat. 'That's enough of that story if you please, your ladyship.'

They continued on their steep drop through ancient pine forest towards the sea. As they approached Strome Ferry, the line ran alongside the edge of Loch Carron, winding in and out under the shadow of a huge rocky cliff with roaring waterfalls.

'Dear me!' Elspeth went pale. 'If the rocks fall we'll all be crushed, or the train will be dashed into the water—'

'It's perfectly safe, Elspeth,' Poppy told her. She indicated through the window of the slowly-moving train a linesman, in dusty clothes and a cap, standing by the side of the track waving a green flag. 'If it wasn't safe to proceed, his flag would be red.'

They travelled along the rocky coastline, around curves and over small bridges; passed through Duncraig Halt, a private station for the use of Duncraig Castle; and finally swept round the shore of a little bay where Poppy could see a cluster of dimly lit cottages as the sun grew low. Plockton.

Poppy glanced at her wristwatch. 'On time,' she said. 'Half past seven.'

As they pulled into the station with a great cloud of steam, a red-haired boy strolled along beside the train, bawling, 'Plock-ton! Plockton Station!'

The stationmaster slipped his watch into his waistcoat

pocket, bustled forward and opened the door of their compartment.

'Good evening, madam.' He touched his cap as he assisted Poppy to climb down. 'I'm afraid the local taxi hasn't yet returned from an earlier fare.'

'Is the village far?' she asked him, as Major jumped down onto the platform.

'A little over half a mile, madam.'

'Then the taxi is of no matter,' Poppy said. 'We have only a small amount of luggage and can walk.'

Elspeth alighted, and handed their tickets and Major's to the stationmaster. 'We need our bags from the luggage rack,' she informed him.

The stationmaster called for the porter and the red-haired boy hurried over, retrieved their luggage from the compartment and set the two bags down on the empty platform. As Poppy tipped him, Elspeth took up the bags.

'I'm perfectly capable of carrying my bag for half a mile, Elspeth,' Poppy said, reaching for the handle.

'It's easier to carry two bags because it evens up the load, your ladyship,' Elspeth told her firmly, keeping hold of both and turning from the station.

Major trotting on the leash beside Poppy, they walked down the leafy hill, past the parish kirk sitting in darkness on their right and the lighted Plockton Inn on their left. Ahead of them they could see Loch Carron shimmering as the last of the sun's rays prepared to slip behind the mountains.

The path curved to the left and the village came into sight, wrapped in the warmth of the summer night. Cottages, of crofters and fisherfolk Poppy guessed, lined the bay, facing the waters of the sea loch. Harbour Street was deserted save for a ginger cat on its nightly rounds. There was no sound to be heard but the gentle murmur of the water and the cry of a lone gull as it settled in its nightly lodgings. Ahead, at the end of the street, a country lane could be seen winding its way uphill.

'How charming it all is!' Poppy declared.

'I hope the hotel is not as *primitive* as the village, my lady,' Elspeth muttered.

'Not primitive, Elspeth,' Poppy observed wonderingly, 'but the sort of quiet, remote place where one imagines dark deeds might be committed...'

TWO

Poppy and Elspeth came to a halt outside a well-lit establishment in the middle of the row of cottages. It looked very much like its neighbours, but it was larger, and the words 'The Harbour Hotel' were painted above the door. They entered the small, plain hall to find a cheerful fire burning in the grate and a cluster of females twittering like agitated sparrows.

A tall, thin woman in a black dress detached herself from the group and came towards them. '*Feasgar math.*'

'*Feasgar math,*' Poppy repeated the Gaelic evening greeting. 'I am Persephone Proudfoot, and this is my maid, Elspeth. We have two rooms booked for tonight.'

'Oh yes, your ladyship. I am Miss Grant, the hotel manageress. You are very welcome.' Despite her words, she looked a little uneasy.

'Is there a problem, Miss Grant?' Poppy asked, when the woman made no move towards the reception desk. 'You *are* expecting us?'

'Indeed we are.' The manageress smoothed back a strand of greying hair which had escaped from her tight bun. Seeing

Poppy glance towards the little group of women, she added reluctantly, 'I am sorry, my lady, we are a little at sixes and sevens this evening.'

'Has something happened?' Poppy asked, a shiver of excitement travelling up her spine.

'Certainly not in this hotel, your ladyship.' The manageress straightened her back. 'Now, I will get the boy to show you to your rooms. Would you like tea to be sent up, and perhaps a late supper in the dining room?'

'That would be delightful.'

The manageress nodded, turned and clicked her fingers at the hotel boy, who hurried over. He led Poppy and her maid up a flight of carpeted stairs, let Elspeth into the first room along the passage and showed Poppy into the one next door. He pocketed her tip with a *'Tapadh leibh*, my lady,' before giving Major's ear a quick tweak and leaving them.

'The bedrooms are acceptable,' Elspeth conceded, coming into Poppy's room. Her gaze went over the old-fashioned furniture, its polished surfaces shining in the firelight from the small hearth. She set Poppy's leather case on the ottoman standing at the bottom of the bed, undid the catch and began to unpack.

Poppy pulled off her beret, dropped it on an easy chair and threw herself onto the bed. She stretched out all five feet two inches of her on the cover, her hands folded behind her chestnut bob. 'I wonder what the manageress meant when she said *certainly not in this hotel.* It sounded intriguing, don't you think?'

'No, I do not think so, your ladyship.' Elspeth paused in the act of slipping Poppy's emerald-green tweed suit onto a hanger to send her a stern look. 'Have a mind to what that inspector said as we were leaving Edinburgh this morning.'

'To have an *enjoyable holiday?*' Poppy enquired in an innocent voice.

'If I remember correctly,' Elspeth said, in a tone of voice that left no doubt she did, 'it was to keep out of trouble.' She turned and hung the suit in the wardrobe.

'He need have no fear, Elspeth. I am looking forward to getting out on the hills, where nothing untoward can possibly happen.'

Poppy climbed off the bed, crossed the floor and opened one of the casement windows. 'Look, Elspeth, there's Duncraig Castle. We passed its private station on the way here.' In the distance she could make out the impressive dark shape with its crenellated towers across the water.

'Aye, my lady, I have the same view.' Elspeth didn't sound impressed. 'I hope you're not proposing to walk to it.'

Poppy smiled as she turned from the window. 'I know your idea of a long walk is the distance from the front door to the Bentley, but—'

There was a soft tap on the door and it opened. A pretty young woman of slight build entered, carrying a tray laden with tea things, her fair hair curling softly around her head. Major looked up, hopeful, from where he sprawled on the blanket provided by the hotel.

'Tea,' Poppy said with enthusiasm. 'Please put the tray there.' She indicated the low table set in front of two armchairs.

The chambermaid did as she was bid, bobbed a little curtsy and turned to go.

'One moment, please,' said Poppy. 'What was the cause of the disturbance in the entrance hall just now?'

'Miss Grant says it's nothing to worry about,' the girl replied quickly.

Elspeth paused in her unpacking.

'All the same, I'm interested,' Poppy went on.

Elspeth set down a jar of cold cream on the dressing table with a thump.

'It's just that one of the guests hasn't returned yet for her dinner, miss,' the girl said.

Oh, was that all? Poppy couldn't quite hide her disappointment. She had graduated with a degree in law when she was twenty-one, four years before women were permitted to train as solicitors, and she longed for real-life puzzles to solve.

'I'm sure Miss Grant is right, in that it's nothing to worry about,' Poppy said. 'Thank you for the tea. What is your name?'

'Katy, miss.'

'Thank you, Katy. We will be down for supper in about fifteen minutes.'

The chambermaid bobbed again and left the room.

Poppy let out a long, heartfelt sigh as Elspeth pulled open the top drawer of the chest of drawers. 'I hope my lady isn't too downcast to discover there is no mystery here.'

'I think I am.' Poppy sat down in an armchair and took charge of the tea tray. 'I've poured out two cups of tea, Elspeth.'

Major gave up hope of anything to eat, sighed heavily and lowered his head to his paws.

'I will just fold away your garments, my lady.' Elspeth paused. 'The chambermaid here is slovenly. There is something at the back of this drawer, which means the girl has not put in clean lining paper after the last resident.' She withdrew several objects, small enough for all of them to fit in the palm of her hand.

'What have you got there, anything of interest?' Poppy asked.

'Nothing, unless you count a cheap earring as interesting,' Elspeth tutted.

'Can I have a look?' Poppy held out her hand.

Elspeth dropped the contents into her mistress's hand. She took the armchair opposite, lifted her cup and saucer and sipped at the hot, deep gold liquid with satisfaction.

Poppy studied Elspeth's treasure haul. A button, a small piece of white card and the small stud earring. She tossed the button and the business card into the waste-paper basket and studied the earring. It was nothing more than a piece of costume jewellery.

'I don't think I need to change this evening,' Poppy said. 'My dress is quite smart enough. As soon as we've drunk our tea, I will wash and we'll go down to supper. I'll give this in at reception. Someone might come back for it.'

In the dining room, as Poppy and her maid ate fluffy omelettes, she realised how hungry she had been. Two elderly ladies, who had been amongst those chattering earlier when she and Elspeth had arrived at the hotel, were also taking a late supper.

'Ellen must be with her mystery man, to be out so late,' giggled a thin woman with flat, grey hair, to her companion. She leaned forward and lowered her voice, which was still perfectly audible to Poppy. 'Did you notice Miss Grant's face when we came in just now? I thought she looked positively sick. I expect she thinks she won't be long running the place if the owners find out she has allowed a loose woman to take up residence here.'

'Dorothy!' snapped her plump friend, who was seated across the table in comfortable-looking tweeds of faded greyish blue. 'The only loose woman in this establishment is you, with your talk.'

Poppy's ears pricked up. Always keen to uncover a mystery, she pretended to consider the customary print of Landseer's *Stag at Bay* on the wall as she ate.

'Oh, I don't think so,' went on the thin woman.

'Do you not?' The chastising tone of the stout woman's question made Elspeth turn to see who was about to disturb their meal. 'Ellen Clark is the middle-aged widow of a Kirk minister, cast adrift by life's hardships. She deserves our fellowship, not our ridicule. Though how a woman with such a sensible background can be sent into a giddy whirl by a wee bit of attention from a man, I'll never know.' She took a sip of her tea.

The smaller woman set her teacup down in its saucer. 'Aye, I suppose you're right. Ellen is such a quiet wee thing. You wouldn't think she was the type to stay out late with this fellow, whoever he is.'

'She has been *most* secretive about him,' her friend went on. Suddenly, she became aware of Poppy and Elspeth at the next table, eating silently. Oh dear, Poppy thought, she knows we are eavesdropping. She sent Elspeth a warning look to stay silent and, giving a casual nod to the two women, turned her attention back to her omelette.

The thin woman leaned towards Poppy and Elspeth's table. 'You must think we are sklaiks,' she said, 'gossiping like this about Ellen Clark.'

'Not at all,' Poppy replied politely.

'The truth is that we're a wee bit concerned about her...'

It didn't sound that way, thought Poppy.

'According to the serving staff, she's never been late back to the hotel before. The manageress, Miss Grant, is most particular about guests giving notice if they will not be here for dinner. My friend and I have been out all day, so we'd requested a late supper.'

Poppy inclined her head. Was this the genuine mystery she hoped for, or just a woman too enamoured with her new beau to care about missing dinner?

The woman in baggy tweeds sat back in her seat and settled her bosom on her folded arms. 'Ellen has changed since she met this man of hers. His attentions have gone straight to her head.'

Poppy felt a brief pang of something surprisingly close to envy. She was also a widow, with her husband Stuart killed nine years ago, in the Battle of Loos in the Great War. Poppy was not yet thirty and there was no man in her life. A part of her thought, good for Mrs Clark for taking a second chance at happiness. But as the manageress of the hotel seemed genuinely concerned for Ellen Clark's non-appearance, perhaps something had happened to this seemingly respectable, middle-aged woman.

The waitress entered the dining room, her face aglow with excitement.

'Has Mrs Clark returned, dear?' the thin woman asked the waitress.

'Oh no, miss.' The waitress was clearly bursting with news and she deemed this question permission to tell it. 'Miss Grant says if the lady is not back by the time the sun sets at half past nine, the hotel will send out a party of men to search for her.'

Poppy glanced at her wristwatch. It was just after nine o'clock. 'It looks like a search party might be needed,' she said firmly.

'Aye, it does.' The waitress straightened her apron. 'Would you both be wanting anything else to eat? There's some nice Dundee cake.'

'We will each take a slice and a cup of tea,' Poppy told her.

The waitress bobbed a curtsy, removed their plates and departed.

'Do you know Mrs Clark well?' Poppy went on conversationally, ignoring the sharp intake of breath from Elspeth.

'Och, no, not at all, really,' replied the thin woman. 'She is a resident at the hotel and Miss Buccleuch and I' – she nodded at her friend – 'are here for a few days' holiday. But we've had the occasional blether with Ellen, of course.'

'She seemed a pleasant sort of woman, if a little shy, and dainty, you know,' put in the tweedy friend. 'Not the type to go gadding about, thither and yon, with some chap she barely knew.'

Seemed? thought Poppy. Miss Buccleuch was speaking about Ellen Clark in the past tense.

The waitress chose that moment to return with a tray

containing their tea and cake, and the two dowdy ladies on the next table excused themselves.

'Cheerio,' said the thin woman as they left the room.

'*Cheerio?*' Elspeth murmured. 'How *common*. And that hole in the back of the heel in the large woman's worsted stocking. Well!'

'Perhaps it's a recent mishap while they were out today.'

Elspeth shuddered. 'It's been darned, and not very neatly at that.'

Left alone in the dining room, they ate in silence, Poppy wondering what the disappearance of the usually respectable Ellen Clark might mean. Elspeth suddenly set her cake fork on the plate with a clatter and said, 'I don't like what you are thinking, my lady.'

Poppy, her cup of tea held in mid-air, looked in astonishment at her maid. 'You cannot know what I am thinking.'

'Maybe not, your ladyship, but I can guess.'

Poppy smiled. 'My thought was that I will now go out...'

'My lady, you cannot mean to join the men in the search party!' Elspeth looked horrified.

'I don't intend to do that. Really, Elspeth! I was about to say I will now go out and walk Major,' Poppy said, being economical with the truth. She finished her tea, dabbed a finger on the remaining few crumbs on her plate, ate them, and rose. 'I won't need you any more this evening, Elspeth. I can see to myself. Good night.'

Before Elspeth could voice any further objection, Poppy strode purposively out of the dining room. In the little entrance hall, the male servants, clean-shaven and in hotel uniform, were gathering. There were other men, too, who she guessed from their full beards and thick jumpers under workman-like jackets were local fishermen. The harassed Miss Grant was attempting to organise the noisy groups.

'Miss Grant!' Poppy called out, 'I wonder if I could have a word?'

'Yes, of course, your ladyship.' Miss Grant hastened over to her. Further wisps of grey hair had escaped from the manageress's bun and the tired lines on her face were deepening. 'How can I be of assistance, my lady?'

'I'm rather hoping it's a case of *my* being able to assist *you*,' Poppy told the other woman. 'I have been training my dog to find various objects and he's doing rather well. Labradors have a particularly acute sense of smell, you know. I haven't yet tried him with finding people, but if you could let me have a personal item from Mrs Clark's room, it's worth a try.'

'I'm sorry, my lady, are you offering the men a loan of your dog?'

'Not a loan. Major is a one-mistress dog. I am suggesting that I take him to search.'

'You, my lady?' Miss Grant was taken aback.

'Yes, Miss Grant. I have some experience of investigating crime, hence training my dog. Only two months ago I helped Inspector MacKenzie of the Edinburgh Detective Branch investigate a murder.'

'Goodness!' Miss Grant stared at Poppy in admiration.

Poppy smiled modestly. 'We must, of course, hope that this is not a case of murder – but my skills might be useful, nonetheless.'

A look of hope entered Miss Grant's eyes. 'It's an excellent idea. I'm sure I can find something suitable in the lady's room.'

Poppy nodded, pleased her suggestion had been received so well. 'I'll fetch Major from my room and meet you down here in a few minutes.'

Poppy hastened up the stairs, Miss Grant on her heels. She turned along the corridor for her bedchamber, while the manageress went in the other direction. As soon as Poppy entered her room, Major, already standing guard by the door, pounced. It would have been impressive, she thought, if his tail hadn't been wagging furiously.

'Honestly, Major,' she scolded affectionately, 'I could be someone entering to steal my jewellery and you would give them a warm welcome.'

Poppy changed into a pair of brogues and pulled on her red coat. She scratched the Labrador under his chin. 'Would you like a walk?' she asked. The dog sat, his tail thumping loudly on the wooden floor. 'That's a yes, I believe.' Removing his leash from the peg on the back of the door, she gave him a serious look. 'You will also be working, so don't think it will be all fun and games.'

He skipped to his feet, gave a small *woof* and followed her down the stairs.

Miss Grant arrived back in the hall within minutes. 'I found a pair of gloves in the top drawer of Mrs Clark's dressing table, your ladyship.' She held out a brown kid glove.

'That will be perfect,' Poppy assured her as she took the soft leather.

'Your ladyship, please take care—'

'I will!'

As she went out the front door, Poppy could hear Miss Grant calling the little search party to order. The village was tiny, so most of the search would take place around the scattering of houses. If Ellen Clark was not found, the loch and the fields which lay beyond the main street would need to be searched the following morning, in daylight.

Poppy paused on the hotel steps. The moon was almost full, rising above the dark hills, its white reflection lying on the surface of the water like a disc of marble. She shivered, and prayed that the missing woman had not slipped into the depths of Loch Carron.

The sounds of the search party in the hall behind her grew louder, more urgent. Clearly the men were anxious to be away and doing their job. Major was of the same opinion. His glossy black nose twitched, his head alert. Poppy held out Ellen Clark's glove to the dog and he sniffed it.

'Major, *find.*'

He sniffed the ground, then set off eagerly, turning right and along Harbour Street. Poppy stuffed the glove into one of the pockets of her coat, the dog's leash in the other, and hurried to keep up with him. His nose to the ground, Major followed the scent as the road curved up and into Innes Street, past the inn on one side of the road and the parish kirk on the other. Major suddenly swerved off the path. He scampered up a flight of roughly made stone steps set in the grassy verge. She darted after him.

They went under a rubble arch and emerged into a grassy amphitheatre. What a curious place, she thought, coming to a halt. It was full of dusky shadows, but as she stood there, her eyes adjusting to the gloom, Poppy could make out that the slopes had been cut into grass-covered terraces where people could sit.

An open-air church, she realised. Some eighty years ago, the Church of Scotland had split over the right of parishioners, rather than landowners, to choose their ministers. The miffed landowners had refused land to the newly-established Free Church on which to build their churches. The Disruption, as it was known, had resulted in a number of open-air churches setting up in the northwest Highlands.

Poppy's gaze went round the little open-air kirk. She could see a corrugated iron shed, which would be used to protect the minister from the elements while he preached to his congregation.

Major, nose still close to the ground, intent on his search, wagged his tail furiously as he made his way around the little amphitheatre. He turned back to the shed and stopped.

'Have you found something, Major?' she cried, hurrying towards him. 'Good boy!'

Her feet sure in the brogues, she crossed the grass to the shed and stared at the door. Was Ellen Clark really inside? Major seemed to be telling her she was.

In the case of the body at the loch in Culross, her dog had found a murdered man, but on that occasion he had simply come across him. This was Major's first *search* for a person, so he could be wrong...

Ellen was the widow of a minister and it was possible she had come here to pray for her late husband, but would she have shut herself into the preacher's shed?

Her heart thudding, Poppy put out her hand, lifted the latch and, holding her breath, slowly pushed open the door. It creaked on its hinges.

A dark object loomed in the shadows. Poppy shrieked and took a step back, feeling nausea rise in her throat.

Then she laughed with relief. 'That's not Ellen Clark, you foolish creature,' she told the dog, 'just the minister's wooden pulpit.' She bent down to tug the dog's ear and gasped, her hand flying to her mouth. 'Oh, dear Lord!'

The moonlit figure of a petite lady lay crumpled on the floor.

THREE

In the bright moonlight flooding in from the door, the woman's face looked as though it were made of marble. A scarf circled her neck.

Poppy gazed at the prone body. 'Mrs Clark?' she whispered, '*Ellen?*' She stepped closer.

Taking care not to disturb the ground around the prone woman, Poppy crouched down, tucking her skirt under her. A pale blue scarf was sunk deep into the skin around the woman's neck. Even without the ligature, Poppy could see this was a case of strangulation. Ellen's face and neck were swollen, her eyes bloodshot.

Poppy rose. There was no doubt about it, she thought, the local policeman must be called. She looked at Major. Could she leave him to stand guard? Best not, they hadn't got to that part of the training yet.

'We'll try in here, men!'

Poppy's head jerked up at the shout of a male voice calling from the street. There were sounds of agreement and flickering beams of electric torchlight. The little group of men tramped in under the rubble arch and stopped when they saw her standing at the open door of the minister's shed.

'Gentlemen,' she said, 'you are a little late, I'm afraid. My dog' – credit where credit is due, she thought – 'has found the poor lady.' She glanced down at Major, who sat on the grass looking from her to the men and back, his tail wagging.

The men stared at Poppy and then at the Labrador.

'Classic signs of strangulation, I believe,' she supplied. 'Would one of you gentlemen be kind enough to lend me a torch?'

Stunned, the man at the front of the party, a slight, clean-shaven fellow, silently handed her his torch.

'Thank you.' She took it, crouched down and directed the beam onto the victim's neck. 'That's better, now I can be more certain. Swollen face and lips, petechiae – that is, small red dots – on nose, and burst blood vessels in eyes.' She gently lifted Ellen's chin. 'Scratch marks under chin, lesions to neck.' She paused to raise one arm of the body. 'Rigor mortis not yet present, so she has been dead for less than three hours.' She examined Ellen's hand, and repeated the gesture with the other hand. 'Bruising on fingertips, where she tried to stop the scarf being tightened.' Poppy got to her feet and stepped outside the shed.

She addressed the gathering. 'With the scarf still in place, there's no doubt of it being ligature strangulation. The police must be informed immediately.'

The slim fellow who had lent her his torch now spoke. 'I am PC Macduff.'

'I am very pleased to see you, Constable.' She handed him back his torch. 'You will wish to take a statement from me, of course.'

'Aye, that I do, miss. But first, if you'll excuse me?' He gestured for her to move aside, then stepped into the shed. He shone the beam of light on the unmoving figure, before stepping out again and turning towards the men. 'Alasdair, you stay here. The rest of you go back to the hotel and tell Miss Grant to get the doctor up here as a body has been found. It's verra likely to be Mrs Clark.'

There were murmurs of agreement as the small search party made their way out. The sound of the men's subdued talking faded into the night air, leaving Poppy and the constable looking at one another. The other man, Alasdair, waited in the shadows.

Constable Macduff switched off the torch and felt for his pocketbook and pencil, before remembering he was not in uniform. 'I need to ask your name, miss,' he said.

'Lady—'

His eyebrows went up.

'—Persephone Proudfoot.'

'And your address, please, my lady?'

'Dunearn Castle, Perthshire. But I am currently staying at the Harbour Hotel.'

He nodded. 'Did you know the deceased?'

'I'm afraid not. My maid and I arrived only this evening, and learned that Mrs Clark was missing.'

'And what made your ladyship enter the open-air kirk at this time of night?' There was a suspicious edge to the policeman's tone. Did he suspect *her* of strangling the woman?

'My dog,' Poppy indicated Major, who had grown tired of sitting nicely and was wandering around the moonlit grassy arena. 'I offered his services to Miss Grant for the search party and he brought me here.'

Constable Macduff gazed at Major. 'It's a pity we havena got a police dog in the village.' He shook his head. 'Did you ken that Glasgow was the first police force in Britain to use dogs? 'Tis a pity they've no' been used for ten years now. Mainly Airedale terriers they were, brave and strong, specially crossbred with collies for their brains. There were a few retrievers, used for their sense of smell.'

'Major embodies all those qualities,' Poppy pointed out proudly.

'But then one of the dogs bit a constable's leg.' Macduff eyed the Labrador worriedly.

'Major would *never* do that,' she said firmly.

Constable Macduff recollected the reason he was there. 'Well now, your ladyship,' he said, sending her a look of admonition for wasting his time talking about canines, 'we need to be thinking about Mrs Clark. So your dog brought you here and you found the lady?'

'That is correct, Constable. He was sniffing around the minister's shed and when I opened the door I discovered her body.'

Constable Macduff switched on the torch again and shone it inside the shed. 'I canna see a handbag,' he said thoughtfully. 'Would a lady go out without her handbag, do you think?'

'Not unless she were walking her dog.'

The constable looked at her sternly. 'It would have been safer for you to stay in the hotel.'

'I had no reason to think I was unsafe, Constable. Mrs Clark was simply a missing woman when we set out.'

'Aye, well... would you say the scarf is likely the lady's own? I'm thinking that it must have been a robbery that got out of hand.'

'I would say that it is a lady's scarf, and therefore likely to be her own,' Poppy agreed.

Constable Macduff sighed as he turned off the torch. 'That's what I thought. I'll let you ken if I'm needing any further information.'

'That's it?' Poppy asked in surprise.

'Nothing can be done at this time of night, my lady,' he told her, an authoritative tone creeping back into his voice. 'The doctor will be here shortly and I'll wait for him. It's my duty to do so, but you'd best be returning to the hotel.' He called to the man waiting in the shadows. 'Alasdair!'

'Aye, Robert?' The man came forward.

'Take her ladyship back to the hotel. We dinna want her to become another easy target for the thief.'

Poppy stared at Constable Macduff. Had the man not listened to what she had said? 'I think you mean another victim of the murderer.'

'She has been killed, I grant you that, but it's no' likely someone would set out to murder a nice, respectable lady like Mrs Clark,' he said. 'A robbery gone wrong is my opinion.'

'And if you don't wish to look foolish, my good man, I'd keep that opinion to yourself,' Poppy said crossly.

Oh dear, had she really said *my good man*? But he was being so stubborn!

'Now look—'

'How many thieves do you know who would drag a woman into a preacher's shed to rob her? I bet the answer is none. Street thieves hit and grab, then run for it. House breakers tend to wait until everyone is asleep or out. No one wants to hang for robbery, so why would this thief of yours bring her here?' Poppy took a deep breath. If the constable wasn't going to investigate properly, then *she* would. She glanced around for her dog.

'Now look here, miss...'

'Major, come!'

The Labrador's ears perked up; he turned from his exploration of the ground and bounded over to where she stood. 'I think Major will be quite enough protection for me over the short distance between here and the hotel, thank you, Constable. Major, heel,' she commanded, and set off towards the arch, leaving Constable Macduff and his companion staring after her.

If only men were as obedient as her dog, she thought, as she passed under the arch and descended the steps.

Poppy turned towards the village. The road was deserted. Slits of dim light showed between the curtains of a few cottages, but most were in darkness. A dog barked somewhere and she glanced down at Major. He sent her a glance that indicated he wanted to answer the distant canine, but at her stern look he decided against it.

'We need to focus on the case, Major,' she told him. 'And find poor Mrs Clark's killer.'

FOUR

Poppy had put Major in her room and was now comfortable in the sitting room of the Harbour Hotel, nursing a glass of whisky provided by Miss Grant, and a notebook and pencil in her lap. Mrs Clark's glove lay on the table between them.

The small room was overcrowded, after the fashion of an earlier day. There were too many chairs, and too many small tables littered with too many wee silver models of animals.

'The men from the other search party have been informed that Mrs Clark has been found and they've returned to their homes, very subdued as you can imagine,' the manageress, perched on the edge of her chair, told Poppy sadly. 'And what a shock you have had, my lady. Indeed, we all have. Poor Mrs Clark. I don't know what she could have done to deserve that.'

'She couldn't have done anything to deserve such a dreadful thing, Miss Grant.'

'And in such a place,' went on Miss Grant. '*A kirk*,' she whispered. Her thin face looked exhausted in the light of the oil lamp.

'That does seem to add insult to injury,' Poppy agreed.

'You don't think it was because of the Disruption, do you, my lady?' Miss Grant's eyes were wide. 'Someone who didn't approve of the creation of the Free Church?'

'The Disruption was in 1843, Miss Grant, so I very much doubt that. Besides, I see there is a kirk in the village.'

Miss Grant nodded distractedly. 'Yes, that was built two years later. But the open-air church is still used occasionally for Communion services.'

And memories can be long in out-of-the-way places, Poppy silently acknowledged as she took a sip of her whisky, feeling its warmth seep through her body.

'Strangled with her own scarf, is what I hear.' Miss Grant's voice was low.

Poppy looked with surprise at the manageress.

'Some of the housemaids are related to the men in the search party,' Miss Grant explained. 'Is it true what they said about her scarf? I ask because you saw Mrs Clark's body...'

'It may well have been her own scarf. It was a pale blue, as far as I could tell.' The face of the strangled Ellen Clark loomed into Poppy's vision like a spectre. 'But moonlight can distort colours.'

The manageress nodded, pressing her thin hands together in the lap of her black dress. 'The poor lady often wore a pale blue silk scarf.'

'Mrs Clark had no handbag with her,' Poppy went on, 'so Constable Macduff thinks it was some sort of a bungled robbery.'

'Do you think that is the case?' Miss Grant asked quickly.

'I don't know. I expect we will learn more tomorrow.' Poppy sighed. 'What was Mrs Clark like?'

'It was a pleasure to have her here. She's been a resident at the hotel for almost a year and was such a quiet and respectable lady.' Miss Grant was adamant. 'She couldn't have had any enemies.'

Someone wasn't too fond of her, Poppy thought. 'Before she went out this evening, did Mrs Clark say anything to you about her plans? Where she was going and with whom?'

The manageress shook her head. 'No, my lady. Though it's fair to say she had been quite lively since she'd' – Miss Grant gave a small cough – 'met this gentleman, and she was always excited about telling me where he was taking her that day. Yesterday, young Malcolm took them out on his boat; he's always happy to provide trips for holidaymakers when he's not fishing. Mrs Clark came back thrilled to have watched seals and dolphins, sailed past Duncraig Castle and Heron Island, and to have seen the magnificent views of the mountains.'

'So in fact she was very happy last night?'

'Perhaps a little too happy...'

Poppy frowned. 'What do you mean?'

'I don't know how to describe it.' Miss Grant sent her a worried look. 'There was a strange sort of glitter in her eyes.'

Poppy nodded. 'Go on.'

'I asked her if she was all right, and she said she was feeling a wee bit tired and would go to bed early as she had a headache. Before she retired, I asked her about her plans for today, and she said Mr Henderson was going away the next day for a week on business, so she had no plans to go anywhere.'

So the mystery man had a name, thought Poppy. 'That's helpful. Do you mind if I jot this down?' Miss Grant didn't object, so Poppy opened the notebook on her lap, wrote: *Day One of Investigation into the Murder of Ellen Clark* at the top of the page, and began to make notes.

'Someone should contact Mr Henderson to let him know what has happened to her,' Poppy went on. 'Is the nature of his profession known?'

The manageress shook her head. 'Mrs Clark never said.' She paused. 'She was rather subdued today.'

'Subdued?' Poppy asked softly. 'Do you think they could have had a disagreement yesterday?'

'Oh no, nothing like that, I'm sure.' Miss Grant sounded a little flustered and she tucked a straying grey lock behind her ear. 'She just seemed to have something on her mind. Probably the fact that she wouldn't see her gentleman friend for a week. Or it might have been nothing at all to do with him.'

That was true. 'What time did Mrs Clark go out today?' Poppy pressed.

'It was some time after tea.' Miss Grant wrinkled her brow as she tried to remember. 'I was on the reception desk and I mind her passing through the hall, dressed nicely as usual. Yes, I glanced at the long-case clock and saw it was getting on for half past six. We serve dinner at seven o'clock and I reminded her of that.'

'What did she say in reply?'

'That she wouldn't be long.'

'And that was all? No indication at all as to where she was going?'

Miss Grant shook her head. 'None. I assumed she simply wanted a walk to work up an appetite for dinner. She showed no interest in her breakfast or lunch today.'

What else could she usefully ask? Poppy wondered. 'Did Mrs Clark receive any letters today that might have brought bad news?'

Miss Grant thought for a moment. 'No, I'm sure she didn't.'

'Or any visitors?'

Miss Grant shook her head. 'Not that I'm aware of.'

'Have you ever met this man, Mr Henderson?' Poppy asked. 'That is, did he come to the hotel in a car?'

'I never saw Mrs Clark's gentleman with a car.' Miss Grant shook her head. 'He would wait for her in reception.'

'Could you describe him?'

'Let me see. Personable, I suppose. Of middle age, quite tall, grey hair and beard.'

As Poppy added this to her notes, another thought occurred to her. 'Miss Grant, do you think you could look in her room and see if her handbag is there? And the blue silk scarf you remember seeing her wear? It's just possible she may have gone out without them. But if they are not in her room, then that lends weight to the notion of a robbery.'

'I suppose I could. Yes, that's an excellent idea, my lady.' The manageress rose, invigorated.

'Oh, and Miss Grant – may I come with you?' Seeing the woman hesitate, Poppy added quickly, 'It's quite possible my trained eye will spot a clue you would miss. And I will make sure that we disturb things as little as possible in case the police want to search the room.'

Miss Grant's brow cleared. 'I'm sure that will be acceptable to Mrs Clark.'

The poor woman isn't coming back to find it acceptable or not, Poppy reflected bleakly.

She closed the notebook, slid it into her pocket and they mounted the stairs. Poppy followed the manageress into Ellen Clark's room. It was as neat and tidy as a pin, which she had expected, given the description of the late occupant's character.

'If her scarf is still here, it would be in the chest of drawers, I imagine.' Miss Grant moved towards it and slid open the top drawer.

'And her handbag perhaps in the press.' Poppy threw open the door of the wardrobe.

A row of dresses, skirts and blouses, arranged according to colour, mainly shades of brown and beige, hung on hangers like soldiers on parade. There was tidy and there was tidy, Poppy thought. She directed her gaze to the top shelf. Arranged neatly in there were two sensible hats, one brown, the other beige, and a large brown handbag.

'Is this her usual bag, Miss Grant?' Poppy asked, as she reached up and took it down.

Miss Grant turned from the chest of drawers and came quickly over. 'It's her usual day bag, my lady, but not the small one she takes out in the evenings. That one is a crocodile-skin clutch bag with a crocodile and marcasite button clasp, quite distinctive.'

Poppy opened the capacious bag, but the emptiness yawned back at her. 'No clues there,' she said regretfully, closing it and replacing it on the shelf.

She gazed around the room as Miss Grant returned to searching the chest.

'I can see no sign of the blue scarf, my lady,' the manageress said, completing her search of the drawers. She turned back into the room. 'I wonder if...' She trailed off.

'If what, Miss Grant?'

'If she had on her blue sapphire pendant when her... when she was found. She wore it every day, you know. If that has gone, then it must have been a robbery.'

Had she seen it on the body? Poppy tried to recall, but couldn't remember if Mrs Clark had been wearing it.

'Then let us search for it.' Poppy stepped over to the dressing table. 'No sign of a jewellery box here.' The surface held only a hairbrush and mirror positioned just so, and a small bottle of some inexpensive perfume. She slid open the top drawer, and there lay a small oak box.

'Is the pendant inside?' Miss Grant asked anxiously.

Poppy lifted the lid on its hinges. She and the manageress stared at the lining of padded cotton in a print of pretty blue poppies in the empty case.

Poppy let out a breath. 'It's not.' She replaced the box and turned back to Miss Grant.

'Oh dear. To be murdered for a pendant, no matter how valuable...'

'Was that the only jewellery she wore?' Poppy asked.

'Apart from her wedding ring? Yes.'

'Given the emptiness of the box, it looks like it was the only jewellery she possessed,' Poppy added thoughtfully.

Miss Grant dropped her hand. 'She was so fond of that pendant, my lady. It was left to her by an aunt, she once told me.'

'So Ellen Clark wasn't a wealthy lady?'

'No, not at all.'

'I was told Mrs Clark's husband had been a minister, is that right?' Poppy said slowly, as a thought occurred to her.

'I expect, my lady, that you got that bit of information from the Misses Buccleuch and Brown. They've been quite friendly with Mrs Clark since their arrival a few days ago.'

'If you don't mind my asking, Miss Grant, how could a minister's widow afford to be a resident at this hotel?'

'I wouldn't share this information if she were alive, you understand, but, well... Her lodging is paid for by a trust that assists distressed gentlewomen of a certain age.'

'That is admirable.' Even as she spoke, Poppy was thinking hard. 'Tell me,' she said, 'how long had Mrs Clark been seeing her gentleman?'

The manageress flushed. 'Oh, I shouldn't have said anything about him, my lady. It was not very professional of me...'

Never mind professional, Poppy thought; there was a more serious matter now. 'I first heard of him from the other two ladies we've already mentioned,' she hastened to reassure the woman.

Miss Grant relaxed a little and considered. 'About a fort-night, I would say.'

'That's a short time to form any sort of attachment,' Poppy mused.

And where, she wondered, had Mr Henderson been staying

for the past two weeks? There was the Plockton Inn, of course. She would ask there tomorrow. Someone in the village must know him...

Ellen Clark's mystery man needed to be tracked down. And quickly.

FIVE

Despite the tragic circumstances, Poppy woke in an optimistic frame of mind the following morning. She was eager to do some investigating.

She slipped out of bed, her limbs feeling delightfully free in the white silk pyjamas, drew back the curtains and stood looking at the shimmering waters of Loch Carron. In the distance she could clearly see Heron Island, the inspiration to J.M. Barrie for his mythical island of Neverland in *Peter Pan*. The sky was clear and a pale blue, with small clouds in the east turned to pink by the rising sun.

What a perfectly beautiful place, she thought. How could something as ugly as a murder have taken place here?

She turned at the light tap on the door, which opened to reveal her maid carrying the breakfast bed tray. Major scampered in with her.

'I took the liberty of—' Elspeth uttered a sound like a dignified gasp as she stared at Poppy's pyjamas. 'My lady, I did not pack those... garments.'

'I know,' Poppy replied gaily, stroking her dog's ears, 'but fortunately I noticed your error in time and popped them into the bag myself before we left Edinburgh.'

'It was not an error, your ladyship,' Elspeth huffed.

'Elspeth. The French fashion designer Gabrielle Chanel has been seen wearing pyjamas in public, on the beach, since 1918. They combine elegance and comfort.'

'Exactly. The woman is *French,* my lady.' Elspeth's long nose gave a disapproving sniff.

'What has been worn for the last six years on the Côte d'Azur can surely now be worn in private in Scotland. Let us pass swiftly over the matter.' Poppy returned to the bed and propped herself up on the pillows.

'As I was saying,' Elspeth said, setting the tray across Poppy's legs, 'I took the liberty of requesting a tray from Miss Grant, thinking you might prefer breakfast in bed this morning.'

'How very thoughtful.' Poppy shook out the linen napkin.

'I guessed your ladyship would prefer this, when I heard last night you had been involved in a murder.' Elspeth's face wore its reproachful look.

'I was hardly *involved.*' Poppy picked up the small silver knife and sliced off the top of her lightly boiled egg. 'It was simply that Major and I found the poor woman's body.'

At the sound of his name, Major looked up from where he lay on the floor and kept his hopeful gaze fixed on the tray. His tail thumped on the rug.

'It's almost half past eight and we have a train to catch after lunch.' Elspeth opened the wardrobe door. 'I'm sure you will be required to visit the police office and give a statement, so I have allowed sufficient time for that.'

'As efficient as ever, dear Elspeth.' Poppy lifted a spoonful of soft yellow yolk.

Elspeth considered the contents of the linen press. 'There is little to choose from, my lady, as the main part of your luggage is in the Bentley. Hopefully Fergusson will be making his way to

Skye today. But your green tweed and brogues are good enough to visit a police office, I'm sure.'

Poppy nodded. 'Could you please run a bath for me while I eat my breakfast?'

'You will need to use the bathroom on the landing, my lady, as the rooms don't have their own. I've already taken possession of the bathroom by turning on the taps and moving the sign on the door to engaged.'

Poppy gazed with admiration at her lady's maid and smiled. 'Thank you, Elspeth. I can always rely on you in my cause.' She took a sip of tea.

'Not always, my lady.' Elspeth gave a tight smile. 'Not if you get yourself involved with this murder investigation. Now then, by the time you have finished your breakfast, the bath will be ready for you.'

Poppy ate the egg, two slices of toast – one with honey, finished her tea, tied the belt of her silk kimono about her waist and strode to the bathroom. Opening the door, she was greeted with clouds of steam, Elspeth arranging towels over the wooden stand and the water drawn to a perfect temperature.

Thanking Elspeth, Poppy locked the door after her maid had left, cast off her dressing robe and pyjamas, and lowered herself into the bath.

'*It had to be you,*' she sang, and then improvised, '*la-la-la...*' She needed to pay closer attention to the words of Gus Khan's song next time she heard it. '*Wonderful YOU-U-U.*'

There was a tap on the bathroom door and she heard Elspeth call sharply, 'Your ladyship, this is a house of mourning.'

Oh dear, Elspeth was right. But she was also well aware that her maid was not fond of Poppy's singing at the best of times.

As she finished her ablutions and began to towel herself dry, Poppy decided not only must she speak to Constable Macduff to ask a few pertinent questions, but she must also suggest he request the help of Inspector James MacKenzie from the Edinburgh Detective Branch.

Was it the song that had brought the inspector to mind? Not that he was *wonderful*, of course. Although... there was something almost *Byronic* about him. She paused in her towelling. He was proud and, she was sure, capable of strong affection. She pictured those coal-black curls, dark eyes, sensual mouth. As to his large and very impressive body...

But of course, she thought, towelling herself vigorously, none of those attributes was why she wanted to work with him again. It was simply because the two of them had dealt so well together in solving the case in Culross. That was, he had eventually worked with her, once he'd realised how successful they were as a team. Men can be so stubborn, she thought as she slipped on her kimono. She, on the other hand, was never obstinate. Or rarely.

Poppy moved on to consider the events of last night. She'd noted these down in her book during her conversation with Miss Grant in the sitting room, and had added the facts of the missing scarf and sapphire pendant before she'd gone to bed. Mrs Clark, a long-term resident of the hotel, had gone out about half past six, saying she wouldn't be long and knowing that dinner was at seven o'clock, and had been found strangled shortly after half past nine. There was no stiffness in her arms, which suggested that she'd been dead for less than three hours. Which wasn't a terribly helpful observation, as there had been only three hours between Mrs Clark's leaving the hotel and her body being found by Poppy.

The woman's handbag and sapphire pendant were missing, presumably stolen by her killer. Why she had been in the open-air church in the evening was a mystery in itself, and who had murdered her an even bigger one. True, Mrs Clark was a minister's widow, so she could have gone there to pray – but what had been worrying her so much to send her there in the first place?

Was it significant that she had taken her evening bag? Probably not, Poppy thought; a woman of Mrs Clark's age and background would be keen to keep up appearances. Besides, she might have intended to go from her walk straight into dinner.

With her robe wrapped tightly around her, Poppy opened the door and looked both ways along the corridor. When she was certain it was all clear, she hastened back to her room. Elspeth had laid out Poppy's elegant, tailored emerald-green tweeds on the bed, and within a short time Poppy was dressed and seated on the stool at the dressing table with wing mirrors.

'Elspeth,' she said, choosing a silver brooch with a diamond spray from the purple velvet interior of her jewellery case and pinning it on her jacket, 'while I am out, could you speak to the hotel staff—'

'I usually do, my lady.'

'I hadn't finished my sentence,' Poppy reprimanded her maid as she searched on the dressing table for the right shade of lipstick to go with green tweed. *Plum...* She uncapped the stick, applied it carefully to her lips and blew a kiss at herself in the looking glass.

She then got to her feet and pulled on her blue beret. 'As I was saying, could you speak to the staff and find out what you can about Mrs Clark's gentleman, about the habits of the lady herself, that sort of thing?' She moved towards the door. 'I'm now off to report to the police office.'

'You are forgetting your gloves, my lady,' Elspeth remarked, taking them from the chest of drawers and hastening after Poppy.

Poppy accepted the soft, pale blue kid gloves and pulled them on. Major had moved to sit blocking the door, waiting for a walk.

'You have been very patient,' she said to him with a smile. 'Now, where is your leash?'

'It's hanging on the peg at the back of the door, your ladyship.' Elspeth unhooked the leather strap, bent and clipped it onto the dog's collar. She handed the leash, with the dog at the other end, to Poppy. 'Do y.ou know where the police office is, my lady?'

'Yes, thank you, Elspeth. I asked Miss Grant last night. I will return later this morning, which gives you plenty of time for sleuthing.'

'*Sleuthing?*' Poppy heard Elspeth mutter as Major led her out of the bedroom. 'The very idea. I never had to do such a thing when I was personal maid to Lady MacCorkindale.'

Lady MacCorkindale! Poppy thought with an inner smile. What a dull employer she must have been.

The day was bright with no wind as Poppy set off jauntily down Harbour Street, seagulls swooping and dipping. The villagers were hanging around in small groups, and they eyed her and Major with curiosity. The news was already out, she guessed, as a woman in a plaid shawl straightened in the act of gathering eggs from the cackling hens in her garden and stared openly at her. She continued past the school, where the sound of the children singing and clapping in time to the music floated out of an open window.

At the town hall Poppy turned right. On a grassy area stood a telephone kiosk, and a little further on a small group of fish-ermen were sitting on wooden crates and repairing nets. Other nets had been set here to dry, and there were barrels used in the salting and packing of herring. The men looked up as she drew near, touched their hats in a respectful gesture, and she smiled and nodded back politely.

Poppy reached the end of the road and there, next to a low, thatched cottage and overlooking the loch, stood the police house. She pushed open the door.

The room was empty. On the counter stood a call bell and Poppy gave it a sharp tap with the palm of her hand. It made a satisfying *ting*. She gazed around the room as she waited for the constable to appear. An attractive little cuckoo clock hung on one wall, while shabby wanted posters and various notices were displayed on another wall.

She wandered over to the notices and began idly to read. One poster showed a portrait sketch of a man wanted for fraud in the USA, describing him as having fair hair, spectacles, of middle years and with a Scotch accent.

A Scottish accent might narrow the number of suspects down in America, but not in Scotland, she thought wryly, when a door opened behind her. She spun round, and the constable from last night appeared from a room at the back, hastily buttoning up his uniform jacket. She caught a glimpse of a comfortable-looking sitting room, before he closed the door swiftly behind him.

'Good morning, Constable Macduff,' Poppy said.

'Och, it's your ladyship.' He straightened his jacket and gave her a forced smile.

Had he actually gritted his teeth? No matter.

'It is indeed,' she continued breezily. 'I have come to give a statement about last night.'

'Aye, my lady, last night.' He came to stand behind the counter and took up a sheet of paper and a pencil. 'I'll be writing it first, my lady, and then will ask you to sign the typed copy.'

'As long as that can be done this morning. I have to catch the 2.22 train to Kyle of Lochalsh.'

How frustrating that she couldn't stay to solve the murder herself, Poppy thought. But she could at least recommend the constable get Inspector MacKenzie on the case.

'Yes, my lady?' Constable Macduff was looking at her, waiting for Poppy to make her statement.

'I am Lady Persephone Proudfoot, at present staying at the Harbour Hotel in the village.' She went on to repeat her account of the previous evening, pausing to indicate Major, sitting nicely by her feet, when she got to the bit about her dog finding the body, and ending with the statement that, as far as she could tell in the dark, there was no sign of the victim's handbag or sapphire pendant. Poppy came to a halt and waited while the constable finished writing.

'The handbag and pendant are missing,' he confirmed. 'Now then, that's all verra useful, your ladyship.'

'Is there anything else I can help you with?' she asked.

'Only to sign your statement when I've typed it up.' He picked up the sheet of paper he'd written on and looked at her, clearly indicating the interview was over.

'Have you taken statements from the other relevant persons?' she asked.

He fixed her with a steady gaze. 'Such as?'

'Well, Miss Grant, the Harbour Hotel manageress...'

'I ken fine who Miss Grant is. And aye, I have taken a statement from her.' He fixed Poppy with an aggrieved eye. 'Not that it is any of your ladyship's business.'

'So you have a description of the missing clutch?'

He frowned. 'Clutch?'

'Mrs Clark's handbag,' Poppy explained impatiently.

'Och, aye, it's listed as a woman's handbag.'

'Quite an unusual handbag,' she persevered, 'made of crocodile skin with an ornate button clasp.'

'I'll add that to the description,' Constable Macduff said, making no move to note it down.

Poppy gritted her teeth and moved on to another question. 'Have you found Mr Henderson?'

The constable frowned. 'And who is Mr Henderson?'

She gave an impatient *tut.* 'Mrs Clark's gentleman friend.'

'I dinna think he can be important, your ladyship. Mrs Clark told the hotel manageress she was going out on her own yesterday evening.'

Poppy took a deep breath. 'Nonetheless, the gentleman might have some useful information.'

'As I told you last night, your ladyship, it was verra likely a robbery that was bungled by some ne'er-do-well on his way from Duirinish to Strome Ferry. There's a lot of those sorts about since the Great War. The perpetrator canna be one of the villagers—'

'Why not?' she asked, astonished.

'Because I ken all of the residents and not one of them would do such a thing—'

'What is the population here?'

'Almost three hundred souls,' he told her proudly.

'Then you cannot possibly know them all,' she said sharply.

'Not all by name, I'll grant you that. Although I'd say that I ken their faces and the family names, and where they stay,' he went on, a stubborn look on his face. 'It'll be an outsider, is my opinion, so I'll be after passing the details on to Inverness.'

'With murder cases, the sooner investigations start—'

'Culpable homicide,' he corrected her. 'That is where someone causes the death of another person without intending to, my lady.'

'Yes, Constable, I do know what the term means.' She had studied criminal law as part of her degree in law. Not that she was going to tell Constable Macduff that. 'Well, then, what did the doctor say about Mrs Clark's death?'

'Strangulation.'

Of course it was murder, Poppy silently seethed.

'Anything else?' she asked as politely as possible.

'She died between half past six and half past nine yesterday evening,' he added.

Poppy sighed. 'That much I already know, Constable.'

'And that's as much as you will ken, my lady. The Procurator Fiscal Depute will be along later today. I will pass my information to Inverness, and they will likely send a detective from there. All is in hand.' He fixed her with a steady gaze.

'Constable Macduff,' Poppy said, in her most authoritative voice, 'you would do well to contact Inspector MacKenzie of the Edinburgh Detective Branch. He comes highly recommended.'

'Recommended by who?' he asked sharply.

'By myself. The inspector and I recently worked together very successfully on a murder case in Culross—'

The constable cut across her. 'I canna comment on that, but I can say that the *police* will do the investigating necessary on this case, and I suggest you go off now and enjoy the rest of your holiday.'

Really! This attitude by police officers was most unhelpful. If he wasn't going to telephone Inspector MacKenzie, then she would.

After all, it was clearly not an accident but a case of murder.

SIX

Poppy turned on the heel of her brogues. The action would have had more emphasis if she'd been wearing a pair of high heels, but it couldn't be helped. A detective worked with what she had.

'To the telephone kiosk,' she told Major, as she closed the police house door behind them.

With the dog trotting beside her, Poppy retraced her steps to the concrete and glass kiosk she'd passed earlier on the edge of the grassy area. The structure was quite ghastly, unlike the bright red models she'd seen in the newspaper, submitted by architects and organisations invited to design a new kiosk.

'Let me see if I have enough pennies for a call,' she said to Major. Taking her purse from her tweed jacket pocket, she opened it. 'Yes.' She removed the money, dropped her purse back into her pocket and pulled at the wooden door.

She looked down at Major. 'Are you coming in?'

The dog trotted into the stuffy little kiosk and Poppy squeezed in beside him. She lifted the receiver and waited for the telephone exchange to answer.

'Operator,' came the male voice at the end of the line.

'The Edinburgh Detective Branch, please.'

'Trying to connect you.' After a short interval of buzzes and clicks, the voice requested her to put her pennies in the slot. Poppy did so, pressed Button A and heard her coins fall into the cash box.

'Hello?' Poppy said. 'I would like to speak to Inspector James MacKenzie.'

'One moment please, madam.' There were more noises on the line.

'Inspector MacKenzie,' a voice said suddenly.

A thrill ran down her back at hearing his deep, mellow tone with its island lilt travel down the telephone line to her ear. 'Inspector, this is Poppy Proudfoot speaking.'

A short pause indicated his surprise – pleasant surprise, she told herself – at hearing from her.

'Good morning, my lady.' Was that a smile in his voice? 'How are you enjoying the Isle of Skye?'

'I'm not there yet,' she informed him. 'My maid and I stopped for the night at Plockton, *en route*, and unfortunately... well, there's been a—'

'Dinna tell me,' he said with a note of exasperation. 'A murder.'

'Exactly, Inspector.' She beamed into the receiver. 'How clever of you to have guessed.'

'It didna take too much imagination to have worked that out, your ladyship. Wherever you go, there is—'

'A murder,' she added helpfully. 'That's not entirely true, of course, although it is in this case.'

'And you are telephoning me because...?'

'Because you are a detective, and the constable here is rather clueless.'

'And you have some ideas of your own, I'm thinking?' He sounded amused.

'Perhaps,' she told him modestly.

'And you find yourself in the thick of it?'

'Major and I found the woman's body at the open-air church. She had clear signs of a ligature strangulation.'

'What sort of a Great War nurse knows about strangulation?' Inspector MacKenzie's tone was wry.

'One who believes in learning as much as possible about any occupation in which she is involved,' Poppy retorted.

Or was involved, she thought. The war had ended five years ago and Dunearn Castle had returned to being the Proudfoot family seat.

'Plus the scarf was still around Mrs Clark's neck, so it wasn't awfully hard to work out.' She heard his soft sigh at the other end of the telephone and hastened on. 'But the important thing is that you are needed here to solve the crime. I cannot do it myself as I have to catch the afternoon train to Kyle of Lochalsh.'

'For that, give praise,' he murmured.

'I heard that, Inspector.'

'Don't get involved any further, my lady,' he said, suddenly earnest. 'Go to see your friend on Skye.' He cleared his throat. 'I might see you there.'

'Oh?'

'Aye, I'm meeting my cousin and an American friend of his for a few days' rambling and I'll be staying on the island.'

How delicious! Poppy felt warm all over at the thought.

A series of pips began on the line. 'Oh, that's my money run out and I have no more change. Do come as soon as you can,' Poppy finished breathlessly, before the line went dead. She hung up the receiver.

'Bother,' she said to Major, who was sitting on her foot. 'I wasn't able to tell the inspector what else I have discovered.'

Major gave her a sympathetic look.

'If you could remove yourself from my foot,' Poppy said

firmly, trying to slide out her brogue from under the dog's weight, 'we can get on with the next thing.'

Major got to his feet and stood, head cocked, alert.

Poppy emerged from the telephone kiosk. The lack of wind meant that the fishermen were not out with their boats, which rode at anchor in the small harbour. She wanted to speak to the young man who had taken Ellen Clark and Mr Henderson for a trip two days ago.

She approached the small group of fishermen mending their nets. '*Madainn mhath.*'

'*Madainn mhath dhuibh,*' came the traditional reply: good morning to you.

'I'm looking for Malcolm.'

A wizened old fellow with a thick beard and wearing a sailor's cap held a net needle, threaded with twine, in his brown speckled hand. 'I'm Malcolm, madam.'

Too old, she thought, remembering Miss Grant had called him young Malcolm. She should have remembered that in some communities a father's Christian name was always given to the first-born son. 'Do you have a son also called Malcolm?'

A younger man, who had been stroking Major's head, took off his battered hat and got to his feet. 'I'm Young Malcolm. Unless it's my bairn you're needing to speak to, Wee Malcolm?'

Poppy ignored the laughter of the other men and considered this Malcolm. He looked to be in his thirties, the skin of his face tanned by working outdoors He was dressed in oilskin trousers with braces over a thick jumper.

'I'm Persephone Proudfoot,' she began.

Young Malcolm nodded, his eyes screwed up against the sun.

'And I wonder if I could have a word with you about two people you took on a boat trip the day before yesterday?'

'Aye, madam.' He turned his hat in his hands. 'What would it be ye were wanting to ken?'

'You know the couple I mean?'

'I'm thinking that I do.'

This way of speaking was charming, if a little exhausting, thought Poppy. She would have to adopt the same pattern if she were to keep her thoughts clear. 'I'm hearing that you took the lady and gentleman to see the wildlife and natural beauty of this part of the world.'

'Aye, madam.'

'Would you be knowing...' She paused, as Young Malcolm was giving her a strange look. Oh, he must think she was making fun of him, which wasn't at all the case. Poppy cleared her throat and began again.

'You've heard that the lady, Mrs Clark, was found dead yesterday evening?'

'Aye, madam. And we were all verra sorry to hear that.' He glanced back at the other men, who had all stopped working on their nets to listen. They nodded in agreement.

'How did they seem to you? Mrs Clark and Mr Henderson? Was there any sort of a disagreement between them, for example?'

Young Malcolm gave a slight shrug. 'I could no' be hearing well enough what they were saying.'

'Well then, was there anything in their behaviour that made you think they were not enjoying each other's company?'

He thought for a while, before saying, 'I'm no' sure there was onything.'

Poppy sighed.

'Although,' he went on with a small frown, 'I'm thinking that the lady was awfa quiet when we finished the trip and returned to the village.'

'Could she have felt seasick, perhaps?' Poppy asked.

Young Malcolm laughed. 'The water was as smooth as a bairn's—' He stopped himself.

'I understand,' Poppy told him. 'I won't keep you from your work any longer. Thank you for your time.'

He replaced his hat and sat again, picking up his needle and net as Poppy took her leave. So something *had* happened on the boat? Mr Henderson was unlikely to have done anything in such circumstances – such as making a pass at Ellen – so it must have been something he'd said. But what could have caused what Miss Grant had described as 'a strange sort of glitter in her eyes'?

She made her way back to the Harbour Hotel. What rotten luck that Inspector MacKenzie would be working on the case without her, especially as she had started the investigation so well.

Poppy hoped that Elspeth had some news for her. Because there was a definite mystery here to be solved.

SEVEN

Poppy found the manageress at the counter of the hotel reception.

'Miss Grant, just the person I require,' Poppy said. 'Can you tell me the time of the next train to arrive here from Edinburgh?'

Miss Grant glanced at the long-case clock on the wall. 'It's now just after half past ten, my lady, and there's the quarter to eleven from Edinburgh. Would that be the train you mean?'

Would the inspector have had time to catch that? It was probably only a ten-minute walk from the police headquarters in Parliament Square to Waverley Station, but he would first have to return home, wherever that was, to pack a bag... Poppy shook her head.

'I think the next train is around half past one.' As Miss Grant spoke, she pulled a *Bradshaw's Guide* from under the counter. 'This book isn't as necessary as it was since the railway companies were grouped into the Big Four last year, but it's still useful.' She leafed through its pages. 'Here we are. Just as I thought,' she said with satisfaction. 'The London, Midland and

Scottish Railway, leaving Edinburgh at 1.32 p.m., change at Inverness, reaching Plockton at 8.21 p.m.'

Poppy hoped that the inspector would at least be on that one. 'And when is the last train from Plockton to Kyle of Lochalsh?'

'That's the same train, my lady. The one that arrives here at 8.21.'

Drat. That really would give her no time at all to speak to Inspector MacKenzie. 'It does connect to the ferry to Skye this evening?'

'It does,' the manageress assured her.

'Thank you, Miss Grant,' Poppy said. 'My maid and I will check out of the hotel later this evening.'

'Very good, your ladyship.'

'Meanwhile, would you arrange to send a telegram for me? To Mrs Catriona MacLeod at the Isle of the Mist Hotel, Portree, to tell her I will be later than expected and ask if a car can pick me up at... What time would be realistic, Miss Grant?'

'Let me see. It's twenty minutes to the end of the line, then a short journey across the water, which means you should be on the island around nine o'clock.'

'Perfect. If you could put nine p.m. in the telegram.'

'Certainly, my lady.'

'Do you know where I can find my maid?' Poppy asked.

'I believe she is in the sitting room with one of the guests.'

Poppy thanked Miss Grant, stripped off her gloves, pushed them into her pocket and entered the small room with its cluttered furniture. Elspeth was seated on the settee, looking strained as the thin woman from last night's dinner chatted to her.

'My lady,' Elspeth said with relief on seeing Poppy, and she got to her feet.

'My *lady?*' queried the woman, a bright look on her inquisitive face. 'I didn't know. And here I am, Miss Dorothy Brown, talking to you as if you were from ordinary folk.'

My father is a sheep farmer in Australia, Poppy thought with a smile. With a title, admittedly, but a sheep farmer, nonetheless. Though, she wasn't inclined to relinquish the natural authority her title gave in the middle of a murder investigation.

Poppy sent Miss Brown a friendly smile and took an armchair. She turned to address the dog. 'Major, come here and sit by me. I'm afraid with your size you might send a small table flying.'

He sat, an offended look on his face.

Poppy looked at the brown teapot on the tea tray. 'Is there any tea left?'

'It'll be cold by now, my lady. I'll order a fresh pot,' Elspeth said.

Miss Brown rose quickly to her feet. 'Let me do that, your ladyship,' she called cheerfully as she hurried to the door.

'That's my job—' Elspeth flushed, moving hastily in the same direction.

The two women jostled in the doorway.

'Elspeth,' Poppy said mildly.

Her maid looked back, and Miss Brown took advantage of the distraction to disappear out of the room, closing the door firmly behind her.

'You've let that auld biddie get the upper hand of me,' Elspeth grumbled, coming back to Poppy.

'Let her go,' Poppy said, 'and take a seat. I want to speak to you in private. There's been a small change of plan.'

'Oh?' Elspeth gave her a suspicious look.

'Instead of the afternoon train to Kyle of Lochalsh, we'll catch the evening one.'

Elspeth gave a small but unmistakeable sigh. 'Is this anything to do with Mrs Clark's murder, my lady?'

'In what way, Elspeth?'

'In any way.'

'Well, yes. I have telephoned Inspector MacKenzie and asked him to come. The constable here clearly needs his help, and I thought it would be a good idea to have a few words with the inspector before we leave Plockton. But,' Poppy went on, 'tell me quickly, before Miss Brown returns, what have you learned from the hotel staff about Ellen Clark and her gentleman?'

'It's not that easy, my lady,' Elspeth said stiffly, 'asking strangers impertinent questions.'

'I'm sure you were able to frame them in a suitable manner,' Poppy told her soothingly.

Elspeth sniffed. 'By all accounts, the gentleman, Mr Alan Henderson, is a charming fellow.'

'So he has a Christian name...' Poppy frowned. 'That takes us a little further forward.'

'The only place we should go *forward* to is Portree,' Elspeth said, her voice firm.

Poppy narrowed her eyes at Elspeth.

'Well.' Her maid fluffed herself out in the manner of a hen. 'I was able to find out something else.'

'Yes?' Poppy gave an encouraging smile.

'I thought the chambermaid, Katy, the one who brought the tea tray when we arrived yesterday evening, was something of a gossip, and I was right. She told me that Mrs Clark was smitten with this chap and that Mrs Clark had told her that life couldn't be more perfect.'

'So no lovers' tiff,' Poppy mused.

'Mind you, that was two mornings ago,' Elspeth added. 'The chambermaid didn't see her that evening, as after the boat trip Mrs Clark went to bed early with a headache.'

'I wonder what happened on that boat trip?'

Elspeth smoothed the skirt of her navy-blue maid's dress. 'I really couldn't say, my lady.'

The sitting room door opened. 'Tea's on its way,' said Miss Brown cheerfully as she entered.

'How kind of you,' Poppy said.

Miss Brown resumed her seat on the settee next to Elspeth. 'Skoosh over a bit and make room for me,' she said to her with a laugh.

Elspeth glowered and moved as far along the settee as was possible.

'That's better!' Miss Brown made herself comfortable.

'Miss Buccleuch is not with you today?' Poppy enquired.

'We're nae joined at the hip, you ken!' Miss Brown flushed, seemed to recollect her surroundings and began again. 'She's gone for a wee walk. Where are you off to next, your ladyship?'

'Portree,' Poppy told her pleasantly. 'And you and your friend?'

'The same!' Miss Brown beamed. 'Perhaps we'll bump into you there.'

Poppy saw Elspeth press her lips firmly together. 'And what takes you to Portree?' Poppy went on.

'Och, a button collection!'

Had she heard that correctly? 'I'm sorry, did you say a button collection?'

'Aye, your ladyship. Miss Buccleuch and I are avid collectors, and there's a button exhibition on Skye shortly, which will feature a rare Russian papier-mâché button. With a picture on it of children ice skating,' she added.

'It sounds very jolly,' Poppy said.

The door opened again, and a waitress brought in a pot of fresh tea and clean cups and saucers.

'You can get some awfully pretty buttons, you know,' Miss Brown went on, clearly settling into her favourite topic, 'but I think the nicest are those with flowers and country scenes hand painted onto enamel and porcelain.'

Elspeth poured out tea for Poppy, then excused herself with

the need to perform some unspecified task Poppy hadn't asked her to do. Poppy was left to listen to the attractions of button collecting while she drank her tea and felt belated sympathy for however long Elspeth had been forced to hear the same.

When Miss Brown at last drew breath, Poppy put down her empty cup. Could she now learn anything about Ellen Clark? 'It is very sad about Mrs Clark.' She sighed.

Miss Brown's face fell. 'It is, isn't it? She was so happy, Ellen was, and then to think this happened.'

'Was she in the habit of going to the open-air church in the evening?'

'If she was, that's the first I'd heard of it,' Miss Brown declared. 'It seems a strange sort of thing to do, don't you think?'

Poppy nodded. Ellen Clark must have gone there to pray, she thought – but for what? People prayed for a number of reasons: peace of mind, strength to deal with something unwelcome, compassion, guidance, understanding... Which, if any, of those was it that Ellen felt she needed?

'Of course, Mrs Clark went regularly to the kirk, though,' Miss Brown continued. 'She told us that on our first night here. Ellen was the widow of a minister, as you know.'

It sounded like the ladies had had some fairly personal conversation, at least. 'Did you get to know her at all?'

'Not really. Although Isabella—'

'Isabella?'

'Sorry, Miss Buccleuch, Isabella Buccleuch. Well, as I was saying, she and I used to pass the time of day with Ellen.' Miss Brown paused as she thought.

'Yes?' Poppy asked quickly.

'Isabella likes to have a walk before dinner and she's told me that sometimes she bumped into Ellen.' Miss Brown shrugged. 'They might have a bit of a blether then. But you'd have to ask Isabella herself what they spoke about.'

Poppy's pulse jumped. Was this a possible lead? 'Do you remember if Isabella went for a walk yesterday evening?'

'Aye, only for about the usual forty-five minutes or so.'

That would be long enough to commit the murder. But surely Isabella Buccleuch would have had nothing to do with it? Although she might have seen something – or someone – that had.

'Did Isabella mention seeing Ellen at all?'

'Och, no,' Miss Brown said cheerfully. 'She would have told me if she had.' She jumped to her feet. 'Well, I'd best be off, your ladyship.' She bobbed a curtsy.

'There is no need to curtsy to me,' Poppy told her gently. 'I am an earl's daughter, not a member of the royal family.'

'Och, silly me.' Miss Brown flushed and smiled. 'Well, see you at lunch!' And with that, she hurried from the room.

Poppy watched her go. Was it possible that Isabella Buccleuch had followed Ellen to the open-air church to meet her there? Or worse still, to murder her? Isabella looked like a strong woman, and Ellen had been described by Isabella herself as a shy, dainty thing. The marks on the victim's hands suggested little resistance, which in turn suggested she knew her attacker.

But what might Isabella Buccleuch's motive be? Perhaps money, Poppy thought, remembering the darned hole in the other woman's brown woollen stocking. The pendant sounded like a valuable one, and the woman must have seen Ellen wearing it if she wore it every day...

But as lovely as the pendant was, was it worth killing for?

EIGHT

While Poppy was alone in the sitting room, a thought occurred to her. Was Miss Brown as guileless as she appeared?

She must have realised that what she had just told Poppy made her friend a possible suspect. Did she have some reason for doing this? But Miss Brown wouldn't know that Poppy was a detective... an *assistant* detective... and perhaps hadn't thought about her comment. At lunch Poppy would follow up the possible clue and speak to Isabella Buccleuch herself.

But before then, more needed to be learned about Ellen Clark. She would start by finding out if Mrs Clark had made a Will. Where better to go for the answer than the local solicitor?

Poppy asked at the hotel reception desk if there was a law agent in the village. Having been given directions to his practice by the young woman, Poppy asked her to take Major up to Elspeth and she set off once again along Harbour Street. She turned left into leafy Frithard Road and at the modest house rang the bell.

A small, elderly woman came to the door, introduced herself as Mrs Paterson and led Poppy through to a room at the back of the house. There she announced Poppy and left her.

Mr Paterson, equally small and elderly but with gingery brindled hair and moustache, sprang to his feet, shook hands with Poppy and waved her to a mahogany chair upholstered in a prickly horsehair.

'Now, my lady, what can I do for you?' he said in a surprisingly deep voice as he resumed his seat behind the tidy desk.

'My visit is concerned with the death of Mrs Ellen Clark,' Poppy began, 'who I believe is one of your clients.' It was a guess, but it was possible Ellen had been his client.

The solicitor shook his head sorrowfully. 'Ah, yes, Mrs Clark. Poor lady.'

Her instinct had been right!

'Is she a friend of yours?' he asked.

'I'm afraid not,' Poppy said, 'but it would be helpful to know if Mrs Clark has any relatives, or the names of the beneficiaries in her Will.'

Mr Paterson's face assumed a stern expression. 'I can't reveal to you the contents of a Will, as I'm sure you must appreciate.'

'I understand, of course, Mr Paterson, but' – Poppy put on her most legal look – 'I am helping Inspector MacKenzie of the Edinburgh Detective Branch.'

'Are you, by Jove?' His face was suddenly alert. 'I'm aware there are now lady police officers. He sobered quickly. 'But from Edinburgh? It must be a serious matter.'

'It is the most serious matter,' she told him. 'Murder.'

'*Murder*! Good heavens. I'd heard only that Mrs Clark was no longer with us.' He steepled his fingers together and looked at her over the top. 'But murdered. And in Plockton, no less. It hardly seems possible.'

Poppy waited a few seconds, and sensing his unwillingness to help her begin to weaken, she added, 'Mr Paterson, like yourself I am experienced in Scots law.' Which was true, to an extent: she had studied law at the University of Glasgow and passed all her examinations with flying colours. 'And naturally what you have to say will go no further than myself and the inspector. He is due to arrive on the Edinburgh train this very evening. The thing is' – she leaned forward and gave him a reassuring smile – 'the first forty-eight hours in a case are the most productive in catching a killer, and by the time he arrives something like twenty-four of them will already have been lost. I assure you that Inspector MacKenzie will overlook a breach in normal procedure in this case, and he will be pleased not to have to disturb you late at night in your own home.'

There, *that* should do it!

It did.

The solicitor dropped his hands. 'Well, in that case, I suppose I could stretch custom a wee bit.' He rang the small handbell on the corner of his desk. 'I'm anxious to do whatever I can to help find the villain who's done such a thing... Murdered. I can hardly believe it.'

Mrs Paterson appeared in answer to his summons. 'What is it ye're wanting, my dear?

'Get me Mrs Clark's papers, my dear, if ye please.'

As sprightly as her husband, she retreated swiftly.

'Thank you, Mr Paterson. The inspector will be able to go over my notes, and if he has any further questions I'm sure he'll be along as promptly as he can tomorrow morning.'

Mrs Paterson returned with a manila folder.

The solicitor hooked a pair of spectacles behind his ears, opened the slim file and consulted the single sheet of paper there. 'Just so,' he murmured. He closed the folder, removed his glasses and cleared his throat.

'Mrs Clark visited me a week ago. She informed me she had made no previous Will, having very little money or possessions to bequeath, and wished to know my fee for drawing one up. I'm afraid that's all, my lady.'

This was disappointing news, even though Poppy's guess

about Ellen Clark's relative poverty had been accurate. But why had she been enquiring about a Will only a week before she was murdered? 'Mrs Clark gave no indication of the person, or persons, she wished to benefit under the Will?'

'None at all.'

'And she didn't mention any relatives?' Poppy pressed.

The solicitor shook his head regretfully.

Poppy could do nothing but thank him for his help, and bid him good day. She walked out of the house and into the sunshine, wondering if Ellen Clark had been about to make Mr Alan Henderson her beneficiary. It seemed the most likely explanation.

On the other hand, if Ellen had virtually nothing of value, which seemed to be the case, then why would she incur the expense of having such a document drawn up?

Poppy returned to the police house and signed her witness statement typed by Constable Macduff.

'Where will you be over the next few days, your ladyship, if I – or Inspector MacKenzie – wish to speak to you?'

Poppy smiled as she slid the sheet of paper back across the counter to Constable Macduff. So the arrangement *had* been made. 'The inspector knows where to find me.'

She returned to the Harbour Hotel for lunch and was just about to enter the dining room when she spotted Miss Brown eating alone at the table. *Dash it!* Isabella Buccleuch must be lunching elsewhere today. Charming as Miss Brown's friends undoubtedly found her, Poppy felt a desire not to have to listen to the further merits and disadvantages of certain types of button while she ate.

She hastily withdrew, thanking her lucky stars that Miss Brown hadn't looked up from her meal and seen her. Poppy raced upstairs and knocked on the door of her maid's room.

Elspeth opened the door, a book in her hand. Poppy just had time, before Elspeth hastily put her hand behind her back, to catch a glimpse of a lurid dust cover featuring a bare-chested fellow in a kilt with a dishevelled serving wench clinging on to him. So Elspeth was reading the famous Miss Taft's latest novel, *All for the Love of a Highland Chieftain*. It had been in all the Edinburgh bookshop windows.

'Yes, my lady?'

From inside the room Major nosed the door open wider and looked up hopefully at Poppy.

'May I come in?' she asked.

'Of course, my lady.' Elspeth stepped back to allow her to enter.

'Have you found out anything else from the servants?' Poppy asked, dropping into an armchair.

'Nothing more than what I told you earlier this morning, my lady: everyone found Mr Henderson a charming fellow; Ellen Clark was as fond of him as he of her; and she had a headache after the boat trip.' Elspeth discreetly slipped her novel into the drawer of her nightstand.

'Miss Brown has told me that her chum, Isabella Buccleuch, likes a brisk walk before dinner and that she went out yesterday evening. But she's of the opinion that Isabella didn't see or speak to Ellen, because if she had, she would have told Miss Brown.'

'It's possible that Miss Buccleuch didn't see Mrs Clark, my lady. But if she did, it might have slipped her mind this morning, or nothing happened that she thought worth mentioning to Miss Brown,' Elspeth pointed out as she perched on the edge of her bed. 'They have little on their minds but buttons.' She sniffed disparagingly.

'You could be right, Elspeth.' Poppy gazed idly around her maid's room. Everything in its place. She had expected nothing less.

'And then when Mrs Clark was found murdered, she didn't want to say anything for fear of what might come next.'

'As in appearing to be guilty?'

'Exactly that, my lady.'

'I really do need to speak to Isabella Buccleuch.' Poppy leaned forward in her chair. 'And here's a piece of news I managed to uncover this morning!'

Elspeth waited, looking unimpressed, to hear it.

'Ellen went to the local solicitor last week to ask about making a Will.'

Elspeth's eyebrows rose. 'Really, my lady? And who was to be the beneficiary of this somewhat impoverished lady?'

Poppy leaned back in the chair and sighed. 'Aye, there's the rub.'

'I'm sorry, my lady?'

'Nothing, Elspeth. It's a quote from *Hamlet*. I mean, that's the problem. Ellen didn't give that information to the solicitor and she didn't return to have the Will drawn up, so we don't know. But her arranging to make a Will is interesting, don't you think? A week before her murder too.'

Elspeth refused to be drawn on the matter.

Poppy, disappointed with Elspeth's lack of response, crossed one leg over the other, dangled her foot and considered her brogue. She waited for inspiration, but nothing of interest to the investigation came to mind.

'Are you taking lunch here?' she asked Elspeth.

'I thought I would.'

'Good. Then if you're quick and go now, you can engage Miss Brown in conversation and see if you can find out anything more about her friend's movements last night,' Poppy said, reaching down to fondle Major's ear. 'We saw Misses Brown and Buccleuch already eating supper when we went down to the dining room about half past eight. We need to know what time the two friends returned to the hotel from their excursion, and whether it was together. And what time Isabella Buccleuch went out again, when she returned, where she might have gone, et cetera.' She straightened and waved an airy hand. 'You know the type of thing.'

Elspeth gave her a frosty look. 'I do *not* know the type of thing, your ladyship.'

'Oh come, Elspeth, you must. Have you never read a crime novel in which the detective grills the suspect?'

'*Grills?*' Her maid looked alarmed. 'Do you mean applies some sort of heated pressure to the unfortunate person?'

'No, of course I don't mean that. Just have a nice wee chat with Miss Brown.'

Elspeth rolled her eyes.

'Think of yourself as assistant to... the assistant to Inspector MacKenzie,' Poppy quickly added.

Elspeth gave a deep sigh. 'Very well, your ladyship.'

Poppy smiled. 'Thank you, dear Elspeth.' She rose. 'Major and I are going to eat lunch elsewhere, and then walk to the castle to see if the fresh air will aid thinking.'

'Your gloves, my lady!' Elspeth said sharply.

'In my pocket,' Poppy called back as she opened the door.

As Poppy descended the staircase to the hall, she noticed that the manageress was back on duty at the desk.

'Good afternoon, Miss Grant,' she said as she approached the desk. 'I was wondering if you could let me have directions to the castle?'

'I'm unsure if the owner is at home or not at present.'

Poppy smiled. 'Thank you, Miss Grant, but I'm not interested in making a social call. As the weather is so fine and I have a few hours before catching my train, I'd simply like to take a stroll up there this afternoon.'

'Of course, my lady.' Miss Grant wrote the directions on a sheet of hotel notepaper and handed it to Poppy.

Poppy took the paper, thanked the manageress and, calling

to her Labrador, stepped out of the hotel and back into the bright sunshine. She stood on the step to read what was written on the note. The route took her past the Plockton Inn. Very well, that was where she would take lunch.

And, with any luck, she'd discover it was where Mr Henderson had been staying in the village...

Poppy ate a pleasant lunch at one of the tables outside the Plockton Inn.

Major had even been given his own dish of a small amount of the baked fillet of haddock. He polished it off in less than a minute, licked his nose and concentrated his unwavering gaze on the busy young waitress. Poppy positioned herself so that she could look down the hill and admire the sparkling waters of the loch with the mountains rising behind.

'Was everything to your satisfaction, sir?' asked the young waitress, winking at Major. 'And madam?' She removed Poppy's empty plate.

'It was, thank you...?' Poppy smiled and left the sentence hanging as she waited to hear the girl's name.

'Aileen, madam.'

'Aileen, do you know if Mr Henderson is still staying here? We're old friends, and I'd heard from a mutual acquaintance that he's holidaying in the area. I thought how jolly it would be if I were to surprise him!'

'Oh, I *am* sorry, madam, but he checked out yesterday morning.'

Poppy sighed. She'd guessed correctly as to where he'd been staying, but it was yet another disappointment. Yesterday morning meant he wasn't the one to have killed Ellen. 'What a shame,' she said with feeling.

'Mr Henderson will be disappointed to hear he's missed you, madam, I'm sure. Are you staying long? Only the gentleman's expected back in a week's time and perhaps you could see him then?'

'He's coming back?' That confirmed what Miss Grant had said she'd heard from Ellen Clark. If this were the case, it seemed unlikely he could be the murderer.

'Shall I give him your name, madam?' Aileen asked.

'Oh no, I don't want to spoil the wonderful surprise.' But, Poppy thought, if Mr Henderson was an innocent party, as he looked to be, then the poor man would indeed get a nasty shock to hear that Ellen was dead.

Poppy paid for her meal and looked down at Major. He looked back at her and raised an eyebrow.

'Well, Major, I have learned a little more, although not, I'm sorry to say, anything that takes the case forward. It is very frustrating. But perhaps Inspector MacKenzie will be able to shed some light on the matter.'

At the mention of Inspector MacKenzie, Major got to his feet.

Poppy laughed. 'You're looking forward to seeing him again?'

Major gave her a shrewd look.

'I confess – but this is in strictest confidence, you understand, Major' – Poppy lowered her voice – 'that I am too.'

His tail wagged. Too late, Poppy realised that Major had tricked the confession out of her. *Really!* If a lady is not cleverer than her dog...

NINE

Following Miss Grant's directions, Poppy set off with her eager Labrador trotting by her side. She walked up the hill, past the open-air church and just before the last house on the left, she took the steps leading down to a path.

Once they had crossed a boggy area at the head of the sea inlet, the path wound along between the railway line and the shore. Soon they came to the short tunnel under the railway that she was expecting to see, and once through it, the track continued steeply up beside a small burn, before she came to a fingerpost pointing to *Duncraig Castle*.

Here Poppy turned left off the track, went through the gate and followed the path between large rhododendrons. How beautiful they must look in May when in full bloom, she thought. Eventually the castle came into sight. A Victorian baronial version of a castle, and nothing like Dunearn, her family's thirteenth-century seat, but a castle, nonetheless. It was impressively large, on the shore of Loch Carron and with views across to the mountains of Applecross and Torridon.

Poppy didn't know the owner and so she stood there,

wondering whether or not to see if anyone was at home to give her tea as it was getting on for four o'clock.

As if in answer, a distant plume of steam appeared, travelling towards her in the direction of Plockton. Below her must be Duncraig Halt, the castle's own station. She could see the octagonal waiting room she'd noticed on the journey to Plockton yesterday. She would take the train back and have tea at the hotel. Could she reach the station in time to catch the train?

There was only one way to find out!

'Major, *run!*' she cried and dashed off along the path. Rather too soon her breath began to come in ragged gulps, but she kept going and reached the platform as the train appeared down the line. The driver had slowed down, alert for any passengers at the request stop, and Poppy stuck out a firm hand.

With a hiss of brakes, the train steamed to a halt. As she stepped forward, the door was opened from inside, and a large male hand reached out to assist her up and into the carriage. Major jumped in behind her.

'Thank you,' she said, then raised her eyes to the man's face.

She gasped.

'Inspector MacKenzie!' Her heart skidded to a stop, before starting again, less steadily. '*Mo chreach 'sa thàinig!*'

'My goodness me,' he translated from the Gaelic with a laugh, the corners of his dark eyes crinkling. 'Your pronunciation is improving, my lady.'

As she took the seat opposite him, her heart danced. He was as tall and broad-shouldered as she'd remembered. *And why shouldn't he be?* she asked herself crossly, given she had seen him only the previous day.

'I have been practising,' she told him with a smile. 'And you managed to catch the earlier train! I didn't think you would have time, given my telephone call gave you such short notice.'

He looked amused.

Oh, that dimple in his left cheek!

'Aye, I caught the mid-morning train. I keep a packed bag at the police office for emergencies.'

Of course he did. She should have thought of that. For now, though, he was wearing his uniform, which simply cried out to be loosened...

'Have you been visiting friends at the castle?' he went on.

'No,' she replied, as the train pulled slowly out of the station. 'I went for a walk and decided to take the train back.'

'I'm verra glad you did.'

Major wagged his tail and sat by Inspector MacKenzie. 'Major Lewis,' said the inspector, giving the dog a gentle tweak of the ear.

'Are you?' Poppy beamed. 'Very glad I am on this train? You said I was to avoid trouble and yet here I am again.'

'Aye.' He gave her a stern look. 'Your catching this train allows me to remind you sooner rather than later that investigating murder is no' a game and needs to be left to the professionals.'

'Absolutely, Inspector. I'm quite happy to, now that you're here. And to be fair, I did say I would do my best, but that I couldn't promise.' Poppy made a show of straightening her skirt impatiently. 'I didn't exactly go out of my way to find the body of Ellen Clark, you know. Major and I simply stumbled upon her when we were out for his last walk of the day. But I do like to be of use. Besides, you were pleased to have my help in the Balfour House case.'

'That's as may be...'

What a ridiculous expression she'd always thought that to be. 'It's perfectly true.' She would take another tack. 'I'm good-natured and wonderfully adaptable.'

Inspector MacKenzie laughed. 'What would you be meaning by that?'

'I'm meaning that you can, on occasion, be... less than good-natured—'

An eyebrow rose. 'Me?'

She ignored his comment. 'And I can open doors that you cannot.'

He laughed. 'I dinna think there is any high society in a fishing village such as Plockton, my lady.'

'That's as maybe' – *ha,* she added to herself – 'but I've already struck up a sort of friendship with various people in the village, and they might be less keen to speak to a police officer from Edinburgh.'

Poppy kept her candid hazel eyes on his dark ones, and felt a little flushed when she noticed those warm eyes were gazing at her mouth. Was her scarlet lipstick smudged? Resisting the temptation to examine her face in the mirror set in the wall above the inspector's head, she reminded herself that she should not be distracted from her purpose.

'Well?' she demanded.

Inspector MacKenzie gave a start. 'I dare say you may be right.'

He might have phrased it better than that! 'Of course I am. And I propose we start immediately.'

Poppy launched into a report of what she knew – which seemed little, now she recounted it – and had just finished when the train pulled into Plockton.

The inspector got to his feet, removed his hat and a small bag from the netting rack overhead and crossed to the window to release the leather strap. The window down, he leaned out and turned the handle. The door swung open, and he stepped down onto the platform, Major bounding after him. While admiring her dog's method, Poppy accepted Inspector MacKenzie's proffered hand and stepped down rather more decorously.

The stationmaster stepped forward and touched his cap. 'Good afternoon, sir, madam.'

Dash it, she didn't have a ticket. She put her hand into her pocket for her purse, but Inspector MacKenzie had already removed his wallet.

'My ticket,' he said, holding it out to the stationmaster, along with some coins. 'And for the lady's journey from Duncraig.'

The stationmaster touched his cap again and moved away. Poppy raised an eyebrow at Inspector MacKenzie. 'You didn't have to pay.'

'It wouldna do for a police officer to be associating with a common criminal.'

Common!

'I meant I could have paid for my own ticket.' That sounded churlish, she realised, so she added, 'But thank you.'

'Now I have to visit the police house. I expect you already know the way, my lady.' He smiled as he settled his hat on his head.

'I certainly do, Inspector,' she told him, and before he could ask her for directions, she stated firmly, 'And to save time, I will escort you there.'

She turned and marched off, Major at her heels. The inspector's long legs enabled him to catch up easily.

'There is the open-air church,' she told him with a wave of her hand as they approached the verge towards the rubble archway. At the sides of the steps leading up, grass of Parnassus, with its ivory-white flowers on long stems, bloomed happily in the sun. 'Would you like to see it now?'

'No' right now, thank you. There is a protocol to follow. Edinburgh agreed to lend me to the Inverness police service, given that I was to be in the area, and the Procurator Fiscal is happy with that, but I dinna want to upset the local man. I'm after first introducing myself to the constable.'

'Yes, of course. What can I say about Constable Macduff, other than I suppose he's doing his best...' She let the sentence hang, to suggest that she knew at least as much as did the constable.

The inspector made no comment.

'That is where I am staying,' Poppy added as they passed the Harbour Hotel. 'I expect it's where you'll be staying too. I'm taking the 8.21 this evening to Kyle of Lochalsh.'

'Just so, my lady.'

What did that *just so* mean? He agreed that she should leave? Or simply that he understood what she had said?

They walked on.

She broke the silence. 'If you need me to clarify any points of the investigation so far, you can find me at the hotel here until early evening, and after that at the Isle of the Mist Hotel on Skye.'

Inspector MacKenzie nodded but said nothing. Bother the man, she thought, vexed at his silence. Was he going to share this investigation with her or not?

'A bonnie position,' the inspector observed as they reached the police house overlooking the loch.

'Shall I come in with you?' she enquired, trying desperately not to show how eager she was to hear what the inspector would discuss with Constable Macduff.

The corner of his sensuous lips twitched. He was laughing at her again!

'That won't be necessary, my lady. I can manage from here.' He touched his hat to her and pushed open the door.

Poppy stood there, staring at the door as it closed behind him.

'Well,' she said to Major, 'there is impolite and then there is Inspector James MacKenzie.'

She was determined to help the ungrateful inspector solve the case, whether he wanted her to or not.

TEN

Poppy returned to the Harbour Hotel, impatient for the inspector to call. While she waited, she sat in an upholstered chair in her room, swinging her legs over the arm and writing in her notebook.

Day Two of Investigation into the Murder of Ellen Clark.

1. Inspector MacKenzie now in Plockton and to travel to Skye.

That piece of information wasn't strictly necessary for her notes, but she liked writing his name in her book.

2. Conversation with Young Malcolm.

He said Ellen Clark seemed quiet at the end of their boat trip.

What had Mr Henderson said to cause this? Something unwelcome, presumably. Now that Poppy thought about it, could the glitter in her eyes, as described by Mrs Grant, have been unshed tears? He might have told her on the boat that he was going away for a week. Would that have been enough to make her weepy? It didn't seem likely, but who knows how she had felt?

> 3. *Miss Brown says Isabella Buccleuch went for a walk during the period Ellen was killed.*

Now that at least was something useful, Poppy thought, although she needed to know more.

> 4. *The solicitor Mr Paterson reports that Ellen visited him recently, but had made no Will.*

Poppy held her pencil poised. What else had she learned today?

> 5. *Alan Henderson has been staying at the Plockton Inn, but checked out in the morning on the day of Ellen's murder. He's expected back there in a week.*

She was looking back over the list when Elspeth entered the room.

'I've come to pack your bag, my lady.'

'Thank you,' Poppy said. 'While you do so, I'll read out what I have written here, and then you can tell me what you have discovered from Miss Brown.' She proceeded to do so and waited for any comments from Elspeth.

'I can help you with some further details for note number three,' Elspeth said.

'Yes?' Poppy said keenly, swinging her legs round into the normal sitting position.

'Miss Brown told me to call her Dotty.' Elspeth shuddered. 'It is short for Dorothy, I believe.' She added Poppy's blue pleated dress to the bag she'd placed on top of the ottoman at the end of the bed.

'Very interesting, I'm sure, Elspeth, but what did she say of relevance to the investigation?' Poppy demanded.

'I am getting to that, my lady.' There was a small smile about Elspeth's mouth. 'Miss Brown – well, *Dotty*,' she went on, the smile disappearing as she twitched her long nose in distaste, 'informed me that she and her friend went on an excursion, booked through the hotel, to Urquhart Castle. Dorothy was quite taken with its ruins on the shore of Loch Ness,' said Elspeth, moving between drawers and overnight bag, 'and especially with the tale of the monster, seen by no less than St Columba in the sixth century.'

'Who are we to doubt a saint?' Poppy murmured.

'When the two women arrived back, they had a wash, then Isabella went out, saying she needed to stretch her legs after strolling about ruins and then sitting in a motor coach for so long. Two and a half hours each way, apparently. By this time it was about seven o'clock,' Elspeth added.

Poppy nodded. 'And what did Dorothy do while her friend was walking?'

'She had an appointment to see a woman in the village about a—'

'Let me guess,' Poppy said dryly. 'A button?'

'Aye, my lady. I dare say Inspector MacKenzie would be impressed by that bit of deduction.'

'Yes, well. Do go on.'

Elspeth placed the last layer of tissue paper on top of Poppy's belongings and closed the bag. 'It seems the woman asked Dorothy to call at her cottage in Frithard Road just after seven. The lady is old and frail and wanted her son to be there.'

'And Isabella wasn't interested in this particular button?'

'Apparently not, my lady.' Elspeth moved the luggage off the ottoman and placed it on the floor.

'What time did Dorothy and Isabella return?'

'About the same time as each other, Dorothy says. Shortly after that they went down to supper together, which was not long after eight o'clock.'

'That fits in,' Poppy said. 'We went down at half past eight. So, Dorothy and Isabella provide an alibi for each other until around seven o'clock. Between then and eight o'clock, Dorothy has an alibi, assuming her story is corroborated by the old lady and her son, while Isabella does not. Thereafter, both the women are seen in the hotel, and Ellen's body is discovered shortly after half past nine.'

'That's about it, your ladyship.'

Poppy looked at her notebook. She hadn't left enough space at number three, so she would add an additional number. What a satisfactory day this was turning out to be!

1. Isabella has no alibi for between seven and eight o'clock.

She would certainly have had time to walk to the open-air kirk, do the deed and walk back for supper with her friend, Poppy thought. And now she came to recall, Isabella had said over dinner last night, before Ellen's body was found, that Ellen had *seemed* – past tense – a pleasant sort of person. Wait until she told the inspector this! She had virtually solved the case already.

'Thank you, Elspeth. Excellent work.'

Elspeth pursed her lips.

Poppy put aside her notebook and hastened downstairs to the reception desk.

'Miss Grant,' she said, 'can you confirm that the Misses Buccleuch and Brown booked through the hotel and took the day excursion to Urquhart Castle yesterday?'

The manageress looked surprised, but she agreed that they had.

'And may I use the hotel's telephone in the office to make a call to the police house?'

'Of course, your ladyship.' Miss Grant gestured to the office.

Poppy thanked her, dashed into the small room and picked up the telephone.

'Plockton police,' came Constable Macduff's voice.

'Constable Macduff, I would like to speak to Inspector MacKenzie,' she said.

There was a pause, before the constable spoke again. 'Is that Lady Persephone Proudfoot?'

'The same.'

'The inspector isna here at the moment.'

'Then where is he? It's very important I speak to him before the murderer gets away!'

'You've solved the crime, have you, my lady?' His tone was dry.

'Very possibly.' She wasn't going to tell the constable about her deductions. 'Where can I reach the inspector?' she asked again.

'I canna say. He is out on police business.' Poppy heard the constable bristle at the other end of the telephone.

She took a breath to keep her tongue civil. 'Well, when do you expect him back?'

'I canna say, your ladyship. But I can say that your help isna needed.'

Infuriating little man!

'Very well, when Inspector MacKenzie returns, kindly ask him to come and see me at the Harbour Hotel, as a matter of urgency.'

Poppy returned the earpiece to the fork on the side of the stick and set the telephone back on the desk. Slamming it down would have been more satisfactory, but it wasn't hers to treat that way.

Instead, she glared at it.

ELEVEN

Poppy quietly fumed as she and Elspeth ate their dinner and still no inspector appeared. Why hadn't he come? Did he think she was – Heaven forbid! – nothing more than a bored socialite? But no, he couldn't believe that. Hadn't she proved she was serious about investigating and that she was good at it?

At eight o'clock, she could wait no longer. Poppy paid the hotel bill, and she and Elspeth walked up the hill. The station was very quiet, with no other passengers waiting to board. The porter touched his cap to her and continued watering the station flower beds filled with a cheerful display of scarlet geraniums, white gladioli and purple heather, their floral, musky scent floating on the evening air.

The train puffed slowly towards them. It stopped, one door opened and a woman and child got out, hurrying off the platform and away. As Poppy climbed onto the train, she cast a last look behind her, half expecting to see Inspector MacKenzie come running, waving his hat at the engine driver to wait. Even Major looked hopeful. But the platform remained empty.

The journey to the West Coast was a short but adventurous one. The line plunged up and down steep gradients, through

Duirinish station and Drumbuie village, twisted around a bay and across a causeway, the towering peaks of Skye looming, before pulling into Kyle of Lochalsh at the end of the line. Carriage doors were thrown open and a few women carrying baskets of shopping stepped down onto the platform and disappeared into the gloaming.

Poppy and Elspeth walked past the Lochalsh Hotel, down to the pier where the small motor boat to Skye waited. A car had already been loaded, balanced on planks placed across the ferry, and taking up most of the space.

'Last ferry of the day! Room for two lassies and one dog!' called one of the boatmen, seeing them hastening towards the steamer.

'Is that fellow shouting at us?' Elspeth's voice was icy as she made a pretence of looking around them.

'It's welcome you are,' the weather-beaten skipper said as they reached the slipway. Major jumped into the boat, as the man took their bags and handed the ladies in. 'The crossing's only half a mile, so you willna get seasick.'

Poppy and Elspeth edged around the motor car, perched precariously on the planks with its driver seated at the wheel.

'That doesn't look very safe to me,' Elspeth muttered.

'It's secured with straps,' Poppy pointed out.

'Even so.'

The Labrador looked with interest at the water. 'Don't even *think* about jumping in,' Poppy warned him. He sent her a guilty look, and contented himself with placing his front paws on the bow, letting the breeze lift and flap his ears.

Poppy sat on the bench. 'Elspeth,' she said, gesturing to the long wooden seat.

'I prefer to stand, my lady. The seat may not be clean.'

The boat began to move and Elspeth toppled forward.

'Steady there,' one of the ferrymen laughed as he caught hold of her. 'Will you no' sit down, lass? It'll be a lot safer.'

Her face flushed, Elspeth removed herself from the man's arms and perched on the bench. As they chugged across Loch Alsh, the Red Cuillin mountains looming over the water, Elspeth produced a small bottle from her bag and turned to pour the contents over the bow.

'Elspeth, what are you doing?' Poppy asked in surprise.

'It's a small gift to Poseidon, my lady.' Turning back, Elspeth shot her an embarrassed look. 'It should be wine, oil, milk or honey, but he will have to make do with water.'

Poppy smiled. 'I'm surprised you believe in the god of the sea.'

'I don't, my lady, but it does no harm to be on the safe side.' A sudden swell hit the boat and Elspeth gave a small shriek, one hand clutching the wooden bench, the other her hat. 'Oh dear, I shouldn't have insulted him with water.'

Poppy smiled and glanced back at the mainland. Much as she was looking forward to seeing Catriona again and to visiting Skye, she felt a wave of frustration at leaving Plockton with a murder still to be investigated. Perhaps, she told herself, she would learn something of use to the case before Inspector MacKenzie arrived on the island. A tourist who may have travelled through Plockton recently might provide some sort of clue.

The sun was low over the water as they approached Kyleakin. Poppy's attention was caught by ruins high on a rock.

'What is that?' she asked the boatman.

'It's aye that remains of *Caisteal Maol*,' he told her. 'The castle was the home of a Norse princess, married to the fourth MacKinnon clan chief around the year 900. She strung a chain across the Kyle passage and demanded tolls from ships wishing to pass through.'

'Enterprising, if not very charitable,' Poppy observed.

'It's said that the princess lies buried at the top of *Beinn na Caillich* – Mountain of the Old Woman – with her face turned towards Norway.'

A picture of the avaricious princess lying in her high, windswept grave came to Poppy's mind, only to be almost immediately replaced by the image of the strangled body of Ellen Clark. Her burial would take place soon, but it would be modest. Poppy hoped that the trust for distressed gentlewomen would pay for the funeral. And that Alan Henderson would hear what had happened to his lady friend and return early from his business trip. Given the lack of family, Ellen's funeral was likely to be poorly attended.

Poppy turned her gaze towards the harbour and saw a woman of her own age in a long coat and with a red hat on her auburn pompadour, standing on the quay and waving furiously.

'Catriona!' Poppy called back, laughing and waving her arm as the boat nosed towards the pier at Kyleakin.

'My lady,' murmured Elspeth. 'Please remember your position.'

'Oh, fiddle-de-dee,' Poppy laughed, pleased to see her old friend again.

The ferry slowed, churning the water as it entered the harbour. As the skipper brought the ferry to rest, rising and falling in the slight swell, the driver started his motor car.

'Foot passengers off first,' shouted the skipper.

The crewman jumped onto the pier and secured the boat's thick rope around a bollard.

Poppy rose, picked up her bag, stepped off the boat and hastened up the wide pier. A lone herring gull screamed overhead, its loud, piercing call sounding eerie in the evening light.

'Poppy, my dear!' Catriona exclaimed, a flush of pleasure on her pale-skinned, freckled face. 'I am delighted to see you!' Her green eyes danced as she put out her arms towards Poppy and they hugged. 'And Elspeth,' Catriona went on, stepping forward to greet her in the same way. Elspeth stepped back quickly, looking alarmed. Major got between the two women and gave a loud bark. Catriona laughed. 'Major Lewis too. How perfect.

Now, you must all be tired after your journey,' she continued. 'It's only about half an hour to the hotel by car, and mine is there.' Catriona pointed proudly at the shiny chestnut-brown car waiting on the harbour as they walked towards it. 'What do you think of her?'

'She's beautiful,' Poppy said, 'but not a model I recognise.'

'A Galloway, a Scottish manufacturer. *A car made by ladies for others of their sex*, says their advertisement. Betsy's got a rear-view mirror, she's lighter and has more storage space than other cars, her raised seat gives the driver better views, and her hand brake is near the driver's seat rather than under the dashboard, so that's more convenient too,' Catriona beamed.

'Betsy is perfectly divine. And thank you so much for meeting us, especially as I had to change our arrival time almost at the last moment.' Poppy smiled at her friend.

Catriona became serious as she stowed their luggage in the back and waited for Poppy to make herself comfortable in the front passenger seat, with Elspeth and Major in the rear seat. The vehicle's windows were already open to enjoy the balmy evening.

'A murder in Plockton,' she said, shaking her head as she climbed into the driver's seat. 'It hardly seems believable.'

'News travels fast, even here,' Poppy said. 'How did you know?'

'We're not a complete backwater!' Catriona smiled. 'It was in the morning paper.'

'Lady MacCorkindale would never have countenanced such a thing as a murder,' Elspeth muttered.

Catriona raised an eyebrow at Poppy and put the car into gear. 'Will you tell me what happened when we get to the hotel?' she murmured. 'There was only a small piece in the *Stop Press* column.'

Poppy nodded, and the Galloway moved smoothly away from the harbour and onto the winding road towards Portree.

'How is Rory?' Poppy asked as they sped along, the sun almost set.

'He's very well, thanks, but he's on the mainland, in Ullapool. His mother became unwell suddenly and he's gone to visit her.'

'I'm sorry to hear that. Nothing serious, I hope?'

'We're not sure yet. He'll telephone me when he has some news. But, Poppy,' Catriona sent her a disappointed look, 'it does mean I won't be able to spend as much time with you as I'd hoped, at least not until Rory returns.'

'Please don't worry. I'm sure I can entertain myself very well,' Poppy reassured her.

'Between you and me,' Catriona went on, 'her illnesses appear when she feels lonely. We asked her to come and live with us when we moved here a year ago, but she has a married daughter and grandchildren on the mainland, and she would miss them if she came to Skye. It's a bit of an impossible situation,' she finished, 'as they don't live that close to her either.'

As they travelled, Poppy admired aloud the lochs, the ancient moors dotted with sheep resting for the night, and the mountains, their tops shrouded by the darkening sky. They passed the occasional cottage in the lee of a hill and flew across a tiny stone bridge over a burn. They drew into Portree, the capital of the island, just as the sun set.

'*Port Righ*,' said Catriona. 'King's port. Or, more likely, since the town predates James V's visit, *Port Ruighe*, meaning slope harbour.' She pulled up in front of a grand, whitewashed hotel on three floors, facing the town square. Oil lamps blazed in every window. 'No electricity on the island and no indication as to when that might change,' she said, 'but here we are, the Isle of the Mist Hotel.'

Poppy gazed up at the magnificent building. Wide, shallow steps led up to the double doors. On each side of the doors standing open in welcome was a shield carved in stone, featuring a triple-towered castle with an arm grasping a sword.

'It's very impressive,' Poppy said with a smile.

'I'm glad you like it. It's certainly bigger than the hotel we had in Ullapool when you last visited us,' Catriona said proudly. 'Forty bedrooms, large dining room, two sitting rooms, billiard room, all bedrooms with Turkish carpets on polished wood floors and mahogany furniture, most bedrooms with own bathroom and W.C. And a servants' hall, scullery, pantry, larders, wine cellar – oh, and a room for the vast and noisy boiler. And servants' quarters in the attic, of course. Stables, a coach house...'

As Catriona paused for breath, Poppy laughed. 'It's *perfect.*' She let out a sigh of relief they had arrived. It had been a long day.

She glanced at her watch. Almost half past nine. Poppy realised with a shiver that this time yesterday the search party had been gathering in the Harbour Hotel to look for Ellen Clark, who, unknown to everyone but the killer, was already lying quite dead in the deserted open-air kirk.

TWELVE

They alighted from the Galloway, and a page boy came running down the steps of the hotel to take the bags from the motor car.

Catriona turned to Poppy as they mounted the steps. 'Would you and Elspeth like dinner? We keep a late cook for guests who arrive after the usual dinner time, so it's no trouble.'

'Thanks for the offer,' Poppy replied, 'but we ate before we left Plockton.'

As the page boy began to carry the bags away, an eager young man in the hotel's smart uniform of grey with red piping hastened down the steps towards them. He stopped by the side of Catriona. 'Shall I put the car in the coach house for you, madam?'

'If you would, Gordon.'

The young man nodded and hurried on towards the car.

'Coffee would be wonderful, though,' Poppy continued, as they reached the front door of the hotel and entered the hall. Catriona had forgotten to mention this, she thought with fond amusement. 'Elspeth, will you join us?'

Elspeth shook her head. 'I will go and unpack, my lady.'

'There won't be much to unpack this evening, Elspeth, with

most of the luggage still in Inverness. Are you sure you won't join us?'

'Thank you, my lady, but I feel I've had enough excitement for one day. If I could have a cup of tea sent to my room, Mrs MacLeod? I would be very much obliged.'

'Of course,' said Catriona.

'Take Major up, will you please, Elspeth?' Poppy asked.

Elspeth looked down at the dog and sighed. 'Yes, my lady.' She called to him and he obediently followed her up the grand, carpeted staircase.

Catriona handed her own coat to the young woman at the reception desk, gave her the coffee and tea order, and led Poppy away. 'The small sitting room at the back of the hotel would be quieter, but it's rather gloomy. I prefer the Palm Court Lounge. We'll go there and you must tell me all about this murder of yours.'

'It's hardly *my* murder,' Poppy said as they entered the lounge and sat together on a comfortably padded wicker settee under one of the palms.

The lounge was a pleasant glassed-in room, the glowing oil lamps making the darkness outside even deeper. Inside there were a number of potted palms and tastefully arranged wicker furniture, a bar, and a trio of ladies playing Strauss waltzes in the corner.

'I wasn't suggesting you were the culprit!' Catriona laughed. 'Only that you might be investigating it. Your cousin Agnes wrote to tell me the shocking news about your role in solving the Balfour case. She said it's the talk of Edinburgh.'

'I doubt the whole of Edinburgh knows about it, but I did have a part in solving the case.' Poppy smiled. 'Agnes is such a gossip. It was rather exciting, to be honest. And such fun, although I probably shouldn't say that. A rather attractive detective was working on the case, and now he's investigating the Plockton murder.'

She noticed a small group of ladies coming through the door of the Palm Court Lounge and glanced around the crowded room. 'You're very busy tonight, Catriona.'

'August is usually a busy month, but this year I've helped to organise a summer programme, which starts tomorrow. Don't laugh, but one of the events is a button exhibition. Anyway, it all promises to be hectic. We're preparing for a rush on afternoon teas.'

Poppy wondered if Inspector MacKenzie, his cousin and the friend had reservations here. She immediately conjured up a pleasant image of Inspector MacKenzie, in a bedroom adjoining hers, propped up against the pillows, smiling at her and...

'Och, I almost forgot,' Catriona put in, dispelling the image. 'Your chauffeur sent a telegram to say the car has been repaired and he will bring it across in the morning.'

'It'll be nice to have a choice of clothes again,' Poppy smiled. 'I know all about the button exhibition. I met two ladies in Plockton who are going to the event.'

A waitress brought a coffee pot with two cups and a little jug of milk. She set them down on the table in front of them. 'And the *Hebridean Evening News*, madam,' said the waitress.

Poppy's eye fell on the headline emblazoned across the top of the page: *Woman murdered!*

Catriona followed Poppy's gaze and picked up the newspaper. 'This is the Plockton case?'

Poppy could see the subheading: *Found strangled!* She nodded. 'I found her body. Or rather, Major did.'

Catriona's eyes widened. 'I guessed you might already be involved in some way. I remember your love of puzzles, and of solving them, when we were just children.'

Poppy laughed. 'I would imagine there was some mystery when we found a broken flowerpot in the greenhouse—'

'And it was simply the castle cat who had got in and knocked it down from the shelf!'

'Or when one of the maids went missing—'

'And it turned out she had gone to visit her parents for a couple of days.'

Poppy gave a melodramatic sigh. 'Oh, how disappointed I was to have my thrilling theories shattered.'

But the murder of Ellen Clark actually had happened, Poppy reminded herself, and it was a real case to be solved.

'Read the piece out to me,' Poppy urged her friend. 'I want to see if they've kept to the facts. Newspapers don't always get things right, you know.'

Catriona lowered her voice. *'Fears are growing for the safety of the inhabitants of the tiny fishing village of Plockton, after a victim was found dead last night in the open-air kirk. Mrs Ellen Clark, a respectable minister's widow...'*

She met Poppy's eye. 'Would the editor have deemed it less shocking if the victim hadn't been a respectable widow?'

It was Poppy's turn to shake her head. 'They want it to be sensational. Murder sells newspapers. What else does it say?'

Catriona bent her auburn head to the newspaper and read on. 'Here we are... *widow of middle years had resided at the Harbour Hotel since the death of her husband a year ago. When she failed to return to the hotel for dinner, a search was instituted. The dreadful discovery of Mrs Clark's body was made last night, when the unfortunate lady was found to have been strangled. "And with her own scarf," said Harbour Hotel manageress Miss Grant.'*

'Really,' said Poppy, 'would it be less shocking if the poor woman had been strangled with another's scarf?'

Catriona shook her head in exasperation. *'Her body was found by Major Lewis, the black Labrador belonging to a leading member of Edinburgh Society, Lady Persephone Proudfoot, daughter of the Earl of Crieff of Dunearn Castle, Perthshire.'*

Constance looked up, aghast. 'Oh, Poppy, how *awful* to be named in this way.'

Poppy took the paper from her friend and read in a low voice. '*The Earl and his Countess are believed to be living on a sheep station in Western Australia.*' She gave a wry smile. 'Thank goodness my parents aren't here to read that. It makes them sound irresponsible.'

She turned her attention back to the news item. '"*It was quite the most distressing night of my life," the Socialite is believed to have told our reporter.*'

'Oh for goodness' sake!' Poppy threw the newspaper down on the table. 'I said no such thing. It *was* very distressing, but I never even saw a journalist, let alone spoke to one. I wouldn't be surprised if Miss Grant also hadn't made that comment they've used.'

'Good evening, Mrs MacLeod,' said a cool voice.

Poppy and Catriona looked up, startled.

'Mrs Harper,' Catriona responded. 'How can I help you?'

Poppy saw a tall, slim woman, perhaps in her late thirties, with her dark hair cut in a structured bob, very short at the neck and the tapered ends at the front cut into sharp points. She wore a black chiffon dress embroidered with blue crystal beads, with blue satin shoes to match. She might have stepped straight out of Morningside.

'I couldn't help but overhear you mention the shocking murder of that widow in Plockton,' Mrs Harper went on. 'Being a widow myself, I am naturally uneasy.' She cast a curious glance at Poppy.

Poppy didn't think Mrs Harper looked at all uneasy, but she could understand the woman's concern. She felt she must try and reassure her.

'It was a dreadful thing to have happened,' Poppy said, 'but there's no reason to think anyone here is in danger.'

'Oh, but perhaps we should be concerned.' Mrs Harper slid

elegantly onto the seat opposite. 'Until the beast is caught, we can't say that any respectable woman is safe.' Her blue eyes moved towards the ring finger on Poppy's left hand. 'Are you here with your husband, Mrs...?'

'This is Lady Persephone Proudfoot,' Catriona put in.

'*Oh*! The lady mentioned in the article. How ghastly for you,' Mrs Harper went on. 'Did you know the dead woman?'

'No, I did not,' Poppy told her.

'I expect your husband whisked you away as soon as humanly possible.'

There was something about Mrs Harper that Poppy didn't like. 'Like you, I'm a widow.'

'So many of us lost our men in the Great War.' Mrs Harper gave a sober nod. 'Then we widows must stick together. And with this latest news, we need to be careful.'

Poppy smiled politely at the woman.

'Everyone is talking about the murder of the widow,' Mrs Harper went on, 'and I wondered if there were any new developments?'

'No, but I'm sure there will be,' Poppy said.

'My dear, how can you say that?' Catriona exclaimed.

'Because...' How much should she say? 'Inspector MacKenzie from the Edinburgh Detective Branch has been assigned to the case.'

'You sound as if you personally know the detective,' Mrs Harper observed.

Poppy almost groaned; she'd intended to tell only Catriona. 'It was something I heard when I was in Plockton today.' That was true, after all.

Mrs Harper gave a soft gasp. 'But surely you must know much more than is in the newspaper.'

'Not really, I'm afraid.'

'But you are quoted—'

'Wrongly, I assure you. You should not believe everything

you read in the newspapers, Mrs...' Poppy waited for the woman to supply her name, although she knew it was Harper. Petty, she thought to herself, but she had never been keen on people insinuating themselves into her company without an invitation.

'Harper,' stated the other woman.

Catriona had clearly sensed Poppy's discomfort, and she rose. 'Lady Persephone must be tired after her journey, so if you will excuse us, Mrs Harper.'

Poppy got to her feet and the other woman had no choice but to do the same. 'Goodnight, Mrs Harper.'

'Goodnight, your ladyship, Mrs MacLeod.'

Catriona took hold of Poppy's arm and steered her out of the lounge, leaving Mrs Harper standing alone in the crowded room.

They crossed the hall and were almost at the bottom of the stairs when they heard a female's urgent voice.

'Oh, excuse me, *please*!'

Poppy and Catriona turned to see a small, timid-looking lady hurrying into the hall after them.

'I couldn't help but overhear what was said just now, my lady. Do you really think we are safe? I'm a spinster, not a widow, but I don't know if that is relevant...' She picked anxiously at a thread in the cuff of her beige velvet dress.

'I'm afraid I cannot say what is in the mind of the murderer,' Poppy said calmly, 'but I can assure you that the finest detective in Scotland is working on the case.'

With a shock, Poppy realised the short, thin woman standing before her must be no older than herself. The timidity and nervousness that she exhibited acted to make her seem older. Especially when put together with her dowdy dress trimmed with its lace collar.

Poppy gave her a reassuring smile. 'I'm sure there's no need to worry.'

'Oh, I do hope so,' the lady murmured. 'Being alone in the world does tend to make a woman rather nervous, you see.'

'You have no family?' Poppy asked.

'No longer, I'm afraid.' She gave Catriona a shy smile. 'This is the nicest hotel I've ever stayed in. I'm tempted to make it my home. I have some money from my father's estate.'

'I'm sure we would be pleased to have you for as long as you wish,' Catriona told her kindly.

'That is good to hear. But I'm interrupting your conversation. I'm going to my room now, but... would tomorrow be too early to speak to you about my future residency, Mrs MacLeod?'

'Not at all,' said Catriona, giving her a warm smile.

Poppy and Catriona watched as she made her way up the stairs. 'That's Miss Scott,' Catriona said, when the other woman reached the first landing. 'Here on holiday. She's spent most of her time alone, although I'm glad to see she's made an acquaintance in a new guest.'

'And who is that?' Poppy asked idly.

'Mrs Harper.' Catriona shrugged. 'Not an obvious combination, I grant you.'

Not an obvious combination at all, Poppy agreed, but perhaps the more confident Mrs Harper would be a good influence on the timid Miss Scott.

But was there any truth, Poppy wondered, in Mrs Harper's apparent belief that widows were in danger?

THIRTEEN

The following morning, dressed in the tailored emerald-green tweed and looking forward to the arrival of her luggage, Poppy descended the grand staircase. Major bounded beside her, his tail wagging and his nose twitching at the delightful aromas coming from the dining room.

'Breakfast smells good, don't you think?' she said to him. 'Perhaps they'll have sausages.'

The dining room was full of people and noisy chatter. A waiter came towards Poppy.

'Table for one with a dog, please,' she told him.

'Certainly, madam.' He was leading her towards a table away from the kitchen doors, when she spotted last night's shy lady sitting alone, wearing a sensible brown skirt and jumper. Pinned to the bosom of the jumper was a rather nice brooch, which Poppy had noticed the night before: a small, square-cut emerald set on a silver bar. Its elegant, open scrollwork made her suspect it was a piece by Carrington.

'I'll share the table with Miss Scott,' she told the waiter, 'if she has no objection to my canine companion.'

He gave a deferential nod of his head and crossed the floor. She saw him have a brief conversation with Miss Scott, who turned her head and smiled at Poppy and Major. The waiter returned and she followed him to the other woman's table by a window.

'Miss Scott, how delightful to see you again. Thank you for allowing Major and me to join you.'

'Oh, it's my *pleasure!*'

Poppy took the seat held for her by the waiter and ordered a glass of orange juice, coffee, scrambled eggs and toast with honey. The dog, settling down on the floor beside her chair, sent her a *don't forget me* look. 'And a sausage or two for Major, if you please.'

She turned to Miss Scott. 'There's nothing like a good breakfast to start the day, don't you agree?' she said brightly. Her gaze fell on the glass of half-drunk orange juice and a plate holding a single slice of toast. 'Oh, but you have almost finished. I suppose I am rather late.'

Poppy didn't think that she was at all late, having noticed the untouched cutlery and china at Miss Scott's place setting, and she had a sudden concern about the other woman's financial situation. True, she had mentioned her father's estate, and that brooch would have been expensive, but her clothes were dowdy and appeared to have been made some ten years ago by a country dressmaker, and the Isle of the Mist was an expensive hotel. No doubt that was why she wanted to speak to Catriona about a rate for a more permanent residence.

'I find I'm not particularly hungry in the mornings, my lady,' Miss Scott was saying apologetically. She smiled down at Major. 'When I was growing up, the family dog was always a black Labrador.'

That sealed Poppy's liking for Miss Scott. 'Please, call me Poppy.'

Miss Scott turned faintly pink. 'Oh, I couldn't possibly do that, your ladyship.'

'Nonsense! I insist,' Poppy smiled. She then looked enquiringly at Miss Scott. There was a pause, and Poppy could see her companion wrestle with her emotions. A look of fear of doing the wrong thing and one of pleasure at finding a new friend managed to cross her features at the same time.

'My Christian name is Harriet,' Miss Scott whispered at last, the pink on her face deepening.

'Harriet. What a delightful name.' Poppy smiled.

'Oh, do you really think so? It's not often I hear anyone use it,' she confessed.

'Then I shall use it as much as possible!' Poppy declared.

'Oh no, please don't.' Harriet looked round in horror, although no one at the other tables was taking any notice of them.

'Occasionally, then,' Poppy reassured her with a smile.

Harriet's face brightened with relief.

The waiter wended his way towards their table with a tray of orange juice, a coffee pot, scrambled eggs and a dish of sausages. Quickly, Poppy turned to Harriet. 'Would you join me in a cup of coffee?'

Harriet nodded, looking pleased.

'Another coffee pot, if you would, waiter,' Poppy told him as he set her breakfast items on the table and the dog's meal in front of him on the floor. Major continued to lie down, but his nose twitched and he kept an eye on his breakfast.

'He knows he is not to eat until I have finished. Leader of the pack and all that,' Poppy explained.

They chatted pleasantly while they ate their breakfast.

'What do you have planned for today, Harriet?' Poppy asked.

Harriet frowned and bit her lip. 'Mrs Harper wants me to visit the shops with her, but...'

'You're not so keen?' Poppy suggested.

'I didn't come to this beautiful island to go shopping.' She smiled.

'Then you and I must do something together.'

'Oh, I didn't mean that,' Harriet said, flustered. 'I don't want to impose on your time.'

'It was my suggestion, Harriet,' Poppy smiled. 'And you would not be imposing. I'm on holiday and I can spend my time as I wish.' True, she had come to see Catriona, but she couldn't expect her friend to spend much time with her, with a busy hotel to run and her husband away. 'What do you say to a visit to the harbour this morning?'

'I've not yet been down there, but from above I can see it has pretty cottages and a small bay.' Harriet returned Poppy's smile. 'That would be lovely.'

'What would be lovely?' Mrs Harper, in a smart royal blue dress with dropped waist, white collar and tie, stood at their table, a lighted cigarette in her hand. She turned to a passing waiter. 'I require another chair to be set here,' she informed him, 'and black coffee.'

What was it about this woman that she didn't quite like? Poppy wondered, as the waiter took an empty chair from a nearby table. Was it just the woman's forward nature, or – and Poppy hated to admit this even to herself – was it because Mrs Harper had a personality strong enough to match Poppy's own?

Mrs Harper lowered herself elegantly onto the seat, and tapped the ash from her cigarette into the ashtray on the table. 'What would be lovely?' she repeated, smiling.

Harriet sat in stricken silence.

'An outing Harriet and I were considering,' Poppy replied carefully.

There was a beat of silence, and Mrs Harper spoke again, looking between Poppy and Harriet. 'Not today, I imagine? Harriet and I are going shopping.'

'Jeanie,' Harriet began to protest, 'I did say I didn't really want to do that...'

'I'm sure you will enjoy it,' Jeanie Harper told her firmly.

Poppy could be equally firm. 'It's another beautiful day and it seems a shame to spend it indoors. I thought a stroll round the harbour would be more pleasant.'

Jeanie's smile didn't quite reach her eyes. 'I quite agree, your ladyship. Harriet and I have admired the view of the harbour from Bosville Terrace, but we haven't yet walked down to it. I think we will all enjoy that.' She drew in the vapour from her cigarette and expelled it through her nostrils, her eyes narrowing in the smoke.

Drat! Poppy hadn't wanted to include Jeanie Harper in the outing. But it would be impolite to exclude her now, and perhaps Jeanie Harper was actually as lonely as Harriet. Poppy accepted the situation as gracefully as she could.

She looked at her wristwatch. 'It's ten o'clock.' She wondered how Inspector MacKenzie was getting on with the investigation without her. She would telephone the police house... No, not there, Constable Macduff was unlikely to tell her anything. Poppy looked up to find Harriet and Jeanie waiting for her to continue.

'So shall we meet in the Palm Court Lounge in half an hour?' she went on brightly. That would give her time to make the telephone call.

'Yes, please, Poppy,' said Harriet in her soft voice.

'Please call me Jeanie,' Jeanie Harper said, looking directly at Poppy.

Poppy drank the remainder of her coffee. 'You may eat your breakfast now,' she told Major. He tucked in with gusto, and all the sausages disappeared in less than a minute.

'I'm surprised your dog doesn't suffer from heartburn,' Jeanie observed dryly, flicking ash from her cigarette into the saucer of her cup of coffee.

Harriet laughed. 'He is a real Labrador.'

Poppy excused herself, stood, and, instructing Major to follow her, left the dining room. She strode over to the reception desk, where the young woman was dealing with an elderly couple who had clearly just arrived. The page boy stood holding their suitcase, waiting to hear which room they had been allocated.

When at last the couple moved away from the desk, Poppy stepped smartly forward.

'Could I possibly make a telephone call?' she asked the young woman. 'It is rather important.'

Well, important to *her*, anyway.

'Och, yes, my lady. We don't usually allow guests to use the telephone because it needs to be kept free for the hotel, but I ken you're a friend of Mrs MacLeod and I'm sure she willna mind.' The young woman slid the instrument across the counter to Poppy and turned away, busying herself with some paperwork.

Poppy picked up the handset, held it to her ear and waited. 'Hello, operator. The Harbour Hotel in Plockton, please... Thank you... Is Miss Grant there?... Oh, good morning, Miss Grant. This is Lady Poppy Proudfoot speaking... Very well, thank you. Have you seen Inspector MacKenzie from the Edinburgh Detective Branch, yesterday evening or this morning?... You have! Wonderful! What did he say?'

Poppy frowned as some half a dozen guests arrived, talking loudly. She pressed her other hand to her ear. 'I'm sorry, can you repeat that?'

'He came in last night and spoke to myself, the staff and the guests who were here,' said the voice at the other end of the line.

'And did he say anything else at all?' Poppy asked quickly, one eye on the door of the lounge in case Harriet Scott or Jeanie Harper came out and were curious.

'I'm afraid not, your ladyship.'

'Well, thank you, Miss Grant. Goodbye.'

Poppy put down the telephone. She would get ready for their stroll to the harbour, and try very hard to forgive the inspector for not telephoning her.

FOURTEEN

Shortly after half past ten, Poppy, with Major padding along happily beside her, led Harriet and Jeanie out of the hotel and into Somerled Square. Across the square, Poppy noticed, were the courthouse and the police office. Conveniently close to run into Inspector MacKenzie if he should visit his island colleagues, she thought.

'Somerled was the first Lord of the Isles in the twelfth century,' Harriet was telling them happily. 'And in 1540, James V held court in this very square.'

Jeanie directed a look of tolerant amusement towards Poppy. Poppy looked away; Harriet was in her element and she could see nothing amusing about that.

They strolled along Wentworth Street with its shops and turned right into Bank Street.

'The Royal Hotel,' Harriet went on, gesturing to an imposing building on the right-hand side. 'It's built on the site of MacNab's Inn, where Bonnie Prince Charlie and Flora MacDonald had their final meeting, on the first of July 1746, before he fled to France.' She gave a soft sigh.

Jeanie laughed. 'Good heavens, Harriet, you are a romantic.'

Harriet's face coloured with embarrassment.

They walked down Quay Street and a row of brightly painted houses came into view, with a cobblestone slipway at the end.

'It's very pretty,' Harriet murmured.

'Isn't it?' Poppy smiled at Harriet. 'Shall we find somewhere to sit in the bay?'

They went down the steps, onto the sandy shingle, and found a sheltered place to sit. Poppy removed her tweed jacket and seated herself comfortably on it. The sun felt warm through her tussar silk blouse, and its bright rays highlighted the deep gold colour of the fabric. Major wedged himself in by her side, Harriet sat next to him and stroked his head, while Jeanie, after placing her handkerchief where she was to sit, lowered herself carefully to Harriet's other side.

Fishing boats bobbed on the water and hills towered in the background. Poppy pulled her sketch pad and pencil from her bag.

'Oh, do you draw, Poppy?' Jeanie asked.

Poppy stiffened at the use of her Christian name. But she had asked Harriet to use it, so she couldn't very well rebuke Jeanie for doing the same.

'Rather badly,' she managed to say pleasantly.

Harriet and Jeanie chatted about clothes, and Poppy listened idly while she drew the scene in front of them. If only she could get the boats right, and the water, and the hills...

She turned over the page and looked for a different composition. Major was lying asleep, so she shifted her position slightly to draw him. After a while she had a passable image of a dog, although not necessarily a Labrador. She turned to a fresh sheet.

Poppy set pencil to paper again, determined to improve her portrait work. Her earlier attempt had been of little, if any, help to Inspector MacKenzie in their last case, but if she could just become more skilful...

From where she sat, she had a three-quarter view of Jeanie, so she would start with her. Poppy sketched a rough outline of the oval shape of Jeanie's face and made a mark where the woman's eyes should be drawn. It was a common mistake, she'd read somewhere, of inexperienced artists to often draw the eyes of their subject too high up.

Having satisfied herself as to their position, Poppy drew Jeanie's eyes. She moved on to sketch the nose and mouth. The natural light did little for Jeanie, Poppy reflected. Perhaps it was her vivid red lips against the very pale skin that made her face look harsh. She finished with Jeanie's cloche hat, and the curl of her dark hair resting on each cheek. Poppy raised her eyes again to study the other woman's face, just as Jeanie glanced up.

'What are you drawing, Poppy?' Jeanie asked, a little sharply.

Disliking Jeanie's tone, Poppy said, 'I thought I might try to sketch you and Harriet. *A study of two ladies.* You know the sort of thing.'

'I'd rather you didn't draw me. I wouldn't want to spoil your picture.' There was a steely edge to Jeanie's laugh. 'Do show us what you have sketched.'

Poppy casually closed her sketchbook. 'I've not started that picture yet,' she lied.

'Oh, but I would still like to see.'

Poppy was determined not to show Jeanie the picture she clearly wanted to see. Instead, she flipped open the book to the sketch of Major and turned it towards Jeanie and Harriet, keeping the pad firmly in her hands.

'That's adorable!' Harriet exclaimed, politely adding, 'And so clearly Major.'

At the sound of his name, Major opened both eyes, got to his feet and stretched out all four legs.

'You're too kind,' Poppy said to Harriet, 'but I think it's a little better than my view of the harbour.' She showed her and Jeanie the first picture, taking care still to keep hold of the sketchbook.

Looking bored, Jeanie now glanced at her wristwatch and got to her feet. 'It's time to leave if we want to be back for lunch.'

'That was a lovely morning, Poppy,' Harriet said shyly, rising unsteadily on the uneven surface of the stones. 'Thank you for suggesting it.'

'Yes, it was rather jolly,' Jeanie added.

Jolly was the last word Poppy would have associated with Jeanie, she thought, as she put away her drawing equipment and got to her feet. 'We must have another outing sometime.'

She regretted saying that immediately the words were out of her mouth, for Jeanie quickly said, 'What a splendid idea.'

Good Lord, didn't the woman recognise an invitation that was civil and no more?

They picked their way off the stony cove and turned onto the road back towards the hotel.

'What about the Fairy Glen?' Harriet asked. 'I've heard there are rocks and ruined fairy castles, rowan trees and a stone circle labyrinth.'

'I'm sure it would make a fascinating outing.' Poppy liked Harriet, but she hoped Jeanie would find something more interesting to keep her from joining them.

'So, Poppy,' said Jeanie, 'have you heard anything more about the murder in Plockton?'

'No, nothing,' Poppy said briskly.

'Really?' Jeanie wrinkled her nose in disbelief. 'I read in the newspaper that you and your dog found the body, so I thought you might have inside information.'

'Jeanie!' Harriet gasped. 'I'm sure Lady Poppy hasn't.'

'I haven't,' Poppy assured her.

Jeanie eyed her carefully. 'But you were in Plockton at the time.'

'Well, yes, I was,' she admitted. 'But I have no idea who strangled the poor woman. The police are investigating and are certain to find the killer.'

Jeanie laughed. 'I've yet to meet a clever police officer.'

'Then you haven't met Inspector MacKenzie,' Poppy retorted. She was surprised at herself – how readily and earnestly she wanted to protect his reputation.

'But clearly *you* have met him,' said Jeanie, one well-shaped eyebrow raised in question as she came to a halt.

Poppy and Harriet were obliged to stop too. Under the inquisitive eye of Jeanie, Poppy felt her cheeks warm. She glanced at Harriet, who cast her eyes down, looking uncomfortable.

It was time to re-establish the normal boundaries of propriety, Poppy told herself. 'That is a very astute observation, Mrs Harper,' she said tersely, 'but I fail to see to what you are alluding.'

'Only to the fact that you have had occasion to become acquainted with a particular officer of the law, my lady.' Jeanie Harper was smiling. 'Did you have some items of your own stolen, jewellery perhaps?'

'No.' Poppy hadn't rattled the woman's aplomb at all. 'And good conscience prevents me from speaking any further on the matter. The incident is not a matter for idle gossip.'

There, she thought, that will keep Jeanie Harper at bay, and if I'm lucky it will also dissuade her from accompanying us on further outings.

As they all turned into Somerled Square, Poppy decided that she would call into the police office after lunch and make enquiries about the inspector. She intended to give him a piece of her mind for ignoring her telephone call.

After all, how could he possibly solve the crime without her help?

FIFTEEN

Back in the hotel's reception, a tall, slim, distinguished-looking gentleman with dark hair, and dressed in a tweed suit, came walking towards them, the smile on his face directed at Jeanie. 'Mrs Harper, I do believe. I cannot believe my good fortune! How long has it been?'

'Mr Hamilton! How pleasant to see you again.' She took his outstretched hand, then turned to Poppy and Harriet. 'This is Mr Hamilton, an acquaintance of my late husband. Lady Poppy Proudfoot and Miss Scott,' she said to Mr Hamilton, introducing each of them in turn.

'Delighted, ladies. And who is this handsome fellow?' Mr Hamilton bent and patted Major's head. The Labrador drew back with a start.

'His name is Major Lewis,' Poppy told him. 'It's best not to pat a dog on its head. Think of it as the equivalent of a giant hand suddenly coming down on your own.'

Mr Hamilton straightened and gave Poppy an apologetic smile. 'Oh dear, yes, I can see what you mean.'

'What brings you to Portree?' Jeanie and Mr Hamilton began at the same time. They laughed.

'You first, dear lady,' Mr Hamilton said.

'I'm taking a few days' holiday. And you?'

'The same. But let us not stand here in the hall, when we could be having a pleasant conversation over luncheon. That is, if you three ladies would do me the honour of being my guests here?' His smile encompassed them all.

'Thank you,' Poppy said, thinking it might be an interesting distraction. And she hadn't missed the genuine pleasure Jeanie had shown at the sight of the fellow.

Harriet flushed and nodded.

'That makes the three of us, then.' Jeanie smiled, giving the impression of being pleased with the arrangement. 'Do be kind enough to give us ladies a moment to freshen up and change.'

Mr Hamilton smiled. 'But you are all perfect as you are!' he protested.

'Nevertheless,' Jeanie insisted.

'Of course.' He gave a slight bow and stepped back. 'I will secure a table in the dining room and wait for you ladies in there.'

As the other two women made their way up the staircase, Poppy went to the reception desk. 'Are there any messages for Lady Persephone Proudfoot?' she asked.

The young woman checked in the pigeonholes behind her, and turned back. 'No, I'm sorry, your ladyship.'

'No telephone call, hand-delivered letter or message given in person?' Poppy went on, half hopefully.

The young woman shook her head. 'I'm sorry, my lady.'

Quietly fuming at the inspector, Poppy climbed the stairs. A glass of dry sherry would be just the thing at this moment, she thought as she opened the door of her room.

'A glass of sherry, my lady?' Elspeth said, turning to the decanter on the chest of drawers.

'You must be telepathic, Elspeth.' Poppy took the glass of pale straw-coloured wine and sank into the armchair.

Major trotted into the bathroom where his water bowl was set, and the sound of slurping could be heard, followed by a loud belch. He padded back out into the bedroom.

'How was your visit to the harbour, my lady?' Elspeth asked.

'Not too bad, except...'

'Except?'

'Except that, although Harriet Scott is a pleasant companion, there's something about the other woman, Jeanie Harper, that I dislike intensely.'

'She sounds a wee bit *forward*, my lady.'

'You are right, Elspeth, but it's more than that.' Poppy took a sip of her sherry. 'This is rather good.' She indicated the glass. 'Won't you join me?'

'No, my lady,' Elspeth said in a voice that indicated a maid should never drink with her lady. 'I wonder if you don't encourage forward behaviour from time to time. I mean, Inspector MacKenzie seems to feel he can call on you at any time, night or day.'

If only that were the case!

'Hardly, Elspeth. And we're not talking about him just now,' Poppy said, a pinch of annoyance in her voice. She took another sip of the sherry. 'Jeanie Harper is a strange creature,' she went on. 'She seems confident on the surface, but I get the impression that underneath she's uneasy. An interesting woman, don't you think?'

'I'm sure I have no opinion on the matter, my lady,' Elspeth said, with an icy look.

'None you wish to express, more like it.' Poppy sipped a little more of the sherry.

'That's because I was not there to make any observation of my own.'

'Good point.' Poppy twirled her sherry glass in her hand. 'Just now in the hall, we met an old friend of her late husband's, and he has invited Jeanie, Harriet and myself to join him for lunch.'

'Has he indeed, my lady?'

'He has.'

'And will you join him?'

'I have accepted. I'm curious about his relationship with Jeanie Harper, and it might be an amusing way to pass the time.'

'I trust the other two ladies will also be present. You would not want to give the wrong impression to a gentleman you have only just met.'

'They will also be there.' Poppy finished her drink and put the glass on the dresser. 'Do you know, when I was sketching at the harbour, Jeanie as good as told me not to draw her?'

'Perhaps she's a wee bit shy about the way she looks, my lady?'

'Have you met the woman?' Poppy's voice rose in disbelief. 'No, of course you haven't. Sorry to burden you with this, Elspeth.'

'Not at all, my lady.'

Poppy looked up sharply. Why was Elspeth being quite so... servile? There was no other word for it. But she had no time to consider the matter at present; she was expected downstairs.

'Has Fergusson arrived with the Bentley yet?'

'Yes, my lady. And I have started to unpack.'

'Oh, excellent news.' Poppy got to her feet. 'I thought I might wear my new headband at lunch.'

'You want to wear the peacock feather headband with crystal beads to impress him?'

'I want to wear it because I like it.'

'That's not going to be possible, my lady, because I have already returned it to Jenners.' Elspeth held Poppy's eye. 'It was not a suitable item for you.'

'Well, really, Elspeth!' Poppy spluttered. 'Don't you think I should be the judge of that?' If anyone exhibited forward behaviour, it was her own maid.

'As the Bard says, *O wad some Power the giftie gie us, to see oursels as ithers see us!*'

'I'm aware of Burns' poem "To a Louse, On Seeing One on a Lady's Bonnet at Church",' Poppy said stiffly, 'but I hardly think it's relevant here.'

Elspeth turned from the wardrobe. 'Your cream cloche is infinitely better, my lady.' She held it out.

Poppy took the felt hat with its biscuit-coloured ribbon and flower and jammed it onto her head. She had to admit it *did* suit her. But so did the peacock headband, she was certain – although perhaps it would have been a little grand for lunch at such a remote hotel.

'Oh, well, I shall just have to order the headband again from Jenners once we are back in Edinburgh,' she said airily.

Elspeth sniffed.

Still wearing the cream hat and smarting, Poppy stripped down to her silk underwear and splashed about in the bathroom, while suppressing her urge to discuss this morning's events with Elspeth.

She returned to the bedroom, and dressed in her cream skirt and matching long belted jacket with a shawl collar. Leaving Major snoozing in his basket, she returned downstairs.

'My lady,' Catriona called softly from the reception desk, gesturing for her to come over. 'Poppy, you may already know, but your chauffeur has arrived. I've given him a room at the top of the hotel and your Bentley is in the coach house.'

'Yes, thanks, Catriona.'

'I'm sorry that we've not yet had time to spend together, but as soon as Rory gets back from Ullapool, you and I will catch up on all our news.'

'Please don't worry about me,' Poppy reassured her. 'How is your mother-in-law?'

Catriona looked relieved. 'Much better, thanks. And so I'm sure he'll be home soon.'

As Poppy turned from her friend to make her way into the dining room, she saw Inspector MacKenzie, splendid in a cream V-neck jumper and dark trousers, a flat tweed cap on his dark curls, stride past the hotel's open front door.

A mix of anger and pleasure surged in her breast. How *dare* he simply pass by the hotel – and how *delightful* that he was here...

She marched in double-quick time to the door. 'Inspector MacKenzie!' she called after him from the top step.

He halted mid-stride and turned back. 'So it's yourself, my lady?' He smiled.

Poppy caught her breath. *Don't even think about that dimple,* she told herself. 'Good day to you, Inspector,' she said coolly.

He glanced behind her into the hotel. 'And is Detective Major Lewis in Portree with you?'

Poppy loved the way he said Portree with his Islander's accent. But she reminded herself she was cross with him. 'He is, and he will be delighted to see you again. I, on the other hand, am less than thrilled.'

Fibber!

He frowned. 'What has happened, your ladyship?'

He looked genuinely surprised. Had she misjudged him? 'I left a message at Plockton police office for you to come and see me at the Harbour Hotel before I left for Skye – and you didn't.'

His frown deepened. 'I did no' receive any such message.'

Well, really! Constable Macduff had failed to pass it on. She should have guessed; the constable was determined to keep her out of the investigation.

'Major is in my room at present, while I have lunch...' Poppy hesitated. Lunch with Inspector MacKenzie would be so *very* delightful. Would he ask her?

He was waiting for her to continue. 'Aye, my lady?'

She pulled herself together. 'Oh, it's just that I'm engaged to dine with others.'

He nodded. 'Verra nice, I'm sure.'

Enough of this chat-chat, she thought. Down to business. 'Tell me, Inspector, how is the case progressing?'

'We are doing all that we can to find the murderer, my lady.'

She pursed her lips. 'As you know, I can be of tremendous help. Women are naturally observant. They pay attention and are not always concentrating on their own matters.' Was that true? She wasn't sure, but it sounded good, anyway.

He thought for a moment, then drew her against the wall of the building and lowered further his naturally soft-spoken voice. He looked down at her, his eyes as dark as night. She looked up at him and heat washed over her. He murmured, 'I am following a hunch...'

'A hunch!' Her voice came out as a squeak. She swallowed. 'What sort of a hunch?'

'I'm concerned there might be more victims of the strangler.'

Poppy felt her eyes widen. 'A repeat killer?' she murmured. 'I've heard of the body snatchers Burke and Hare...'

'Aye, who murdered sixteen people in Edinburgh to meet the medical demand for corpses, and of course to line their own pockets.'

'But that was one hundred years ago.'

'And you are thinking that makes a difference?'

'One would at least hope this is a more civilised century.'

'There is nae harm in hoping. Meanwhile, I've put men on to examine the police files for other murdered women in the Highlands, and to be on the lookout for any suspicious characters. I'm after doing the same on Skye.'

'Is that why you're not in uniform?' Not that it mattered to her in the slightest what he wore.

'Aye, I dinna want to alarm the culprit if he's in the town.'

Poppy shivered at the thought. 'So you really think we are dealing with a... repeat killer?'

'I dinna ken yet,' the inspector reminded her, 'or what his motive might be.'

'He stole Ellen Clark's jewellery and handbag,' she pointed out.

'Aye, but she was a slightly built woman, and if he could have crept up on her quietly from behind, why not simply knock her out and take anything of value?'

'A hatred of women, perhaps?' Poppy shuddered.

'It has been known,' he said.

'A fellow guest is of the opinion that the killer might be targeting widows.'

'That can no' be concluded on the basis of one murder,' he pointed out.

'Then it's even more important that you use me in this investigation, Inspector.'

'Dinna suggest you act as a lure, to entice him into a trap,' he said grimly.

'Heaven forbid!'

'But we are getting ahead of ourselves.' Inspector MacKenzie straightened. 'And someone is staring at us.'

Poppy glanced round and saw Jeanie standing in the hotel doorway. Let the wretched woman wonder! Immediately, Jeanie disappeared back inside. 'That is one of my lunch companions. Very well, Inspector, let's meet for dinner this evening and we can exchange what information we have. Would you like to call for me here at seven o'clock?'

'Aye, but until then, dinna do anything dangerous, my lady,' he warned her.

'I will keep my wits about me,' she promised. Feeling considerably more cheerful, Poppy returned to the hotel and entered the dining room.

She smiled at the curiosity etched on Jeanie's face as the
waiter held Poppy's chair. Curiosity killed the cat, she thought,
as she took her seat. Then she was struck with a sudden,
dreadful notion. Perhaps Jeanie Harper was right to be
concerned. If there really was a repeat killer, then Jeanie, a
clearly affluent widow, might well be his next victim.

The presence of Mr Hamilton at lunch made Harriet quieter
than ever, so Poppy did her best to draw the shy woman into the
conversation.

'When did you arrive at the hotel, Harriet?' she asked.

'A week ago,' Harriet told her, before lowering her eyes
again to her plate of chicken rissoles.

'And where have you been so far?' Poppy persevered
gently.

'To the harbour with you and Jeanie this morning.' Her
voice was barely above a whisper. 'Otherwise, only in the town.
I know every shop.' She gave a self-deprecating smile.

'Then perhaps you would be good enough to show me
around?' Mr Hamilton suggested pleasantly.

Harriet's cheeks pinked. 'Oh!'

'It looks like Miss Scott would be delighted.' Jeanie said.

Nasty little cat! Poppy thought.

Harriet's cheeks went a deeper shade of pink. 'Well, I—'

'Come, come, Harriet,' Jeanie pressed. 'You are the perfect
guide to the island. I'm sure Mr Hamilton would benefit from
your historical knowledge of the area. Wouldn't you agree, your
ladyship?'

'Mrs Harris is correct, Mr Hamilton. Miss Scott is most
informed in her studies of the island. Though—'

'You should come along with the three of us on an outing,'
Jeanie cut in. 'Although we do have to be back before dinner.
Harriet has no liking for staying out any later.'

'Then we will have to find some form of amusing entertainment to rectify that,' said Mr Hamilton cheerfully.

Harriet, her face a fiery red, studied her plate with intensity.

How dare Jeanie make Harriet feel so uncomfortable, Poppy thought as she forked up a piece of chicken rissole to hide her annoyance. Even if the Hamilton fellow was simply being kind to Harriet, then let him be so without the interference of Jeanie. And *she* had no interest in going hither and yon, when there was a murder to solve.

'Please,' Mr Hamilton was saying, 'call me Algernon. It must be time for you to do so, dear Mrs Harper, and I'm sure the rest of us will soon be good friends too.'

'Do you own a car, Algernon? Only it would be terribly useful for trips around the island,' Jeanie purred.

'Alas, I was not able to bring my Morris Garage motor,' he said. 'It developed a fault, and I had to leave it for repairs. But a two-seater would have been inadequate for three such charming lady passengers. I will ask at the desk about hiring a suitable vehicle.'

'I'm not sure you would have very much luck with that idea. There seems to be a distinct lack of motor vehicles on the island. Jeanie turned to Poppy, 'I apologise if I'm being too forward, but I couldn't help overhearing Mrs MacLeod say your chauffeur had arrived with the Bentley?'

Was she to have no privacy from the woman? She hadn't seen Jeanie when Catriona had given her this news, so had Jeanie been eavesdropping? And positioning Poppy into offering her car for their use... The woman really was too much!

'We don't need to go anywhere,' Harriet said quickly, seeing the flush on Poppy's face. 'I'm quite happy staying here, in Portree.'

Poppy smiled at her, then addressed Jeanie. 'You are correct, and I'm sure we can all have an outing somewhere.' She needed to take control of the conversation before she ended up agreeing to drive them all goodness knows where. 'You were saying earlier, Mr Hamilton...'

He raised an eyebrow at her.

'Algernon,' she continued, 'that you are here for a few days' holiday?'

'That's right. I'm not long back from a visit to New York City, visiting a wealthy client of mine, and I've promised myself a break in the Islands.'

'Do you have plans to visit other Scottish islands too?'

'That depends on how much I find myself enjoying Skye.' He smiled round the table, but finished with his eyes and smile directed, not at Harriet, but at Poppy herself.

'A client in New York?' Poppy went on, swallowing her annoyance at his obvious flirtation. 'What is your line of business?'

He shook his head. 'Nothing that would interest a lady such as yourself.'

'I disagree. As it happens, I am interested in many things, so do tell me.'

'If you wish, but I assure you it's hardly a subject for lively discussion. I'm in finance,' he said reluctantly. 'There, I told you it would not be of interest.'

'You work in a bank?' Harriet asked suddenly.

'No, I'm in investments.'

'My husband was a banker,' Jeanie said, her hand touching her hat.

'And he would have agreed with me wholeheartedly, dear lady, that it's not at all an exciting profession.' Algernon indicated to the waiter to replenish their wine glasses.

'Not for me, thank you,' whispered Harriet. 'One glass of wine at luncheon is more than enough.'

'Nonsense. Same again for all of us,' he told the waiter with a broad grin.

'Mr Hamilton – Algernon,' Poppy said sternly, eyeing the waiter as he refilled the glasses, 'if a lady tells you something, please do her the courtesy of listening to her.'

A silence fell around the table.

'It's all right, Poppy, I don't mind.' Harriet quickly picked up her glass and took a gulp of the white wine.

'My apologies, dear Miss Scott,' Algernon said, contrite. 'Of course you should not drink if you do not wish to.'

Poppy was relieved when the meal came to an end. She excused herself as soon as she could politely do so, promising to drive them all to wherever they wished the following day.

She'd had a stupendous idea and wanted to speak to Elspeth about it right away. If her hunch – the inspector wasn't the only person to have one! – was correct, she would be able to prove that other women had also been the victim of the person who had murdered Ellen Clark.

SIXTEEN

Poppy ran up the stairs and burst into her room, just as Elspeth was removing the last few items from Poppy's suitcase.

'Good afternoon, my lady,' Elspeth said stiffly, placing on a hanger a pale pink backless evening dress with crystals around its dropped waist and cascading down the skirt. 'I took a short break from the unpacking to eat my lunch at a different establishment. I trust your ladyship doesn't mind.'

Dash it! From her tone, Elspeth was clearly still miffed about the peacock headband. Poppy would have to jolly her maid along.

'Elspeth,' she began.

'My lady?' Elspeth hung the dress in the wardrobe.

'Am I right in saying that you have a cousin who works for a newspaper in Edinburgh?'

'You are, my lady,' Elspeth said coolly and turned her back on Poppy. She busied herself taking a pair of Poppy's evening shoes from their soft cloth bag and placing them in the bottom of the wardrobe.

Good Lord, this woman could hold a grudge! If anyone

should be grudge-holding, it ought to be her, Poppy. 'How useful to have a cousin like that,' Poppy smiled.

Elspeth sighed. 'What is it you would like Beathag to do, your ladyship?'

'That's the ticket, Elspeth! Could you ask her to find out if there are any reported cases of women in Scotland who have been attacked and robbed?'

'That is likely to turn up a huge number, I would have thought, my lady, especially in such places as Glasgow.'

'Sadly, you are probably right. Let me explain the situation and perhaps you can suggest a better way of framing the search.'

Elspeth looked mollified, as Poppy had intended, so she ploughed on before Elspeth could change her mind.

'I bumped into Inspector MacKenzie outside the hotel just before lunch,' Poppy went on. 'He thinks there might be more victims of the strangler.'

Elspeth's hand flew to her neck. '*Oh!*'

'And it's occurred to me that your cousin Beathag might be able to do some research in the newspaper's archives – not only for women strangled, but perhaps those attacked and robbed.'

Elspeth narrowed her eyes as she thought. 'I could ask her to look at the Highlands and Islands for the last year, my lady.'

'Excellent!' Poppy beamed. 'Thank you, Elspeth.'

'As soon as I have finished your unpacking, my lady, I will go downstairs and make the telephone call.'

'Do you think you could you do it now, Elspeth?'

Her maid put down Poppy's bright green dancing shoes she held in her hands. 'Yes, my lady. Is there anything else you require before I rush off?'

Poppy had never seen Elspeth rush anywhere in her life. 'No, nothing else at present, Elspeth.'

. . .

Poppy had the entire afternoon to herself. Beathag wouldn't be able to come up with the goods immediately, so there was no point in her waiting around for that.

She wandered downstairs, nodding pleasantly to guests who were on their way up the staircase, and she was pleased to see Catriona on the desk.

'Who was that attractive fellow you were speaking to outside the hotel before lunch?' her friend asked with a smile. 'I could see you both through the window.'

Poppy decided to ignore Catriona's delightfully accurate description of the inspector. 'He,' she lowered her voice, 'is the detective investigating the Plockton strangler.'

'Good Lord!' The colour drained from Catriona's face, making her freckles even more pronounced. 'Do you mean to say there's been another murder... *here?*'

'No, Catriona,' Poppy quickly reassured her friend. 'Inspector MacKenzie is on a planned holiday on Skye. He is also following a hunch.'

'I see.'

'I wish I did,' Poppy said bitterly. 'I don't suppose you've heard of any women on Skye who've been attacked and robbed in, say, the last year?' she asked.

Catriona shook her head. 'Nothing like that at all, I'm glad to say. The Islands have very little crime.'

'Well, that's good news,' Poppy said, disappointed. If she could just find some clue that might lead her to the murderer, that would show Inspector MacKenzie she could be as good a detective as he. 'Anyway,' she went on, 'can you suggest something I might do this afternoon?'

'Take your pick,' Catriona laughed and indicated the poster on the wall behind her. 'These events are part of the summer programme I mentioned to you. It's a way of drawing more people to visit Portree. The events will culminate with the annual Isle of Skye Highland Games.'

'Very enterprising,' Poppy said with admiration.

'There are two yoga classes, both in the hotel, one this afternoon and the other tomorrow afternoon. And as you can see from the poster, there's also a show with a medium—'

'A medium what?'

'Someone who claims to be able to communicate with the spirits of the deceased. Oh, but she won't be here for a couple of days yet. And of course, there's the button exhibition...'

'Ah yes, the famous button exhibition!'

Catriona laughed. 'When the local button society heard of the summer programme, they wanted to be included, and I thought, why not?'

It was Poppy's turn to laugh. 'Why not, indeed. I think, though, that I will try the yoga. It will remind me of that short time we had as children in India.'

Catriona smiled fondly. 'Weren't we fortunate to have met when we visited there with our mothers all those years ago?'

She and Catriona may have been only six years old at the time, Poppy reflected, but for both of them, the heat and the sounds, the people and the sights, had all created lasting, wonderful memories.

'How did you manage to persuade a yogi to come to Skye?' Poppy asked, bringing herself back to the present.

'Yogis have been travelling to the West for the last forty years, but we are lucky to have him here – although of course the Western Isles are known for their rich spiritual history. When I heard there was to be a yogi travelling through the Highlands and Islands, I offered him a free stay at the hotel in return for the yoga classes.'

Poppy smiled. 'I'm impressed that Portree has so many activities on offer: yoga, a medium, the button exhibition...'

Catriona laughed. 'Och, well, we're midway between Belgium and Iceland, you know, so we're very central!'

'Why don't you come with me to the yoga class?' Poppy said

suddenly. 'That is, if there is someone who can look after the hotel for an hour?'

'Tempting... I wonder if I can ask Sorcha. She works in reception when I can't be here, you see.' Catriona made up her mind. 'She can come and fetch me if anything happens that she can't deal with. Give me a moment.' She picked up the telephone and Poppy heard her friend's pleased response when Sorcha agreed to take over.

Catriona put down the receiver. 'The poster says to wear loose clothing, so we will need to change.'

'I'll be back shortly.' Poppy ran up the stairs and opened the door to her room. Elspeth had finished unpacking and was stowing the suitcase away.

'I'm going to have a lesson in yoga,' Poppy told her.

'Yoga?' Elspeth stiffened. 'What precisely is that, your ladyship?'

'It's an exercise class designed to strengthen muscles...'

Elspeth stared at Poppy. 'Such a thing would be most unbecoming to a lady.'

'And to improve posture,' Poppy added.

Elspeth relented a little, as Poppy knew she would.

'If you want my opinion, my lady,' Elspeth began.

'Not really, thanks.' Poppy flung open the wardrobe door.

Elspeth was not to be put off. 'Balancing a book on the head would work just as well, and it can be done in the privacy of one's room.'

'I need something loose to wear,' Poppy said, examining the contents of the linen press.

Elspeth sighed. 'Can I suggest your pale green cotton blouse, pleated skirt and tennis shoes, my lady?'

'Jolly good idea.'

Poppy stepped back as Elspeth removed the garments from the wardrobe and laid them on the bed.

'What did Beathag say when you telephoned?' Poppy stepped out of her cream outfit.

'That she would be happy to oblige, if in return I gave her the full story in due course.'

'Oh yes, of course she can have that,' Poppy said airily, as she drew on the pale green skirt and blouse.

She had no idea what the inspector would say, but she would deal with him when the time came.

In the hotel's small sitting room, rugs had been set out on the floor ready for the class. A bearded Indian man of slight build, his eyes closed and breathing deeply, sat cross-legged at the front of the room. He wore a turban, a long white robe, and slippers on his bare feet.

Some of the mats were already occupied by other women, their corsets creaking as they attempted to copy the teacher's pose.

'Let's sit here,' Catriona whispered, gesturing to two empty rugs in front of the yogi.

As soon as they had settled themselves, he opened his eyes. There was an excited stirring amongst the ladies.

He rose, put his hands together and bowed. '*Namaste.*'

An undignified scramble to stand followed and a self-conscious muttering of '*Namaste.*'

'Gracious ladies,' he said in a soft voice, 'this afternoon we will do some simple exercises.'

'Nae levitation, then?' came a familiar voice.

Poppy glanced round and saw a smiling Dorothy Brown, the button woman from Plockton. She nodded her recognition at Dorothy, looked briefly for the woman's friend Isabella but couldn't see her, and turned back to face the yogi.

'Breathing is most important in yoga. Kindly place one finger on the side of your nose to close the nostril.'

He demonstrated, and they all did the same.

'Please now inhale through the other nostril, hold your breath, count to six...'

Gasping could clearly be heard, followed by snorting and coughing.

'Breathe out, and repeat on the other side.' He did so.

'I feel wobbly,' called Dorothy.

'Me too,' said another woman.

'For this first lesson,' the yogi went on unperturbed, 'we should perhaps do the breathing exercise while seated.' He gracefully resumed his earlier cross-legged position.

They all did the same, although with considerably less grace.

There followed an hour of breathing and various unfamiliar postures accompanied by gasps and giggles, creakings and coughs.

'We will finish, gracious ladies, with a salute to the sun. Kindly do as I do.' The yogi put his hands together as if in prayer. He stretched his arms up and leaned backwards, bent forward and touched his toes. He lay prone on the floor and raised the top half of his torso, and then reversed the position by sticking his bottom in the air, rather like Major waking up, Poppy thought. The yogi rose to his feet, bent forward and touched his toes. He stretched up his arms, dropped them and stood straight again.

He put his hands together and bowed. 'Peace be unto you.'

'That was invigorating,' Poppy said to Catriona with a smile.

'I hope the others feel the same,' Catriona murmured. She and Poppy turned to gauge the reaction of the rest of the class. A number of the ladies had very red faces, and judging by the strange lumps under their clothing, their corsets had come adrift. All but one in the class were hastening towards the door.

'We meet again, your ladyship,' Dorothy said, smiling and coming towards Poppy.

'Your friend, Miss Buccleuch, is not with you?' Poppy asked as she greeted her acquaintance.

'Yoga isn't for her.' Dorothy pulled a comical face. 'I missed the yogi's class in Plockton, so I wanted to try him here, but I'm nae sure it's for me either.'

Poppy introduced the two women to each other. 'This is Mrs MacLeod, the owner of the Isle of the Mist Hotel. Miss Brown, who stayed at the same hotel as me in Plockton.'

'Pleased to meet you, Miss Brown,' Catriona said. 'But I must go. I promised Sorcha I wouldn't be longer than an hour.'

'And I should find Isabella,' added Dorothy. 'It's almost tea time and she hates to wait for her tea.'

The two women departed, and Poppy saw that she and the yogi were now the only people left in the room.

'Thank you for a most enjoyable class, yogi,' she told him.

He smiled, showing beautiful white teeth.

'I feel that yoga is so much more beneficial than the physical jerks that are growing in popularity,' Poppy went on. 'Mrs MacLeod tells me that you are touring Britain giving lessons.'

He bowed in acceptance of her statement. 'I am travelling the country, spreading the philosophy of yoga. Everything in the universe is connected.' He spread his arms to emphasise his words. 'Through practice, the mind, body and spirit can be unified, to achieve inner peace.' He drew his arms together across his white-robed chest.

'Where will you be visiting after Skye?'

'The Isle of Iona, a most spiritual place.'

'The birthplace of Christianity in Scotland,' Poppy agreed. St Columba had arrived there in 563 AD and founded the abbey, which still stood.

'A kind lady on Iona has invited me to stay at her house for a week and give lessons to her friends,' the yogi told her.

This was how the man survived, Poppy realised, being given free board and lodging in return for instruction. A sort of pilgrim, or a mendicant.

'Wherever I go, everyone is so kind.' He smiled.

'Where were you before this?' she said idly, thinking of her cup of tea.

'In Plockton, gracious lady.'

Poppy suddenly remembered what Dorothy had said: *I missed the yogi's class in Plockton.*

'When were you in Plockton?' she enquired, the hair prickling on the back of her neck.

He blinked. 'Let me try to remember... I meditate between classes and one day can seem very like another.' He closed his eyes. He opened them. 'Two days ago.'

The day Ellen was strangled.

'Were you aware of a murder in the village that evening?' Poppy pressed.

'I have not heard of such a terrible event.' He shook his head slowly and sadly. 'I must have left before it took place.'

Or perhaps before Ellen's body was found, Poppy thought. Could she ask him what time he'd taken the ferry to Skye, without looking like she was interrogating him?

'You were on the late afternoon ferry that day?' she asked casually.

'I cannot be certain,' he said slowly. 'Time has little meaning for me.'

How convenient, she thought.

'But I do remember in Plockton I saw the small lady and the large lady together. It is most unfortunate that the small lady's large friend could not also have come to this class today,' he went on. 'She seemed to be in great need of inner peace.'

'Small lady? The one who spoke to me at the end of the class?'

He dipped his head in agreement.

'What makes you say that her friend seemed to be in great need of inner peace?'

'I heard her arguing with another small lady on the afternoon of my departure.'

Another small lady? This was getting complicated. The world was full of large and small ladies, and ladies of medium height...

Could he mean Ellen Clark?

Poppy had never met the living Ellen, but she had been described as 'wee' by Dorothy and 'dainty' by Isabella, and the body she'd found in the preacher's shed had been of petite stature. 'Can you describe this other small lady?'

He gave a small shrug. 'She was small, and slim; she looked like all the other small, slim ladies of middle years.'

'Was she wearing any remarkable jewellery, for example?' Dash it, she was asking a leading question of her own witness, which would not be allowed in court. But the man might be more than a witness; he might be the accused. Had it been an indication of guilt when he blinked before telling her when he'd been in Plockton?

The yogi had closed his eyes again. When he opened them, he said, 'She wore a sapphire pendant.'

So it *was* Ellen Clark! Isabella Buccleuch and Ellen had been arguing on the afternoon before Ellen's murder.

'And when you're saying you *heard* them arguing, what do you mean exactly?' She needed to be absolutely certain of her facts.

'I saw the two ladies enter the sitting room in the Harbour Hotel, and then I heard raised voices.'

'How can you be sure it wasn't two other female voices you heard?' Poppy asked.

'Because, gracious lady, I had just come out of the room, leaving it empty.'

Poppy was trying to imagine the shy Ellen raising her voice

in an argument when the yogi spoke again. 'When I say raised voices, I mean it was the same voice being raised each time.'

'Isabella's. it must have been hers. 'Do you know what the argument was about?'

'I cannot say, gracious lady.'

That was disappointing – but it was still a clue! And one Poppy doubted Inspector MacKenzie had.

'Thank you, yogi. I will leave you to your meditation.'

She crossed to the door. When she glanced back, the yogi was standing on one leg, his other leg bent behind and his hands together in the prayer position. His eyes were closed. Was that an indication of a clear conscience, or of a man desperately seeking spiritual help for a deadly crime?

As Poppy mounted the staircase, she realised she now had three possible suspects for Ellen's murder: the mystery man, Alan Henderson; the button woman, Isabella Buccleuch; and the yogi. Although if she could confirm the yogi had been on the afternoon ferry, then he would no longer be a suspect.

Alan Henderson had said something to Ellen the day before her death, which had caused her to want to be alone and given her a headache, and now he wasn't to be found. Isabella Buccleuch had been seen arguing with Ellen what must have been some hours before she was murdered, if the yogi was telling the truth. As for the yogi himself, he'd been in Plockton on the day Ellen was strangled, but he was vague about what time he'd taken the ferry across to Skye.

But Hindu philosophy was one of non-violence to *any* living creature. If he literally wouldn't kill a fly, was he likely to strangle a woman?

Poppy had a lot to discuss with the inspector this evening. She was looking forward to it.

It would be rather thrilling to see him again.

SEVENTEEN

Inspector MacKenzie called for Poppy at the hotel promptly at seven o'clock. Poppy had dressed in orange-red chiffon, the bodice cut in a low V edged with gold beads. An orange-red lipstick and a black headband with a rosette of glass beads on the side completed the look.

Inspector MacKenzie raised his fedora and smiled with that sensuous mouth when he saw her. 'You look bonnie.'

Poppy had been hoping for a little more enthusiasm, but that would have to do. She took in his dark, fitted suit and waistcoat, the crisp white shirt and black bow tie. The result was to emphasise his height and broad shoulders. She had a vivid image of the powerful body under the garments and for a moment her mouth went dry.

'Thank you,' she managed to say. 'So do you.'

His freshly shaved face flushed. The man was not used to receiving compliments, she realised.

'Where are you taking me?' she asked, passing him her coat.

'There is a wee restaurant no' far,' he told her, holding out the coat as she slipped it on.

Poppy took his arm and was immediately aware of the

muscles concealed beneath the dark sleeve. *Focus!* she told herself. 'Have you managed to track down Alan Henderson?' she asked as they left the hotel.

'The fellow seems to have vanished. My men are still trying.'

They turned out of Somerled Square. 'I've made some progress of my own in the investigation,' she said proudly.

'Have you now, my lady?' He sounded amused.

'For heaven's sake,' she burst out, 'do try and give me a little more encouragement with this case than you did at Culross!'

The dark eyebrows rose and he looked down at her. Heat flashed through her. 'Oh, did I say that aloud? I didn't mean to.'

He laughed and she was torn between feeling ridiculously pleased and rather annoyed.

'Here we are,' he said, ushering her into a delightful little restaurant.

A waiter came over, took Poppy's coat and showed them to a candlelit table for two by the window, set sufficiently apart from the other diners.

'Pleasure before business,' Inspector MacKenzie said when they had been handed menus.

'Isn't that the wrong way round?'

'Not on this occasion, your ladyship,' he said, amusement in his voice.

Was he actually flirting with her? How delightful!

The waiter returned and they placed their orders. They sat silent for a little while, then Poppy said, 'Tell me about where you come from.'

'Harris? What is it you are wanting to know?'

'Anything, really. I've never been there.'

He cleared his throat. 'Well now, as you no doubt ken, Lewis and Harris is the largest island in the Outer Hebrides. Harris is to the south, Lewis to the north. No' many folk live in the northern part of Harris, while the southern part has miles of unspoiled white sandy beaches. It's known for its tweed, hand-woven by the islanders at their homes—'

Poppy laughed. 'I can get that from the *Encyclopaedia Britannica*. Tell me something about your life there.'

He frowned. 'I'm thinking it canna be of any interest to you, my lady.'

'Oh, but it is,' she assured him.

He sent her a puzzled glance. 'I was born on Harris, where my father is a minister of the kirk. I studied theology at the University of Glasgow... But you ken this, your ladyship.'

'Then add some fresh details.' She sat contentedly looking at him. She loved his throat with the Adam's apple, and the way his dark eyes narrowed when he was thinking.

'I have four brothers. I play the bagpipes...'

Ah, something personal at last! At that moment the waiter brought their plates of soup and Poppy had to be patient while he returned with bannocks. Left alone again, she prompted him to continue.

'Are you any good at the pipes?' She liked the image of Inspector MacKenzie playing the instrument, his kilt swinging in time to the music.

He smiled. 'I'm invited to play at Burns Suppers and the like, so I suppose I must give satisfaction.'

Oh, yes, I'm sure you do.

'Do you stay in Edinburgh?' she went on, casually taking up her soup spoon.

'Aye, I have a flat in the city.'

'I seem to remember' – she remembered very well – 'that you said you weren't married.' She flushed at her audacity in asking such a bold question.

'I have a daily maid-of-all work, your ladyship.' The inspector's cheeks coloured and he hastily swallowed a spoonful of his soup.

'You mean you don't want a wife because you have a daily maid?' she half teased, astonished at her boldness.

'I never said I dinna want a wife.' He smiled. 'Will there be anything else your ladyship wishes to ken?'

An almost-forgotten conversation came back to her mind. They had been in the butler's pantry at Balfour House when he'd told her he'd witnessed a serious crime while studying at Glasgow. And that had decided him not to follow his father into the church but to join the police service.

'You told me you joined the police service as a result of witnessing a serious crime when you were a student in Glasgow...'

'Aye.' He suddenly looked wary.

'What was it you saw?' she asked.

His face clouded and he lowered his eyelids. 'Nothing I wish to talk about, your ladyship.'

In the candlelight his long eyelashes made shadows on his cheeks and he looked so very vulnerable. How could she have been so stupid as to ask that question, when it should have been clear that it was something still painful to him?

She murmured, 'I'm sorry.' She had been too direct, asking him like that. And they had been getting on so well. She took a sup of the cream soup to hide her embarrassment.

He cleared his throat. 'Now, tell me about yourself.'

'You'll find the public side of my life in *Who's Who*, but considering you're an excellent detective, you will have already looked me up.' It felt good to see the slight reddening of his cheeks.

'I was born in Perthshire,' she went on, 'have no siblings and studied law at the University of Glasgow. I was married, briefly, before my husband was killed in the Great War. I draw badly, but I like to sing. My father is the Earl of Crieff and he owns Dunearn Castle. When he inherited the title and property from his brother, he and my mother promptly left for Australia to run a sheep farm. He had no interest in running a country estate in Perthshire, but a sheep farm in Western Australia was his idea of heaven. Personally, I can't see much difference between the two.'

'Except for the weather, perhaps?' the inspector said with a smile.

'Except for the weather.' She smiled, then asked, 'Do you like your job?'

He considered the question. 'Aye, I do. I know it to be useful and I'm able to do it sufficiently well to take a pride in it. It's full of variety and it forces my brain to stay active. Aye, I like it, my lady. Why do you ask?'

'Oh, nothing,' Poppy said. 'Detection is a hobby to me, I suppose.'

'I had noticed.' The inspector gave a wry smile.

'I took it up when I realised life was passing me by,' she told him. 'Stuart and I married in the summer after my finals. After he was killed in France, I went through the usual stages of grief: shock, anger, loneliness. Acceptance.' Her voice wobbled. The concern in the inspector's dark eyes was almost too much to bear; she looked down at her plate. *Detectives do not cry.* She would not cry. 'The truth is our marriage could never have lasted; people marry unsuitably in times of war. The hospital for wounded soldiers I set up in the family castle gave me direction. But since then I've felt a lack of purpose.'

He reached across the table for her hand and she raised her eyes to his.

'With your degree in law, you could have returned to your studies and trained to become a solicitor,' he said softly.

Poppy shook her head. 'I'm not the same woman I was when I graduated. But I still love working out a puzzle.' She smiled, then felt the loss of his warmth when he withdrew his hand. 'Although when it comes to catching a real person, someone that you've met, and wondering if they will be found guilty' – she bit her lip, thinking of the Balfour case – 'and be hanged...'

'I understand,' he said earnestly, 'but someone has strangled Ellen Clark and that person needs to be found. I'm thinking that we all have a duty to society to find out the truth... But I dinna think you should be involved in searching for a murderer,' he added softly.

'Because I'm female, or because I have a title?' she demanded. 'Oh, never mind.' She didn't want to fall out with him again. 'I'm already involved because I've questioned some of the suspects. Now, there's Isabella Buccleuch, for instance,' she went on, warming to her theme. 'If she is the killer, then I'd feel bad about being the one to uncover her and to say nothing.'

'Wait, my lady!' the inspector exclaimed. 'What has Isabella Buccleuch to do with Ellen Clark's murder?'

'Hush.' Poppy looked around the little restaurant; he followed her gaze, and they became aware that the waiter was glancing towards their table.

'He will return soon for our soup plates,' said the inspector. 'We will no' discuss the matter until after our main course.'

They worked their way through an excellent poached salmon, keeping the topic neutral and chatting about Skye and Edinburgh.

'Coffee?' he asked, when they had finished their meal.

'Please.'

'Do you mind if I smoke my pipe?'

She shook her head, and watched as he took the pipe and a tobacco pouch from his pocket, filled the bow, struck a match from the matchbook on the table and lit his pipe.

The waiter served their coffees and when the man had departed, the inspector said, 'Now, tell me about Isabella Buccleuch.' He deposited the spent match in the ashtray on the table, sat back in his chair and puffed on his pipe.

'There's so much to report about Isabella,' Poppy said, stirring her coffee. 'I'll start with when I spoke to the yogi this afternoon—'

He removed his pipe. 'Sorry, my lady, you spoke to a what?'

'A yogi, a teacher of yoga, which is a form of exercise developed in India. I spent a couple of months in that country as a child, visiting my grandparents, you know. I have fond memories of the place, so I thought I would go along to the yogi's class at the Isle of the Mist Hotel. He told me that he'd overheard Isabella arguing with a small, slim lady in Plockton on the afternoon in question.' Poppy paused for breath and smiled, pleased she'd been able to use a suitably police-officer-type phrase.

Inspector MacKenzie raised an eyebrow. 'You are knowing that description could verra well fit her friend, Miss Brown?'

'Yes, but he was quite clear it wasn't Dorothy Brown. He also said she was wearing a sapphire pendant.'

'*Mo chreach 'sa thàinig!*' The inspector sat up in his chair, laid his pipe in the ashtray and looked earnestly at her. 'Are we knowing what the disagreement was about?'

'Sadly, we are not.' Poppy hid a delighted smile at her easy use of the plural, first-person pronoun. 'The yogi said he didn't hear the words, but it was clear one of the women – it must have been Isabella, because Ellen was reportedly rather shy – shouting at the other.'

'You said there was much to report about Isabella Buccleuch?'

'When she was talking about Ellen, before the body was found, Isabella referred to her in the past tense. She told me Ellen *seemed* a pleasant lady.'

The inspector leaned back in his chair and folded his arms across his broad chest.

'And,' Poppy went on, slightly distracted by how his jacket strained over his biceps, 'Dorothy Brown told me that her friend went for a walk on her own between seven and eight o'clock... Oh.' Poppy saw the surprised look on the inspector's face. 'You didn't know that, I can see. That was what I wanted to tell you when I left the message with Constable Macduff, and it is exactly the reason why you should keep me informed so I can help you solve this case.'

'I see,' the inspector said grimly. 'I'm needing to have a wee word with Macduff.'

Poppy took a sip of her coffee. 'This means that Isabella has no alibi for that hour, which was within the time Ellen was murdered. Before that, the two were on an outing arranged by the Harbour Hotel, and after that, Elspeth and I saw them in the dining room.'

'And what is Isabella herself saying about this hour?' he asked.

'I haven't had a chance to ask her yet. But you must send a man to check Dorothy's alibi for the same time. She told me she went to see an old lady in the village. Dorothy can give you the address.'

'I'm no' wanting to alert either of the two ladies that they are under investigation.'

'Of course not. What was I thinking?'

'I canna answer that particular question for you, but I'll get Constable Macduff on to finding out who this old lady is and take it from there. Is there anything else, my lady?'

'Yes. This means that we have three suspects.'

'And they are?'

'You must know!' she exclaimed.

The corners of his lips twitched. 'Perhaps I do, but as you never fail to surprise me, my lady, I would verra much like to ken your three suspects.'

'Absolutely, Inspector! We have Alan Henderson—'

Inspector MacKenzie nodded. 'Ellen Clark's mystery man.'

'Isabella Buccleuch, the button collector—'

'Button collector?'

'Yes, she and her friend are here on a button expedition...'

'Now I have heard everything.' He drank his coffee in one gulp. 'And your third suspect?'

'The yogi!'

The inspector frowned. 'Your witness to the argument?'

'Yes, but – and here's the crucial thing – he was in Plockton at approximately the time Ellen was strangled.'

'Approximately? Can you be a wee bit more precise, your ladyship?'

'The yogi told me the argument he overheard took place on the afternoon before his departure.'

'Which could mean he left in the afternoon or later...'

'Yes, I realised that immediately too,' she remarked without a blush. 'Unfortunately, he was rather vague about what time he caught the ferry.'

'No one in the Harbour Hotel mentioned the yogi to me,' the inspector said thoughtfully.

'He must have left the hotel by then – but that doesn't mean he had left Plockton. He is travelling to Iona tomorrow, but not until after his yoga class, so you still have time to question him.'

'Are you telling me how to carry out my job, your ladyship?'

'Just trying to be helpful, Inspector!'

He laughed. 'It seems that we do make a good team.'

She beamed. Then for one glorious moment, she imagined the two of them *together* in another way... Her heart began to race.

She forced the thought away and sat up straighter. 'And so, Inspector MacKenzie,' she said, 'who is on *your* suspect list?'

'I have only Alan Henderson as a suspect, and that as a poor one,' he admitted. 'He has no' been seen since the murder, but apparently he'd told Ellen Clark he would be awa' on business, so his disappearance could be misleading. Talking of red herrings, how is Major Lewis?'

Poppy knew this term had come about thanks to a recommendation to use a smoked herring to distract a dog from a rabbit. 'A raw sausage would be more accurate in Major's case,' she suggested. 'He's very well, thank you.'

'I look forward to working with him again.'

'I will tell him. I'm sure he feels the same.'

They smiled at each other in silent amusement. Poppy felt the familiar flutter in her stomach at seeing that dimple appear.

'And so, Inspector,' she said quickly, to distract her thoughts from him as a *man*, 'what is our next move?'

'What do you mean, what is our next move?'

'I should have thought that was obvious. You have the advantage of your official position; I have the advantage of my natural warmth and social standing. *Ergo*, we are a perfect combination.' She beamed. 'Together we will catch the killer.'

EIGHTEEN

Inspector MacKenzie raised an eyebrow. Poppy looked at him.

'My dear Inspector,' she said, raising an eyebrow of her own, 'we have been through all this before. I am not a susceptible female but a grown woman keen to work as a detective.'

He sighed. 'It seems my eyebrow has failed.'

Poppy laughed. 'Have you learned anything of interest from the local police files?'

The inspector was immediately sober. 'No' one of the women murdered in Scotland over the last five years matches our killer's method of operation. The victims have been either in a domestic incident—'

'A *domestic incident*? A husband murdering his wife? How desperately sad.'

'It is, or the victims have been what are known in polite circles as ladies of the night.'

'Oh dear.'

'Aye. It's a good world, and what a mess we men make of it.'

Poppy couldn't disagree. 'My maid, Elspeth,' she told him, 'has a cousin who works for one of the Edinburgh newspapers.

Beathag is going through their records to find any mention of women attacked and robbed in the Highlands and Islands over the last year.'

'No' murdered?'

'I thought the search could be widened a little, to see what came up. The strangler may not have murdered before. At least, one can hope it was his first time, can't one?'

'His first and last, we must hope. Aye, it's possible a wee piece could be in a newspaper, and that the victim had no' reported it to the police,' he said thoughtfully. 'Verra good, Detective Proudfoot.'

She felt a smile tugging at the corners of her mouth, but went on, 'If we accept that all three of our suspects may well have had the opportunity to commit the crime—'

'Do we accept that?'

'Alan Henderson was in Plockton on the day of the murder, but we can't be sure what time he actually left the village,' she said. 'The same applies to the yogi. Isabella Buccleuch was not only in Plockton that evening, but she has no alibi for part of it. So, back to motives: what do we have?'

'Money is the obvious one, given that Ellen Clark's jewellery and handbag were stolen.' The inspector considered a moment. 'Let's look first at Alan Henderson. He is supposedly a businessman. Say his business has failed and he is needing money. What if he asked Ellen Clark for a loan and she refused?'

'She didn't have any money to give.' Poppy set down her cup in its saucer. 'Miss Grant, the manageress of the hotel in Plockton, told me that Ellen's accommodation was paid for by a trust for distressed gentlewomen.'

'Then perhaps she refused to sell the pendant to bail out his business, so he took it, killing her – accidentally or otherwise – in the process.'

'Yes, that's possible,' Poppy agreed. 'And it would certainly explain why she was subdued after her last meeting with him, the day before she was murdered. She could have been questioning his real feelings for her. But if it was an accident, that doesn't fit with the tightness of the scarf around her neck. You saw the bruises on her fingers?'

'Aye, I did, and I do think the strangling was intended. I just like to keep an open mind when working on a case.'

'That sounds sensible.' Did she keep an open mind? Poppy wondered.

'Next, Isabella Buccleuch.' The inspector paused briefly. 'Now here I canna think of what to suggest.'

'What would you say were the main motives for murder in general?'

'Money, as we've just considered, and personal feeling – either hate or jealousy. We have a financial motive for Alan Henderson. Shall we try that for Isabella Buccleuch too?'

'She needed money for...' Poppy suddenly had the answer: 'The button! Miss Brown told me there is some sort of rare Russian papier-mâché button on Skye. Suppose Miss Buccleuch had heard it was for sale and was desperate to buy it. I've no idea of the price of such a thing.'

'If an item is truly unique, then a seller can ask whatever he or she likes for it.'

Poppy remembered the hole in Isabella's brown worsted stocking. 'And I think Isabella's fairly hard-up.'

'And the yogi? Could he be needing money too?'

'I imagine that he doesn't make much travelling around the country. He stays at the invitation of wealthy folk as their guest and in return gives classes.'

'Does he have a name?'

'Catriona has told me that he likes to be known simply as the guru.'

Inspector MacKenzie frowned. 'Staying with the same motive – financial gain – why would he want to kill Ellen Clark?'

'That, I admit, is difficult to answer.' He lived a nomadic sort of life, but didn't that fit in with his philosophy?

'What about another motive?' suggested the inspector. 'Personal feeling, such as hate or jealousy?'

Poppy shook her head. 'I can't believe that. Yogis spread the word of peace, after all.'

'I suppose he really is a yogi?' Inspector MacKenzie asked hopefully.

'If he's not,' she retorted, 'he's giving a jolly good impression of one.'

'When this case is solved, my lady, I'd like to hear more of your time in India.' He smiled at her. 'Meanwhile, let's go back to the first two suspects and apply personal feeling as a motive for them. Alan Henderson strangled Ellen Clark because she had spurned his love and Isabella Buccleuch because Ellen...'

'Had a row of attractive buttons on her suit and wouldn't give them to her?' Poppy scoffed.

'Was her suit minus its buttons?' he enquired.

'I didn't notice.' *Dash it!*

'A good detective notices things,' he pointed out.

'Actually, it was rather dark in the shed.' Poppy fixed him with her gaze. 'So, tell me. *Did* her suit still have its buttons?'

'It did – and they were no' special as far as I could tell.'

'*Mo chreach 'sa thàinig!*' Poppy exclaimed. 'I have the motive, Inspector. Ellen's clutch bag had an unusual button clasp of crocodile skin and marcasite.'

'Is there anything you dinna ken, your ladyship?'

'I couldn't say,' she answered modestly. 'But listen, Inspector. Perhaps Isabella wanted the button, offered to buy it – bag and all – but Ellen wouldn't sell. So Isabella followed her to the open-air kirk, there was a wee stushie and Ellen ended up dead.'

'It's difficult to imagine *a wee stushie* resulting in a strangulation.'

Poppy sighed. 'Perhaps Constable Macduff was right and Ellen's murder was the act of a stranger.'

'Come, your ladyship, you dinna really believe that!'

She sat up straighter in her chair. 'No, I don't. And we must remember what Burns had to say about men as well as mice.'

'*The best-laid schemes… gang aft agley*. Often go awry. It's no' really of much help here.'

'No, but unlike a mouse, we can look forward.' Poppy knew the poet had gone on to say he could only guess and fear the future, but she chose to skip over that. 'Elspeth's cousin may turn up some news items of interest.'

Poppy certainly hoped so.

'Good evening, my lady,' said Elspeth, waiting in Poppy's room when she returned.

'You didn't need to wait up for me, Elspeth.' Poppy pulled off the headband and dropped it on the dressing table, 'although it's very kind of you to have done so.'

'I thought Major might want some company,' Elspeth said.

From his blanket, the dog raised his head and gave her a questioning look. Elspeth, not fond of time-wasting, hurried on. 'And this came, my lady.'

'A telegram!' Poppy took the buff-coloured envelope. 'But it's addressed to you, Elspeth.'

'I believe it may be from my cousin in Edinburgh.'

'Quick work, Beathag,' she said approvingly as she tore the envelope open. 'You're right, it is from your cousin in Edinburgh. I'll read it aloud:

'*Hello Elspeth stop sorry nothing like you asked for stop only three of possible interest stop one on Skye in Broadford stop.* Elspeth, we passed through that village on our way here yesterday!' Poppy exclaimed, smiling at her maid. 'She's given us a woman's name and address. Then the message goes on, *will send the news articles in the post stop hope to see you again before too long and hear more stop Beathag.*

'That's awfully good of your cousin to find this out and to send such a long telegram too. That's, what, some forty words including the stops. It must have cost her a bit.'

'I told Beathag you would reimburse her, my lady.'

That was a bally cheek of the woman to have been so chatty at her expense, Poppy thought, but no matter. 'Pop out tomorrow and arrange that, would you, Elspeth? There's a bank in the square.'

Poppy lifted an arm and submitted to Elspeth undoing the various hooks and eyes at the side of her orange-red chiffon. She wiggled out of the delicate garment, letting it fall into Elspeth's waiting hands, and stepped out of the dress.

'Are you going to Broadford, my lady?' Elspeth carefully smoothed out the dress and hung it up.

'If that's where the woman stays, then yes.' Poppy sat on the edge of the bed and kicked off her heels. 'I wonder what Beathag means by "of possible interest". It's very cryptic, don't you think?'

'I suppose it is, my lady.' Elspeth picked up the shoes.

'Leave them until morning, Elspeth. We each need to get our beauty sleep.'

Elspeth pursed her lips. 'Did you have a pleasant evening with the policeman, my lady?'

'Yes, thank you.'

'With a nice chat about murder and the like?'

'We discussed the case, if that's what you mean.'

'I was afraid of that. You are getting too involved again, my lady.'

'No doubt that paragon Lady MacCorkindale wouldn't do such a thing?'

Elspeth gave an exasperated sigh. 'Certainly not, my lady.'

'Then I will go to Broadford first thing tomorrow morning!' Anything Lady MacCorkindale wouldn't do, Poppy was sure *she* should. 'Order my breakfast to be sent up, would you? I can't face being ambushed at breakfast by Jeanie Harper for a second morning.'

She crossed to sit at the dressing table and smiled to herself as she unscrewed the glass jar of Pond's cold cream. All in all, it had been a good evening.

As soon as Elspeth had left the room, Poppy climbed beneath the bedcovers, drew the oil lamp closer to her, opened her notebook and wrote:

Day Three of Investigation into the Murder of Ellen Clark.

1. Beathag might have found something of interest in newspaper records. An address to visit tomorrow.

2. The yogi was in Plockton. He left in the afternoon or – importantly – the evening on the day Ellen was killed. He's vague about time.

3. The yogi says he heard Isabella arguing with Ellen in the hotel that afternoon. If he's telling the truth, could the fancy button on Ellen's bag be the reason? And is that reason good enough to resort to murder?

4. Inspector MacKenzie plays the bagpipes. I'm sure he's awfully good at it.

The bed was comfortable, the day had been a long one, and the lines swam before her eyes. She put the notebook into the nightstand drawer, extinguished the lamp and drifted off into a fitful sleep.

. . .

Poppy awoke the next morning as Elspeth entered the room.

'Good morning, my lady,' her maid said as she placed Poppy's cup of tea on her bedside table.

'Morning, Elspeth.' Poppy sat up in bed and made herself comfortable. 'How is the weather for the drive to Broadford?'

Elspeth drew back the curtains and daylight flooded in. 'Pleasant enough, my lady. So pleasant that I have decided to come with you.'

Poppy almost spilled her tea on the counterpane. 'Did I hear that correctly?'

'I believe you did, my lady.'

There was a knock at the door. Elspeth opened it and took the tray from the maid who stood there.

'Grilled kidneys and bacon, toast and honey,' Elspeth said, bringing the breakfast tray over and arranging it on Poppy's lap.

'Delicious!' She tucked into the food with relish. 'There's something about investigating a crime that gives one an appetite.'

'If you say so, my lady, although I could not eat more than a slice of dry toast, with the thought of what is ahead of us.'

'Then don't come, Elspeth,' Poppy said through a mouthful of bacon.

'I must, my lady. I need to see that you come to no harm.'

'In Broadford?' She dabbed her mouth with the napkin and took a long drink of tea. 'It looked like a law-abiding sort of village to me.'

Elspeth narrowed her eyes. 'Those are probably the worst kind. I will draw your bath. And then I will tell Fergusson to be ready to drive us this morning.'

She disappeared into the bathroom, and Poppy heard the clatter of pipes as the taps were turned and the water began to run.

It must be only half a dozen miles from Broadford to Kyleakin, she thought. If Elspeth was determined to accompany her, and it looked as though she was, then her four-legged companion should also come for the ride. He enjoyed visiting new places. Her chauffeur could be in charge of Major while Poppy was engaged in investigating. Elspeth... she had no idea what role Elspeth saw for herself, apart from fending off murderers, which she doubted it would come to.

While Poppy bathed, Elspeth cleared away the breakfast things and went off to deal with the business at the bank. Poppy emerged from her bath to see her pale pink silk blouse and grey pinstriped flannel suit set out on the bed.

She was in the process of exchanging the pale pink blouse for her pale blue one, when the door opened and a red-faced Elspeth entered, an apologetic-looking Labrador on the leash beside her.

'He saw a C-A-T,' gasped Elspeth, 'and dragged me along the pavement before I could get him under control again.' She unclipped the leash from his collar.

'Really, Major,' Poppy admonished him.

He hung his head and crept onto his blanket, not sure why he was in trouble but recognising all the same that he was.

'I've a good mind to leave you behind this morning...' Poppy continued to address the dog.

'A very good idea, your ladyship,' Elspeth said, still a little breathless.

'But then, with you coming, Elspeth,' she added thoughtfully, 'there will be no one here to keep an eye on him.'

Elspeth pressed her lips together.

'We will leave in fifteen minutes,' Poppy said brightly.

Fergusson drove the Bentley slowly and steadily along the twisting roads. Poppy, seated in the front next to her chauffeur, was delighted as little had been visible when they'd arrived in the gloaming two evenings ago.

Now she saw, between lochs and stony moorland, stooks of harvested oats drying in the fields. They were for winter animal feed, but the wood pigeons didn't know this, or care, and were pecking what seeds they could.

The car passed a farm cart with elder leaves tucked into the head harness of the carter's horse. Poppy knew the elder had a strong, distinctive smell disliked by flies, so it was an excellent way of keeping the insects off the horse. A flock of starlings were eating blackberries by the roadside, and they rose in a flutter of wings as the motor car drove past.

After a while, the increased number of cottages dotted along the side of the road signalled they were drawing close to the village.

'Broadford is the second-largest settlement on the island, I'm told, my lady,' Fergusson said.

'I hope it won't be too difficult to find *Baile Mhicheil*,' Poppy responded. 'It could so easily be a croft on the outskirts.'

The chauffeur drove very slowly and they peered through the open car windows. They went through the village with no sign of *Baile Mhicheil*.

'Oh dear, I hope we haven't got the wrong name,' she murmured.

'If we have, it won't be my cousin's fault,' Elspeth declared from the back seat. 'The sort of people who work at the General Post Office can't be trusted to write down a name properly.'

'There it is!' Poppy exclaimed.

They had travelled about a mile or two outside the village. The name *Baile Mhicheil* had been painted on a piece of wood, and the post secured into the ground. At least, it had been secured at one point. Now it leaned sideways and looked uncared for.

Fergusson turned onto the rutted track. They bumped

down it for less than half a mile and then, rounding a bend, came to a drystone dyke. It looked like the tumbledown stone wall had at one time marked off a croft. The cottage stood a short distance away. It looked desolate, and once again Poppy felt this was a place that held secrets.

She took a deep breath. What would she find inside?

NINETEEN

'I don't like it,' Elspeth said.

Poppy knew what she meant. There were no animals or crops in the fields. A silence seemed to brood over the whole place, punctuated now and then by the twittering of a skylark.

Fergusson stopped the car and climbed out. He opened the door and Poppy alighted.

'I'm staying put,' Elspeth said firmly, holding on tightly to the handle of the door.

Poppy let Major out from the back seat next to Elspeth and he scampered around joyfully, sniffing at everything.

The gate in the stone wall stood open and Poppy walked through, the Labrador bounding after her.

'Don't be long, my lady,' Elspeth called nervously after her.

So much for her maid ensuring she came to no harm!

'Wait here, Fergusson,' Poppy told her chauffeur, 'and protect Elspeth from any marauding chieftain.'

Fergusson smiled. 'Yes, my lady.'

Poppy walked the short distance up to the door. Like the gate, it stood open.

'Hello?' she called into the silence. Standing on the

threshold, she could see a door that led off the tiny hall, with a steep little staircase in front of her that she supposed led to the bedrooms. The woodwork and walls were painted brown, and the lino on the floor was also brown. It was very dispiriting.

The place was utterly abandoned. What had happened to the woman who had once lived here? And why had Elspeth's cousin thought Poppy would be interested in speaking to her?

'Wait!' cried a voice from outside and she turned to see a young man in a well-worn waistcoat and trousers, with his sleeves rolled up to the elbows, striding down the rutted track.

He reached the Bentley and came to a halt. 'I heard the motor car.' He looked between Fergusson in his chauffeur's uniform standing by the Bentley and Poppy in her bright blue beret and pinstriped suit at the door of the cottage. He frowned. 'What is it ye're wanting?'

She hastened towards him. 'I am looking for Miss Mairi MacKay, sir, but it seems that she hasn't lived here for a while.'

'This is *Baile Mhìcheil*, Michael's Farm, but Mairi MacKay is no longer with us,' he said bitterly. 'I farm yon neighbouring croft.' He pointed to some well-tended fields. Seeing Poppy's puzzled look, he added, 'She was taken in by some smooth-tongued rogue.'

'What do you mean?' Poppy asked.

'She was persuaded to lend him money, every penny she had, as it turned out. She even sold her beasts.' The young man indicated the croft's empty fields. 'That was how much she was taken in by him. When he disappeared with her money, Mairi was in despair. Nae cattle left or money to work the place.' The young man rubbed a hand over the stubble on his chin. 'She threw herself off the sea cliffs by Glasnakille.' He swallowed. 'She was a good Presbyterian, ye ken, so to have done that... It shows how desperate she must have felt.'

'I am so sorry.' Poppy's voice was gentle. 'But why would

she have lent so much money to what sounds like a relative stranger?'

The young man stuck his hands in his trouser pockets. 'Because he turned her head! Said he wanted to marry her, but first was needing money for something or other. *Mac an diabhoil!*'

That was easy for Poppy to translate: son of the devil. 'Did Mairi have no family who could have helped her?'

He shook his head. 'She inherited the croft from her faither, Michael. She worked it herself, and never married.'

Why had Beathag thought the suicide of a crofting spinster had anything to do with the strangling of a minister's widow? Poppy couldn't make the connection.

Poppy thanked the young man, called to her dog and climbed back into the car. As she looked back at the unloved cottage, she silently promised Mairi MacKay she would find answers.

'To Kyleakin,' she instructed Fergusson firmly.

'Kyleakin?' asked Elspeth sharply, leaning forward in her seat. 'Why there?'

'To see a man about a yogi.'

She sniffed. 'Who is being cryptic now, my lady?'

'More specifically, to speak to the ferryman about a certain passenger.'

The young man stood and watched as Fergusson turned the Bentley and they bumped off down the track.

'It'll be another wild goose chase,' Elspeth muttered.

'We don't know that the visit to Mairi MacKay's was a waste of time.'

Elspeth said nothing more, but Poppy wondered if her maid might not be correct. She would have to wait until the newspaper articles arrived from Beathag to learn more.

Within a short time, the motor car was pulling into Kyleakin. Fergusson drove down the wide pier, where the ferry could be seen at the end waiting for passengers. He drew to a halt and parked.

'What luck, Elspeth,' Poppy said, 'that the ferry is here.' She jumped out of the Bentley and hurried across to the ferryman.

'*Madainn mhath*,' she greeted him.

'*Madainn mhath dhuibh.*'

'I would be very grateful if either of you gentlemen' – she nodded politely at the second ferryman, who stepped forward, curious – 'could tell me which boat the Indian gentleman took from Kyle of Lochalsh to here three days ago.'

The first ferryman spoke. 'A terrible lot of people travel on the boat.'

'I'm thinking you mean the man in a white robe, wearing a turban,' said the second man.

'That's him!' Poppy smiled with relief. 'Do you happen to remember if he took the ferry in the afternoon or the evening of that day?'

'I wouldn't be remembering the time,' the second man replied.

Poppy's heart sank.

The first ferryman spoke again. 'I'm remembering that it was the day my wee bairn fell in the keech.'

Keech? she wondered. Did that mean the sea?

'Oh dear, I hope she wasn't badly hurt?'

'Och, no,' the man laughed. 'We cleaned her up and she's right as rain.'

Too late, Poppy remembered 'keech' meant horse's excrement. *Drat!*

'Aye,' he went on, 'the fellow was on the last ferry. I mind that too because he was the only passenger that evening.'

Before the men had a chance to ask why she wanted to know, Poppy thanked them both. As she moved away, she wondered if she should have tipped them. Wasn't that what one did with police informers?

'Give them some money, Fergusson,' she murmured to her chauffeur when she reached the car.

'Aye, my lady.' He touched his cap, strode down to where the two men still stood and dropped some coins into each of their hands.

'Not a wild goose chase, Elspeth,' Poppy chided as they waited for him to return. 'Now we know that three days ago the yogi caught the last ferry to Kyleakin. As that's the boat we took the following day, which we know met the train leaving Plockton at 8.21, it means he *did* have time to murder Ellen Clark.'

Elspeth's long nose twitched. '*Only* if he spent the evening in Plockton. He might have been elsewhere during the day, arriving back in the village in time to take that train. Or he might have taken an earlier train altogether, then enjoyed the amenities of Kyle of Lochalsh until it was time for the ferry to leave.'

Poppy heard the note of triumph in Elspeth's voice. Dash it that she hadn't considered those herself.

'They seem very unlikely, but yes, they are a possibility,' she conceded.

A smile hovered around Elspeth's mouth.

'We'll take an early lunch here,' Poppy said, 'and then I will be back at the hotel for my yoga class this afternoon.'

After all, she still had more questions to put to the yogi.

When Poppy arrived back at the hotel, she saw with dismay that the word 'Cancelled' had been written across the poster advertising the yoga class.

Catriona was once again on the reception desk and, seeing Poppy's look as she gazed at the notice, said, 'It's so unfortunate, but it seems while in Dingwall this morning to visit a friend, the poor man met with some kind of an accident so he has stayed there to see a doctor.'

How very convenient, once again, Poppy thought wryly. But she immediately chastised herself; after all, the man could genuinely be hurt.

'Will he come back to hold the class another day?' she asked, already sure of her friend's answer.

'It's not possible, I'm afraid. He's due on Iona tomorrow.'

How *very* convenient. Swallowing her disappointment, but not her suspicion, she told Elspeth to take the Labrador to Poppy's bedroom. She would go immediately to the police office and tell Inspector MacKenzie he needed to track down the yogi in Dingwall and question him.

Poppy hastened out of the hotel, marched across the square and, tugging her beret to a jaunty angle that implied a keen and inquisitive mind, she entered the police office.

There he was, Inspector MacKenzie, wearing a cream waistcoat and with his black curls tousled. He looked up from reading the contents of an open file. 'My lady.' He closed the file and smiled.

She wanted to press her lips against his curved, sensuous mouth. She wanted to...

'Have you come with some valuable information?' he asked.

'I believe I have,' she told him, stirring herself from her thoughts. 'You will recall the three suspects we discussed yesterday evening?' There was no one else present in the office, so she felt no qualms about mentioning them.

He raised an eyebrow. 'Aye, I do.'

'Regarding the third one...'

'The yogi?'

'Yes.' She put both her hands on her waist. 'You know, Inspector, I will be able to let you have this important information more quickly if you don't interrupt.'

He bowed his head. 'I stand corrected.'

When his dark eyes met hers again, she could see amusement dancing in them. Poppy dropped her hands.

'To continue,' she said quickly, before she lost the thread of what she was saying, 'I found out this morning that the yogi was on the last ferry from Kyle of Lochalsh to Skye the evening Ellen Clark was murdered.'

'I need a wee bit more evidence than that, my lady.'

'Here is something else, then. He has cancelled his class this afternoon because he's had an accident in Dingwall! What do you think of that?' she demanded.

'I think it's possible he may have had an accident.'

'A bit convenient, don't you think? And why has he gone to Dingwall today, when he is due to go to Iona in the morning?'

'I can't answer that at present.'

She drew a breath. 'Well, here's an answer for you. He may have realised I am on to him.'

Inspector MacKenzie looked up at the clock on the wall.

'I'm not saying that you should go immediately to Dingwall to question him,' Poppy said in a tone that suggested she very much was.

'Something tells me that if I don't go, you will,' he said in a resigned voice.

'Oh, how well you know me, Inspector!'

He reached for his hat hanging on the coat stand. 'What would I do without your ladyship to direct the investigation?'

She beamed, then said, 'I don't suppose you'd let me come with you?'

'You suppose correctly, my lady.'

'Well then, do let me know how you get on.'

She wouldn't mention her visit to Mairi MacKay's croft, because it might be a red herring and she had no wish to waste Inspector MacKenzie's time. On the other hand, a detective could not afford to overlook even tiny details, so she would consider Beathag's findings.

Leaving the police office, Poppy marched back across the square to the hotel.

'Sorcha,' she asked the young woman on duty, 'what time does the afternoon post arrive?'

'Around four o'clock, your ladyship.'

Poppy glanced at her watch. It was now almost half past two; rather a long wait, and it was unlikely the newspaper cuttings from Beathag would arrive today.

She strolled into the Palm Court Lounge, intending to have a cup of tea while she had detectivey thoughts.

'My lady!' Algernon Hamilton rose from his chair and came towards her, taking her hand warmly. 'I'd quite given up on seeing you today. Please, do come and sit with us.' He indicated Harriet and Jeanie and two empty cane chairs set around a glass-topped table holding tea things.

It would be pleasant to see Harriet again, she thought, so she followed him and joined the little group.

'What can I get you to drink?' he asked.

'Tea, please.'

'Have a Gin Cobbler, Poppy!' Jeanie exclaimed, raising her cocktail glass containing a liquid of layered colours, the ice chinking. 'Gin, port, sherry, blackberries, slice of orange. Very refreshing.'

'Now then, Jeanie,' Algernon Hamilton chided her. 'If her ladyship would prefer tea in the afternoon, as do Harriet and I, then that is what she will have.'

'You needn't be so formal, Algernon,' said Jeanie with a laugh. 'Poppy has said we can use her Christian name.'

No, she hadn't actually.

'Have you had an enjoyable morning?' Algernon asked her, once the order for more tea had been given to the waitress.

'Not particularly. I had a visit to make in Broadford.'

'Broadford?' he remarked.

'Have you been there?'

'I passed through it on my way to Portree.' He shrugged. 'Everyone does. Now then, the ladies and I were just talking about an outing. Harriet would like to see the Fairy Glen, and Jeanie favours Dunvegan Castle.' He smiled at Poppy. 'Do you have a preference, my dear?'

Poppy's skin crawled. How she hated being called *my dear* by a man she barely knew. She was tempted to say her preference was for Inverness, where she could track down the yogi and question him herself, but that would involve a lot of explanation, which really was none of his business.

Harriet had looked hopeful at the mention of the Fairy Glen, so Poppy said, 'The Fairy Glen must be worth a visit. It will be something a little different, after all.'

Jeanie took a sip of her cocktail. 'Different?' she asked slyly. 'I suppose you have your own castle, Poppy?'

Poppy thought of her beloved Dunearn in Perthshire, with its tower and turrets, twisting passages and spiralling staircases. Totally impractical, but endlessly enjoyable. 'My family does have a castle,' she admitted.

Jeanie looked down into her drink, and Harriet's brown eyes grew wide.

'Delightful, most delightful, I'm sure,' Algernon said.

Poppy thanked the waitress, who set down a fresh pot of tea and a clean cup and saucer in a pretty floral pattern.

'The Fairy Glen it is, then,' Algernon continued with a smile. 'If we are all free this afternoon, then I propose we leave when we have finished our drinks.' He hesitated. 'Oh, how disappointing, I have just remembered my present lack of a motor car.'

He had 'just' remembered, had he? thought Poppy. Honestly, the man was so obvious!

'My car is available,' she felt obliged to say. 'As there are four of us, and a dog, of course, I will drive.'

'It will be wonderful to see Major again,' Harriet said, beaming.

'It will,' added Algernon.

Jeanie said nothing, but continued to sip her Gin Cobbler.

Poppy drank her tea and thought about receiving the newspaper cuttings from Elspeth's cousin. She needed to know what exactly was the link between Mairi MacKay, the two other women Beathag had referred to in her telegram, and the poor, strangled Ellen Clark.

TWENTY

When they had finished their drinks, Poppy drove the Bentley out of Portree, heading northwest.

'So tell us, Harriet,' Poppy heard Jeanie say in the back seat, 'what is so special about the place we are visiting?'

'It's believed that fairies live deep within the heather of the glen,' Harriet replied.

'Believed by whom!' Jeanie laughed. 'You cannot really believe that?'

'Well, no, I don't really,' Harriet replied in an uncertain voice.

'But how delightful it would be if they did, eh, Harriet?' Algernon said from the front passenger seat.

Poppy couldn't see Harriet's face, but she was sure the woman would have flushed cheeks and bright eyes from being singled out by Algernon.

They had covered some miles, following the road marked to Uig, when Algernon said, 'There is Uig Tower on our left.' He gestured to a small round tower with arched windows and arrow-slits.

'What is it?' Harriet asked, intrigued.

'It looks Norman but in fact it's a nineteenth-century folly,' he told her. 'We must take the road on the right here, just before the hotel.'

'You must have been here before,' Poppy said.

'Not here, but as a lad I once spent a short walking holiday on Skye with my father and have fond memories of sleeping in a bothy on the Knappach Estate.'

Poppy glanced at him and, for a moment, saw an unguarded look of nostalgia on his face. Almost immediately he reverted to his usual charming manner. 'I always make it my business to find out about a place before I go there.'

Poppy turned into the road signposted to *Bail nan cnoc*.

'The name means *village in the hills*,' Algernon added.

She raised an eyebrow. 'Do you speak Gaelic?'

He smiled. 'No, but as I said, I like to do my homework.'

A well-prepared man indeed, she thought.

They followed the narrow, winding road for a mile or so.

'There!' he said. 'Park there. This is likely as close as we can get by motor car.'

Poppy pulled into the grassy area he'd indicated and they all climbed out.

'Livestock roam freely around the area, so you might want to keep your dog on his leash,' Algernon told her.

'You must have been here to know that!' she exclaimed.

He laughed. 'I simply asked Mrs MacLeod at the desk.'

Poppy chided herself as she bent to clip Major on his leash. That was an obvious explanation. And one she should have asked Catriona herself.

'Allow me, dear ladies.' Algernon offered one arm to Poppy and the other to Harriet. Harriet took it with a shy smile.

'Thank you,' Poppy said, 'but I prefer to walk unaided.'

'Of course. Jeanie?'

Jeanie sent Poppy an unfriendly glance, took his other arm and they set off.

They strolled past a lochan, sparkling in the sunshine, and came to one of the strangest sights Poppy had ever seen. Grassy hills, of various sizes but all of a strange cone shape, were dotted about the landscape.

'These must be the hills of the Fairy Glen,' Harriet breathed as they came to a halt.

'And see here, ladies.' Algernon pointed down a path. 'Glen Conon.'

Poppy took a few steps down the path, her dog sniffing excitedly at every opportunity, and she caught her breath. The Glen itself was a splendid sight, but a breathtaking series of glittering waterfalls plunged down the far side.

'It's quite a prospect, is it not?' Algernon asked, coming to stand beside her. 'And the adventure isn't over yet.'

Not liking the way he was standing so close to her, she said cheerfully, 'Then let us move on and see what else there is to admire.'

'I already admire what I see,' he murmured, looking down at her.

Poppy stepped further away.

'Algernon,' Jeanie said, coming up behind them, 'we should see the rest of this place before the sun sets.'

He laughed. 'There must be a good five hours yet before that happens, but come.'

Jeanie took his arm again as the little group retraced their steps and continued walking.

Jeanie didn't need to worry that Poppy had designs on Algernon; she was welcome to him, Poppy thought. Although, she reflected, he seemed to prefer Harriet to Jeanie, so perhaps the fellow had some sense. But what game was he playing?

Before long they came to stone boulders covered in moss and surrounded by ancient, gnarled rowan trees. Algernon and Jeanie glanced at them and continued to stroll.

'The fairy ring, I think, Harriet,' Poppy said, taking her arm and tucking it into her own. 'The stones look haphazard, but perhaps it amused the fairies to arrange them like that.'

'Fairies are known to be mischievous,' Harriet smiled.

'Are you going to make a wish?' Poppy asked softly, sure that Jeanie would mock Harriet if she heard their conversation.

Harriet flushed deeply. 'No, I don't think so. I wouldn't know what to wish for...'

But Poppy saw Harriet's eyes flick towards Algernon ahead of them, and she knew the man's attentions hadn't been lost on the lonely Harriet.

They followed Algernon and Jeanie, who were conversing in a low tone, up a steep path. At the top they found themselves on a flat area of grass.

'Oh, look!' Harriet cried, pointing up. 'We're standing at the foot of a castle.'

'It's not really a castle, but a natural basalt outcrop,' Algernon told them. 'But I agree it has the appearance of a crumbling medieval fortress.'

'I'm going to climb to the top,' Poppy suddenly declared.

'I would advise against it, dear lady.'

Dear lady again! That determined her to climb the outcrop. She would not be patronised.

'I'm told the drop is very steep at the top,' he added.

'I'd rather stay here,' Harriet said nervously.

'I don't see the point of climbing up there,' Jeanie stated. 'The view will just be more of the same from down here.'

'Major will take the easiest route up and I will follow him.' Poppy unclipped the Labrador's leash. 'Off you go,' she said, gesturing to the gravel path winding upwards.

The dog didn't need to be told twice. He bounded forward, climbing the track with four-footed confidence.

Poppy followed on two feet. It *was* steep, but that would not deter her. The climb would be good exercise – and her yoga class had been cancelled this afternoon. It was a scramble to reach the very top, but she did it. And it was worth it. Major sat and stared with interest about him, his pink tongue lolling out of the side of his mouth.

'The view is magical from up here!' she called down to the others, a breeze ruffling her grey pinstriped skirt, but they seemed not to hear. Before her spread an enchanting landscape: an irregular pattern of grassy cone-shaped hillocks, random boulders and tranquil lochans. Sunlight played over the scene, casting patches of light and dark over the land below. It was otherworldly and, standing there, she felt it possible to believe in fairies.

She turned to gaze at the small figures of Algernon, Harriet and Jeanie below. What did she know of them, any of them, other than a very general impression? Jeanie was overbearing, but if the surface of that worldly exterior were scratched, what would be found? A woman who was controlling, or one that was perhaps as lonely as the quiet and unassuming Harriet? As for the dashing Mr Hamilton, was he really nothing more than a charming man who made a good living out of investing other people's money? He appeared as cast adrift as the two women who hung on his every word.

Poppy sighed and drew in a deep breath of clean summer air, the tang of the sea carried on the breeze. What were they each thinking, *really* thinking? How interesting it would be if she could read minds. How useful it would be if the spiritualist Catriona had mentioned could really communicate with the departed. How wonderful it would be if she, Poppy, could solve the case of Ellen's murder.

At that moment, Jeanie looked up, shading her eyes with her hands. She called out something it was impossible to hear, but Poppy guessed the other woman wanted to leave.

With a small sigh, Poppy began the scrambled descent. Major pushed past her and loose stones slipped from under her boots, but once she was back on the rough path, she found her footing again.

'I thought you would never come down,' Jeanie grumbled. 'I'd like to have a bath and then a cocktail before dinner.'

As the little party made their way back to the motor car, Poppy put aside thoughts of Algernon, Jeanie and Harriet, and reflected on the disappearance of the yogi – another man who had vanished – and on the button women. The exhibition was on today and tomorrow. She wanted to speak again to Isabella and Dorothy, and the exhibition might be the place to observe them in their natural habitat, so to speak. If she didn't see the two women this evening at dinner, she decided she would catch them at the exhibition tomorrow.

Meanwhile, Poppy fervently hoped the newspaper cuttings she was waiting for had arrived at the hotel, and that they would reveal the link she desperately sought between the murder in Plockton and the events on Skye. She had a good feeling about finding something of use inside the envelope, or at least she told herself she had a good feeling. Positive thinking was how she propelled herself through life. She'd done enough negative thinking since the day the boy arrived on his bicycle with the telegram informing her of Stuart's death.

She shook her head. She was making a fresh path for herself. If nothing else, she needed to make a new discovery before the very capable Inspector MacKenzie beat her to it, if she was to make him take her seriously.

The afternoon post hadn't brought the articles from the newspaper that Poppy longed to see, and she had to curtail her disappointment.

She and Elspeth had dinner in the hotel. As they ate, Poppy couldn't help but think that dinner with the inspector would have been a sight more uplifting than her maid's frowning face opposite her at the table.

'It's not my place to criticise, my lady...' Elspeth began.

'That's never stopped you before,' Poppy observed.

'But it would be better if, instead of chasing criminals, you spent more time with your new friends.' She glanced across the dining room.

Poppy followed Elspeth's glance and to her surprise saw Algernon and Harriet dining tête-à-tête. 'I don't think they would welcome me this evening,' she retorted. 'I'd be playing gooseberry.'

They certainly did look very intimate. Harriet was flushed and smiling, while Algernon appeared enchanted with his new companion.

'I wonder where Jeanie is,' Poppy went on. 'I don't think she would approve.'

'What makes you say that?' Elspeth took a bite of her bread roll and chewed.

'Jeanie's been making a play for Algernon.'

Elspeth caught a ladylike belch in her napkin. 'A *play*, my lady?'

'Yes, you know. Putting herself in his way and so forth. But he seems distinctly uninterested in her. Well, if the fellow makes Harriet happy, there can be no harm in a little casual flirtation.' She snatched another quick glance across to their table. Algernon was smiling and nodding at his dining companion.

'Although,' Poppy went on, 'there's something about Algernon that I can't quite trust...'

'He's not a gentleman.' Elspeth took another sip of her wine.

'I'm not sure that's a consideration for Harriet. But still, I would choose someone better for her if I could. He's the sort of man who enjoys the chase. Not a steady chap at all. You know,'

Poppy continued, 'he came on a bit strong with me this afternoon at the Fairy Glen.'

Elspeth sniggered. 'A strong man at the *Fairy Glen*.'

Good Lord, Poppy thought, had the wine gone straight to her maid's head? True, Elspeth usually drank only water, but she'd asked for wine because they were on holiday.

'It's not that funny,' Poppy admonished.

'No, my lady.' With an effort, Elspeth pulled herself together.

'As I said, it's my belief that Algernon is something of a cad. Perhaps he thinks that Harriet is a wealthy spinster, and he must know that I am from a fairly well-off family, so he sees the two of us as financially more attractive than Jeanie. And of the two of us, in Harriet's favour would be her malleable nature.'

'Indeed,' muttered Elspeth.

'And remember,' Poppy added, sending her maid a sharp look, 'that he knew Jeanie's husband, so he must have some idea about her financial position.'

'He's a gold-digger!' Elspeth exclaimed.

'*Wheesht!*' Poppy said in a low voice. She glanced across the dining room and was thankful to see Algernon and Harriet were still engaged in conversation, giving no indication they'd heard.

'You are best to keep away from him then, my lady.' Elspeth finished her soup with a satisfied sigh. 'I told you, you need someone to keep an eye on you. It's a dangerous world out there for such as you.'

'Such as me?'

'Rich, beautiful, available. *Hic.*'

'You should revert to water, Elspeth,' Poppy said disapprovingly. 'The wine has gone to your head.'

'You are probably right.' Elspeth drew the water carafe towards her. 'But I'm correct about staying away from that man. I don't like the look of him. His eyes are too close together.'

'I can look after myself,' Poppy told her firmly. It was the unworldly Harriet that Poppy was more concerned about.

There was no sign of the button women in the dining room, so Poppy supposed they were eating elsewhere this evening. She would seek them out at the exhibition tomorrow.

Poppy and Elspeth had just finished their meal, when Harriet caught sight of Poppy and she gave her a happy little wave. Shortly afterwards, Harriet and Algernon rose from their seats and made their way across the room.

'Would you both join me for coffee in the lounge?' Harriet asked, an excited flush on her cheeks.

'I have some business letters to write and the dear lady doesn't like to sit alone,' Algernon said.

'We'd be happy to join you, Harriet,' Poppy told her, getting to her feet.

Algernon bid them goodnight and excused himself.

Elspeth had also risen, and now she said, 'I have some mending to do this evening, my lady.' She nodded at Harriet and left the room, walking a little unsteadily.

Oh dear, thought Poppy. I do hope she is safe to be left alone. But then she remembered Major. He could be trusted to keep an eye on Elspeth.

'Shall we go into the small lounge?' Poppy suggested. 'It will be quieter there than the Palm Court.'

Harriet agreed, and Poppy ordered coffee from a passing waiter in the dining room.

'Would you also like a liqueur?' Poppy asked her.

'Oh, no. I've already had two glasses of wine,' Harriet confessed, shamefaced.

The small lounge, gloomy after the brightly lit dining room, was unsurprisingly empty, and they made themselves comfortable on the Chesterfield in front of a small fire. The lamps standing on side tables had been lit and they also helped to make the room feel cosy. The two women talked about inconsequential matters until the coffee had been brought and the waiter left, closing the door quietly behind him.

'You look as though you've had a very pleasant evening,' Poppy said, stirring her coffee and blatantly fishing for information.

'Algernon was very attentive.' Harriet smiled. 'And I think I've come to a decision.' She paused and continued. 'But can I ask for your advice, Poppy?'

'Of course!' *Please do!* she silently urged.

'Algernon is very experienced in investments and I wonder if I should ask him to look into my financial affairs. I've already mentioned something to him about it.'

Poppy frowned, feeling very uncomfortable. Wasn't there something a little suspicious in a virtual stranger willing to provide financial advice? Could the man be trusted? But it appeared that Harriet had already made up her mind.

'Harriet, you hardly know him,' Poppy cautioned.

'I know we met only yesterday, but we get on very well and I feel I can trust him. He said virtually the same as you, Poppy, when I mentioned it,' Harriet added eagerly. 'That he appreciated my confidence in him, but he couldn't advise me. That I didn't know anything about him and I mustn't risk my money to someone who is, after all, almost a stranger. That's what he said! A dishonest person wouldn't say that, would they?'

Would they not? 'Do you...' Poppy began carefully, 'do you have much money to invest?'

'Some,' Harriet admitted. 'I have no brothers or sisters, and when my father died he left me well provided for.'

'And your mother?'

A cloud passed over Harriet's face. 'She died giving birth to me.'

Poppy looked at Harriet. 'Do you really want my opinion?'

'I do. I have no one else to advise me—'

'No one else to advise you about what, Harriet?' Jeanie asked with a smile, dropping into an armchair beside them.

Good Lord, that woman could enter a room quietly when she wished to!

Harriet flushed. 'Just something I had been discussing with Algernon over dinner.'

'I'm so sorry I couldn't join you,' Jeanie said, 'but I think I had too much fresh air this afternoon.'

Was such a thing possible? Poppy wondered. 'I do hope you're feeling better?' she enquired politely.

'Much better, thank you. But tell me, Harriet, what is this advice that's required?' Jeanie pressed.

Harriet clearly felt she had no choice but to tell Jeanie. 'My father passed away a few months ago, leaving everything to me, and now I have money simply sitting in the bank. As a single woman with no prospect of marriage, I need to invest it wisely. I'm thinking about asking Algernon to recommend somewhere.'

'Then he is the very man!' Jeanie exclaimed. She looked around her and, despite there being no one else in the lounge, she lowered her voice. 'I don't mind telling you ladies, but I had been struggling financially after the death of my husband. Then one day I bumped into Algernon and he helped me by investing a small sum – which produced a very good return.' She opened her blue eyes wide. 'That's how I can afford to stay in such a splendid hotel.'

Jeanie held out her right hand and the firelight caught the red sparkle of a ring she was wearing. Poppy recognised it as a Belle Époque design.

'What a beautiful ring,' Poppy commented, in genuine delight. She had always had an eye for jewellery, and this piece was particularly special.

'Thank you.' Jeanie turned her hand in the light of the flames for them to admire the ruby and diamond curved bombé ring, constructed out of stylised ivy leaves in platinum. Poppy was sure it couldn't be worth less than three thousand pounds.

'Oh,' Harriet whispered.

'You should have asked *me* about Algernon's business sense,' Jeanie went on, withdrawing her hand and with a glance at Poppy to suggest there was no need to have asked *her*.

An uncomfortable silence fell between them all.

'I wish I could ask my father if he approves of my investing the money,' Harriet said wistfully.

'Then why don't you ask him?' Jeanie said casually.

'Jeanie!' Poppy frowned. 'You know perfectly well that is not possible.'

'Isn't it? I can see what looks like a planchette box over there.' Jeanie nodded in the direction of the bookshelf.

Harriet rose from the settee in excitement. 'I've never tried a planchette board, but I am interested in spiritualism.' She crossed to the bookshelves and took down a small wooden travel box shaped something like an envelope, with a brass handle on the top, and carried it to the circular table in the shadowy corner of the room.

Poppy and Jeanie joined her. The three women pulled out chairs and stared at the box as Harriet opened it with trembling fingers. Nestled in the red velvet inlay was a heart-shaped piece of flat wood, a pencil and some sheets of parchment paper. Gently, Harriet withdrew the contents. On the table she placed the planchette board, resting on its two brass castors attached at the wide end. After a moment's hesitation, she wedged the pencil into its hole at the thin end of the board, in the writing position.

'It's very impressive,' Jeanie said.

'Certainly a beautiful piece of workmanship,' Poppy agreed.

'It must have been here for a while,' added Harriet. 'I remember my father telling me that, some time ago, the boards were popular. Sir Conan Doyle believes the spirits can be contacted, you know.'

'Conan Doyle, the author of those ridiculous Sherlock Holmes stories? They're utter nonsense!' Jeanie pronounced.

'Are there any instructions in the box?' Poppy asked. She didn't want to encourage Harriet to believe that spirits could communicate by way of a piece of wood and a pencil, but it was clear that the other woman wanted to try the board.

Harriet felt inside the travel case and pulled out a folded sheet of paper. She opened it and placed it on the table.

'*Stand the board on a sheet of paper*,' Poppy read. '*Rest one hand lightly on the board, allowing the tip of your forefinger to touch the pencil.*'

Jeanie went first, then Harriet placed her finger on Jeanie's and Poppy followed suit, her forefinger resting on Harriet's. They waited.

Nothing happened.

'Oh, what a pity,' Harriet said, crestfallen.

'Wait,' Jeanie urged.

They gazed in horror as the planchette on its swivel wheels suddenly rushed across the paper. It proceeded to perform a series of movements until the paper was almost completely covered with pencilled whirls.

'The planchette is moved by the presence of spirits,' Harriet whispered. 'One of us must have psychic powers!'

'A useful attribute,' Poppy mused, 'but not one I have.'

Jeanie put in a fresh sheet of paper. 'We must ask it a question. Who will go first?'

'You,' said Harriet nervously.

'All right. Let me think... I'll ask after my deceased husband.' Jeanie cleared her throat and spoke clearly. 'Is Harold's spirit close tonight?'

The pencil began to move.

TWENTY-ONE

Poppy saw Harriet shiver as the planchette scrawled rapidly. It came to a halt. A large *yes* had appeared across the sheet of paper.

'That's clear enough,' Jeanie said.

'Another question, one requiring an answer other than *yes* or *no*, would be helpful,' Poppy suggested.

Again, Jeanie spoke in a clear voice. 'Please ask Harold how life is treating him on the other side.'

The planchette scribbled again and they all stared at the result.

Harriet frowned. 'What does it say?'

'It's just a series of squiggles,' Poppy said.

'It clearly says *well*,' Jeanie told them.

If that was the best Harold had to say, Poppy thought, the other side couldn't be *that* wonderful.

'Ask the question again, Jeanie,' Harriet urged.

This time the planchette moved slowly. When it stopped, they all gazed at the writing.

'I was right,' Jeanie said, with a little gasp.

Despite her best endeavours, Poppy couldn't make out if the scrawl read *well* or *ill*. Even so, it was a reply.

The planchette remained motionless in the middle of the shadowy table. They continued to sit with the tips of their middle fingers on the pencil.

'We need to ask it another question,' Jeanie said. 'Your turn, Harriet.'

Harriet swallowed. 'This is Harriet Scott here.'

'You need to ask a question,' Jeanie reminded her.

'Oh, yes.' Harriet swallowed again. 'I have met a gentleman who can invest my money and I want to know if my father thinks it is a good idea.'

For another minute or two, the planchette remained inactive. Then it twitched.

'It *is* Father,' Harriet breathed. 'He always cleared his throat before he spoke.'

'Mine too,' Poppy murmured.

Slowly the pencil began to move across the paper, leaving behind its message.

'*Don't invest*,' Poppy read aloud.

'*Do invest*,' exclaimed Harriet and Jeanie, leaning over the table.

'It couldn't be clearer,' Jeanie added with a nod.

'I think so too,' Harriet added. 'Father wants me to invest.'

'I don't think it says that at all,' Poppy insisted.

The pencil gave a little wobble.

'The messenger has more to communicate!' Harriet quickly lay down a fresh sheet of paper.

Almost at once the planchette started writing. It rushed about all over the paper and finally stopped, after covering it with undecipherable scrawls. They waited, but nothing further happened.

Harriet suddenly looked very tired. 'I think I'll go to bed.' She got slowly to her feet.

'Are you quite well?' Poppy felt alarmed. Harriet looked white as a sheet.

'Yes, just a little tired. It's been an exciting day.'

'It most certainly has, Harriet.' Jeanie also stood. 'I think I shall also retire.'

Harriet smiled at Poppy. 'Thank you for taking us to the Fairy Glen. It's made today one to remember. Goodnight.'

'Harriet is right,' Jeanie said. 'What a day it has been. I'll see you both tomorrow.'

Alone in the room, Poppy looked at the planchette. A ridiculous piece of wood, she thought, putting the pieces back in its box. But one that seemed to have had an influence on Harriet, who was sure her father had spoken to her.

But had he?

Back in her own room, Poppy took her notebook out of the nightstand drawer and sat on the edge of her bed in her silk pyjamas.

Using the planchette had not been a good idea, she decided. There could be only two explanations for what had happened this evening. One was that the spirit of Harriet's late father had guided the pencil, which Poppy couldn't believe. The other alternative was that one of the three of them had been responsible for the writing, in which case it had to be Jeanie. But she had seemed as surprised as the rest of them. Hard as it was for Poppy to accept, the other woman might really have Harriet's best interests at heart, and had thought this a way to reassure Harriet.

Reminding herself of the need to ensure Harriet did nothing to her disadvantage, Poppy climbed into bed and turned her thoughts to her notebook entry. She propped herself up on the pillows and wrote:

Day Four of Investigation into the Murder of Ellen Clark.

She thought for a moment, then wrote in a firm hand, unlike the ridiculous scrawl of the planchette:

1. Mairi MacKay took her own life after a man let her down. What is the significance of this?

2. The yogi was on the last ferry on the night Ellen was murdered. But did he remain in Plockton until he caught the train?

3. The yogi may have gone missing in Dingwall.

4. Inspector MacKenzie at the police office listened to what I had to say and acted on my information, while wearing a cream-coloured waistcoat and recklessly allowing his black curls to become tousled.

It was satisfying to see the facts written down – but she was dashed if she could see how they all fitted together.

The following morning, Poppy and Elspeth entered the dining room to find Isabella and Dorothy already down and halfway through their breakfast.

'The button exhibition calls,' Poppy muttered to Elspeth as they followed a waitress to a table, thankfully in a corner far away from Isabella and Dorothy.

They took their seats and the menus were handed to them by the waitress.

'I wanted to be sure they attend the exhibition today,' Poppy went on, holding her leather-bound menu card and peering over the top at the two women. 'And now they will be off before we have finished eating.'

'As your ladyship knows, I have the appetite of a bird,' Elspeth murmured. 'So I can tail them if your ladyship wishes.'

'*Tail* them?' Poppy put down her menu in surprise. 'Where did you learn such a word?'

The waitress reappeared, and they both ordered coffee, scrambled eggs and bacon.

'I confess to a liking for the very occasional crime novel, my lady,' Elspeth told Poppy, arranging her napkin on her lap.

'So you approve of crime detection in a novel, but not in real life?'

'Naturally, my lady.' Elspeth said demurely. 'I approve of the detecting of crimes and the chasing down of criminals, but never by a lady.'

'What about...' Poppy sought her memory for a suitable female police officer. 'Lady Molly of Scotland Yard?'

'A fictional detective,' Elspeth said with obvious triumph.

'Written by *Baroness* Orczy!' Poppy cried gleefully.

'Yes, but she is the author, my lady, and not the detective, and of course she is foreign. It is better that I, rather than you, follow the suspects. Ah, here is our breakfast,' Elspeth said in a voice that brooked no further conversation on lady detectives.

As Poppy ate her breakfast, she kept a wary eye on the Misses Buccleuch and Brown. She and Elspeth had just finished their eggs and bacon, when the other two women dropped their napkins onto the table.

'They're making a move, Elspeth,' Poppy hissed.

'So I see, my lady.' Elspeth set her knife and fork tidily on the plate, finished her coffee and dabbed her mouth with the napkin. 'Bide in the hotel.'

'Thanks awfully, Elspeth.'

Barely had Elspeth left the dining room than Inspector

MacKenzie entered. As soon as she saw him, Poppy was glad she had chosen to wear her flattering pink silk dress with tiny pleats below the low waist, and the pink cloche with a white lace flower.

He came over to her and she gestured for him to take a seat. 'Would you like anything to eat, Inspector?' she asked. 'Eggs and bacon, or toast and honey?'

'No, thank you, my lady. I have already eaten.' He shifted to try to make his large frame comfortable on the delicate cane chair and placed his hat on his knee. 'I'm thinking that there are two things you would like to ken.'

'Yes?' Poppy looked up from spreading a layer of honey on her toast.

'I returned from Dingwall last night having spoken to the Indian gentleman, and I'm now officially taking a break from the investigation.'

She stared at him, her knife poised. He was no longer on the case? 'But you and I work so well together! Good detective work is teamwork!'

'I didna say I wasn't working on the case. Only that I'm officially taking a break.' He smiled.

And was that a wink? *Surely a wink!*

'So, unofficially we continue to work on solving the murder?' Poppy asked.

'The honey is dripping off your knife, my lady.' He nodded at the thick, golden sweetness threatening to ooze onto the tablecloth.

Hastily she finished spreading the honey on her toast.

'I'm away to start the walking holiday,' the inspector went on. 'Constable Macduff will continue with the investigation in my absence.'

'Oh.' Poppy was disappointed. 'But a walking holiday means you will be...?'

'Walking hither and yon? Aye.'

'Then how will I contact you when I have further clues?'

'When?' He raised an eyebrow. 'You anticipate finding more clues?'

'Absolutely, Inspector!' She bit decisively into her toast and honey.

'From Saturday I will be staying at the Portree Inn. You can leave a message for me there.'

Her face brightened. 'Right you are! So, Inspector, you were telling me about the yogi.'

'Aye, my lady. I spoke to the hospital in Inverness and learned that the Indian gentleman had gone there with a suspected broken arm yesterday after taking a tumble. It turned out to be nothing more than a severe sprain. He'd given the address of a lodging house in the town where he was to spend the night and I found him there. His lady benefactor on Iona had sent him a telegram to say she was sending her motor car to collect him and take him across to the island.'

'So it was genuine.' She should have asked Catriona if he'd checked out and paid his bill, before she had told the inspector about this. 'But what about his being on the last ferry from Plockton the night Ellen was killed?'

'He was after telling me he'd intended to take the earlier boat, but had been meditating and the time had run away with him.'

She met the inspector's dark eyes. 'Do you believe him?'

'I'm giving him the benefit of the doubt for the present. He'll be safe on Iona for the week, I'm thinking.'

Poppy pointed to her coffee cup. 'Are you sure you won't join me, Inspector?'

He shook his head.

Just then the hotel's page boy trotted over to her table. 'A letter for you in this morning's post, your ladyship.' He held out a small silver salver containing a thick envelope.

Poppy thanked him and took up the package.

'I'll leave you to your correspondence, your ladyship.' Inspector MacKenzie took hold of his hat and went to rise.

'No, wait, Inspector. I think I know what this is, and if I'm right, you might find it of interest as well.'

The inspector reached for Elspeth's unused knife and handed it to Poppy.

'Thank you.' She slid the blade under the envelope flap, slit it open and took out a small number of newspaper cuttings.

'These do look interesting,' the inspector agreed, drawing his chair closer to Poppy's. His thick, dark curls bent close to her sleek, brown bob.

Her heart picked up speed, her skin prickled and her nerve endings quivered. She took a deep, surreptitious breath of his delicious scent of soap and clean linen, and keeping her voice steady, she said, 'These are from the newspaper where Elspeth's cousin works in Edinburgh.'

The inspector moved her empty plate and coffee cup to one side, and Poppy smoothed out the three cuttings on the table in front of them. He settled into reading.

Poppy quickly scanned the items. 'One on Mairi MacKay, of course, and two others.'

'You sound as though you ken Mairi MacKay.'

'I know *of* her. Yesterday morning, following a tip-off—'

'A tip-off?' He raised an eyebrow.

'You know what the word means. I have my sources too, Inspector,' Poppy said with a smile.

'Your maid's cousin?' he asked wryly, gesturing to the cuttings in front of them.

Poppy was not to be deflected. 'As I was saying, I visited Mairi MacKay's croft yesterday and discovered she had died.'

'Murdered?' he asked quickly.

'No, she'd thrown herself off a cliff.'

The inspector frowned. 'That's verra sad for the poor lady and her family, but how is it connected to the case?'

'I don't know, Inspector, but I do know from her neighbour that she was destitute and had no family to help her. Now we need to find out what, if anything, links these three women to Ellen Clark.'

Poppy and the inspector together examined the news items.

'They have no' been murdered or taken their own lives or been attacked, my lady,' he said, straightening.

'But here is the link. Look.' Poppy leaned over and singled out one clipping with her forefinger. 'Mairi MacKay committed suicide after she lost all her money to some affable fellow. And this woman in Eyemouth, and this one in Dumbarton,' Poppy pointed to each cutting in turn, 'were also swindled out of their life savings.'

'Two women in southern Scotland and at opposite sides of the country to each other,' the inspector pointed out, 'and one here on Skye. It's likely a coincidence.'

'Don't spurn coincidence in that casual way,' she said severely. 'Look again.' She tapped her finger on two of the newspaper cuttings. 'Neither the Eyemouth victim nor the Dumbarton one appears to have any close family.' Poppy looked up at the inspector. 'Mairi MacKay had no family either. There is a pattern!'

'Just because no family is mentioned, that doesna mean they had none,' he pointed out. 'And although it's a sad fact that there are men who prey on such women, that doesna make these three situations connected to each other – and much less to the murder of Ellen Clark.'

'I have a strong feeling about this, Inspector,' Poppy told him, not willing to be dissuaded.

'My lady, just because you hit on the truth in the Balfour case...' he ventured.

'Hit on the truth? I reasoned out every step in the case and drew the most brilliant deductions!'

Inspector MacKenzie ran an exasperated hand through his

hair. *Oh,* she thought, watching him with delight, *I must exasperate him more often.*

'Verra interesting, your ladyship. I will bear in mind everything you have told me.' He picked up his hat and rose. 'If you'll excuse me, I will take my leave and begin my walking holiday.'

'You are excused, Inspector.' Poppy waved a hand dismissively. 'I need to get on with the investigation.'

She had a good mind to let Inspector MacKenzie get on with the case himself, if she weren't almost sure she was on the right track.

Now, she just had to prove it.

TWENTY-TWO

Elspeth returned later in the morning with the news that Isabella and Dorothy were happily engaged in talk of buttons with the various exhibitors.

'I'm sure they'll be there for some time, my lady, if you want to go.'

'I can't say I want to go to a button exhibition, but needs must,' Poppy said, pulling her cream felt cloche well down over her chestnut-brown bob.

'You've already had a walk this morning,' she told Major, who looked as hopeful as ever at the thought of an outing, 'and I don't think you'd be welcome where I'm going.'

Elspeth gave a little cough. 'I took the liberty of asking if a dog were permitted in the hall, my lady, and was told a well-behaved dog would be.'

'That rules you out, Major.'

The Labrador's face seemed to suggest her assessment of him was incorrect. Poppy could feel herself relenting.

'Oh, very well!' she told him. 'But you absolutely must behave yourself.'

Poppy clipped the leash onto the dog's collar and they set

off for the hall. Major trotted along beside her, deliberately turning aside from any enticing smells they passed on the way.

A poster in a shop window caught Poppy's eye and she stopped to look. It depicted the profile of a young woman with waved hair, clad in a black evening dress and wearing a diamond necklace and earrings. In her hands she held up a glass ball, and a scarf was tied across her eyes.

Poppy gave a slight shiver at the sight of the scarf. She read the words at the side of the drawings of the woman.

'SHE SEES ALL,
KNOWS ALL'
Mistress Moodie, SPIRITUALIST MEDIUM
Portree Inn
This Saturday at 3 p.m.

The Portree Inn, where Inspector MacKenzie and his two walking companions were staying. Poppy was certain that the inspector wouldn't attend the session tomorrow, and just as certain that Harriet would.

Poppy walked on and soon reached the hall. A handwritten sign stuck on the door proclaimed the exhibition.

BUTTON EXHIBITION – LAST DAY!

She pushed the door open and entered.

Tables had been set out on either side of the small hall, and row after row of buttons lay displayed on trays covered in black velvet.

Poppy glanced around, taking the opportunity to look for Isabella and Dorothy. The room was surprisingly crowded and she didn't spot either of them immediately. Motes of dust floated in the sunlight coming through the single, high window. Then she caught sight of Isabella by one of the tables, but there was no sign of Dorothy. That was good, she thought, as she wanted to speak to Isabella alone.

Leading Major, who looked less than impressed with his walk, Poppy eased her way through the little knots of chattering women.

'Isabella!' Poppy said with a smile. 'I thought I might see you here.'

Isabella looked up from reading the handwritten inscription on a small white card at the display. 'You wanted to see me, my lady?'

'I happened to be passing the hall and thought the exhibition might be jolly. But now I find myself absolutely parched. Would you like to go somewhere for a cup of tea?'

'I suppose I could,' Isabella said reluctantly. 'I've seen all the exhibits now, anyway.'

'Is Dorothy also here?' Poppy asked.

'Did you want to speak to her as well?' Isabella eyed Poppy suspiciously.

'I thought she might like to come for tea too.' Which was not at all what Poppy wanted.

Isabella shrugged. 'Dotty's got something else on this morning.'

'Anything interesting?' Poppy asked in a careless voice as the two women and the dog made their way out of the hall.

'Not really,' came Isabella's unhelpful reply.

A tea shop sat directly opposite the town hall and they crossed the road, entered and took seats. Major sat by Poppy's chair, a disappointed look on his face. Clearly, this was not the sort of walk he'd envisaged.

'Isn't this pleasant?' Poppy began when they had placed their order.

'I suppose so.'

Goodness, the woman was surly! It was going to be hard to

draw her out on the subject of her pre-dinner walk on the night Ellen's body was found.

'Have you been interested in buttons for long?' Poppy asked mildly.

Isabella stared at her. 'You're not the slightest bit concerned with buttons, so why don't you just come out and say what's on your mind?'

'Perhaps because I was brought up to avoid hurting people's sensibilities,' Poppy said with a well-practised smile.

'Very nice, to be sure, but I prefer plain speaking.'

Poppy had noticed. 'I'm beginning to see that for myself. In that case, where did you walk between arriving back from the excursion to Urquhart Castle and dinner at the Harbour Hotel on the evening Ellen was murdered?'

Isabella gave a harsh laugh. 'You are asking me if I killed poor Ellen, aren't you? You think yourself quite the little detective. I think you'll find it takes more than a title and a lifetime of privilege to make a good detective, my dear.'

Hardly a lifetime, Poppy thought. Merely the last four years, when her father had come to the earldom upon the death of his older brother in the Great Influenza epidemic. 'I am assisting Inspector MacKenzie of the Edinburgh Detective Branch,' she said, tilting her determined chin and holding the other woman's gaze.

'Maybe you are, maybe you aren't, but either way it has no bearing on the matter because I've nothing to hide.' After a long pause, Isabella said coolly, 'I took a brisk walk to the end of Harbour Street, then I turned and walked in the opposite direction to Bank Street, and back to the hotel. Which means I was out for about three-quarters of an hour, as no doubt Dorothy has already told you.'

'So you didn't see Ellen?' Poppy pressed. 'Or go to, or walk past, the open-air kirk?'

'If that's the best you can do, your ladyship, I fear Ellen's killer will never be brought to justice.' Isabella got to her feet. 'Do you know, I think I'll forget that cup of tea. Good morning, my lady.' Narrowly missing Major's tail, she strode out of the tea shop.

'Well, I didn't make a good job of that interview, did I, Major?'

Her dog declined to comment. But Poppy noted that Isabella had also not answered her question. Which meant that she was still firmly on Poppy's suspect list.

A long morning stretched ahead. Poppy's feeling that Ellen Clark and the three women in the newspaper articles had been tricked by the same man was growing stronger, but where did that take her?

As she was trying to make sense of her thoughts and wondering what to do next, the door of the coffee shop opened and in came the tall, thin figure of Algernon Hamilton. *Drat*, she really didn't want to see him. She bent her head to her teacup and thanked her lucky stars that Major was lying down on the opposite side to the door and that the place was now busy.

Algernon was so deep in thought that he failed to see her. She surreptitiously watched his progress as he took a table on the other side of the tea shop. He slid onto a chair and took off his hat, placed his order and, before long, was drinking his cup of coffee and reading the newspaper he had brought with him.

Poppy had a sudden urge to work on her portrait skills. She removed her sketch pad and pencil from her bag and started work. After a while she had a rough likeness of the dark-haired, clean-shaven Algernon, which she was more than pleased with. She was confident that her skills as a quick sketch artist were improving.

She put away her pad, signalled to the waitress and paid

her, then got to her feet. The coffee shop was now busier than ever and it didn't seem fair to take up a table any longer. In his eagerness to get back outside, the Labrador's large body knocked against her chair leg; it scraped on the floor and heads turned her way. One of them was Algernon's. *Dash it!*

He immediately rose, folded his newspaper, dropped some coins on the table and crossed to where she stood.

'Poppy, my dear, I see you also find yourself in here this morning.' He took her hand and very gently pressed her fingers.

An idea came at once to Poppy. If he wanted to flirt with her, let him try! He would get nowhere and it would show her how serious were his feelings for Harriet. Poppy was more concerned than she liked to admit for her new friend. Did all professional men behave in this manner? Chasing the best financial prospect, rather than a woman to love and cherish?

'Poppy?' Algernon's soft tones interrupted her thoughts.

'As you see, Algernon, I can't deny that I am here.' Very gently she returned the pressure.

His eyes lit up and he smiled. 'Would you care to adjourn to the hotel? The coffee served there is the vastly superior Colombian, and the small sitting room is less noisy and much more intimate.'

'That would be delightful,' she murmured, dropping her eyes modestly. Good Lord, she thought, it was as if she were acting out a passage in one of Miss Taft's novels.

'Take my arm, dear lady.'

Poppy gritted her teeth at his expression and accepted his arm. They crossed the road, Major walking beside her, and entered the Isle of the Mist. He guided her past a visibly surprised Catriona, along the corridor and into the small sitting room. It must face north, she thought idly, as even in daytime the small fire was burning and the lamps lit on the side tables.

'Please sit down,' he said with a smile.

She sat on the Chesterfield and he lowered himself next to

her. Major stretched out in front of the hearth with a deep sigh. I know, Poppy thought, me too.

'It's very kind of you to invite me for coffee, Algernon,' she said, smoothing the soft pink silk of her skirt. 'I had been wondering about asking you for some financial advice. Jeanie tells me you are the very man.'

'I understand how hard it must be when you are a widow and have no man to advise you,' he said softly, his grey eyes gazing at her face. 'What you want is equities, by which I mean shares in companies. Not in the big companies, but in the small ones that might do well very soon. But you should know that I'm happy to assist you in *any* way I can.'

Good Lord, she thought, he didn't hang about. She dropped her eyes. 'Really?'

'Really,' he replied.

'Of course, you've heard about the terrible affair in Plockton, Algernon?' she went on with a little flutter.

'Yes, I have. As you say, terrible,' he said, shaking his head. 'I do hope you do not go out alone in the evenings? I would be very happy to escort you wherever you wish.'

She allowed her hand to drop from her lap onto the couch between them.

'That is so... thoughtful of you.'

'Not at all.' He closed his hand over hers, and again his fingers tightened in a very gentle squeeze.

'Oh, but the waiter will be here shortly,' she breathed, withdrawing her hand.

'I haven't yet ordered the coffee,' he pointed out.

The devil he hadn't! Poppy cast around to find something to distract those compelling eyes of his. Finding nothing, she glanced at her watch. 'Goodness, is that the time?' she said, starting. 'I have to fly. Come, Major.'

Poppy rose, despite Algernon's warm protests. She was satisfied that he had no real feelings for Harriet. But how to let

Harriet know that, when the other woman had declared she trusted him implicitly?

And, equally worrying, was the thought that had crossed her mind just a moment ago as Algernon offered to put his manly protection at her disposal. Were Mairi MacKay's confidence trickster and this distinguished-looking fellow one and the same?

TWENTY-THREE

Elspeth had taken an early lunch, so Poppy gave the Labrador into her care and went down to the hotel's dining room. She was about to enter when she saw Harriet hovering in the doorway, looking a little lost without her newly acquired friends, Jeanie and Algernon.

'Harriet,' Poppy said, going up to her, 'please join me for lunch. It's so much nicer to have a dining companion than to eat alone. My treat!' She smiled.

'That's very kind of your ladyship... Poppy,' Harriet corrected herself. 'Are you sure you don't mind?'

'I would not have asked you if I didn't mean it.' Poppy took Harriet's arm and they entered.

Harriet looked as if something was on her mind, so although the dining room was quiet today, Poppy requested a table at the side of the room.

No sooner were they seated than Harriet began. 'Poppy, you remember I asked you for your opinion of my investing some money?'

Oh dear, thought Poppy. Please let her not say she'd already done so on the basis of a recommendation from Algernon.

'Shall we order first?' Poppy said gently, picking up her copy of the lunch menu. She perused it. 'What would you like, Harriet?'

'What are you having, Poppy?'

The waiter reappeared. 'I'll have the steak and kidney pie,' she told him.

'The same for me, please,' Harriet added.

'And to drink, my lady, miss?' he asked them.

'What do you say to champagne, Harriet?' Poppy asked.

'Champagne?' Her face lit up, before the familiar anxious look returned. 'Oh, I would like to, but I don't know if my father would approve of drinking champagne at lunchtime.'

But he was not here to approve or disapprove, Poppy thought. 'I'm sure he wouldn't object to one small glass. Two glasses of Perrier-Jouët, please.'

The waiter bowed and withdrew.

'Are we celebrating something?' Harriet asked Poppy.

Perhaps her progress in the case, Poppy thought, slight though it was. 'I simply feel like some bubbly,' she told Harriet.

'I do have something to celebrate, Poppy,' Harriet said shyly.

'Yes?' Poppy tried to sound encouraging, but she guessed what was coming.

'I've told Algernon that I want to invest the money my father left me, and I asked if he could recommend somewhere.' Harriet straightened her already straight cutlery. 'I know what you think, Poppy, but he was truly reluctant at first.'

Had she misjudged him? Poppy wondered. Not about being a cad, because he was surely that, but about being a fraudster?

'But eventually,' Harriet went on, 'he suggested a railway company in South America that's looking for investors.' She looked up at Poppy and said in an earnest voice. 'Algernon told me he's happy to help me invest my money and that he would forego his commission. He gave me his business card.'

Harriet opened her brown leather clutch bag lying on the

side of the table, removed the card – white with a fancy border – and showed it to Poppy.

'He's being very kind and helpful, Poppy,' Harriet added, putting away the card.

Poppy was saved from any immediate comment by the arrival of the waiter with the two glasses of champagne, which he set on the table. She lifted her glass and the bubbles popped, spraying tiny droplets of champagne into the air and tickling her nose. She took a sip.

'Harriet, I cannot tell you what to do with your money, but I do think advice from another party, such as your bank manager, would be useful before you go ahead with such a transaction.'

'It's not necessary, as I'm sure *Compañía Ferroviaria* would be a good investment.'

Poppy tried again. 'Fledging railway companies are not a safe bet, Harriet. Some fail to raise enough money to build the railway, while others manage to build them but then find there are insufficient passengers to make any money for the investors.'

'And others are built *and* are successful, which means I will get a good return on my investment. And I'll be helping people in poor countries who need it, Algernon said.' There was a note of defiance in Harriet's voice. 'My father always tried to help those less fortunate than ourselves. He would approve, I'm sure of it. So I've made up my mind.'

The waiter brought their portions of pie. Poppy did her best to chat with Harriet of inconsequential matters, but she was so worried that the food seemed tasteless and the conversation was strained.

And then her thoughts were disrupted by the arrival of another diner, a middle-aged man with a cheerful face.

'Afternoon, ladies,' the man said in a hearty voice as he followed the waiter past where they sat and took a seat at a nearby table.

Poppy and Harriet nodded politely at the new arrival.

Seeing he had their attention, he called across to them. 'Lovely weather, is it not?'

'It is, sir.' Poppy turned back to Harriet.

'The name is Bertram,' he continued loudly. 'Travelling salesman in ladies' fashion accessories. Just you ladies let me know if there's anything you require.' He beamed.

Harriet's face turned the colour of beetroot.

'Thank you. We will bear that in mind,' Poppy told him, turning firmly to Harriet and engaging her in a conversation about her plans for the rest of her holiday.

The lunch continued in a pleasant but slightly strained fashion. Poppy and Harriet were taking their coffee in the Palm Court Lounge, when their fellow guest, the hearty salesman, burst into the room.

'Here we are again!' Bertram smiled. 'I'll just take a seat with you ladies, if that's all right?' Without waiting for an answer, he sat in one of the cane chairs. 'Och, this is not a comfortable fit for a gentleman built like myself.' He laughed.

He was dressed in a tweed suit, but otherwise was most unlike the hotel's usual clientele, Poppy thought.

'It gets a bit lonely travelling on the train on your own all the time, so I like to strike up a conversation with the ladies at the hotels,' Bertram went happily on. 'I find they are better company than the gentlemen.'

Harriet gave her an anguished look, which Poppy interpreted as wanting the man to leave, but Poppy wasn't so sure she wanted that. A travelling salesman might have some useful information.

'It must be an interesting life,' she began, 'visiting so many places and people.'

'Och, aye, it can be, but not everyone is as friendly as you two ladies. Take this auld biddie I was speaking to recently in Attadale...'

Attadale. Only three stations from Plockton!

'Ah, Attadale,' Poppy mused fondly, as if she were very familiar with the estate. 'You must have also visited Strome Ferry, Duncraig, Plockton...'

'Strome Ferry, aye, but not the other twa places you mentioned. I've nae had much luck with sales there in the past, so I gave them a wide berth this time.'

Dash it, that wasn't what she wanted to hear.

'Now then, ladies, what can I get you to drink?' He rubbed his hands together. 'I'm sure you'd like something a wee bit stronger than coffee, eh?'

Poppy considered the man. How could a travelling salesman afford to stay at an expensive hotel like the Isle of the Mist? Business must be very good indeed.

Or did he have a sideline, she thought darkly, such as charming wealthy single women out of their money?

TWENTY-FOUR

'Do you have a regular route on your travels,' Poppy asked Bertram, 'or do you go wherever the next train takes you?' She sounded ridiculously flippant to her own ears, but the man let out a loud guffaw of laughter.

'I like to keep flexible in my business dealings, but I do have a bit of a route. One where the customers are regular and willing to spend a little to obtain their heart's desire. If you get my meaning.'

'I think I do,' said Poppy, stopping herself in time from giving him a confidential wink.

Was he lying about not having been to Plockton? Could he be Ellen's mystery man? How had Miss Grant at the Harbour Hotel described Ellen's beau? Personable, the manageress had supposed, middle-aged, tall, with grey hair and beard. Some might see the fellow seated here as personable. He was middle-aged and tall. Beards could be shaved off and hair dyed. And he could call himself Bertram, or Alan, or any other name he chose. If he was Ellen's mystery man, then he could also be her killer. It all seemed very unlikely, but Poppy mentally added Bertram to the bottom of her suspect list.

She was refusing Bertram's offer of a stronger drink for them both when Jeanie appeared in the lounge. Poppy glanced over at Harriet and was disturbed to see that she looked very relieved.

'Harriet,' Jeanie said, coming over to where she, Poppy and Bertram were seated, 'have you forgotten that we are going to Mistress Moodie's event this afternoon? We still need to purchase tickets from the hotel desk, and then leave to be sure of good seats. Are you ready?'

She looked doubtfully at Harriet's loose brown dress that resembled nothing as much as a sack, relieved only by the presence of her small but beautiful emerald brooch.

'Oh, yes, Jeanie, I am.' Harriet rose, picked up her wrap and turned to Bertram. 'Do excuse us.'

'Who is this gentleman you are keeping from me?' Jeanie said, suddenly coy.

In an instant Bertram was on his feet. 'Good afternoon, miss.'

'Mrs,' Jeanie corrected him, then added, 'A widow.'

Bertram smiled. 'Do you ladies have to depart so soon? Won't you join us for a cup of coffee – or perhaps something stronger?'

Jeanie slid into one of the seats. 'A cocktail would be lovely.' She smiled at him.

'What can I get you?' Bertram asked.

'You choose. I like a man to make the decisions.' Jeanie's voice was silky.

He laughed and went off to the bar at the end of the lounge.

'Jeanie,' Harriet hissed, sitting down again, 'I thought you said we had to go or we would be late?'

'There's time for a wee cocktail. What is the matter – were you trying to keep him to yourself, as if Algernon isn't enough?'

Harriet looked shocked. 'I've done nothing to encourage—'

'That is not very kind, Jeanie,' Poppy said in a low voice.

Jeanie hesitated. 'Sorry, you're right. I'll have this drink and then we'll go.' She sighed. 'The planchette last night produced nothing of interest, so I hope this afternoon's event is better.'

'Jeanie wants to ask more about her deceased husband,' Harriet explained to Poppy. 'Would you like to come with us? Although I don't know if there is anyone you would like to speak to on the other side...' She tailed off uncertainly.

'There is someone who comes to mind,' Poppy said, thoughtfully. 'Not my husband.' She had no wish to try to conjure up the spirit of Stuart. 'But my father.'

He was on the other side, all right – the other side of the world. She would dearly like to know what he had done with the key to the small room in the turret before he and Poppy's mother left for Australia.

Harriet and Jeanie were staring at her with interest, but before she could explain, Bertram reappeared with a pint of beer and a vivid blue cocktail.

'Here we go,' he said, 'to match your eyes. A Blue Moon, as served in Times Square.'

'Times Square?' Jeanie accepted the proffered glass and took a few sips.

'You've been to New York?' Poppy was astonished. *How could a travelling salesman afford such a trip?*

He winked. 'You don't have to go there to ken about the cocktail.'

No, of course not, she thought, noticing that he hadn't actually answered her question.

'No, thank you, Harriet, I can't join you this afternoon, as I'm going with Mrs MacLeod to the reverend's for tea,' she said. 'Is Algernon not going with you both?'

'He's got a business appointment, unfortunately,' Harriet said.

'A man after my own heart,' Bertram said. 'Perhaps you

could introduce us this evening. It would be refreshing to talk to a man in the same line. Is he a purveyor of fancy goods like myself?'

'No, he is not,' Harriet told him with a degree of pride. 'He's an investment broker to the great and wealthy.'

'Ah,' was all Bertram said, as he settled further back into the chair.

'It's a pity Algernon isn't free to accompany you,' Poppy added. 'He is here on holiday, is he not?' There, maybe that would make Harriet a little less trusting of the man, she thought.

'It's probably not his sort of thing,' Jeanie said.

'He told me he's heard of barefooted pilgrims walking over burning coals and small boys shinning up ropes tossed in the air,' Harriet stated, 'so he doesn't laugh at people who believe in the spirit world. He's very sympathetic and understanding,' she added softly.

Jeanie tossed back the cocktail and got to her feet. 'Now, we really should go. Nice to have met you, Bertram.'

Poppy echoed the pleasantry, and the three women left him to his beer, Jeanie and Harriet to buy tickets for the medium, and Poppy to go to her room to change for tea with the minister.

Would she learn anything of interest from the Reverend Greene? she wondered. Ministers famously saw and heard most things going on in their parish.

The fine summer's day continued as Poppy and Catriona walked the short distance from the hotel to the manse for tea.

'How is Rory's mother doing?' Poppy asked.

'Much better, thanks. He's expecting to return to the island this afternoon.'

Poppy smiled. 'That's good news all round.'

'I had to give bad news earlier to your two friends, though, Harriet Scott and Jeanie Harper,' Catriona told her. 'All the tickets to the medium's show are sold out.'

'What a pity!' Poppy exclaimed. 'Harriet in particular was looking forward to it.'

'She did look quite distressed. So I told the two of them that Mistress Moodie had a few private consultations available, but that they were more expensive – and,' Catriona arched her eyebrows, 'are for tomorrow.'

'On the Sabbath! That won't go down well.'

'I know. The ferries don't run that day, of course, which means the medium has to stay on the island until Monday, so she told me she would do a small number of private – very private, in the circumstances – consultations in the afternoon. Harriet and Jeanie must be keen, as they paid for two.'

Poppy smiled. 'I'm glad, for Harriet's sake. She seemed so desperate to go this afternoon. I just hope she asks about investing her money with a Spanish railway company and the medium says a very definite no.'

'I suspect, Poppy, that all mediums are charlatans, but...' Catriona paused to bid good day to an acquaintance of hers they passed in the street. 'What do you think of our using another two of the consultations? Just to check on the woman's authenticity, I mean.'

'Catriona, I never thought you would believe in such a thing as spiritualism!'

'I'm not saying I do, and I'm not saying I don't, but I am intrigued to know how she works.'

'In that case... why not? Book the consultations, Catriona!'

'I already have,' she admitted with a laugh. 'One never knows if an opportunity like this will appear again. But for goodness' sake, don't mention it to the minister! The shock might bring on a heart attack.'

They reached the manse, knocked on the door and it was opened by a young girl in a black dress with white apron.

'Come away in,' the maid said, with a little bob. 'The master is expecting you.'

She led them into a small sitting room. Open French windows took up most of one wall and through them the sweet scent of roses wafted in.

The Reverend Greene turned from contemplating his garden. He had a lean brown face, and a long sharp nose. A pair of gold pince-nez perched on said nose, and his pullover and trousers hung from his lanky frame.

He came forward, his long, bony hands extended.

'*The bee that thro the sunny hour, sips nectar in the opening flower*, as the bard puts it. Ah, isn't it a beautiful day?' He smiled.

Poppy subdued the laugh she felt bubbling up. Burns' "Philly and Willy" was not usually recited by a minister to parishioners, being a teasing song about love and courtship.

'Mrs MacLeod, delightful as always to see you,' he went blithely on. 'And you have been kind enough to bring your friend. I have been looking forward to meeting you, your lady-ship. Rambling Rector, ye ken,' he added.

'I beg your pardon?' asked Poppy, startled.

'Yon climbing rose.' He gestured to the creamy-white roses that could be seen climbing on the outside trellis. He breathed in deeply. 'Och, such a *wondrous* fragrance.'

He indicated they should take a seat, then he took up from the mantelpiece a little silver lady in a crinoline. He shook her and the silvery tinkle of a bell rang out.

As he waited for the maid to answer his summons, he looked out into the garden and sighed. '*A garden is a lovesome thing, God wot!*'

Good heavens, was he going to quote poetry at them all afternoon?

'Thomas Edward Brown, of course,' the Reverend Greene added. 'What a pity the man was not a Scot, but we can't have everything.'

The sitting room door opened and the maid appeared.

'Ah, Elsie. Tea, if you please.'

'Yes, sir.' She bobbed and disappeared from the room.

'Now, where were we?' The minister sat in an armchair, positioned so that he could see his garden as well as his visitors.

'The garden...' Catriona offered.

'Ah, the purest of human pleasures.' He gave another sigh. 'But I didn't invite you here to discuss gardening, close though it is to my heart. No, it was about another matter entirely. *Man's inhumanity to man*, or rather to woman. In his poem "Man Was Made to Mourn", Burns was talking about class inequalities...' Reverend Greene faltered as he recollected Poppy's status.

Poppy felt her face flush, and reminded herself that she mainly used her class position for the greater good. To help the delicious but annoying Inspector MacKenzie track down murderers, for example.

Reverend Greene carried on briskly, 'But today I am concerned with Exodus chapter 20, verse 13. The sixth commandment,' he clarified. '*Thou shalt not kill.*'

'You are thinking of the lady in Plockton?' Poppy suggested.

'Aye, that poor lady. I heard you found her body and I was wondering if there has been any further news.'

'Nothing to speak of,' Poppy said. She wasn't averse to telling a wee white lie on occasion, where it was necessary, but this answer was entirely true. She couldn't possibly speak of the progress she was making.

'I see.' He sounded disappointed.

The door opened again and the maid came in bearing their tea. The minister brightened. 'Och, more of God's bounty.'

Shippam's, more like, Poppy thought, accepting a dainty sandwich and biting into potted fish paste.

Cups of tea were handed to them by the maid.

'Och, there is nothing like a nice cup of tea,' the minister said, and drank with relish.

They discussed gardens, gardening and poetry with specific reference to nature. Eventually, the topic seemed to have run its course.

'Are you going to any of the events in the summer programme, Reverend Greene?' Catriona asked, refusing another sandwich but taking a slab of Dundee cake.

'I don't think so, my dear. I'm thinking that neither yoga nor button displays are for me. As for that so-called spiritualist-medium...' A red flush crossed his thin cheeks. 'Balderdash! Oh dear, apologies for my language, ladies, but it is an expression first used by the poet Samuel Butler. Balderdash, indeed! As if the woman could communicate with the deceased!'

Poppy decided not to point out that was what in essence the minister did, but she supposed it wasn't quite the same thing. She contented herself with saying, 'She is proving popular, at any rate. All the tickets have been sold.'

Perhaps, she thought suddenly, the medium could tell her who had killed Ellen Clark. Now, *that* would be very helpful!

'People today,' continued the minister, 'have no sense of... Do you know,' he added as a related thought occurred to him, 'only today, when I was taking my post-luncheon constitutional, I saw a couple come out of your hotel, Mrs MacLeod, and disappear round the back of the building. They were canny enough not to come out together, you understand, but close enough. I'm afraid they could only have been up to no good.'

Poppy's pulse jumped. Who could the minister mean? Of course it might be none of her business, but on the other hand it could be very much her business...

Catriona frowned. 'I don't like the reputation of my hotel to be threatened. Could you describe them to me, minister? And I will have a discreet word.'

'Quite so, my dear. I ken I can rely on you to keep up standards in this charming wee town of ours, Mrs MacLeod. The lady, if I can call her that, was tall, of a slim build, well-dressed, with one of those modern, angular haircuts.'

Jeanie! Poppy thought.

'And the' – he gave a small cough – 'gentleman would be about the same height but a wee bit older, wearing a tweed suit...'

'Bertram!' Poppy burst out.

The Reverend Greene sent her a sharp look. 'Ye ken the man?'

'I believe I do,' Poppy admitted. 'And the lady.'

Jeanie and Bertram? She could hardly believe it. But Jeanie had seemed put out by Algernon's attention to Harriet, so had she transferred her affections to the travelling salesman?

'I will see if these two persons attend kirk tomorrow, and I have every intention of addressing from the pulpit such behaviour,' he said darkly. 'And now, dear ladies, I need to expand my sermon on that matter forthwith. If you will excuse me.'

He rose, teacup and saucer still in hand, and without waiting for the maid, ushered them out. 'I look forward to seeing you both at kirk tomorrow forenoon.'

The minister smiled, bowed, quoted, '*Adieu! a heart-warm, fond adieu!*' and closed the door behind them.

'"The Farewell"...' Catriona laughed.

'By Burns, who else?' Poppy smiled, but she didn't feel like laughing. The minister had inadvertently given her something else to think about.

If that had been Jeanie and Bertram behaving indiscreetly behind the hotel, what did it mean? That Jeanie had made quick progress with him, or that the two of them already knew each other, but for some reason had kept it quiet?

A third thought crossed Poppy's mind. If Bertram *was*

Ellen's mystery gentleman, was he now making love to Jeanie, after whatever money she had? Although the back of an hotel seemed a most unlikely place for a seduction, and not something she could imagine impressing Jeanie.

What, then, were they up to?

TWENTY-FIVE

'Catriona,' said Poppy, as they walked from the manse back to Isle of the Mist Hotel, 'I am feeling uncomfortable about something Harriet Scott has told me.'

'Yes?'

'She didn't say it was in confidence, so I feel I can tell you a little about it.'

'Go ahead,' Catriona said, looking intrigued.

'Harriet has a sum of money, left to her by her father, and she wants to invest it.'

'That doesn't sound like a problem so far.'

'No, but she has asked for advice from another hotel guest, Mr Hamilton, and he has recommended an overseas railway company.'

Catriona frowned. 'Why has she asked Mr Hamilton?'

'Apparently he works in investments.'

'Then he must know what he is talking about, surely?'

'But Harriet hardly knows him!' Poppy burst out. A man they passed on the street gave her a startled look, and Poppy lowered her voice. 'I suggested to her that she approach her bank manager for another opinion, but I'm very much afraid that she is about to ask Mr Hamilton to invest the money on her behalf.'

'I can see why you're wary,' Catriona replied. 'He arrived at the hotel only two days ago, so she's not had time to form a realistic opinion of him.'

'Exactly my thoughts, Catriona.'

'Has he approached you about investing any money? Between you and Harriet Scott, I'd have thought it would be your business he'd want.'

'Harriet says that she approached him.'

'I see. Well, if you put that aside for a moment, you're still the most financially attractive guest we have staying at present.'

Poppy caught hold of Catriona's arm and stopped, the action turning her friend to face her. 'Tell me, what does your female intuition tell you about this situation?'

Catriona took a moment to think. 'It tells me Miss Scott should take your advice and speak to her bank before parting with any money to a man she hardly knows.'

'Then we are in agreement.' They started walking again and after a few moments Poppy asked, 'How long is Algernon Hamilton booked in for?'

'It's quite a nice long booking, for three weeks.'

A lot could happen in three weeks, Poppy thought soberly. 'Perhaps I can persuade her to wait another week.'

'That would be best, Poppy. By the way, she and I have agreed terms for her to be a long-stay resident at the hotel.'

'I'm pleased for you, but I feel saddened for Harriet. She isn't so old as not to hope there might be marriage and children in her future.'

'No, she is not,' Catriona observed. 'And neither, my dearest Poppy, are you.'

Poppy sent her friend a startled glance. 'What brought on that comment?'

'Only that I've noticed there appears to be a wee spark

between you and the police inspector,' Catriona murmured with a smile.

Poppy was saved from replying as they reached the hotel, and inside found Rory working at the reception desk. He looked up as they approached, with a smile on his intelligent, agreeable face.

'You made it back,' Catriona said fondly to her husband.

'Aye. My mother is doing grand, and I thought you'd probably need some help back here.'

'Not that you missed me, then?' she teased him.

Rory came out from behind the desk, his kilt in the colourful MacLeod tartan of green, navy, black, red and yellow, and planted a husbandly kiss on the cheek she offered.

He grinned. 'That too, of course.' He turned to Poppy. 'And Poppy too. 'Tis grand to see you again.' He gave her cheek a chaste kiss.

'How have things been while I was away?' he asked Catriona.

'Busy,' she told him. 'I think my idea of the summer event is working.'

'Och, that reminds me,' Rory said. 'I've booked the last two sessions of that medium's private consultations.'

'Keep that under your hat,' Catriona told him. 'Reverend Greene was quite vociferous on the subject a short while ago.'

Rory's laugh rang out through the hall, and in her mind's eye Poppy saw him on his and Catriona's wedding day. What a fine match the pair made, and how fortunate that he had returned from the war unscathed.

'I should leave you both,' Poppy said, 'as I'm sure you have a lot to talk about.'

'Do find time to join us for dinner in our private apartment one night, Poppy,' Catriona said. 'Perhaps tomorrow?'

'Perfect.' Poppy smiled and crossed to mount the staircase to her room.

It was time to discuss with her maid what was fast becoming the Plockton-Portree case.

Poppy rapped smartly on Elspeth's door.

'Elspeth,' she said, when her maid answered, 'please come to my room. I need to think through the suspects in Ellen's murder, and you are the very person to help me.'

Elspeth sighed. 'Very well, my lady.'

Major pushed his way out of Elspeth's room and she closed her door behind them.

'Make yourselves comfortable,' Poppy said to Elspeth and Major when they entered her bedroom. Elspeth perched on the edge of an armchair; Major threw himself onto his blanket and lay on his back, his upside-down face stretched in a gleeful smile. Poppy sat at the little writing table with her notebook and pencil.

She half turned to address Elspeth. 'Right, Elspeth, who do we have as suspects so far?'

'I have no suspects, your ladyship. Perhaps you are using *we* in the royal sense?'

'Think that if you wish.' Poppy turned back to her notebook, opened it to a new page and wrote:

Day Five of Investigation into the Murder of Ellen Clark.

Underneath, she wrote:

Suspects.

'I have identified four suspects.' Poppy jotted down the information as she spoke. 'One is Alan Henderson. His week away on business will be up on Monday. If he reappears in

Plockton in two days' time, Constable Macduff will interview him and inform Inspector MacKenzie.'

'Will one of the policemen also inform you, my lady?' Elspeth managed to make her question sound both innocent and knowing.

'Perhaps. I don't know.' Probably not. 'If Mr Henderson doesn't return, then that is a sure sign of guilt.'

'Unless he has met with an accident, or has died, or simply changed his mind about wanting to see Mrs Clark again.'

Poppy swivelled round in her seat. Was Elspeth being facetious? 'There are those possibilities, of course,' she said sharply. 'Well, moving on.' She returned to her writing. 'Two is Isabella Buccleuch.'

Elspeth's thin brows puckered. 'Why is Miss Buccleuch a suspect, my lady?'

'Because,' Poppy explained, 'she wanted the button that decorated the clasp on Ellen Clark's clutch.' In theory, anyway.

'Would she *kill* for a button?' asked Elspeth, astonished.

'People have murdered for less,' Poppy told her with authority in her voice. Was that true, though? She tried to think of any cases in her Criminal Law lectures where such a thing had happened and drew a blank. If she had more time, a case would have come to mind, she was sure. She was even more sure that not one case would involve a button. No matter how rare.

Might kill for a button she desires, Poppy wrote against Isabella's entry. 'Although perhaps Isabella should be number three on the list,' she added, her pencil hovering over the number two. 'The yogi is still looking pretty suspicious to my mind.'

'The yogi! My lady, aren't you clutching at straws?'

'That's what we detectives have to do, Elspeth.'

'Clutch at straws?'

'No,' Poppy said a little crossly. 'I mean consider every

avenue, no matter how implausible it may seem. It is what's known as,' she added, remembering the inspector's expression, 'keeping an open mind.'

She decided to leave Isabella at number two, but only because to cross it out would spoil the look of her notebook. And besides, there was something about Isabella's caustic manner in the tea shop that could be described as suspicious.

'Number three,' Poppy went on firmly, and said as she wrote: '*The yogi. In Plockton at the right time and lives from hand to mouth.*'

'I thought he was no longer a suspect and is now on Iona, my lady.'

'And if another woman is found strangled on that island, it would point the finger at him. If the strangler goes for well-off women, there must be some wealthy folk at the house where he is staying.'

'Assuming he is actually on Iona,' Elspeth pointed out.

'Inspector MacKenzie saw the telegram from his new hostess with the travel arrangements.'

'I dinna doubt that, my lady, but it doesna mean he went there.'

Elspeth was surprisingly good at this, Poppy thought rather crossly. Turning back to look at her maid, she raised a questioning eyebrow.

Elspeth replied by raising one of her own. Then she remembered her place, as the brow went down and she asked, 'Has the police inspector checked that the yogi hasn't done a runner, my lady?'

Poppy started. Elspeth wouldn't have got that expression from one of Miss Taft's romances. It must be something she'd picked up from the crime novels she said she read occasionally.

'I'm sure he has,' Poppy said doubtfully, and saw a little smirk on Elspeth's face.

Poppy took a breath and returned to her page.

'Four,' she said, writing it. 'Bertram.'

'The common fellow travelling in ladies' accessories?'

Poppy didn't need to turn in her seat again to know that Elspeth was looking down her pointed nose.

'I could believe almost anything of such a man, but... murder?' Elspeth said.

Poppy realised she hadn't yet told Elspeth about what Reverend Greene had said. 'The minister at tea this afternoon was incensed at seeing a man who fitted Bertram's description disappear around the back of the hotel with a woman who fits Jeanie Harper's description.'

Elspeth's hand flew to her thin cheek. 'Glory be! Nothing should surprise me about that woman, but this is not the behaviour of a respectable woman.' She dropped her hand. 'But I cannot see what a dalliance between the two of them has to do with Mrs Clark's murder.'

'I agree, Elspeth. It does seem remote. But my thinking is this: he denies visiting Plockton, but is a fast worker on women's affections.' Poppy added her words to her list as she spoke.

'I see,' Elspeth said, dryly. 'Considering every avenue. Doing the inspector's job for him, while he's off striding through the land in the sunshine.'

Poppy chose to ignore that comment. No one liked an opinionated maid. 'They are our four suspects, as far as I can tell. Now, what about motive? Inspector MacKenzie told me the obvious motives for murder are money or personal feeling.'

Motive, she wrote at the top of the next page, and continued to write as she spoke. 'One. Alan Henderson could have wanted Ellen's pendant and the contents of her bag because he needed money for whatever reason. The pendant could have caused him to think she had money, so he asked her to help him out with a loan and she refused.'

'That's possible,' Elspeth agreed. 'She had none to give. And Isabella Buccleuch?'

Poppy nodded. 'Two, Isabella Buccleuch could have wanted the button on the clasp of the bag. Ellen refused to give it to her, and after Isabella had killed Ellen she took the pendant to hide the real reason for the theft.'

'That sounds like a reasonable assumption, my lady.'

'Three, the yogi,' Poppy went on, still writing, 'could have wanted money so that he could continue his tour around the Highlands and Islands. And Bertram...'

Elspeth pursed her lips.

'Four, Bertram,' Poppy said, jotting it down. 'Needs money to fund his lifestyle. He seems to live beyond the means of a travelling salesman.' Even if he hadn't been to America, the Isle of the Mist was the most expensive hotel in Portree.

'And in all these situations,' Elspeth suggested, 'Mrs Clark would not have meekly handed over her jewellery and bag. Not with her in such financial straits and the pendant being valuable. I think she would have fought her attacker, or at least called out. That must have made the attacker panic, and use Mrs Clark's own scarf to stop her and in the process strangle her.'

'Exactly, Elspeth!' Poppy said admiringly. 'You are really rather good at this, you know.'

'I don't know what your ladyship means, I'm sure.'

Poppy could almost see Ellen fighting off the assailant, but she couldn't quite make out the person's features in the dark of the kirk. It was so frustrating!

'All your suspects would have to sell the jewellery,' Elspeth pointed out, 'preferably with no questions asked.'

'Except Isabella Buccleuch, if she took it to hide the real reason for the crime. Although she might have wanted the money to buy a rare button. But anyway, assuming the suspects don't know the right people, they will be found out by the inspector. Now we should consider opportunity.'

Poppy wrote the next heading: *Opportunity.*

'Alan Henderson had been with Ellen the day before her murder,' she continued, 'and something he had said or done caused her to want to spend some time alone, which is why she went to the open-air kirk.'

'But you said it yourself, your ladyship: *the day before.* There was nothing to suggest he'd remained for another day.'

Poppy had to agree. 'The hotel where he'd stayed, the Plockton Inn, confirmed he had checked out the morning of Ellen's murder.'

'Should he still be on the suspect list?'

'Yes. Ellen knew him, and she wouldn't have been surprised – at least, not very surprised – if he'd appeared at the wee church. And he might have guessed she would be there.' Poppy wrote:

1. Alan Henderson left Plockton before Ellen's murder – but they knew each other well.

'Mrs Clark would have known Isabella Buccleuch too, but not as well,' Elspeth added thoughtfully.

'That's right. So Ellen would have wondered why the other woman was there, but she would have waited to see what she wanted. Isabella had no alibi and that means we must credit her with opportunity. And the two women were overheard arguing by the yogi.'

'Two,' Poppy said as she scribbled, 'Isabella denied being at the kirk that evening – but admitted she had been for a walk around the village.'

Poppy frowned as she continued with her list. 'The yogi is more problematic. It seems he'd stayed at the Harbour Hotel and held a yoga class, but Ellen hadn't been to it. And he'd left the hotel in the afternoon before Ellen was killed that evening. Except that he'd not taken the afternoon ferry to Skye, but the evening one, claiming he'd been lost in meditation.'

'But as Mrs Clark didn't know the yogi, it's unlikely she would have remained in the open-air kirk as he approached her,' Elspeth added.

'The same argument must go for Bertram,' Poppy said with a small sigh, 'even if he had been to Plockton, which he denies. The few bruises on Ellen's fingertips suggested she'd not attempted to fight off her attacker, but had tried only to stop the scarf from tightening around her neck.'

Poppy added to her notes:

3. The yogi was in Plockton at the time of the murder – but claims he was meditating.

Under that, she wrote:

4. Bertram?

He was on her suspect list simply because he'd been seen with wealthy widow Jeanie in Portree, which was hardly evidence of any illegal behaviour.

'Of course there could be other suspects we know nothing about,' Poppy mused.

'The Lord preserve us from suspecting every person in Plockton and Portree,' Elspeth muttered.

'Tell me, Elspeth, just thinking for a moment of character alone, which of the four on the list would you pick as the murderer?'

'I couldn't possibly say, my lady.'

'Do you think you could try?'

Elspeth smoothed the skirt of her navy-blue lady's maid costume. 'I've never met Mr Henderson or the yogi, and have only been aware of the salesman in passing, so I really cannot comment.'

Elspeth was correct and she shouldn't have asked her,

Poppy realised. She herself had also never met Alan Henderson, so she could have no opinion of his character either. Both the yogi and Bertram seemed unlikely murderers, the first because he espoused peace and the second because of his cheerful demeanour.

The most likely candidate for the role of murderer seemed to be the button-minded, short-tempered, alibi-less Isabella Buccleuch. Not exactly the most convincing list of suspects.

As Poppy closed her notebook, she decided she needed to speak to Inspector MacKenzie. He might at the very least be able to help her narrow down her list of suspects.

TWENTY-SIX

Later that afternoon, Poppy gave Major an early dinner, then took him for a walk. She clipped on his leash, descended the stairs and asked the young man working at the desk where he would recommend.

'The Lump, my lady.'

She frowned down at Major. 'The Lump? Are you referring to my Labrador?'

The young man smiled. 'No, my lady. It doesna sound verra bonnie, but it's a place where your dog can have a grand runabout and you can admire the views of Loch Portree. The Isle of Skye Games are held there every year. Will your ladyship be attending them next week?'

'I intend to.' Although perhaps that depended on whatever happened with the investigation, she thought.

'Public hangings used to take place there,' the young man went on conversationally. 'All you'll see today though are the ruins of an old lookout tower.'

'The tower sounds a lot more pleasant than a hanging. How do I get to The Lump?' she asked.

'It's the grassy hill behind Quay Street,' he told her and gave her directions.

Poppy thanked him, and she and Major set off. A five-minute walk brought them to the wide, tree-lined track the young man had described, and she turned into it. Rabbits bobbing about on the grass verges stopped and sniffed the air as she let Major off the leash. Immediately he scampered after them.

'Major!' she called.

He gave a start of affected surprise. *Did I hear someone call my name?* his face said, his ears pricked.

'Don't chase the rabbits,' she told him sternly.

He shot her a careworn expression, before turning back, only to find they'd all gone to earth.

Poppy strode up the track, Major trotting beside her. At the top of the hill, the rough path opened out into an amphitheatre rising above Loch Portree. With spectacular views of the loch on both sides, Poppy could see it was a splendid site for the annual Games. She strolled on the grass around the amphitheatre while Major ran and sniffed in equal measures.

It was quiet today, but she imagined it as it would be for the Gathering. The stalls and tents set up in the field, the bustle of the excited men, women and children. The platform for the dancers, performing the Highland Fling and the Sword Dance, the Reels and the Hornpipe, their arms raised, kilts swirling to the music.

The heavy events must take place in the amphitheatre itself, she thought, and she could almost hear the silence of the crowd as a competitor crouched to balance upright the mighty caber, twenty feet long, the man's muscles bunching in his singlet, the sweat on his face as he stood to lift the one hundred and fifty-pound pole in his cupped hands, walk a few paces forward and throw it, the caber turning end over end and landing as it should, pointing away, to the roar of the crowd.

At night, after the Gathering, as the sun was setting and above the hills the sky aflame, would be the dance. The sound of the fiddle and accordion through the open door of the hall growing louder as she and the inspector approached, the flickering lights inside welcoming everyone, Inspector MacKenzie, his dark curls dishevelled and looking down at her with smiling eyes.

She decided she would stay for the Isle of Skye Highland Games.

Back at the hotel, she gave Elspeth the evening off and took a leisurely bath in lavender-scented water. When she emerged from the steamy bathroom, she found Elspeth had laid out her blue-grey velvet with white collar and a white bow at the neck. Whatever had her maid been thinking of to have packed such a garment?

'That is not at all what I want to wear on a Saturday night to dine with the inspector,' she told Major. 'I need something much more... *delightful.*'

The dog raised an eyebrow.

'There is no need to look at me like that. I mean only that it will be more pleasant for him to look at an attractive dress, instead of that abomination,' she explained.

Major gave her a *you don't fool me* look.

She ignored his insolence and pulled from the wardrobe a sleeveless dress in black and white. With it she would wear her long white gloves, rope of pearls and dangling diamond earrings. There was something about the contrast between the soft, rounded pearls and the sharp, brilliant diamonds that created a particularly appealing combination.

As she dressed she hummed an approximation of a tune she'd heard on the gramophone at some party or other in Edinburgh. Then a light dusting of powder on her face, a careful application of pink to her lips, the white beaded cloche in position on her glossy bob, and with her mink fur stole loosely around her shoulders, she trod lightly down the staircase.

Outside the hotel, Poppy crossed Somerled Square, turned along Wentworth Street and soon came to the Portree Inn. Pushing open the door, she entered and followed the delicious smells of roast meats to its small restaurant.

The dining room proved to be less stylish than that of the Isle of the Mist Hotel, but it looked clean and comfortable, and it was certainly busy. The maître d' at the lectern bid her good evening.

Raising his voice a little over the general hubbub of people chatting and laughing, he asked, 'Do you have a booking, madam? It is Saturday evening, and I'm afraid we have no tables available.'

Poppy scanned the room. If Inspector MacKenzie wasn't here, she was going to look dashed silly.

There he was! His coal-black curls and broad shoulders were easily spotted among the other diners. And, wonderfully, he was alone. No sign of his cousin or any other companion.

'I'm dining with the gentleman seated by the potted plant,' she told the maître d'.

'Of course, madam. Would you like me to take your stole?'

He signalled to a waiter as Poppy slid off her fur.

'If you would follow me, madam,' said the waiter.

He led her across the room, weaving between tables. When she reached him, Inspector MacKenzie looked up in surprise.

'My lady.' He rose hastily, a flush mantling his cheeks as his eye flickered over her dress. She knew it had been the right thing to wear.

'Thank you,' Poppy said to the waiter as he pulled out the chair for her. 'I will have whatever the gentleman is having.'

The waiter bowed, departed and Poppy smiled at Inspector MacKenzie across the table. 'It looks very jolly in here.'

The inspector took his seat again. 'This is an unexpected pleasure,' he said politely.

'I'm so glad.' Her smile widened. 'You are wondering what I am doing here.'

'It's as if you can see into my mind.' He raised an eyebrow. 'How do you ken such a thing?'

'I am a detective,' she said. 'Few mysteries are impenetrable to the trained mind.'

The inspector's lips curved into a smile.

'That's better,' Poppy said. 'You look quite nice when you smile.' He looked dashed more than *that* when he smiled.

The wine waiter appeared and poured them both a glass of ruby red claret.

'What shall we drink to?' the inspector asked her as he picked up his glass.

'Finding villains,' she replied without hesitation.

He lifted his glass and they chinked them. 'Finding villains,' he repeated. 'And on that subject, I presume that is why you are here?'

'It is, but pleasure before business, as you said not so long ago.' She looked around for the waiter. 'I wonder what we are to eat?'

On cue, the waiter returned with plates of mutton cutlets.

'I find I am very hungry,' Poppy said, picking up her knife and fork. 'It must be all this detective work.'

'What have you been up to now, my lady?' the inspector asked warily, taking up his own cutlery.

Poppy chewed and swallowed a mouthful of the mutton. 'Are you going to the Games next week?'

'Now that is what you legal people call a non sequitur, if ever I've heard one!'

Poppy blushed. It was true; her statement bore no connection to what he had said. 'It's the way the legal brain works,' she said airily. 'Able to hold and consider many thoughts at the same time.'

'That will be an asset, I'm thinking.'

'You haven't answered my question, Inspector.'

'Aye, I will be at the Games.' He nodded.

'I *love* the Games!' she said. 'I hope I will see you there.' She took a mouthful of the claret to stop herself babbling on like a schoolgirl.

'Och, you will, my lady. I've been invited to play a solo on the bagpipes.'

The wine threatened to go up her nose. She swallowed quickly. 'You have? But that's wonderful! And quite an honour.'

She pictured the lone piper, standing on a high rocky crag, piping across the vast highlands, through valleys and over mountains, spurring soldiers to action or lamenting the loss of fallen comrades. A symbol of Scotland's cultural resilience, its history, and the deep connection between the Scottish people and their land.

Not that Inspector MacKenzie would be calling people to arms at the Games, of course, but the thought of him standing there, a lone, brave, honourable man – which he was – stirred her blood. A shiver ran down her spine.

'Why would you be staring at me like that, your ladyship?' he said with a smile. 'Wasn't I after telling you I play the pipes?'

'Yes, but...' His black locks were tousled, as if he were standing on a mountain top, the wind in his hair...

He raised an eyebrow as he sipped his wine. 'But what?'

'Oh, I don't know.' She did know. 'I *love* the bagpipes!'

He laughed. 'There's no' many will say that.'

'Tell me more about the Games.'

'You must surely be knowing yourself, my lady?' He cut another portion of mutton.

'I know that in the eleventh century, Malcolm III called what became the first Highland Games. He'd summoned men to race up *Creag Chòinnich*, overlooking Braemar, to find the fastest runner in Scotland to be his royal messenger.'

Inspector MacKenzie nodded. 'Years later, clan chiefs were holding competitions to test their strongest warriors.'

'And later again,' Poppy went on with a smile at him, 'musicians and dancers were encouraged to display their talents, to be a credit to their clan. What will you play at the Skye Gathering?'

'I thought I'd do a 2/4 march, "Highland Laddie",' he told her.

'A very lively tune.' She smiled. 'There will be a dance in the evening?'

'I'm thinking there will be.' He returned her smile, as the waiter topped up their wine glasses.

This was all going swimmingly well, Poppy thought, as he spoke about the events of the Gathering. She relaxed into her second glass of wine and felt how easy it was to talk to the man seated across the table from her.

'When does your cousin and his friend arrive?' she asked, as he took a sip of wine.

'I dinna ken about my cousin's friend, only that he is travelling from America and is to meet us here,' he told her. 'Ewan was supposed to arrive this evening, but he was delayed by some business at home and so he missed the ferry.'

'And the next one isn't until Monday.'

The inspector nodded.

'I'm sorry for Ewan and chum, but pleased that I was able to prevent you from the ignominy of dining alone.'

'I don't find it embarrassing to eat dinner alone, my lady.'

'You are quite a self-contained man, aren't you, Inspector?'

He looked amused at her assessment. 'I would describe myself as... sober and steady.'

'And intelligent,' she went on.

He raised an eyebrow. 'I hope so. It's a requisite of detecting, that and having principles.'

Their empty plates were removed, and shortly after, the waiter arrived with their main course.

'This smells delicious,' Poppy said, inhaling the aroma of rabbit stew with brandy, prunes and herbs.

'It does.' The inspector drank some of his claret. 'Shall we move on to business now?' he asked. 'It was your reason for coming here this evening?'

'Oh yes,' she lied. Well, it was *partly* the reason. 'Elspeth and I have been examining the evidence—'

'You have reviewed the case with your maid?' His knife and fork were poised over his dinner.

'Why not?' Poppy retorted. 'You haven't been frightfully keen to do so and I must discuss it with someone, or go mad!'

'Hardly that, I think, my lady. Why not discuss it with Major? At least he isn't likely to accidentally reveal any information that could send our culprit fleeing.'

'Well, yes, all right. Major *is* the soul of discretion. But deprived of your expert input, I have discussed the case with Elspeth. I can trust her to say nothing. This case is very much on my mind, and I wanted to consider some aspects.' That sounded less dramatic.

He seemed to think so too, for the inspector said, 'Go on.' He resumed eating the aromatic rabbit stew.

'This morning I bumped into Isabella Buccleuch at the button exhibition—'

'Bumped into?' He smiled. 'You just happened to be visiting the button exhibition?'

'Absolutely, Inspector!' Poppy said airily. 'And I took the opportunity to quiz Isabella about her pre-dinner walk on the evening Ellen was killed. She admitted it took her from one end of the village to the other, but she avoided answering my question as to whether she had seen Ellen or if she had gone into the open-air kirk.'

'And what do you think?'

'I think that she's awfully short-tempered, so I wouldn't put it past her to be violent if needs must.' Poppy ate some more of the stew.

'But no hard evidence?'

'Not yet.'

The inspector nodded. 'Anything else you have discovered, my lady?'

'There is a new guest at Isle of the Mist Hotel,' she said tentatively. 'He's a travelling salesman. Bertram Something or Other. I haven't learned his surname yet.'

'And what about this Bertram Something or Other?' The inspector forked up a piece of meat.

'The Reverend Greene told me—'

'You've no' been questioning the minister?' he exclaimed.

'Certainly not,' she bristled. 'Catriona and I were invited to tea with him, and while we were chatting he said he'd seen Bertram disappear behind the Isle of the Mist Hotel with Jeanie Harper.'

'And?' Inspector MacKenzie picked up his wine glass and took a sip.

'And nothing.'

The inspector looked at Poppy. 'Is that it?'

'That's it.'

'The last I kent, that wasna a crime.'

'No, I know. It's just that I thought, with the other victims of the trickster...'

'Don't tell me. You are referring to your pattern?'

'Yes,' she said firmly.

'You are worried that the travelling salesman could be our conman, and is going to try the same thing with Mrs Harper?'

'Yes,' Poppy repeated. 'Although, I must say, that she's quite a hard sort of woman, and I don't think Bertram will find her an easy target.'

'Then perhaps you have nothing to worry about there. But your concern does you credit.'

Poppy beamed, pleased the inspector had noticed her caring nature.

'What conclusion did you and your maid come to about the suspects?' Inspector MacKenzie asked.

'First, Inspector, may I ask you a couple of questions?'

'I'm at your service.'

Her heart fluttered a little at that statement, but she recovered quickly and got down to business. 'First, has Dorothy Brown's alibi – the old lady in Plockton with the button for sale – been checked?'

'Constable Macduff spoke to Mrs Stewart and she confirms Miss Brown kept their appointment and bought the button.'

'Second, is the yogi actually on Iona?'

'I got one of my men to check that, and he is there.'

'Third—'

'You said two questions, my lady,' Inspector MacKenzie pointed out, amused.

Poppy ignored that comment. 'Third, have you identified any suspects other than Alan Henderson, Isabella Buccleuch, the yogi and Bertram? If the latter *can* be considered a suspect,' she added hurriedly.

The inspector shook his head.

'To answer your question, then, I think that the most likely of these to have killed Ellen Clark is Isabella Buccleuch. She had motive – the button; means – she's strong and has a bad temper; and opportunity – her evening walk.'

'You present a plausible case, but I can't be persuaded that Mrs Clark was killed for a button.'

Poppy sighed. 'I know.'

So who on earth was responsible for the murder of Ellen Clark?

TWENTY-SEVEN

On Sunday morning, Poppy and Elspeth crossed the square to the kirk and slipped into seats near the back.

Inspector MacKenzie was already seated in the pew in front of them. Poppy scanned the kirk to see who else was there. She spotted Harriet, Jeanie and Algernon sitting at the front of the church, but there was no sign of Bertram, or of Isabella or Dorothy.

Reverend Greene's Rambling Rector roses with their sweet, musky fragrance, decorated the sanctuary. Their large heads of small creamy-white flowers with pretty yellow stamens looked beautiful amongst the green foliage.

Her gaze moved on to consider the nape of the inspector's neck. There was something so... manly about it, she thought idly, like his Adam's apple. How strange that such things could be fascinating. His hair, too, she thought, wondering how it would feel if she could just put out a hand and run her fingers through his thick, dark curls...

The primary school choir began singing the introit, reminding Poppy they were in church, the minister was arriving and that such thoughts as the inspector's physical attributes had no place during the service. The congregation sang "I to the Hills Will Lift Mine Eyes", Poppy singing quietly so that she could enjoy Inspector MacKenzie's thrilling, rich baritone. A prayer followed, then a reading.

Poppy sat forward with interest as the minister stepped up to the pulpit. He cleared his throat, leaned over the top and glared down his thin, sharp nose at the upturned faces below. 'It is my sad duty to have to comment on the lack of morals by some in this wee town of ours,' he began.

There was an uncomfortable shuffling of feet, and Poppy was reminded of hearing something that the popular magazine *Tit-Bits* had reported. Sir Arthur Conan Doyle, convinced that a skeleton lurked in every household, no matter how respectable, had once sent a telegram to an archdeacon, reading, 'All is discovered! Fly at once!' And the man had done exactly that, never to be heard of again.

True to his word of yesterday, the Reverend Greene went on in the same vein as he'd started, his dark eyes under their thin dark brows roving suspiciously over the congregation. They settled on Jeanie for some minutes as he spoke, but whether she looked uncomfortable or not, Poppy couldn't tell. All she could see of Jeanie was the purple beret perched on the back of her head.

After some fifteen minutes, the minister wound down his sermon and descended the pulpit. Another prayer, and they moved on to sing the hymn "Ye Servants of God". Oh, good, Poppy thought, one of my favourites.

She sang with gusto:

> *'All honour and blessing, with angels ABO-O-*
> > *O-OVE,*
> *And thanks never-ceasing, and infinite love.'*

The four verses came to an end and Poppy stopped singing.

'Praise the Lord,' she heard Elspeth murmur next to her.

The minister pronounced a blessing, and made his way to the door of the church. The congregation rose chattering from the pews, the men taking up their hats and the ladies their handbags.

Elspeth was commenting on the service to the woman sitting the other side of her, when Inspector MacKenzie turned around from his pew. 'My lady,' he said. 'It was you who charmed us with such a spirited rendition of "Ye Servants of God".'

'It was.' Poppy beamed. 'I do like a rousing hymn, don't you?'

'I certainly feel much better for having heard you sing it.' He smiled.

Before she could reply, Poppy found herself being carried along with the rest of the congregation, pausing to shake Reverend Greene's hand at the door and thank him for the service, then out of the church and into the square. Elspeth appeared soon after, but Poppy couldn't see the inspector. Perhaps he had been invited to tea in the vestry. She was sure the inspector would be keen to speak to Reverend Greene, to rule Bertram in or out of the investigation.

'An uplifting service, my lady,' Elspeth said. 'The minister was quite right to address us on the topic of declining morals. I was heartened, though, to see so many in the congregation – but not, I observed, the travelling salesman or either of those two button women.'

'I noticed that too,' Poppy said. 'They might be of a different faith, of course.'

'The Roman one, you mean?' Elspeth gave a small shudder. 'Nothing would surprise me about followers of that religion with its idolatry.'

'That's not actually true, Elspeth,' Poppy admonished. 'The

Roman Catholic Church doesn't believe that idols have any power in themselves.'

'And the Episcopalians are almost as bad,' Elspeth went on, as if Poppy hadn't spoken.

'We must be tolerant of all faiths,' Poppy told her.

'I am an extremely tolerant person. Although I wouldn't be surprised if' – Elspeth dropped her voice to a whisper – 'the two suspects we've just mentioned were of *no faith* at all.'

Poppy declined to comment. Her thoughts were already on the afternoon ahead and the consultation she and Catriona had booked with the visiting medium, Mistress Moodie.

Perhaps the spiritualist would be able to shine a light on the case at last?

TWENTY-EIGHT

'You know, Catriona,' Poppy said as she and her friend walked along the empty Sabbath streets to the Portree Inn that afternoon, 'how useful it would be if the medium could communicate with the spirit of Ellen Clark, as Ellen could then tell me who killed her.'

'I'm surprised the police don't make use of mediums.'

'I imagine that's because people can't really have a conversation with the dead.'

They had almost reached the inn when Poppy spotted Bertram coming out of the premises. Hastily she drew Catriona into the doorway of a closed shop.

'It's Bertram,' she whispered, and Catriona followed her lead in turning to face the goods displayed for sale. It was a pity it was a pharmacist, Poppy thought, with rows of bottles containing coloured liquids, and blue and white jars labelled with such alarming-sounding contents as *MIEL DE BORAX, UNG. SULPHATE* and *EMP. CANTHAR.*

'What are we doing?' Catriona whispered.

'Hiding,' Poppy hissed.

'Why? Would it really matter if he saw us about to enter the Portree Inn?'

'Yes.'

'Just because he's *persona non grata* in the eyes of Reverend Greene...'

'I wonder what he's been doing at the hotel.'

'I can answer that for you,' Catriona said, keeping her voice low. 'The same as we are about to do. Rory told me who'd booked the last session with Mistress Moodie: Bertram Knox.'

'That is interesting.'

'Is it really? I have to say, Poppy, you're being very mysterious. Is this how you always behave when you're investigating a case – skulking in shop doorways?'

'Just so,' Poppy found herself murmuring.

They heard the sound of a man's footsteps pass the shop.

'I must say, it's quite thrilling,' Catriona breathed. 'I don't wonder that you like to help the inspector. What an exciting man he must be.' She gave Poppy a keen glance.

Poppy laughed as she linked her arm through Catriona's, and they turned towards the inn.

Catriona nodded good afternoon to the young man at the reception desk of the Portree Inn as they crossed the hall and sailed up the staircase.

'Mistress Moodie is in Room Twenty-Two,' Catriona told Poppy. 'The ticket says we're to go straight there.'

On the second floor, they followed the brass numbers on the doors until they came to Room Twenty-Two. With a quick, mischievous glance at Poppy, Catriona knocked on the door.

The elderly woman who opened it looked nothing like the stylish young lady on the poster. This woman wore a drab brown dress draped across with brightly-coloured tulle scarves, and had a large mole on her chin.

'Mistress Moodie?' Poppy asked, wondering if the woman was simply the doorkeeper.

But no, she wasn't. She nodded, stepping back and gesturing for them to enter. When the door was closed, she spoke in a tired, reedy voice.

'We need to be quiet,' she told them as she took their tickets. 'No business to be transacted on the Sabbath.' She led them over to a small round table covered with some heavy green fabric in the centre of the room. 'If anyone asks, you must say you're my guests, here to thank me for the event yesterday.'

'No crystal ball?' Poppy asked, seeing the table empty.

'That is a theatrical prop,' the elderly woman snapped. 'As a true medium, I rely only on my sensitivity to connect with spirits.'

'Sorry,' Catriona said in a soothing voice. 'This is our first time, you understand.'

Mistress Moodie's eyes narrowed as she assessed them, then she nodded again and indicated they should each take a seat at the table.

'I hope you are not expecting materialisation of a spirit,' she warned as she took her own seat. 'I do not deal in ectoplasm.'

Poppy was hugely relieved. She didn't believe in spiritualism, but the last thing she wanted was to see any viscous substance exude from the medium's body.

The woman placed her hands palm down on the table, and they all sat in silence for a while.

Mistress Moodie spoke. 'I am tuning in to the other world by listening for or sensing spirits,' she said softly.

They remained seated in silence.

Suddenly Mistress Moodie's eyes rolled back in her head alarmingly. 'Someone is coming through,' she murmured, closing her eyes. 'It is... it is a gentleman, well-spoken. One moment...' She appeared to be listening to something or someone. 'He is clearing his throat, preparing to speak.'

Poppy's mouth suddenly went dry. Her father *did* have the habit of clearing his throat before he spoke. Was he dead? She sent an alarmed glance at Catriona, who frowned and shook her head.

Poppy swallowed hard but said nothing.

'I have a message from your papa,' went on Mistress Moodie. 'He wants to tell you to trust the stranger and you will have secured for yourself a bright and prosperous future.'

Poppy's eyes grew wide. What on earth did the woman mean?

'Do you wish to say anything to your father on the other side, Harriet?'

Harriet! That explained it. The spiritualist thought she was Harriet. What a *fraud!* Well, Poppy thought, she would put on a little show of her own and get out of there.

Poppy and Catriona exchanged a glance.

'Does Papa remember,' Poppy asked the medium, 'where he put Mama's diamond earrings, for I cannot find them anywhere and would dearly wish to have them. They were so important to her and therefore also to me.'

Her eyes still closed, Mistress Moodie paused as if listening, and sighed. 'He says he regrets that he does not remember.'

'But he is happy?'

'He is content.'

'Does that mean he is happy?' Poppy grabbed at the woman's hands and dissolved into pretend tears. 'Do *you* think that means he is happy?'

Mistress Moodie opened her eyes, as Poppy dashed from the room, leaving the door open to the hallway.

'I must go after my friend,' Catriona said, hastening towards the door.

'But there may be someone else in the spirit world who wishes to contact you, Jeanie!' the elderly woman called.

Catriona slammed the door shut behind her. She turned to Poppy. 'She's a fraud.'

'Quick, let's go.'

They sped down the stairs and only when they were out of the hotel did they slow their pace.

'She obviously mistook you for Harriet,' Catriona said, a little breathless with excitement, 'and me for Jeanie – but how did that happen?'

'She had been expecting two women who wanted to have joint consultations. Harriet and Jeanie must be after ours, and when we entered the room together she made the wrong connection.'

'How sick she will feel when Harriet and Jeanie turn up and she discovers her mistake.'

'Not as sick as I felt for a moment,' Poppy said, 'when I thought my father had died in Australia.'

'Yes, how ghastly for you, Poppy.'

The wretched Mistress Moodie telling her the 'spirit' was clearing his throat before he spoke had caused the confusion. When had Harriet talked of her father having that same habit? During the game of planchette. Jeanie had been present that evening of course, but Harriet might have mentioned the throat clearing to Algernon, or Jeanie to Bertram.

'Never mind that now, Catriona. We know that someone is trying to trick Harriet out of her money. At this moment, it's Bertram Knox I want to consider.'

'Because he had the appointment before us? Do you think he bribed the medium to help him defraud Harriet?'

'I mean to find out.'

'Do you think he was set to use the same method to defraud Jeanie as well?'

'Dash it all. I forgot about that.'

'Probably because you don't like the woman.'

'You may be right. But for now we will follow the evidence

for Harriet. I have a feeling Jeanie Harper is more than capable of looking after herself.'

As they strode towards the square, Catriona said, 'I can't think why Bertram Knox would have primed the so-called medium to recommend Harriet invests her money – unless the two men were in the confidence swindle together.'

Poppy came to an abrupt halt. 'Catriona, you could well be right!'

Somehow she must discover if Bertram and Algernon were in league with one another.

Poppy pondered the spiritualist question over dinner with Catriona and Rory in their private apartment above the hotel that night.

'I think there are some people who possess second sight,' said Rory, helping himself to a large portion of vegetables from the dish on the table. 'Take the Brahan Seer, for example. *Coinneach Odhar* – Grey Kenneth – was born in the early seventeenth century on the Isle of Lewis, and he foresaw all sorts of things. A black metal horse belching fire and steam through the glens; that's the railways, of course. And the Battle of Culloden, the Highland Clearances, the building of the Caledonian Canal—'

'I can't explain those prophesies,' Poppy admitted, 'but I do think second sight is different to communicating with spirits. And after this afternoon's escapade, I know that Mistress Moodie is simply out to make money from gullible people. What kind of true medium would mix up the relationship between her earthly client and the spirit coming through for a chat?'

'I agree with what you say, Poppy,' put in Catriona. 'The woman was a complete fraud.'

'This investigation is becoming rather complicated,' Poppy

said. She separated a green bean from the others on her plate. 'First there was the murder of Ellen Clark on Plockton—'

'Aye, I heard about that,' Rory said, tucking into the Chicken Lyonnaise. 'You and Major found the body, Catriona tells me. Clever boy,' he added, addressing Major on the hearth rug.

At the mention of his name, the Labrador, who had been lying with his head on his paws, looked up with an unconvincing bashfulness.

Poppy laughed. 'I must say that I am pleased with how his training is progressing.' She cut into her chicken. 'I've identified at least four suspects—'

'*You* have, Poppy?' Catriona asked. 'Not that nice Inspector MacKenzie?'

'He seems to be agreeing with me, on this at least.'

'Who are these people?' Rory enquired, lifting his glass of Chablis. 'Or aren't you allowed to say?'

She thought back to Inspector MacKenzie's reaction to her discussing her findings with Elspeth and paused for a moment, then looked from Rory to Catriona and back again. 'I'm telling you this in confidence, you understand,' she warned.

Rory and Catriona both nodded.

'Ellen Clark had a blue sapphire pendant which disappeared at the time of her murder. She also had a man friend who is not at present to be found, so he has to be one suspect. The other three suspects are Isabella Buccleuch, the yogi and Bertram Knox, all of whom may have been interested in the valuable pendant. But, Catriona, you said something about how a confidence trickster could have persuaded Mistress Moodie to give out false information that would encourage Harriet to entrust her money to another to be invested, and that brings—'

'Algernon Hamilton to mind.' Catriona beamed.

'Exactly.' Poppy smiled. It was good to see her dear friend enjoying herself in this way, but she must keep her distance from her over the next few days. Her mind flashed back to the young woman who was stabbed in Princes Street just because she was wearing one of Poppy's coats. A case of mistaken identity according to Inspector MacKenzie, and she had no reason to doubt his assumption.

'Mr Hamilton, Miss Buccleuch and Mr Knox are all guests at the hotel, dear,' Catriona told her husband. 'And so was the yogi.'

Rory lowered his wine glass. 'Good grief! Do you mean to tell me we are harbouring criminals?'

'Possible criminals,' corrected Poppy. 'A list of suspects is only a list, after all. Innocent until proven guilty.'

'If this gets out—'

'Don't they say there's no such thing as bad publicity, dear?' Catriona said in a soothing voice.

'I'm not so sure,' Rory remarked grimly. He waited for Poppy to continue.

'I then discovered – well, Elspeth's cousin who works at an Edinburgh newspaper did – that three women in the last year in the Highlands and Islands have been tricked out of their life savings. And now,' Poppy went on, 'there's this spiritualist racket. I can't help thinking that somehow they are all related.'

'What does that nice inspector say?' Catriona asked.

'You don't need to keep calling him *that nice inspector*,' Poppy replied. 'He can be annoying as well sometimes, you know.'

Catriona laughed. 'So can we all, Poppy dear.'

'He doesn't agree that the three tricked women have a connection to the murdered woman,' Poppy admitted, 'but I'm certain he is mistaken. As to Bertram visiting the spiritualist, he doesn't yet know about that.'

'So you'll be seeing him soon to tell him?' Catriona prompted.

'No, I will not,' she said, keeping as calm as possible. 'He is now off the case while on a walking holiday on the island.'

'Is this a cover to pretend he's not investigating, in order to catch the murderer?'

'Nothing so dramatic, Catriona. He had already arranged to come to Skye for the holiday and to play the bagpipes at the Games.'

'You mean Mr James MacKenzie, the piper from Edinburgh, and your Inspector MacKenzie are the same man?'

'I do. And that is why I will be working on the investigation myself.'

TWENTY-NINE

The following morning, dressed in her green tweed suit for the day's walking, Poppy entered the dining room to find Harriet seated and in a state of excitement. She beckoned Poppy to join her.

'Jeanie and I are going shopping in Inverness today,' Harriet said, her eyes shining, as Poppy took a seat.

'I thought you didn't like shopping, Harriet?' she asked with a smile, pleased to see her new friend so animated.

'I don't usually.' Harriet flushed and spoke in a whisper. 'But Algernon said how nice I would look in a bright colour, and I want to please him.' Her flush deepened. 'Jeanie thought I should buy a new dress and she's offered to go with me to help me choose.'

'I'm sure you'll both have a delightful time,' Poppy said, hiding her grave concerns. 'Will Algernon also be helping you shop?'

'Don't be silly, Poppy!' Harriet giggled. She actually *giggled*, Poppy thought. 'Gentlemen don't go shopping.'

A waiter appeared with a teapot and milk jug for Harriet. He set them on the table.

'What would you like for breakfast, madam?' he asked
Poppy.

'Kidneys, bacon and coffee, please.'

He bowed and withdrew.

'Can I tell you something?' Harriet went on, breathless. 'I'm
so excited that I cannot keep it to myself, despite what Algernon
said.'

What Algernon said? The hairs on the back of Poppy's neck
immediately prickled. 'I won't let on,' she told Harriet.

'Jeanie has confessed that it's clear Algernon admires me!'
Harriet's eyes shone with excitement. 'I have never had an
admirer before...'

Oh dear, Poppy thought. Harriet was smitten. And Jeanie
was encouraging her.

'I think I have fallen in love with Algernon,' Harriet
announced.

It had gone much further than Poppy had realised, and in
such a short space of time. 'Do you think,' she began carefully,
'that you are rushing matters with Algernon and ought to wait
until you know him a wee bit better?'

'I know all I need to know about him!' Harriet protested.
'Jeanie has had a longer acquaintance with him and she trusts
him – not only his knowledge of investments but also his
character.'

The waiter returned with their breakfast orders, and as he
set them out, Poppy wondered about the best way to deal with
Harriet's revelation.

'You said something about despite what Algernon said?' she
asked Harriet when the waiter had gone.

'Yes,' she said, a little reluctant now. 'He has given me a
token of his esteem.' Harriet reached for a fine chain around her
neck, and from under her beige velvet dress with its lace collar,
drew out a pendant.

Poppy stared at it.

A sapphire pendant.

'It is beautiful, isn't it?' Harriet went on, cheered by what she clearly saw as Poppy's admiration of the jewellery. 'It was his mother's – and now he's given it to me! He asked me to keep the pendant a secret, but I had to tell you as you've been so kind.'

Poppy couldn't take her eyes off the piece. A beautiful double cluster blue sapphire pendant. It looked like the work of Garrard, the Crown Jeweller of the United Kingdom, which meant it was very valuable. Was it Ellen Clark's pendant? It had to be!

'It's exquisite,' Poppy breathed.

Harriet slipped the pendant back inside the collar of her dress. 'It is surely a prelude to a marriage proposal, don't you think?'

'I think...' *I think it very likely the jewellery was taken from the neck of a murdered woman.* 'I think that it's only a matter of days since you met...'

'Poppy, I cannot believe it of you.' Harriet went pale. 'I thought you would be happy for me.'

How to even suggest her real concern to the love-struck Harriet? 'It's just that—'

'I have decided to invest in the South American railway company,' Harriet rushed on, 'and I have written to my bank in Edinburgh to say I want a cheque made out in Algernon's name. And now I'd rather not talk about this any more, if you don't mind.' Harriet bent her head and fumbled for her napkin. As she did so, Poppy saw tears start to her eyes.

'Oh, Harriet,' Poppy said softly, reaching out a hand. She hoped there would be time to cancel the cheque. And she needed to tell Inspector MacKenzie about the pendant.

'Don't,' Harriet said brusquely, moving her own hand out of reach. She blinked back the tears and pulled herself together.

'Sorry I'm late, Harriet,' Jeanie said, appearing as if out of nowhere and taking a seat at the table. 'Don't worry, though, we'll still be in time for the train to Inverness.'

Elspeth hurried into the dining room and joined them. 'My lady, a word if you please.'

An idea came to Poppy. 'I think Elspeth would love to join you both on your shopping expedition. She works too hard in my service and could do with the day off.'

'My lady,' said Elspeth, a look of horror on her face. 'I wanted to wash your tussar silk blouse after breakfast, my lady.'

'Nonsense, Elspeth. You deserve a day off. Take three pounds out of my purse, and whatever you need for the train fare, and spoil yourself with a day in town.' And keep an eye on the slippery Jeanie, she thought, giving her maid what she hoped was an eloquent smile.

Clearly Elspeth didn't see it that way. 'I don't think—'

'Think on it no further, Elspeth,' Poppy went on breezily. 'The blouse can wait. Fergusson can take you all in the Bentley. He's been twiddling his thumbs for the last two days, and it will be good for the motor car to have a bit of a run.'

'That is very kind, Poppy.' Harriet sent her a grateful look.

'Very,' Jeanie added dryly.

The waiter reappeared to take Jeanie and Elspeth's orders, and Poppy gestured to the reluctant Elspeth to sit down.

Keen to move the conversation on and knowing Harriet's love of history, Poppy said, 'It's a pity Inverness Castle isn't open to the public, but at least you can see it from the outside. Although,' she added, 'you can go inside the courthouse, which is housed in the castle.'

'We don't want to visit that, do we, Harriet?' Jeanie said with her brittle laugh. 'Why don't you come with us, Poppy? It promises to be a jolly day out.'

'I think Elspeth would benefit from my absence. She finds it hard to relax when I am about, don't you, Elspeth?'

Elspeth snorted.

'No, Major and I will spend the day walking, and I will do some sketching.' Despite her breezy tone, Poppy felt dispirited by the news Harriet had just given her. Especially since Inspector MacKenzie was out of communication. He would be waiting for the ferry at Kyleakin to meet his cousin, or already striding over the heather like the lone piper of old.

She was desperate to tell the inspector about the pendant she had seen. But now she'd had time to think about it, she was equally determined to be certain of all her facts before doing so.

A walk in the fresh air would clear her head, allow her to think about what Harriet had told and shown her, and how it might fit in with her pattern.

Algernon Hamilton was now her prime suspect for the murder of Ellen Clark.

After giving her maid instructions as to what to listen out for, Poppy saw off Elspeth, who looked pleased to be seated in the front seat of the Bentley with the uniformed Fergusson at the wheel. Harriet and Jeanie in the rear smiled and waved to her as the car rolled away.

Poppy slipped her sketchbook into the knapsack she had borrowed from Catriona, along with a map and a bottle of lemonade, and set off, Major dancing by her side.

They strode out of Portree, Major pulling on the leash slightly in his excitement. She bent and set him free once they were out of the town, and followed a track north into the countryside. The day was pleasant, not too hot, and she swung her arms as she walked, enjoying the freedom that her box-pleated tweed skirt and the brogues gave her. Passing the occasional farmhouse or croft, she heard the barking of dogs from time to time, and at one croft where the track passed close, she stopped for a moment to watch beautiful fat brown hens scratching in the yard.

After a while, she came to a crossroads without any helpful signpost. She took out the map and consulted it. The road to the left led to a small wood, straight ahead to some hamlet, and the road to the right was marked with a ruin. Tempting as the wood was, for there were very few trees on the island – felled over centuries to provide fuel, building materials and grazing, Catriona had told her – she decided on the ruin. There was always something enticing about a ruin.

Poppy took this path, following the mossy track that ran by its side. Before long the path began to climb, away from the burn, and ahead of her she saw the ruins of a stone cottage over-grown with ivy. She went closer. To the front of the ruin lay two graves side by side.

She crouched down to examine the headstones. They were so covered with lichen that it was impossible to read the inscrip-tions. She slipped the knapsack off her back and from her pocket took out the Swiss Army knife her mother had given her as a present before leaving for Australia. 'You never know when you might need to open a bottle of wine, my dear,' her ever-practical mother had said with a smile.

Poppy pulled out the small blade attachment and set to work, carefully scraping off the lichen. She had barely completed the first line of one of the stones when she noticed Major was standing and staring along the track they had used, a low rumble coming from his chest.

'What is it, Major?' Poppy asked, rising.

He ran forward a few steps then stopped, raised his nose and sniffed at the air, before giving a joyful bark.

'I take it that a friend is about to appear,' she said as his tail wagged and he moved forward a few more steps. It was then she heard the sound of two men chatting and laughing. Inspector MacKenzie and a shorter man with red hair and a pink face came into view. Each wore old Norfolk jackets and flat caps, and carried knapsacks.

'*Mo chreach 'sa thàinig!*' Poppy and the inspector exclaimed in unison.

The other man looked quizzically between them both. '*Goodness me?*' he said. 'What have I missed?'

'Lady Persephone Proudfoot and I are—'

'Old friends,' she finished.

'Your ladyship, this is my cousin, Ewan Macdonald, from Harris.'

'How do you do, your ladyship,' Ewan said.

'Delightful to see you again, Inspector, and to meet you, Mr Macdonald.'

Ewan Macdonald looked a little bemused. 'You say you are old friends and yet you address each other as your ladyship and Inspector.'

'That we do, and this is Major Lewis,' went on Inspector MacKenzie, scratching Major behind one ear.

'Major for short,' Poppy added.

'Good morning, Major,' Ewan said. 'Are you enjoying your walk, my lady?'

'Absolutely. Although I've just been wondering about these two graves.' Poppy gestured to them.

''Tis a verra sad story,' Ewan told her.

'Dinna bore the lady, Ewan. He kens just about everything historical on all the islands, my lady, and doesna need any encouraging to show off his extensive knowledge.'

'All the same, I'd like to hear it, this bit of history.'

'Well then,' Ewan began, a smile on his pleasant face. 'One day long ago, when Ranald,' he nodded at the stones, 'was out hunting, he saw the daughter of his clan's ancient enemy, and then and there they both fell in love. One nicht, verra dark it was, Ranald called his clan together, entered the enemy's settlement and carried off his lady-love from under her faither's nose. They married and were verra happy together.' He paused to look at the two graves in respectful silence.

'That's a delightful story,' Poppy said, 'not a sad one.'

'Aye, at first. But then, one day,' Ewan went on, 'out hunting with a kinsman, Ranald heard a lassie screaming for help in the depths of the forest. No' thinking of himself, he plunged into the forest. In a clearing was a wee lass tied to a tree. He leaped off his horse, cut the ropes and set her free. Too late it was he heard the other clan's battle cry, and a dozen or more of them burst through the undergrowth and fell upon the two men. It was an ambush, right enough.' Ewan shook his head.

'What happened next?' Poppy asked, enthralled by the story.

'Somehow his kinsman escaped and brought back the news,' he continued. 'The next day, Ranald's body was found near to the cottage where they bided. His lady, bent on revenge, called her husband's clan together and that nicht she led the men into the others' settlement. They laid about the enemy with their claymores, but in the end they were all slain and their bodies thrown into the loch. The next morning, washerwomen found the lady's body in a wee bay. The brave lass was carried back to the cottage and buried here beside her husband.'

'Man's inhumanity to man,' Poppy murmured.

'Aye,' Ewan agreed sadly.

Poppy brought her thoughts back to the present, and suddenly remembered that the cousin was to have brought a friend. 'Shouldn't there be three of you?'

'Och, my cousin's friend has failed to turn up,' Inspector MacKenzie said.

'That's no' strictly true,' Ewan amended. 'The thing is, my lady, he appears to have gone missing.'

THIRTY

'I'm sure you're worrying unnecessarily, Ewan,' Inspector MacKenzie said calmly. 'He is a grown man and he will return in his own time.'

'Eugene has disappeared,' Ewan insisted. 'Something has waylaid him, though I canna mind what it might be.'

Poppy looked from Ewan, to the inspector, and back again. 'Could there be a lady involved?' she asked Ewan, thinking of the story he had just told her.

'It's more complicated than that,' he said ruefully.

'This is intriguing,' Poppy murmured.

'It's nothing for you to concern yourself with, my lady,' stated the inspector quickly.

'Oh, but I am good at solving mysteries, as you well know, Inspector.'

'You are?' Ewan regarded her with a hopeful look. 'Then can you help me find my missing friend?'

'I'd be delighted to,' she told him, ignoring the exasperated glance the inspector sent her.

Ewan smiled. 'Thank you, your ladyship.'

'Please, call me Poppy,' she said.

Inspector MacKenzie eyed the blade in her hand. 'Why don't you put away the knife, your ladyship, and we will walk on a little way?'

She closed the blade of the Swiss Army knife and returned it to her pocket. The three of them, with Major dashing hither and thither, retraced their steps down the track until they came to the burn.

'Let's follow this a little way to find somewhere to discuss the situation of your missing friend and have a drink,' Poppy suggested.

They followed the burbling water until they came to a part of the bank with a scattering of slender trees. The day had grown warmer still and the silver birch would provide dappled shade from the sun. Major immediately dashed into the burn and lowered himself into the water.

'Allow me, my lady.' Inspector MacKenzie shrugged off his jacket and squatted down to spread it on the grass for Poppy.

For the first time she noticed that his white shirt was open at the neck, revealing a strong throat. Her eyes unconsciously travelled down to his thighs, where the material of his trousers was stretched taut. Goodness, he was a big man.

'Thank you,' she said, her voice suddenly hoarse. Was she expressing appreciation at his kindness in providing his jacket, or at his unconscious display of his attributes...? She felt herself flush.

He lowered himself to the ground beside her. 'It is warm today.'

Poppy tore her gaze away from the inspector. Had her thoughts been visible on her face?

'It is,' she said in what she hoped was a cool, calm voice, and pulled out her bottle of lemonade and the Swiss Army knife to extract the corkscrew.

'Let me do that,' he said, holding out his hand for the bottle and corkscrew.

'I can manage, thank you.' Good Lord, she thought, if a girl couldn't open her own bottle of lemonade, she could die of thirst.

She screwed the implement into the cork wedged into the top of the bottle and withdrew it with a satisfying *pop*. Turning to give him a smug smile, she found the inspector propped up on one elbow, staring at the water. How disappointing; her display of competence had been wasted.

Ewan had seated himself on the grass to her other side and she turned to him. 'You were saying about your friend?'

'Aye.' Ewan pulled a bottle of beer from his knapsack and extracted the cork using his teeth. He took a long draught of his drink and frowned.

'Just begin when you're ready,' Poppy said kindly. She drank some of her lemonade while she waited for him to begin.

Major splashed out of the burn, shook himself and padded over to them. He found a spot to his liking on the grass and stretched out there, his eyes just sufficiently open to see if anyone produced food.

'Eugene is, or was, a farmer in the United States,' Ewan began.

'One moment.' Poppy was determined to be thorough. 'What is his surname?'

'Miller.'

'And can you describe him, please?'

'About my height, in his thirties, muscular build, close-cropped light-coloured hair. Will that do?'

'Thank you. Please continue.'

'Some months ago, at home in the United States, he was befriended by a Scot calling himself Angus Haliburton.'

'That wasn't his real name?'

'After what Eugene told me, I doubt it.'

'And can you describe this man?'

Ewan shrugged. 'Clean-shaven, fair-haired and wearing spectacles.'

'No distinguishing marks? A tattoo, broken nose, cauliflower ear...?'

Behind her, Inspector MacKenzie let out a guffaw of laughter. 'No' all criminals have those, my lady.'

'I know that!' Poppy retorted without turning round. 'Please go on, Ewan.'

'It seems this fellow, Haliburton, swindled Eugene out of what little he owned,' Ewan went on. 'By the time my friend realised what had happened, it was too late. Things were already hard for him in Manhattan. During the Great War, farmers over there took out loans to increase production and meet the need for food in Europe. After the War, the market situation improved, the demand for American food decreased and the farmers were unable to pay back their loans. After Haliburton, Eugene was left with barely enough money to travel here by steerage.'

'Steerage,' Poppy murmured. The lowest category of long-distance steamer travel, used by people trying to escape destitution at home. Passengers travelled in the hold, packed like cattle, and had to provide their own bedding and food. 'How utterly miserable that must have been.'

'I feel bad about his disappearance,' Ewan went on, 'as I was the one who persuaded him to come here.'

'So it was a bit more than a holiday for Eugene?'

'He was hoping to find employment.'

'You said he used to farm?'

'Aye, he was a duck farmer on Long Island.' Seeing Poppy's look of surprise, Ewan added, 'Apparently that part of Manhattan has the perfect conditions for duck farming.'

'Not much call for duck farming in Scotland...' she ventured.

'Eugene knows that and he's willing to turn his hand to any

kind of work. Anyway, when I arrived at the Portree Inn, I found he'd left a note for me, dated three days ago, saying that he'd arrived early on Skye and was going to try to find Haliburton before meeting up with me and James.'

James? Poppy knew that was the inspector's name, but somehow it felt strange to hear it spoken with a manly affection from one cousin to another. Strange, but rather lovely.

She needed to concentrate on the missing Eugene. 'What makes your friend think the fellow is on Skye?' she asked.

'Apparently Haliburton had mentioned the area to him.'

'And that's all your friend knows about him?' It wasn't much to go on, she thought.

'Aye. That and the fancy business card the trickster had given him.'

'Do you have the card on you?' she asked, without much hope.

'I do. I've been trying to track the fellow down myself, without success.'

'May I see it?'

'In the note Eugene left for me, he said I was to keep the card in case anything happened to him, but I can show it to you.' Ewan leaned his beer bottle against the trunk of the tree and pulled the card from the pocket of his Norfolk jacket.

'And this is why you believe he has gone missing? You think he's found his quarry in Portree and, as a result, has come to harm.'

'Aye, I do, Poppy.'

'One moment, while I find my sketchbook.' She rammed the cork back into the lemonade bottle, rummaged around in her knapsack and withdrew the pad and pencil.

'I imagine your drawing skills have improved since last I saw them, my lady,' she heard the inspector observe in an amused voice.

Poppy ignored him. 'Can you hold the card while I draw it?' she said to Ewan, settling the pad on her knees.

It was the usual sort of business card: small, rectangular and white, with the name printed in the centre. Poppy drew the outline of a business card and in the centre wrote *Angus Haliburton*, sloping to the right as on the card.

'Under his name it says in upper case the words *investment adviser*,' Ewan said.

Poppy added to the sketch the words INVESTMENT ADVISER. She considered again the card. It had a bold black line around all four sides with a stylised triangle in each corner. She drew this in.

'What do you think?' she asked, tilting the pad towards him.

'It looks just like the card.'

'Is the name of the printers on the reverse side?' she suddenly thought to ask.

Ewan turned it over. 'It's no' there.'

'That is a pity.' She could have contacted the printers and found out who had ordered this style of card.

Then, as she considered her sketch, she realised it appeared similar to Algernon's card that Harriet had shown her, except that the name was different. But surely this was a standard card for businessmen, the design replicated thousands of times for different clients? Perhaps the two men used the same printers. It sounded highly plausible, as weren't Angus and Algernon in the same line of business? How thick on the ground were investment brokers in Scotland?

She would have to find a way of asking Algernon for his card. Maybe she should ask him if he knew of this chap or – and then a dreadful thought struck her – could Algernon and Angus be one and the same person? The physical description of the men didn't match, but Angus might not have needed the spectacles; surely plain glass could be inserted into the frames. And hair colour could be changed. Goodness knows there were a number of society women who changed theirs.

Perhaps she should now tell the inspector about Harriet and the pendant? But Poppy had wanted her facts straight first and that was still the case. She would ask Harriet about the card Algernon had given her. Harriet was sure still to have her card; she probably had it wrapped in a handkerchief and kept close to her heart. Poppy chided herself for such an ungenerous thought. And she thought of Harriet's newly acquired blue sapphire pendant, and shivered as if a cold breeze had blown down her spine.

Yes, Poppy would have to ask Harriet to see the card again, if only to put her own mind at rest. She wanted to be certain it didn't match the one in her sketch, although she was almost sure it would. But Harriet was already suspicious of Poppy's intentions towards Algernon and was likely to refuse. She was positive Harriet thought that she, Poppy, would have liked to have the man for herself. She shook her head; how was it some women could be so gullible when it came to dealing with men? But wasn't that exactly what had befallen Ellen Clark? That thought made up Poppy's mind: she would ask Harriet and risk being rebuffed.

Poppy suddenly realised Ewan was looking at her, waiting to hear what she had to say next, and that behind her the inspector was very quiet. Had Inspector MacKenzie gone to sleep?

'Thank you,' she said to Ewan, and he returned the business card to his pocket. 'I'll make some enquiries about your friend and the card, and let you know what I find out.'

She turned back towards Inspector MacKenzie. He'd removed his cap, his tousled hair shining like a blue-black raven's wing, and he was sitting and reading a newspaper he must have had in his knapsack.

'Inspector,' she said, 'would you mind if I glanced at your paper? There's something I would like to check.'

'Help yourself, my lady.' He closed *The Scotsman* and handed it to her.

She glanced at the headline: *Treaty of Lausanne into Effect.* It referred to the peace treaty between Turkey and the Allied Powers, which had been signed the previous year, and meant that the restoration of peace following the Great War was now complete. That was good news, and she would read more about it later, but at present it was the list of share prices Poppy was interested in. Now, what was the name of the company Harriet had mentioned?

Compañía something... Poppy scanned the overseas opportunities columns, but she couldn't see anything she recognised.

Seeing her frown, Inspector MacKenzie asked, 'What is it you are looking for, my lady?'

'A South American company... something to do with a railway.'

'*Compañía Ferroviaria?*' he suggested.

'That's it! Do you know anything about them?'

'I wasna saying a company name, I was merely translating "railway company" into Spanish.'

She stared at him. Would a genuine railway company really call itself that? It didn't seem likely. She must speak to Harriet as soon as she got back to the hotel.

The inspector was watching her face. He's wondering what this is all about, she thought – and he can jolly well carry on wondering. There were too many goings-on at present in Portree, not to mention Plockton, for her to think the events weren't related. Inspector James MacKenzie may believe each was an isolated event, but *she* didn't. She wasn't going to try to tell him again her thoughts on this, because she didn't wish to appear foolish in front of him.

When she had gathered sufficient evidence, *then* she would share her findings with him.

But time was running out. She must fathom everything before Harriet lost her life savings – or, worse, her life.

Poppy made her excuses and left the inspector and his cousin to continue their walk.

Her next step was to return to Portree, visit the inn where the men were staying and find out from the staff what she could about Eugene Miller's disappearance. The walk was not too long but the day seemed unusually hot, and she was in such a hurry it surprised even Major, who couldn't stay long snuffling the bank of the track for anything exciting. He ran to catch her up as she hastened down the hillside.

She entered the Portree Inn, perspiring in what she trusted was a ladylike manner. She told Major to sit, and asked the young man at the reception desk for the manageress.

'One moment, please, miss.' The young man turned and knocked on the door behind the desk. He opened it and Poppy heard him say, 'Mrs Bruce, there's a lady here asking for you.'

'Thank you, Donald,' Poppy heard the reply.

A short, neat woman with a demure look and a soft step came bustling out of the office.

'Yes, madam?' she asked politely. 'I am the manageress, Mrs Bruce.'

'Mrs Bruce, I am here on behalf of the Edinburgh Detective Branch.'

Mrs Bruce paled and put her hand to her thin chest. 'Police?' she whispered.

'Please don't worry,' Poppy hastened to reassure her. 'No crime has been committed here.' Apart from the fraudulent medium, she thought ruefully.

Mrs Bruce relaxed a little, but she looked puzzled. 'How can I help you?'

'My name is Lady Persephone Proudfoot. I've had a report that one of your guests, Eugene Miller, has disappeared.'

'Och, yes. The nice American gentleman. I don't know about disappearing, my lady. Although...' She hesitated, before admitting, 'It is a wee bit strange. We've never had this situation in the hotel before.'

Poppy gave an encouraging nod. 'I understand that Mr Miller arrived here three days ago, but he failed to meet his walking companions.'

'That's right, your ladyship. When Mr Macdonald arrived this forenoon, he asked for Mr Miller and I told him that the American gentleman hasn't been seen since Friday. Mr MacKenzie...'

Of course, the inspector wouldn't have used his detective title on holiday, Poppy realised.

'...checked in on Saturday, but I hadn't realised he was one of the walking party.'

'Do you have any idea where Mr Miller might have gone?'

Mrs Bruce shook her head regretfully. 'When Mr Miller arrived – a day earlier than expected, I should add' – she pursed her thin lips – 'he was lucky we had a vacancy, as the summer programme is bringing in additional visitors. Mr Miller asked after Mr Macdonald and I informed him that his friend had been delayed until today. Mr Miller then gave me a note for Mr Macdonald, said he would use the three extra days he had to explore the area, and that he would walk in the hills and might camp overnight. So I wasn't unduly concerned when he didn't reappear...' The manageress's voice wobbled. 'Och, now I'm thinking that the American has maybe met with an accident.'

An accident – or something more sinister? Poppy thought with misgiving.

As she tried to decide on her next move, a smartly dressed woman entered the inn and came up to the desk. Poppy stepped to one side, so that the manageress could deal with the customer.

'My key, if you please, Mrs Bruce.'

'Certainly, madam.' Mrs Bruce turned to the wall of keys, each with their own number, lifted one off and handed it to the guest.

As the other woman took it, she tucked her clutch bag more firmly under her arm. Poppy stared at the bag. It was made of crocodile skin. Just like Ellen Clark's missing bag.

'Excuse me,' she said to the woman, stepping forward with a smile. 'I have been admiring your clutch bag.'

As Poppy expected, the woman looked pleased and held it out for Poppy to admire further. 'Such workmanship,' the woman added. 'I couldn't believe my luck when I saw it for sale.'

There was a marcasite button on the clasp, just as Miss Grant had described the one on Ellen Clark's bag. Did this mean Isabella was in the clear – or was it simply a different bag?

'I would love one for myself,' Poppy gushed. 'Where did you find such a treasure?'

'You will never believe it!' The woman smiled.

Just tell me! Poppy wanted to cry. She returned the woman's smile. 'I cannot guess.'

'A travelling salesman, in Portree for the Games!' Seeing Poppy's mouth drop, she added, 'There, I knew that would surprise you.'

'I must see if I can find him,' Poppy said. How many travelling salesmen were there in Portree at present?

'You should find him easily. He's a rather loud gentleman by the name of Bertram Knox.'

A chill went down Poppy's back. So it *was* Bertram who

had sold Ellen's handbag. And yet she still felt certain that Algernon Hamilton was her prime suspect.

This could be the proof she needed that Algernon and Bertram truly were working together.

THIRTY-ONE

Poppy's sense of satisfaction that she had a further, strong clue to follow fought for supremacy with her relief that she hadn't told the inspector about the business cards and pointed the finger at Algernon without sufficient proof. Next, she had to question Bertram.

Poppy thanked the woman for the information about the bag and turned to leave the Portree Inn. At that moment, the door opened and in walked Inspector MacKenzie and Ewan Macdonald.

'Good Lord!' Poppy exclaimed. 'You must have followed in my footsteps.'

'Almost,' Ewan said with a touch of embarrassment. 'We found ourselves in need of lunch and James assured me the inn keeps a good table.'

The inspector frowned at her in such a way as to suggest he thought she was keeping something from him.

'Would you care to join us, Poppy?' Ewan asked.

'The dining room is this way, my lady,' Inspector MacKenzie said, gesturing towards the door.

Poppy was about to retort that naturally she knew where

the dining room was, since they had eaten there together two nights ago, when she realised with a start that he didn't want his cousin to know. Was he ashamed of their friendship, such as it was, or did he want to protect her reputation in some sweet, Victorian way?

She allowed herself to be guided into the room, slid off her knapsack and took the seat the inspector held out for her. When the two men were seated and Major tucked under the table, she spoke again.

'I came here to have a word with the manageress. Mrs Bruce has confirmed that Eugene arrived on Friday, a day earlier than expected, and that he went out later that same day and didn't return.'

'Aye, because he'd told her he might camp out in the hills,' Ewan added, 'she wasna too concerned when he didna return.'

The waitress appeared and Poppy chose a cheese soufflé; she had work to do this afternoon and didn't want to feel sleepy after a heavy lunch. Major showed no such concern and tucked into the large bowl of biscuits set down for him under the table.

'I must just freshen up,' she told the men. 'I won't be long.'

'The powder room is along—' began Ewan.

'Thank you, I know!' Poppy said cheerfully as she got to her feet, sending the inspector a pointed look and picking up her knapsack. 'I have been here before.'

In the powder room, she washed her hands and face, combed her hair, powdered her nose and applied a fresh layer of plum lipstick. The face in the mirror looked presentable, she decided. Perhaps a wee bit more than *presentable*, she liked to think. The candid hazel eyes sparkled, the chestnut-brown bob shone, the chin set at just the right angle to suggest determination without taking anything away from her feminine features. She might be only five feet two inches, Poppy thought, but the reflection in front of her was definitely the face of a plucky sort of girl, a solver of puzzles.

She strode jauntily back to the table. Her dining companions rose politely until she was again seated.

'We have decided,' Ewan said, 'that if Eugene hasna appeared by this afternoon, the police will search for him.'

'Very sensible,' Poppy said, sending an *I should think so* look at the inspector. 'It might be summer, but three nights in the hills without news is long enough.'

Ewan shot her a grateful look.

'Where do you think he might have gone, Ewan?' Poppy asked as they waited for their meal.

'It could be anywhere.'

That was also Poppy's thought, but it wasn't helpful.

'Ewan, see if there's anything in his room, any notes or similar, that might point to the route he intended to take,' Inspector MacKenzie said.

'Mrs Bruce willna let me have the key,' Ewan replied. 'I asked her this morning, when there was no sign of Eugene.'

'I think she's worried enough now that she'll give you the key,' Poppy said.

Ewan looked doubtful, but he left the dining room anyway.

'Are you not concerned, Inspector?' Poppy asked.

'That I am,' he admitted, 'but I didna want to worry Ewan. I had to wait the requisite time before making it a police matter. But now that time has almost passed, we can start the search shortly.'

'On a related matter, what about the search for Ellen's gentleman, Alan Henderson? It's been a week now and I presume he hasn't reappeared.'

'He hasna. I've already instructed Constable Macduff to step up the search for him.'

Poppy glanced out of the window into the busy street. The sun shone, there was a holiday atmosphere, and it was hard to imagine anything bad could happen in such a place.

Ewan stuck his head round the door of the dining room,

directly in Poppy's eyeline, and with a smile brandished the key. He immediately withdrew his head, presumably to disappear upstairs.

'There must be *something* in Eugene's bedroom,' Poppy said thoughtfully. 'He can't just be wandering the hills in the hope of bumping into Angus Haliburton.' She must join Ewan in his search of his friend's room. 'Perhaps Eugene made a list of possible places and put it in his drawer...'

About to get to her feet, Poppy stopped. She had remembered another occasion where she'd seen a business card. It was in a drawer in her room at the Harbour Hotel, and she'd casually tossed it into the wastepaper basket.

The cards given to Harriet and Eugene looked the same as the one she'd found in Plockton.

She suddenly felt horribly cold.

'Do excuse me, Inspector!' Poppy jumped up and, grabbing her knapsack and calling to Major to come with her, dashed out of the dining room. She needed to telephone the manageress at the Harbour Hotel immediately.

It took Poppy only minutes to reach the Isle of the Mist Hotel. She burst in and was relieved to see her friend at the desk.

'Catriona!' she gasped, 'can I use your private telephone, please? It's desperately important!'

A few guests were milling about in reception and they stopped chatting to stare at her.

'In the office at the back,' her friend said quickly, opening the door for her.

Poppy hastened in and dropped her knapsack. She snatched up the stand in one hand and with her other unhooked the receiver and held it to her ear.

'Operator,' came the voice at the other end of the line.

'The Harbour Hotel in Plockton,' Poppy urged.

'Trying to connect you,' came the infuriatingly calm reply.

'Harbour Hotel,' said Miss Grant.

'Oh, Miss Grant, I am so pleased to hear you! I have a very important question to ask you. It's Lady Persephone Proudfoot, by the way,' she added.

'Yes, my lady.' Miss Grant sounded distant, but clear enough.

'Please listen carefully. When I stayed with you, can you tell me who had the room before me?'

There was a slight pause before Miss Grant answered. 'Actually, my lady, it was

Ellen Clark. Why do you ask?'

'I found something in one of the drawers in my room and I thought it might be a clue to Ellen's murder.'

'Och, I see what you mean. Mrs Clark *used* to have your room, but then she asked for another, thinking it might be pleasant to have a change. She moved into the other room only a couple of nights before... she was murdered. Her original room remained vacant until you arrived, my lady.'

'So she *had* used the room I stayed in!' Poppy could hardly keep the excitement out of her voice. 'Thank you so much, Miss Grant. I think I might now be close to discovering the identity of her murderer.'

She quickly replaced the receiver on its hook and set down the telephone candlestick. She was certain that Ellen Clark, Mairi MacKay and the other two women identified by Elspeth's cousin Beathag from the newspaper, and goodness knows how many others, were victims of the man calling himself, variously, Alan Henderson, Angus Haliburton and Algernon Hamilton. Hadn't Algernon said he was not long back from a trip to New York City? Eugene Miller's farm had been in Manhattan, which was part of New York City. He and Harriet were the confidence trickster's latest victims.

Harriet was still safe at present, thank God, but Eugene... Eugene knew the man, had spent time with him, and could recognise him. Had he spotted Algernon Hamilton in Portree and...?

Poppy didn't want to think about what might have happened to Ewan's friend. All she knew was that she had to find Eugene as quickly as possible in the hope that it wasn't already too late.

She dashed out of the office, Major on her heels, calling her thanks to the astonished Catriona, and headed up the stairs to her room. There was no sign of Elspeth, so she hadn't yet returned with Harriet and Jeanie from Inverness.

Poppy looked frantically around the room; she needed an electric torch and a first aid kit... Where were they kept? She wrenched open drawers, frantically searching for the items.

'My lady!' Elspeth, standing in her open doorway, looked aghast. 'Have you gone quite mad?'

'Not yet, but I fear I will soon if I don't find a torch and a first aid kit—'

'First aid kit?' Elspeth hurried into the room. 'Are you hurt?'

'No, not me, but an American, Eugene...'

Elspeth's nose twitched. 'What extraordinary names these people have.'

'It may already be too late for bandages. Do help me, Elspeth!'

'Of course, my lady. I have no idea who this person is, but if you're concerned about him, that is good enough for me. Bide here a moment; I have an electric torch and an accident emergency case in my room.'

'And tell Harriet and Jeanie to stay in the hotel, where she will be safe!' she called to the departing Elspeth.

Poppy pulled the map out of her knapsack, knelt on the floor and spread it open on the rug. *Think,* she told herself, *think!* She didn't know where Eugene might have gone, but what about Algernon? There must be somewhere he had mentioned...

The bothy, that was what she needed to look for! She remembered the look of nostalgia she'd seen on Algernon's face on their journey to the Fairy Glen, when he'd mentioned one he had stayed in as a young child when out on the hills with his father. It was probably the only true thing he'd told them. A bothy was a basic shelter in a remote spot, originally built for labourers on large estates, but since the decline of hill farming they were left unlocked for walkers to stay in overnight free of charge.

What was the name of the estate? She stared at the map, racking her brains. It wasn't to the north of Portree, given that Algernon had said he'd not been before to that part of the island. It could be to the west, or to the south. She would start with the south. It must be somewhere that could be walked to from the wee town. One mile, two miles, five, ten? Algernon, or whatever his real name was, didn't appear to be much of a walker these days, so she'd try no more than five miles out.

Major walked across the map and sat on it.

'Get off, you great gowk!' she exclaimed, trying to push his large, heavy body away.

He shot her a *then don't forget me* look and got to his feet, padding across the thick paper.

Poppy bent her head again. How many bothies were there? A wee brown square caught her eye. A building, of course, but too small to be a cottage, much less a house. A bothy. She looked for the name of the estate. *Knappach*. That was it!

Oh, but how would Eugene have known this? She thought again. What had Ewan said about Haliburton in the United States? That he'd mentioned the Isle of Skye to Eugene...

The bedroom door opened and Elspeth entered. 'Miss Scott and Mrs Harper have been advised as requested, my lady. They will stay in the Palm Court Lounge or the dining room until they retire. I have brought a torch and a medical aid kit.'

'And I have identified the place where I think Eugene might

have gone.' Poppy stabbed her finger triumphantly on the map. 'The bothy on the Knappach Estate.' She folded the map and jumped to her feet. 'We need to leave now, unless we want to spend the night on the hills.'

'Certainly not,' Elspeth shuddered. 'Wait, what do you mean, *we* need to leave now?'

'Exactly that. Best foot forward, Elspeth.' Poppy was already pushing the torch and medical tin into her knapsack. 'Best paw forward, Major.'

'Shouldn't we let the inspector know what we are doing?' Elspeth asked.

'He knows,' Poppy replied. By which she meant he knew she was investigating.

Even as she dashed out of her room, Poppy knew that chasing a murderer into the hills without leaving a message for Inspector MacKenzie might not be the wisest thing she'd ever done.

Poppy, Elspeth and Major took the road leading southwards under a cloudless blue sky and followed it for a mile or two, Poppy bringing her maid up to date with events as they hurried along. When they reached a signpost, Poppy consulted her map.

'We should turn right here,' she said, pointing to a narrow, uphill track.

'Perhaps we should call out for the gentleman, my lady?' Elspeth suggested. 'Then we might not have to go as far as the bothy.'

'Good idea. *Eugene!*' Poppy shouted.

'Mr Miller!' came Elspeth's thinner voice.

Major joined in with a bark.

They followed the track through a group of trees, calling as they went. When they emerged on the other side, the track became grassy.

Poppy glanced at the map again. 'We're on the right path.'

'That's good to know,' Elspeth said without enthusiasm.

'Look, here on the grass!' Poppy suddenly exclaimed, pointing. 'See those marks, Elspeth? Unless I'm very much mistaken, they've been made by something being dragged along.'

'Such as a heavy body?' Elspeth faltered.

Poppy nodded excitedly. 'And they look quite recent.'

'Are we near to the bothy, my lady?' Elspeth whispered.

'I think so. We need to continue along this track.'

'Do we actually need to?' Elspeth peered ahead. 'I mean, can't we go back and get some help?'

'Not now we've come this far. And besides, we'd look foolish if no help is needed.'

'Better than looking dead if it *is* needed,' Elspeth retorted, her voice wobbly.

Poppy strode on for about a hundred yards, following the marks in the grass, with Major sniffing the air and Elspeth muttering about the saintly Lady MacCorkindale.

'There!' Poppy breathed. She put out a hand to stop Elspeth's reluctant steps. 'Major, sit!' she hissed.

The Labrador sat, his nose twitching, his ears cocked, waiting for further instructions.

In front of them stood an old single-storey building, slate-roofed and constructed out of stones. At the front was a low wooden door, with a small grubby window just visible to the side.

'There's obviously no one there, my lady,' Elspeth said, looking up at the single, smokeless chimney. 'We might as well go back.'

'Wait here,' Poppy said. 'I'm going in.'

'If you are entering that place, then I am entering with you,' Elspeth said firmly.

'Thank you, Elspeth.' Poppy was touched. 'That is very kind of you.'

'Well, I'm not staying here on my own.'

Poppy allowed herself a wry smile. 'I will go first, and then you follow.'

'As befits a lady and her personal maid.'

Poppy glanced at Elspeth. Was she being facetious? No, for the look on Elspeth's face was one of trepidation. Had she done the right thing in bringing her? She knew that a police officer shouldn't go alone into a dangerous situation, but she and Elspeth were hardly the long arm of the law.

'Major, *heel*,' Poppy murmured, creeping forward in the grass. She could see Major close by her side and hear Elspeth breathing heavily behind her.

'This isn't safe, my lady,' Elspeth whispered.

'We will naturally take care on entering the building,' Poppy assured her.

'We don't want to get killed.'

'That goes without saying.'

'I'd rather it was said.'

They continued to approach cautiously.

'Are there any snakes on the island?' Elspeth whispered again.

'Only adders,' Poppy replied, her voice low.

They stole towards the bothy, the descending notes of a meadow pipit eerie in the silence.

'Are adders poisonous?' Elspeth continued.

'Yes, but their bite is unlikely to kill you.'

'Och, that's good to know.'

'And they're shy.'

'Aye, and so am I, so let's hope we dinna meet.'

'*Hush!*'

They drew closer to the small building. Nobody came to the

door or looked out of the window, but that didn't mean it was empty.

Poppy shivered in the late afternoon sunlight. There was no turning back now, and besides, Eugene might be lying inside and injured, in need of their help. She motioned to Major to stay, then turned the handle and pushed open the door.

It scraped on the uneven stone floor. A musty smell hit her nostrils. The bird had fallen silent, and all she could hear was her own thumping heart. Elspeth stood so close to her it felt like her maid was glued to Poppy's back.

In the gloom, Poppy could make out a single room, with a raised platform to sleep on. With relief she saw the platform was empty; no straw or sleeping bag or person. An incoming shaft of dim sunlight from the tiny window showed her the room contained only a rough wooden table and two chairs. In the small fireplace lay the remains of a long-dead fire, a few twigs burned to charcoal.

A low growl rumbled in Major's chest as he slowly entered the bothy through the open door.

'What is that?' Elspeth breathed into her ear. 'There, in the corner?'

Poppy looked around with more care and saw against one wall a pile of old hessian sacks. 'Wait here, both of you.' With slow steps she crossed the floor. As she drew closer to the sacks, a sickly odour hit her nostrils. She crouched down, took hold of one of the hessian bags and moved it away.

She couldn't be sure of the age or height of the body lying there, but he was muscular with fair, close-cropped hair – and with a bloody gash on his forehead.

'Oh, Eugene, I am so sorry,' Poppy whispered.

THIRTY-TWO

Poppy's work as a nurse during the Great War meant that she wasn't new to death, but she still felt nausea.

She felt the man's neck. A spark of hope went through her when she found a pulse – a faint one, but it was there.

'Elspeth!' she cried, turning round to where her maid and the Labrador waited in the doorway. 'Perhaps we are not too late. The emergency kit, please!'

Elspeth hurried into the bothy, pulling the small yellow tin marked *ACCIDENT EMERGENCY CASE* from her pocket. Poppy examined the wound carefully. The blood no longer oozed from the gash, but it remained a bright, glistening red. Close by lay a poker, its end bloodied.

Poppy took the tin and, with hands not as steady as she would have liked them to be, managed to open it. She went through the contents. 'Ammonia for insect bites, Carron oil for burns, arnica for bruises... Ah, here we are: a plaster, packet of lint, two rolls of bandages, safety pins, scissors, tube of boric ointment – good, that's an antiseptic.'

Feeling more in control now, Poppy unscrewed the tube and smeared some of the ointment onto a square of lint. As gently as she could, she positioned the piece of cotton over the wound on Eugene's forehead. She held her breath, waiting to see if there was any reaction – a fluttering of his eyelids, perhaps – but there was nothing.

Bandage next. 'Can you hold his head a little off the ground, Elspeth?'

Elspeth knelt on the floor and carefully took hold of the man's head.

Poppy unwrapped one of the rolls and wound the length of bandage around his head, securing it at the side with a safety pin. She nodded her thanks at Elspeth.

'I can't just put his poor head back on the hard ground,' Elspeth said.

'You're right, of course.' Poppy gazed around the bothy, but there was nothing suitable. 'I have the very thing!' She got to her feet and wriggled out of her petticoat.

Elspeth gasped. 'My lady...'

'You suggested it,' Poppy said, stepping out of the lacy white garment.

'I did not, your ladyship!' Elspeth cried indignantly.

Poppy gave her a quick smile. 'I know. In fact, it was another American who gave me the idea.' She bundled up her petticoat and placed it in position. 'Mr J. Franklin Emmett.'

'That director of moving pictures we met at Balfour House,' Elspeth said disparagingly as she gently lowered Eugene's head and sat back on her heels.

Poppy looked down at Elspeth. 'One of us needs to go back to Portree for a doctor and a stretcher.' She glanced over to where her dog still sat on the threshold. 'I don't think Major can yet be relied upon to carry a message in his collar.'

He sent her his most intelligent look, but Poppy wasn't fooled.

'You go, my lady,' said Elspeth. 'You can run faster than me.'

'Are you sure, Elspeth?' She was certain her maid would not

want to stay here alone. Well, almost alone. A near-dead man probably didn't count as company, much less as protection should, Heaven forbid, the killer come back to finish the job. 'I can leave Major with you.'

'Much good is that creature,' Elspeth scoffed, but Poppy had seen a look of relief cross the other woman's face.

'Major, *stay*,' Poppy instructed him.

Don't be too long, the dog's face seemed to suggest. *It's almost dinner time.*

'I'll be as quick as I can,' she said to Elspeth, who had taken hold of Eugene's hand and was giving it a reassuring stroke.

Poppy squeezed past the Labrador in the doorway, and flew out of the bothy and down the hill towards the Portree Inn, praying that the inspector was there.

Poppy burst into the reception hall of the hotel. Inspector MacKenzie and Ewan, kitted out for the search, whirled round.

'Thank goodness I haven't missed you, Inspector!' she cried, her breath coming in painful gasps. 'We've found Eugene Miller – he's injured – alive but only just – in a bothy on the Knappach Estate.'

'Sit down, my lady,' the inspector said, guiding her towards an armchair, 'and catch your breath.'

'I can't!' Poppy shook off his arm. 'I've left Elspeth and Major with him, and who knows what might happen if Algernon comes back?' she cried.

'Algernon?'

'Oh, never mind now! I will explain as we go. Come on, I'll take you there.'

She darted to the door of the lounge and looked back. '*Hurry!*'

As they hastened through the hall, Poppy called to the astonished young man at the desk, 'Send a doctor immediately to the bothy on the Knappach Estate! And tell him to bring a stretcher and two men. It's a matter of life and death!'

They hurried out of the door and along the road.

'It was the mention of a drawer in Eugene's room at the hotel that gave me the notion,' Poppy explained to the inspector and Ewan. 'The business card that you showed me, Ewan, was very like one I had seen in two other places. One in the hand of Harriet Scott, a fellow guest at the Isle of the Mist Hotel, and the other in a drawer in my bedroom at the hotel where I stayed in Plockton.'

'I kent nothing about the other cards,' Inspector MacKenzie said with a frown.

'No, well, you were on holiday. I rang the manageress at the Harbour Hotel and what she told me confirmed my suspicion,' Poppy went on. 'Ellen Clark had stayed in the same bedroom as myself until a couple of days before she was murdered.'

The inspector nodded. 'Go on,' he said, his voice grim.

'I was certain she'd been given the card by her missing gentleman friend, Alan Henderson. Then Harriet Scott showed me the business card she'd been given by Algernon Hamilton, also a guest at the Isle of the Mist. And Ewan has the card his friend Eugene had been given by Angus Haliburton. All three business cards, bar the name, are the same. And then,' Poppy drew in a great breath, 'I remembered Ewan saying Haliburton had mentioned Skye to Eugene when in the United States, and Algernon commenting on his fond memories of a bothy on the Knappach Estate.'

'So you put the two facts together and found Eugene?'

'Yes.'

'You have learned an impressive amount, my lady,' Inspector MacKenzie said, sending her an appreciative look.

Poppy's pulse skipped deliciously, but she managed to puff out as they increased their speed. 'A detective needs to be inquisitive... and I have always been interested in matters which were none of my business.'

'Quite so.'

'And Inspector, we must hurry not just for Eugene's sake, but for Elspeth's too. Major is with her, but...' Poppy's voice trailed off. There was only so much a lady's maid and a dog could do in the face of a returning murderer.

The inspector shot her a concerned look. 'We had best save our breath now,' he said. 'The track is beginning to climb.'

There was still the matter of Bertram selling Ellen's handbag, Poppy thought. Oh, and of him and Jeanie together behind the hotel, and perhaps his communication with the medium, and Isabella's argument with Ellen, but she would consider those later. The important job now was to lead the men to Eugene and Elspeth.

'There,' she panted, when at last they had gained the hill and emerged from the small group of trees. 'Marks in the grass, where something heavy has been dragged. You can see they go along here, towards the bothy.'

Inspector MacKenzie paused to examine the marks before those who followed trampled the evidence beyond recognition. 'Aye, something heavy has been dragged along here, right enough.'

A shout rang out from Ewan as the small stone building came into sight.

'Pray God all inside are safe,' Poppy murmured.

'Let me go first,' the inspector ordered.

For once, Poppy didn't feel like arguing with him.

'I'm coming too.' Ewan stepped forward.

'Elspeth, it's Inspector MacKenzie,' he called as he turned the handle of the door.

Poppy watched the two men enter the bothy. But she couldn't stand outside doing nothing. 'It's me too, Elspeth,' she called and followed them in.

Elspeth looked up from where she sat on the floor, Eugene's bloodied head now in her lap. Major, his tail wagging, ran towards Poppy. She stroked his head, but looked towards the man on the floor, still half covered by the hessian sacks. Elspeth held her gaze and shook her head.

'He's gone,' her maid said softly, getting to her feet.

Ewan groaned. 'All because of Janet,' he murmured.

Poppy moved quickly towards him. 'Who is Janet?' she asked softly.

'The lassie Eugene fell in love with back home, Haliburton's sister.'

Inspector MacKenzie strode forward, squatted down and checked for a pulse. He shook his head in agreement with Elspeth, rose and glanced at the poker lying nearby.

He moved away from the body to stand beside Poppy, and Ewan took his place, kneeling down beside his friend. He bent his head in respect.

'This is now a murder investigation,' the inspector said. 'I should have taken Ewan's concerns more seriously.'

'Well, as they say,' Poppy murmured, 'ye ken noo.'

He looked at her. 'Aye, I ken noo.'

'I'm certain Algernon Hamilton is behind this murder, and that of Ellen Clark, and many cases of fraud besides,' Poppy said, her voice low. 'I know Algernon wasn't on my list of suspects, but Ellen's mystery man was, so I wasn't completely mistaken. With each persona he changed his appearance, but it is one and the same man. He used the same initials, A.H., just as it says in *The M. McIntyre Detective Agency's Casebook* that people tend to do, when choosing a new name for themselves.'

The ladies of the M. McIntyre Agency would have noticed that clue immediately, Poppy chastised herself – although perhaps not in the *early* days of their detective work.

'The motive for the frauds and Mrs Clark's murder was money,' Inspector MacKenzie said. 'As for Eugene, the killer had already tricked him out of a large sum, and that should have been the end of it as far as Algernon Hamilton was concerned. But when the American came after him, to Scotland, he must have spotted Eugene in Portree and felt he had to silence him. Having murdered one person, what had he to lose by murdering another?'

Poppy knew no answer was expected. Murder attracted the death penalty – and a convicted man could not be hanged twice.

'I need to find and arrest Hamilton,' the inspector added. 'But first, I need to wait with the body for the doctor to arrive. I'll get Ewan to walk back with you.'

'Elspeth and I – and Major – can find our own way back very well, Inspector, thank you.'

'I do believe you can, my lady.' He looked at her. 'And if you see Algernon Hamilton, for goodness' sake keep away from the man.'

'I'm certain the murderer has been identified, Elspeth,' Poppy told her as they made their way back down to the town.

'I heard what you told the inspector,' Elspeth said quietly, 'and I'm sure you are correct.'

'There are just a few matters to be cleared up.'

'And what would those matters be, my lady?'

'One,' Poppy counted the numbers off on her fingers as she strode along, 'what, if anything, had Bertram to do with the spiritualist medium.'

'The medium? Are you talking about Mistress Moodie?'

'Yes, Elspeth, but we'll discuss that later. Two, what was Bertram doing with Jeanie behind the hotel, and three, most importantly, how did he come into possession of Ellen's clutch? For I'm certain it was her missing bag.'

'The fellow needs to be spoken to. I always thought he was

not to be trusted. Could we walk a wee bit slower, your lady-ship?' Elspeth added. 'This stony track is playing havoc with my feet.'

'Sorry.' Poppy slowed her pace. 'One final question. Where is my petticoat?'

'In my pocket. I couldn't let the poor man bleed all over it. Dried blood can be very difficult to get out of lace.'

Elspeth had been a brick this afternoon, Poppy thought, and she must repay her in some way. Suddenly it came to her. 'About that peacock feather headband with crystal beads.'

'Aye, my lady,' Elspeth said warily.

'I've decided I won't order another from Jenners.'

'That is just as well, as I've telephoned them to check on their stock of the item, and it's sold out.'

'Elspeth!'

'My lady?'

Poppy was silent for a moment. Then she said, 'You are probably right, that it is rather over the top.'

'Outrageous in the extreme,' Elspeth agreed with satis-faction.

When they reached the door of the Isle of the Mist Hotel, Elspeth excused herself to have a lie down after all the excitement.

'Could you take Major and put him in my room, Elspeth? I can see Bertram Knox in the hall and I want to clear up those few things.' Poppy pushed open the door. Bertram turned from chatting to Sorcha at the desk.

'Afternoon, your ladyship,' he called, staring in surprise at her and Elspeth's bedraggled state.

Elspeth had folded the sides of her dress together to hide the bloodstain from Eugene's injury, and now she called to the

Labrador. He glanced back at Poppy, then padded up the stairs after her.

Poppy, unkempt as she was, approached Bertram. 'Ah, Mr Knox, could I have a few words, please?'

'You can have as many as you like, my lady.' He grinned. 'What can I do for you?'

Poppy gritted her teeth. 'Perhaps we should go somewhere more private?'

'I dinna mind if I do.'

She led him along the passage to the small sitting room and was thankful that, as usual, it was empty.

Bertram dropped into an armchair by the hearth and raised an eyebrow. 'What is it you want to ken?'

Poppy took the chair opposite. She decided to come straight out with it. 'On Sunday I believe you had a consultation with Mistress Moodie.'

Bertram immediately stiffened. 'Oh, aye?'

'Did you?' Poppy demanded.

'Maybe I did and maybe I didn't,' he said evasively.

She fixed him with her gaze. 'You should know.'

He hesitated before replying, then sighed. 'Aye, I did.'

'I'm not interested in the fact that you consulted a medium on the Sabbath' – *goodness knows, I did,* she thought – 'but I would very much like to know if you mentioned Miss Scott or Mrs Harper to the woman.'

'What would I want to do that for?' he asked.

'You tell me.'

'Well, I didna. Although...' A light came into his eyes and he passed a hand over his mouth. 'Och, I have such a dry mouth.'

'Beer?'

'A pint, if you would, my lady.'

She rose and went into the Palm Court Lounge to order a pint of Scotch Ale from the bar. There was no sign of Algernon, but she spotted Harriet and Jeanie in conversation and resolved to return there as soon as she'd finished speaking to Bertram Knox.

'The waiter will bring your drink shortly,' she told him as she resumed her seat in the small sitting room.

He smiled and said nothing. Poppy tapped her foot as what seemed like minutes ticked by. The door opened, the waiter entered, put down Bertram's beer on the table beside his chair and a glass of water by her, then departed. Bertram took a long draught and wiped the froth from his mouth with the back of his hand.

'That's better. Now, what was I saying, my lady?'

'Your consultation with the medium,' she prompted him. 'You said you didn't mention Miss Scott or Mrs Harper to the medium, but you were about to say something else?'

He nodded. 'It was a strange thing, but as I was going into the room, that posh fellow, Algernon Hamilton, was coming out. I say strange, because he'd told me the whole spiritualist thing was a load of keech. Oops, pardon my exuberance, your ladyship.'

What a busy afternoon Mistress Moodie had enjoyed. Poppy sat forward and moved on to her next question. 'And what were you doing behind this hotel a few days ago with Jeanie Harper?'

'Me?' He grinned. 'She's a braw-looking lass, but no' really my type. It must have been some other fellow with her.'

Another man, and not Bertram? Poppy had no idea how many men were staying at the hotel, but the minister's description had seemed to fit the salesman. What had Reverend Greene said? Poppy tried to remember. The gentleman wore a tweed suit and was about the same height and only a little older than the lady. The female's description matched Jeanie exactly, down to the clothes she wore that day. What had the minister said about the man's build? He hadn't mentioned build at all.

Poppy had just assumed that. How could she have been so *careless?*

Bertram was not slim like Algernon, but a large man – although not as splendidly built as Inspector MacKenzie, of course.

Who else among the men that Poppy knew fitted the Reverend Greene's description? Algernon. And when the minister had been glowering down from his pulpit on Sunday, had he been addressing not just Jeanie, as Poppy had thought, but also Algernon, who was seated next to her?

'One final question, if I may,' Poppy said. 'The crocodile-skin clutch bag you sold recently.'

'Eh?' He slopped the beer he had been drinking.

'It looked more expensive than the sort of thing a salesman in ladies' fashion accessories might usually sell,' Poppy said delicately.

He brushed the spilled beer from the front of his jacket. 'I didna steal the bag, if that's what you're thinking, your ladyship.'

'I'm not suggesting you did,' she said, 'but I would like to know how you came by it.'

'I bought it, all legal and proper.'

'Yes, but from whom?'

'A lady staying here.'

'At this hotel?' she persevered. 'Could you identify her?'

He hesitated. 'There are a lot of ladies staying in the hotel.'

He knew who it was, Poppy thought, but he didn't want to get involved. No matter, the inspector would call both Bertram and the woman who bought the bag from him as witnesses in Algernon's trial.

Perhaps the purpose of the meeting behind the hotel was so that Algernon could pass the bag to Jeanie, who had then sold it to Bertram. A lady selling a handbag would look much less suspicious than a gentleman doing so. No doubt Jeanie would do what Algernon asked.

'Enjoy your beer, Mr Knox,' Poppy said, getting to her feet. 'Oh, by the way, have you ever been to Times Square?'

He winked at her. 'No, I say it because it seems to impress the lassies.'

She left him and made her way to the Palm Court Lounge. Thankfully, Harriet was safely there. Jeanie was with her and they were drinking cocktails before dinner.

'Do join us, Poppy,' Harriet said, her face shining with happiness.

'Are we celebrating something?' Please let it not be an announcement of Harriet and Algernon's engagement, Poppy thought, her heart sinking with sympathy for Harriet.

'Just a satisfactory shopping expedition,' Jeanie said, as Poppy sat down. 'Doesn't Harriet look smart in her new dress and hat?'

'She does, indeed,' Poppy said with a smile at Harriet. The dress was in burgundy wool with a low waist, white buttons down the front and a black bow at the neck. On her head she wore a black cloche with a dainty red flower pinned to the side.

'I was surprised to find such a nice, well-made dress in Inverness,' Harriet admitted shyly. 'But both Jeanie and Elspeth said it suited me, so I bought it.'

'Just wait until Algernon sees it,' Jeanie promised.

Harriet blushed. 'Oh, I don't want him to get the wrong idea,' she faltered.

'What do you mean, the wrong idea?' Jeanie cried. 'My dear, he admires you tremendously!'

Here was the opening she wanted. 'Where is Algernon?' Poppy enquired.

'In his room, dressing for dinner, I imagine,' Jeanie replied. 'He'll join us soon, no doubt.'

'Have you had a pleasant day too, Poppy?' Harriet asked.

'Yes, and no. I met an old friend this morning when I was walking in the hills, but then I came across a body.'

Harriet went white. 'A body? Not another lady?' she whispered.

'No, a man, but a person who'd been murdered, none-theless.'

Jeanie gave Poppy a look of panic. As she met Jeanie's gaze, Poppy thought, *I'm sure I know who you are, Miss Whatever your real name is.*

THIRTY-THREE

Poppy had to endure a good fifteen minutes of inquisition from Jeanie, who incessantly flicked ash from her cigarette into the tray on the table, as well as worried comments from Harriet, all while she wondered if Inspector MacKenzie was back at the police office in the square. She was about to rise when the long-case clock in the hall struck half past six.

'I wonder what is delaying Algernon? He said he would be here by now.' Harriet checked the time on her wristwatch. 'I'll go upstairs and knock on his door.' She got to her feet and left the lounge.

Jeanie drew on her cigarette, tilted her head back and blew smoke out of her mouth. Poppy sipped her cocktail and kept a covert eye on Jeanie. The other woman had turned and was watching the door of the Palm Court Lounge warily. She suspected something, Poppy was certain.

Harriet rushed back into the lounge. 'Poppy! Jeanie!' she cried. 'Algernon's door was open, all the drawers and cupboards are open and bare, his belongings strewn about the room, and *he's not there!*' she wailed.

Jeanie went pale. Now, that was something the woman hadn't expected, Poppy thought.

'What if he's been taken by the person who killed the man today?' Harriet went on, stricken. She sank into a chair. 'He's been murdered, I'm sure of it.'

'You can't know that, Harriet,' Poppy said comfortingly.

'I do, I just do!' She began to weep. 'I'm going to the police.' She rose again. 'There's a murderer on the loose in Portree.'

That was true, Poppy thought, but she was confident that Algernon Hamilton was unlikely to find himself the next victim.

'I'll come with you, Harriet,' Jeanie said, stubbing out her cigarette in the dregs of her cocktail glass on the table. 'Wait here while I get my coat.' She hurried from the room.

'Poor Algernon.' Harriet searched up her sleeve for a handkerchief. 'It's awful that this has happened to such a kind man.'

'Take mine.' Poppy held out her own clean handkerchief. 'Jeanie will be back in a few minutes.' While the two women were across the square at the police office, she would go upstairs and examine Algernon's room for any clues as to where he might have gone.

The lounge was emptying as the guests left to go to the dining room. Some of them, aware of a disturbance, glanced at the distraught Harriet, who had again sunk back in her chair, Poppy's handkerchief to her eyes.

'Is everything all right, dear?' asked an elderly lady, coming over.

'No,' whispered Harriet. 'The man I love has disappeared.'

The elderly lady shot Poppy a glance as if to say, *This is what men do*. Poppy gave a slight nod as if in agreement; she had no wish to spread alarm amongst the guests in Catriona's hotel. The elderly lady nodded back and moved away. It wasn't until the room had emptied of people that Harriet broke the silence between them.

'Where is Jeanie? Why is she taking so long? Algernon could be dead by now!'

Poppy's heart thudded. Harriet was right; Jeanie had been gone for longer than was necessary to collect a coat.

Jeanie... Janet, Haliburton's sister, Poppy thought. How could she have let such an important clue slip her mind just now in the bothy? Jeanie was not Algernon's old acquaintance, but his sister.

'Let me go upstairs to check on Jeanie,' she told Harriet, getting to her feet. She hastened out of the lounge and up the wide staircase to the first-floor landing. What she discovered didn't surprise her. Jeanie's room was empty. The drawers and cupboards were empty; the room had been stripped of its resident's belongings. On one wall hung a Victorian improving text stitched in wool proclaiming: *The hand of the diligent maketh rich.*

This was not the hasty departure of Algernon's, Poppy realised, but one Jeanie had planned for. They had to have been working together. There was no other explanation that made sense. But was Jeanie a victim, forced into crime by the man – her brother – or was she an equal partner?

Poppy turned from the doorway and almost bumped into the chambermaid on the landing.

'Sorry, miss,' the girl said. 'I'm to turn down beds while the guests have their dinner.'

'Is it Katy?' Poppy exclaimed.

The girl looked startled. 'Yes, miss.'

'You were our chambermaid at the Harbour Hotel in Plockton, were you not?' she said. 'You've changed jobs?'

'Yes, madam. I fancied a change and Skye is awfa bonnie.'

'I don't know if you remember me. Lady Persephone Proudfoot.'

'Oh, my lady, yes. I recognise you now.' Katy stared into Jeanie's empty room. 'Has Mrs Harper left?'

'So it would seem,' Poppy said.

'But she wasn't due to leave today.'

'I guessed as much.'

Fear flashed across Katy's face. 'She can't have paid her bill, as Mrs MacLeod would have told me.'

'You won't be held to blame,' Poppy tried to reassure her.

'You don't understand, my lady.' Tears came to the chambermaid's eyes.

'Come now, Katy. I can't believe Mrs MacLeod is such a fierce employer,' Poppy said with a comforting smile, and wishing she had a second handkerchief to give to the girl.

'She's not, not at all. But... but if only I'd gone to the police. I thought I recognised...'

'Recognised who, Katy?' Poppy urged the girl. 'Mrs Harper, Mr Hamilton? This is important. Who did you recognise?'

'It wasn't just a *who*, my lady, it was a *what*,' Katy burst out. 'I thought I recognised the pendant. It's the same sapphire pendant!'

'The sapphire pendant?' Did the girl mean the one Ellen had been wearing when she was murdered and which Harriet now had? Poppy needed Katy to say this, if so.

'I've seen the pendant Miss Scott is wearing – she showed it to me yesterday, saying it was a secret – and I'm sure it's the same one worn by Mrs Clark, the poor lady who was strangled.' Katy gulped. 'And I think Mrs Harper stayed in the Harbour Hotel, although she wore her hair different – and I can't be sure, but I don't think she was calling herself Mrs Harper then.'

If Poppy had any doubts left about the case, they were now removed. She had not seen Ellen's pendant, so this was the confirmation she had been waiting for, that the pendant Harriet had shown her was one and the same. Algernon Hamilton and Jeanie Harper were in league with one another.

'If you go further along the landing and look in Mr Hamilton's room,' she told the chambermaid, 'I'm afraid you will find that he also has absconded.'

Katy's tear-filled eyes grew larger.

'Let Mrs MacLeod know what has happened and tell her I have gone to the police office to report this. Don't speak about it to anyone else, Katy. We don't want to upset the guests.'

The chambermaid nodded, turned and ran down the stairs.

Poppy followed her, grateful that all the other guests were making a great deal of noise chattering in the dining room. She found Harriet waiting anxiously in the lounge, twisting Poppy's handkerchief in her hands.

'Is Jeanie all right?' Harriet asked.

'I'm sorry, Harriet, but she has also gone.'

Harriet frowned, unable to take in this latest piece of information. 'What do you mean – gone?'

'Just that, I'm afraid. And all her belongings have left with her.'

Harriet shook her head, as if to clear it. 'I don't understand. We need to report this to the police.'

'I agree. We'll go now.' Poppy picked up her bag, took Harriet's arm and they crossed the square to the police office, Harriet sobbing and repeatedly saying she didn't understand. There would be time enough later to explain everything to her, Poppy thought, but first she must speak to the inspector.

'Has Inspector MacKenzie returned yet? If so, I would like to see him,' Poppy announced to the red-haired sergeant on duty.

'Here's no' here at present, miss.'

'I'd like to report a missing person,' Harriet said.

'Aye, madam.' The sergeant rifled through a sheaf of papers in a folder on the counter and pulled one out. He took up a pencil. 'Can you give me his name, please?'

'His name is Algernon Hamilton and he's staying at the Isle of the Mist Hotel.'

'And can you give me a description of Mr Hamilton?'

'He's very good-looking,' Harriet offered.

The sergeant looked up. 'That's no' much to be going on.'

'Oh, yes. He's also tall and slim, with dark hair.'

'Would you be knowing his age?'

'In his forties, I think.'

The sergeant frowned. 'That's an awfa general description you're giving me.'

'I know, I'm sorry.' Harriet bit her bottom lip.

'Your name, madam?'

'Harriet Scott, Miss Scott. I'm also staying at the hotel.'

'And what is your relationship to the missing gentleman?' he enquired.

'He's my intended,' she whispered.

The sergeant looked at her. 'Aye, just so.' He made to slide the sheet of paper back into the folder.

Poppy intervened. 'It's a wee bit more complicated than you might think, officer.'

'And you are?'

'A friend of Miss Scott's. Lady Persephone Proudfoot.'

The sergeant straightened and clicked his heels. There was no need for that, Poppy thought, but he did need to take Harriet's report more seriously.

'Mr Hamilton and his sister have both disappeared—' she began.

'His sister?' Harriet interrupted Poppy's account. 'You've got that wrong, Poppy. Jeanie's an old acquaintance of Algernon's, nothing more.'

'I'm sure she's his sister, Harriet,' Poppy said gently.

'She can't be.' Harriet was adamant. 'She hadn't seen him for years until a few days ago, when he arrived at the hotel.'

'When you've made up your mind if she's his friend or his sister,' put in the sergeant, 'you can let me ken. Until then, I'd better take a description of her too.'

'Tall and thin, with dark hair,' Harriet said.

The sergeant sighed. 'So you're telling me it's two missing persons of a similar description, but one male and the other female. Would that be right?'

Harriet nodded soberly, doubt as to their relationship clearly crossing her mind for the first time.

The officer made a few more notes on the sheet of paper and set down his pencil.

'To continue my report, Sergeant,' Poppy went on smoothly, 'the pair have fled the hotel, leaving both their bills unpaid. But more importantly, I have every reason to believe they are wanted in connection with a number of other crimes, namely fraud, both in this country and in the United States, and the murder in Plockton of Ellen Clark...'

Harriet gasped. 'Poppy, you don't know what you're saying!'

'I do, Harriet. You must trust me on this.'

The sergeant was watching them both closely. 'That's quite a tale you're after telling me, my lady.'

'True, nonetheless. Inspector MacKenzie will confirm it.'

'As the inspector is no' here at present, we will have to wait for that. The missing persons will be looked into as soon as we have the time.' He put the report in the folder and, with a decisive hand, closed it.

'Sergeant, there has been a murder on the island, which Inspector MacKenzie is currently dealing with,' she told him. 'I was the one to find Eugene Miller and I think the missing Algernon Hamilton is the killer.'

'No, Poppy!' Harriet was distraught. 'It can't possibly be him!'

The sergeant eyed them both impatiently. 'Why don't you two lassies go back to your hotel and leave it to the police to find the murderer?'

'*Mo chreach 'sa thàinig!*' Poppy exclaimed in frustration,

turning to go. As she did so, her eye caught a poster pinned to the wall.

INVERNESS-SHIRE CONSTABULARY
Wanted for questioning in connection with the murder of Mrs Ellen Clark in Plockton:
ALAN HENDERSON
Age mid-forties, above-average height, slim frame, hair and whiskers going grey, grey eyes, gentlemanly appearance and address.

She paused and looked at the sketch of the man on the poster. There had been a similar wanted poster at the police house in Plockton. What exactly had it said? With a sinking heart, she remembered it was a man with a Scottish accent wanted for fraud in the USA. The sketch on the Plockton poster had shown a clean-shaven man with spectacles, as Ewan had described.

'That's *him*!' she pointed at the poster.

'That's no' Algernon Hamilton,' the sergeant said sternly. 'If you read it properly, it plainly says that the villain's name is Alan Henderson.'

'But that is what I am trying to tell you! They're one and the same fellow!'

The sergeant stared at her, his brow furrowed as he folded his arms across his chest. What could she do to persuade the dolt? Then, remembering she had her sketch of Algernon, she marched up to the poster and snatched it off the wall.

'Hey!' The sergeant's face turned as red as his hair. 'You canna do that. That's police property you are damaging.'

Harriet looked aghast. 'Come on, Poppy, let's go back to the hotel,' she begged.

Poppy put the poster on the counter in front of the sergeant. Then she quickly opened her bag, pulled out her sketchbook and turned to the page where she had drawn Algernon.

'There!' She slammed the open book on the counter, next to the poster. 'What do you say now, Sergeant? If you ignore the hair colour and spectacles, are they not the same person?'

He peered at the two sketches. 'One's a dog.'

Poppy looked. The draught caused by her action had wafted the page over to the portrait of Major.

'Sorry.' She turned to her sketch of Algernon and set it side by side with the poster.

The sergeant peered again. 'Aye, I admit there's a certain similarity...'

'Indeed there is! And I have another drawing to show you.' She tore the picture of Algernon from the pad and turned the pages until she came to the one of Jeanie. She placed this portrait between those of the two men. 'Now you can see the family resemblance.'

The sergeant started. 'You have persuaded me, my lady.' He turned to the door behind him and called, 'Constable! Here this minute!'

A young officer hastened through. 'Aye, sir?'

'Take Miss Scott here back to the Isle of the Mist Hotel and ensure that she's looked after. She's had a wee bit of a shock.'

Harriet did indeed look as if she might faint. 'Oh, Poppy,' she whispered.

Poppy gave her hand a squeeze. 'I'm so sorry, my dear.'

Harriet let herself be led out by the young constable, and the sergeant turned to Poppy. 'I'm Sergeant Girvan. No doot ye'd best see Inspector MacKenzie, my lady. '

'You need to stop the ferry, to prevent Henderson and his sister escaping.' Poppy almost stamped her foot in frustration.

'Stop the ferry?' the sergeant said, shocked. 'I canna be doing that without the say-so of the inspector. Now then, we'll be after asking Mrs MacLeod of the hotel across the way if we can borrow her motor car, as we havena yet got one of our own, to see if we can find him. Come with me.'

The door to the police office was flung open and Ewan hurried in.

'Ewan!' Poppy cried. 'I am so pleased to see you. Where is the inspector?'

'The doctor has arrived,' Ewan told her, 'and James has gone to interview folk at the cottages on the estate, to see if anyone saw or heard anything.'

'A policeman has taken a rather distressed friend of mine, Miss Harriet Scott, back to the hotel across the square. Would you mind going there and seeing that she is all right, Ewan?'

'Of course I will.'

'Thank you.' Poppy turned to the sergeant. 'We'll take my car,' she said, as she picked up the drawing of Alan Henderson and slipped it on top of her sketch of Algernon. She pushed her book back into her bag. 'Come with me.'

Ten minutes later, Poppy and the sergeant had scrambled into the Bentley and, with Poppy at the wheel, were speeding out of the town.

'This motor car can certainly move,' muttered Sergeant Girvan.

The speedometer needle wavered on forty.

'No' like the doctor's motor car,' the sergeant added. 'A Rolls-Royce Silver Ghost.'

'That is built for comfort and elegance,' she told him, 'not speed. Kindly direct me to the Knappach Estate. I know the route only cross-country, on foot.'

They had soon fled by the cottages along the road and were into open country. Poppy put her foot down.

'You're breaking the law, my lady,' the sergeant suddenly thought to say. 'You're now doing fifty!'

'Don't worry,' she told him, pressing the accelerator more firmly, 'this model is capable of doing up to seventy-five miles per hour.'

He held onto his cap. 'That wasna what I meant. The speed limit under the Motor Car Act 1903 is twenty miles per hour.'

'But it's widely ignored, Sergeant,' she pointed out. 'And this is an emergency.'

They came to a crossroads and she slowed down.

'Go right here,' he told her.

She turned the wheel and they roared off in that direction.

Now there was only an occasional cottage or farm to be seen, with fields of grazing sheep stretching on either side, with the ever-present hills on the horizon. All was bathed in the glorious golden light of that time of day.

Before long, they were approaching a fork in the road.

'Where now?' she asked him.

The sergeant tore his gaze from the speedometer. 'Turn right again.'

As they passed a cottage on their right, set well back from the road, Sergeant Girvan yelled, 'Stop!'

Poppy pressed hard on the brake. The car shrieked and came to a shuddering halt.

THIRTY-FOUR

Poppy put the Bentley into reverse, backed up to the cottage and collected Inspector MacKenzie, whose unmistakably large form had been spotted through the cottage window.

She drove the inspector and the sergeant back to Portree. Once in Somerled Square, Sergeant Girvan saluted the inspector and disappeared inside the police office.

Poppy turned to the inspector. 'How jolly frustrating that no one on the Knappach Estate saw anything. Never mind, we will team up to find the missing pair.'

The inspector raised an eyebrow, but didn't object.

'We'll start with the bus,' Poppy said. 'Without a car, that's the only way of leaving Portree fast.'

Well, relatively fast, she thought.

The shops around the edge of the square had closed for the evening and apart from the two motor buses in the square itself, it was quiet. A young man stepped into one of the vehicles, and from the other bus a few passengers were climbing down.

The inspector strode over to the first of the buses, its driver ensconced behind the wheel, door open. The man had just turned over the engine and the headlights were illuminating a patch of the darkened square, when Inspector MacKenzie put his foot on the bottom step.

'*Feasgar math,*' he called up to the driver.

'*Feasgar math,*' Poppy called, not to be left out.

The driver returned the evening greeting.

The inspector spoke to the man in Gaelic, and the driver replied in the same tongue, shaking his head.

'*Tapadh leat,*' called Poppy. Her Gaelic was coming along nicely, she felt.

'*Tapadh leibh,*' the inspector said to the driver, stepping back down.

'Why did your thank you sound different to mine?' she asked, curious.

'It should have been *tapadh leibh*, my lady, as you dinna ken the fellow,' he said gently.

How annoying to have made that mistake. 'At the end of our last case, you promised me some lessons in the Gaelic,' she reminded him.

'I did, didn't I?' He smiled. 'I have no' forgotten.'

Thrilled to have an excuse to see him again, Poppy tore her gaze away from the dimple in his left cheek. 'I can guess what the driver said, but tell me anyway.'

'When I asked if he would be after seeing a man and a woman, both tall and with dark hair, taking a bus this evening, he replied that he would not.'

She reconstructed the sentence in her head: the driver had not seen the pair. 'That bus was going north. Let's try the driver over there; he has come from the south of the island.' She gestured to the other bus. The driver was operating the handle that turned the sign at the front of the vehicle, changing it from *Portree* to *Kyleakin*.

As Poppy hastened across, the man had jumped down onto the road and was turning away. 'Excuse me, driver,' she called.

The man turned back. 'Aye, lass?'

'We're looking for a tall, dark-haired, smartly-dressed couple in their thirties or forties. Have you seen them?'

'I've just returned from taking folk to the ferry and there was no couple of that description on this bus.'

Poppy could have hit her forehead with the palm of her head. What was she thinking? There might have been time for Algernon to travel to Kyleakin and for the bus driver to return, but certainly not for Jeanie.

'This afternoon I had a male passenger who might have been the one you're looking for,' the driver was saying, 'but he wasna with a lass.'

'Are there any more buses going to Kyleakin this evening?'

'I'm the last one, and I'm awa' home now.'

Poppy thanked him and stepped back, meeting a large, solid body. A pair of strong arms steadied her, and she felt her face flame.

'Careful now,' came the inspector's soft lilt.

The driver laughed and walked off, whistling "My Luve's Like a Red, Red Rose".

'Is there something you are needing to tell me?' Inspector MacKenzie said grimly.

'I forgot to mention that Algernon fled the hotel a while before Jeanie. She bolted only a short while ago.'

'Which means that he is either waiting for the ferry or already on the mainland.'

Poppy nodded. 'And that she is still on the island.'

The inspector took Poppy's arm and led her across the square.

'Am I under arrest?' she asked.

'A night in the cells here might do you some good,' he said wryly.

'I doubt it,' she said and removed her arm from the inspector's.

'*Mo chreach 'sa thàinig!*' he said in exasperation.

'So what are we going to do now? Once Algernon is on the mainland, he'll be able to disappear easily.'

'No' so easily,' Inspector MacKenzie told her. 'No' if we circulate both sketches of him. But I'll get the sergeant to telephone Kyleakin and stop the ferry. Your drawing is coming on, by the way, my lady.'

In the police office, Sergeant Girvan was back at the counter.

'Sergeant,' the inspector ordered, 'please telephone the police office at Kyleakin—'

'There's no police office at Kyleakin, sir. The nearest is Broadford.'

Inspector MacKenzie frowned. 'That would no' be quick enough.'

'Do you have any friends or relatives in Kyleakin?' Poppy asked the sergeant.

'Aye, my lady.' He smiled. 'My brother Lachy and his wife and their five bairns bide there. He's a chippie.'

Poppy frowned. 'Chippie?'

'A joiner, your ladyship.'

'That's verra interesting, Sergeant,' the inspector said impatiently, 'and it's a grand thing to be having so many children, but can you contact him? Does he have a telephone?'

'Bless you, no, sir.'

'What about the boat?' Poppy asked. 'Do they have an office in Kyleakin?'

'Oh, aye, your ladyship.' The sergeant picked up the telephone on the counter and waited for the operator to respond. 'Is that yourself, Dougie? ... Aye, I'm grand, thanks. And yourself? ... Grand, grand.'

'Sergeant!' warned the inspector.

'Now listen, Dougie, this is urgent, ye'll understand. I need to speak to the ferry office, to stop two passengers getting on the ferry... suspects, aye... No, I dinna want anyone to make a citizen's arrest – just stop the boat...' The sergeant looked up at Inspector MacKenzie, and shook his head. He returned to addressing the unseen Dougie. ''Tis a great pity. *Mar sin leat.*' He replaced the receiver.

The inspector raised an eyebrow. 'Well?'

'Dougie, he's the telephone operator, says the ferry is back, having already deposited its passengers at Kyle of Lochalsh. They're finished for the day.'

'Wireless telegraphy!' Poppy suddenly exclaimed. 'Crippen was caught that way on a boat when he was escaping from England after murdering his wife.'

'That was on a ship crossing the Atlantic, my lady,' the inspector pointed out. 'The ferry from Skye is no' the same thing.'

'No,' she admitted, crestfallen.

'And the ferry has already crossed.'

'Yes.' She had been too enthusiastic in making the suggestion.

'Sergeant,' the inspector went on, 'get the mainland police on the telephone. I need to instruct them to continue the investigation, while I fulfil my obligation to play at the Games.'

'Aye, sir.' The sergeant picked up the receiver again.

Inspector MacKenzie drew Poppy towards the door. 'Now, my lady, can I trust you to return to the hotel and not to start a search of your own?'

'It would be difficult for me to search in the dark...'

'Just so. But I will instigate a police search tonight. And you will not search tomorrow?' he said, his voice stern.

'Absolutely, Inspector.' She smiled up at him. 'I'll be at the Gathering. I have no intention of missing your playing the pipes.'

. . .

The following morning dawned bright and fair. A bonnie day for the Skye Highland Games, Poppy thought, as she left the hotel.

Buses filled the square, bringing the country people from their villages and farms. With what seemed like the entire population of Portree and beyond, she marched towards The Lump. Major on his leash trotted beside her, his tail swinging jauntily from side to side.

There was a holiday feeling in the air, and the smell of whisky wafted about the stream of people. The crowd, with Poppy among them, turned into Bank Street. She had dressed in a new short-sleeved lemon dress with black collar and matching band around the hem, and a new cloche, also in lemon with a black band.

Farmers and labourers strode along, tackety boots on their feet and the straps of nicky-tams tied around their trouser legs below the knees. Old women padded along, their equally old husbands hobbling beside them in thick suits and stiff collars. Young men and women laughed as they walked arm in arm, and small children dashed around in high spirits.

To Poppy's pleasure, Harriet had blushingly told Poppy at breakfast that she and Ewan would be along later. Poppy tried to spot Jeanie, but it was impossible in the throng. And now she'd thought about it, she didn't really expect to see the woman there. Jeanie might be a thief and a fraudster, but would she be foolish enough to risk picking pockets in the circumstances?

Above the bobbing heads in front of her making their way to the games ground, she caught a glimpse of the tree-lined path that led to The Lump. She smiled at the distant sound of inflating bagpipes above the hum of voices, and her pulse gave a little skip, picturing Inspector MacKenzie in his Prince Charlie jacket cut to the waist, and his swaying kilt.

And before she knew it, she and Major were through the entrance. All around the edge of the amphitheatre were brightly decorated stalls. Poppy saw 'Guess the Number of Currants in the Cake' displayed on one table and 'Guess the Weight of the Ham' on another. A tray of toffee apples for sale glistened at yet another stall, with children pushing each other in an attempt to get to the front of the queue.

Major's nose twitched with the excitement of so many enticing smells and Poppy took a tighter hold on his leash. A Labrador, she knew from past experience, would eat whatever food he could wrap his jaws around. Any resulting stomach ache would be well worth the risk, in Major's opinion.

In the games field, nervous little girls, with one or two wee boys, were limbering up around the edge of a wooden stage for the Highland dancing competition, their anxious mothers flapping by their sides. The less artistically inclined bairns were happily practising for their wheelbarrow races and pillow fights, and already feathers flew in the warm, noisy air.

While laughing at their antics, Poppy noticed people were beginning to take seats in the grassy amphitheatre, ready for when the heavy events began at midday. Others were heading towards the lunch tent and feeling a little hungry herself, she followed.

'Lunch tickets!' called a boy seated behind a small table at the entrance to the large tent. Poppy paid and entered. Inside the dim place was a seething mass of people, some sitting and eating, others trying to push their way out, yet others struggling to find seats at the long trestle tables.

Keeping Major close to her, Poppy forced her way through the chattering crowd. Waitresses moved between the tables, carrying laden plates and brimming glasses. Her heart jumped in her chest at the sight of a woman who looked awfully like Jeanie Harper, but then she disappeared back into the crowd. It wasn't likely to be Jeanie.

A huge roar from outside the tent heralded the start of the Games. Keeping her lunch ticket to use later when it would be less busy, Poppy managed to slip through the mass of bodies and out into the fresh air again. She squeezed into a place in the amphitheatre and instructed Major to lie down.

A muscled fellow in a white singlet and kilt strutted into the centre of the arena, to a roar of cheers and good-natured boos. He stuck his fists on his hips and turned in a complete circle to encompass all the audience, before he made a mock bow. Laughter rang out. He stood at the line marked on the ground, his feet slightly apart, ready to perform the standing long jump, to test the quick bursts of strength which had been necessary all those centuries ago. The crowd hushed, waiting.

He launched his body, swinging his arms and bending his knees to propel himself as far forward as possible, and landed on both feet. A burst of applause went round the audience.

After the long jump came the high jump. By the time the events had moved on to throwing the heavy hammer, Poppy had decided, fascinating as the sixteen-pound light hammer and the twenty-two-pound heavy stone undoubtedly were, she wanted a cup of tea and a slice of the veal and ham pie she'd noticed earlier.

She and Major made their way back into the lunch tent. It was less busy than before and she was able to squeeze into a space on a bench at one of the long tables. Major immediately crept under the table, where Poppy was sure the grass was littered with bits of food being enjoyed by the boisterous diners. They included her in their conversation, chatting about the events and the participants as they consumed their lunch, and she had a pleasant time.

She had finished her simple meal when she spotted Katy, the chambermaid from the hotel, looking anxiously around her. Poppy gave her a friendly wave; the girl's face cleared and she crossed to the long table.

'You can have my seat, Katy,' she told her with a smile, standing and stepping over the bench. 'I'm just leaving.'

'Thank you, my lady,' Katy said, her brow creased again. 'I heard you were here and I was hoping to find you.'

'Is something the matter? Is there a problem at the hotel?' Poppy asked quickly.

'No, it's not that. I thought I saw Mrs Harper coming out of the lunch tent and going towards the Highland dancing.'

Poppy's pulse jumped. So she hadn't been mistaken when she thought she'd seen Jeanie earlier. 'Thank you, Katy. I'll let the inspector know. Enjoy your lunch.' She called to Major, who crept out reluctantly from under the table, and pressed through the people milling about in the tent to the exit.

Outside, the crowd around the amphitheatre had thickened. There were men in plus fours, women in smart tweeds, girls in berets and brogues. Cigarette tips littered the grass. Poppy caught sight of Harriet, arm in arm with Ewan, and waved at them. They beamed and waved back, but there was no sign of Jeanie Harper.

She should tell Inspector MacKenzie that both she and Katy thought they'd spotted Jeanie in the crowd, but dash it all, where was he? Poppy made her way through the throng, looking for a sight of any pipers, Major keeping close to her heel.

A small group of Highland dancers were performing on the stage in the games field, including a wee toot of a boy, who couldn't have been more than four, in a tam o'shanter and kilt.

A bellow of enthusiasm rose from hundreds of spectators, as the master of ceremonies announced through his megaphone that the hill race was about to start.

'Up to Fingal's Seat and back!' the man shouted, his words washing over Poppy as she scanned the crowd for Jeanie. 'By any route as ye care to devise,' he continued, pointing to a flag just visible on the hill on the far side of the bay.

A pistol fired and Poppy froze. A rush of wild figures, bare hairy legs and tennis shoes, pounded the corner of the games field as the men set off. The crowd let out a joyous roar and Poppy breathed again.

She took a moment to pull herself together. And suddenly she saw him, Inspector MacKenzie, standing proud in the MacKenzie Ancient tartan in green and blue, and preparing to play his solo piece! She watched as he lifted the pipes and tucked the bag under his arm. He threw the drones over his shoulder, put the blowpipe to his lips and settled his grip on the chanter. He took a deep breath. The drones started up, and then the first note came, clear and steady.

Poppy recognised the ancient Scottish folk tune: "Highland Laddie". The crowd in the amphitheatre fell silent, listening to the march for all Highland regiments confidently announcing their arrival. The inspector set off around the arena, playing steadily as he marched. She waited for him to draw alongside where she stood and then marched behind, Major doing his best to keep in step. She was dimly aware of the crowd's good-natured laughter. *Oh yes!* she thought, admiring the way the inspector's kilt swung in an authoritative manner as he strode.

Suddenly Major turned his head in the direction of the trophy tent they were passing and gave a low growl.

Poppy came to a halt and looked towards the small tent. Through the opening, she caught a glimpse of Algernon holding open a sack and Jeanie in the act of dropping in a silver trophy.

THIRTY-FIVE

'It's Algernon and Jeanie!' Poppy yelled. Inspector MacKenzie stumbled at his piping, and the criminal pair paused at the sound.

Poppy sprinted towards the tent, Major at her heels.

'Run!' cried Algernon, dropping the sack as he pushed past Poppy.

Poppy made a grab for Jeanie, but she dodged her and ran after her brother.

'Inspector!' Poppy shrieked.

Inspector MacKenzie had seen the pair and was running through the crowds, tearing off his bagpipes as he went and dropping them to the grass. Poppy was briefly aware of the gaping faces of the crowd, before she saw Algernon and Jeanie sprinting towards the exit. Algernon was making good progress, but the inspector was closing in. The crowd roared with enjoyment at this new spectacle.

Poppy's ancient clan blood was up. She let out the war cry, '*Proudfoot and strong, we stand tall!*' and launched her five feet two inches after the fleeing Jeanie. Giving a loud bark of his own, Major bounded after Poppy, quickly overtaking her and getting in front of the woman she was chasing. The crowd cheered them on.

As she dodged out of the Labrador's way, Jeanie's foot slipped on the grass, but she recovered herself and ran on. Major darted forward to cut her off as Poppy took a flying leap, tackled Jeanie to the ground and sat on her back. Major wheeled round to the two women and pounced on Jeanie's kicking legs. He lay his full weight on them, a satisfied look on his face.

'Well done, Major Lewis,' Poppy said with a grin, before turning to see how Inspector MacKenzie and Algernon were getting on.

All eyes were now focused on the inspector pounding across the grass. He overtook Algernon before he reached the exit and seized hold of him. Algernon broke away and turned again towards the way out. The inspector whipped his skean-dhu from the top of his hose and threw it.

The crowd gasped as it shot between the other man's legs and the shocked Algernon came to an abrupt halt. The inspector snatched up his knife from where it had embedded itself in the grass, pushed it back inside his sock and took hold of the ashen-faced Algernon. He removed a pair of handcuffs from his sporran and snapped them on Algernon. The crowd broke into laughter. There was whistling and applause as the inspector pulled his prisoner to his feet and led him back to where Poppy and Major waited, seated on Jeanie.

Poppy didn't have a specific command for her dog to get him off people – such an occasion hadn't risen before – so she got to her feet and said, 'Arise, Major Lewis.' And he did.

Poppy allowed Jeanie to climb to her feet, but she took a firm grip on the other woman's arm.

'Damn you both,' said Algernon, his voice breathless, looking between Poppy and the inspector.

'Whatever your real names may be,' the inspector said, 'you're both under arrest for fraud, murder, and now theft.'

Jeanie scowled at her brother. 'I told you that second murder was a mistake.'

Finally the crowd quietened down and the master of ceremonies came over to join Poppy, the inspector and their charges.

'What's going on?' he asked, his ruddy face puzzled.

An idea came to Poppy. In *The M. McIntyre Detective Agency's Casebook*, the two lady private detectives ended each case with a denouement. She would do the same!

'May I borrow your megaphone?' she asked the master of ceremonies. 'And I will explain all.'

Perplexed, he handed it to her.

'*Feasgar math*,' she began, speaking through the trumpet. She saw Harriet in the crowd, and a little further away Elspeth, and she smiled at them both. 'Good afternoon, ladies and gentlemen. My name is Lady Persephone Proudfoot and I have the honour of drawing together for you the strands of a vile series of events. In capturing this couple, I have been assisted by Inspector MacKenzie.' Poppy paused to indicate the inspector by her side. Not daring to look at his face, she hurried on. 'And by my dog, Major.' The crowd cheered and Major sat straighter, a delighted look on his face.

'This man and woman here are thieves and worse,' she continued through the megaphone. 'His real name is...' She paused. What was his real name? She held out the instrument to him.

'Athelstan Haig,' he muttered.

'Speak up!' Poppy ordered.

'Athelstan Haig,' he said reluctantly.

'Oh, dear,' Poppy said, 'I am so sorry.' That was rather a grim name. 'And this is his sister...' she went on, proffering the megaphone to Jeanie or Janet.

'Jessie Haig. But I am innocent of all charges!'

The ridiculous woman had effectively just confessed to being art and part in the two murders, thought Poppy.

At that moment a photographer pushed his way through the crowd towards them. 'Smile for the camera, miss!' the man called.

Jessie turned and gave a defiant smile. 'Send me a copy!' she called back.

'Care of Duke Street Prison, Glasgow,' Poppy added.

She addressed the crowd again. 'Athelstan and Jessie Haig' – the woman had got off lightly when her parents came to name her, Poppy reflected – 'work together: she finds a female victim, strikes up a friendship and learns about them; so that when he arrives a few days later, it is easy to strike up a rapport, appearing to be the perfect mate for the lady from the information gained by Jessie. He then charms money from the unsuspecting lady, enabling him and his sister to live comfortably for a while.'

'Shame on you!' cried a woman in the crowd, and there were murmurs of agreement.

'It was all going well,' Poppy continued, averting her eyes from Harriet, 'with his latest victim being persuaded to invest in a non-existent company, until it transpired that a lonely man in America had been tricked by Jessie's charms and the pair left him virtually destitute. The unfortunate gentleman came to Skye to track them down. For his pains, he was brutally murdered.'

'It's a lie!' Athelstan shouted.

Poppy took no notice of him. 'Alas, the siblings had murdered before. In a place not so far from here. In Plockton, Athelstan befriended a lonely widow and proposed marriage' – Poppy knew this last was a guess, but she thought a reasoned one, remembering the mention of the strange glitter in Ellen's eyes and her quietness after the boat trip – 'and, being a devout Christian, Mrs Clark went to the open-air kirk to pray for guidance. Athelstan and Jessie had spent all the money they'd earlier obtained from the American, Eugene Miller, and were again struggling financially.

'When this man' – Poppy pointed at Athelstan to make sure there was no mistake – 'discovered Mrs Clark had no money, he decided to take the one valuable item she owned and always wore: a sapphire pendant. This was a treasured gift from a deceased aunt. In his greed, he followed her and strangled her with her own scarf.' Perhaps he had simply panicked when Ellen resisted. Or perhaps, after all his confidence tricks, Athelstan had started to feel invincible, and emboldened enough to take a step further and kill a victim.

'He still had the pendant with him,' Poppy continued, 'when he decided it was the perfect wooing gift for his latest victim. No doubt he intended to take the jewellery back from her when he had achieved his aim. But then Mr Miller appeared on the scene. And Athelstan killed a second time.' That was rather a good summing up for a jury in the circumstances, Poppy thought.

A man in the crowd lobbed a piece of veal and ham pie at Athelstan. Major swooped down and swallowed it in one gulp.

Athelstan gestured for the megaphone and spoke into it. 'First of all, the money was just resting in my account.'

'Aye, that'll be right!' yelled a man.

'As to the American, I had no choice,' Athelstan went on sullenly. 'I saw him enter the Portree Inn and I knew it was only a matter of time before he spotted Jessie and me, and gave the game away. What else could I do?'

'You could have no' killed him, that's what you could have done,' shouted another man in the crowd. The place erupted with jeers, and one enthusiastic child standing at the front hurled her toffee apple at him. It hit Athelstan on the nose before falling to the ground by his feet. Poppy sent Major a look that said *don't even think about it.* Athelstan glared at the wee girl and she burst into tears.

'I think that's enough, my lady. We need to take the pair away,' the inspector said, 'before it turns nasty.'

'Thank you for your attention this afternoon, ladies and gentlemen.' Poppy beamed at the spectators. 'You will be able to read more about this pair of criminals in the newspapers after the trial.' She lowered the megaphone in time to see Jeanie lunge towards her. Poppy stepped swiftly back.

'*Awa' and boil yer heid!*' Jessie screamed.

The siblings were led away by Sergeant Girvan and the constable, both dressed in singlets and kilts in anticipation of their participation in the tug of war. Elspeth nodded at Poppy, before melting into the crowd as it dispersed to watch the various delayed events, leaving behind four faces now familiar to Poppy.

'I can't believe what has happened,' Harriet said, holding on to Ewan's arm and coming forward.

Isabella and Dorothy were also there. 'You did an awfully good job,' Isabella said, with a grin at Poppy.

'Thank you. While you're here, Isabella, can I ask you a question?'

'Go ahead.'

'I've been told that you were overheard shouting at Ellen Clark on the afternoon before she was murdered. It's been puzzling me. What was the argument about?'

Isabella let out a hoot of laughter. 'We weren't arguing, my dear. I was trying out my talk for the button exhibition. I wanted an impartial listener, and so naturally I had to raise my voice.'

'You never thought Bella here had murdered poor Ellen?'

Dorothy shrieked. 'That's too ridiculous. She's a pussy cat.' She smiled fondly at her friend.

Poppy couldn't imagine anyone less like a pussy cat, although they both did have sharp claws.

'You noticed that Bella's been a wee bit short-tempered lately?' Dorothy added.

Poppy gave a very small, non-committal nod.

'That's because Dotty wrote to old Mrs Stewart in Plockton before I did and bagged a jolly decent button,' Isabella admitted. 'It was boorish of me. But we've made up now, haven't we, Dotty?' She returned her friend's smile.

'That is good to hear,' Poppy said.

Isabella took hold of Dorothy's arm and led her away. Ewan nodded at Poppy and the inspector and turned to Harriet with a warm smile. 'Shall we return to the Games, Miss Scott?'

Harriet blushed. 'Please call me Harriet.'

Poppy and Inspector MacKenzie watched as Ewan led his companion back to the activities.

'What do you think might be going on there?' the inspector asked, nodding in the direction of the couple.

'Something good, I hope. Harriet's had precious little happiness in her life, as far as I can tell.'

'Shall we find a place away from all this and I'll play you a lament on the pipes?' the inspector suggested.

Poppy looked up at him. 'That sounds wonderful. I'm awfully sorry you weren't able to finish your moment in the sunlight.'

'Och, I'm thinking after that performance, they'll be asking me back next year.'

Poppy laughed for what felt like the first time in days. They wandered over to where the inspector's bagpipes lay and he picked them up. They looked for a quiet spot away from the spectators, and found a seat overlooking the bay. Major settled himself at their feet. For a while they watched in silence the boats bobbing in the water below. The sun beat down and Poppy felt happy.

'I haven't felt quite as alive as this in years,' she admitted softly. *Not even when I was with Stuart*, she thought.

'You did verra well there just now, my lady,' the inspector told her, a glint of amusement in his eyes. 'Though perhaps a little theatrical in your delivery.'

'Proudfoot by name, Proudfoot by nature,' she found herself saying.

'Someone with a strutting gait?' he enquired, the smile still there, the sun exaggerating his dimple.

'And why not?' She smiled back. 'The first known bearer of the name was a sheriff, a person who might be justified in walking with a proud step.'

Inspector MacKenzie laughed, before turning his attention back to the events of the last few days. 'I think we have a good case for court.'

Poppy listed the evidence. 'Ellen's pendant and handbag, the business cards, and witnesses who can identify Athelstan, if not Jessie.'

'No' to mention the confessions in front of an entire audience!'

Poppy smiled. How clever the woman had been until then, she realised. The only witness to her part in any of the crimes might well have been Eugene Miller, and he was dead. The planchette, too, must have been manipulated by Jessie. She, Poppy, had been so focused on the writing that she foolishly hadn't paid sufficient attention to the other woman's control of the pencil.

'The spiritualist medium,' Poppy went on, adding to the list of evidence, 'and the two surviving women who were tricked out of their savings.'

Now she thought about it, Poppy realised that Athelstan, then known as Algernon, hadn't actually denied being to Broadford, where Mairi MacKay had lived. He'd said only that he had passed through it on the way to Portree. She must get better at reading between the lines.

'Aye.' The inspector gave a small sigh. 'There are two things we havena cleared up. That's what prompted the siblings to run from the hotel yesterday, and their journey after that.'

'I think I can answer the first one, Inspector,' Poppy confessed. 'Before Elspeth and I went looking for Eugene in the hills, I asked her to tell Harriet and Jeanie – Jessie – to stay in the hotel where they'd be safe. That must have alerted Jessie, even if she didn't then know to what exactly. She must have assumed that what I knew, the police would know, and so she got word to her brother.'

'Which of the two are you thinking was the boss of their operation?'

Poppy shook her head. 'I don't know. With Jessie's brittle laugh, she'd struck me as a woman on edge. As it turned out, she had her bags packed, ready for flight. Unlike the supremely confident Algernon, who ended up packing in a hurry.'

'I've given some thought to the second matter,' the inspector remarked. 'He must have no' stayed on the bus all the way to the ferry, but got off earlier and at some stage, perhaps this forenoon, made his way back. No doubt feeling bad about leaving his sister behind.'

'Honour among thieves, Inspector?'

'Something like that.' He hesitated, before speaking again. 'My lady, you put yourself in danger once again.'

'I couldn't simply stand by and leave it all to you.'

'*When shall we three meet again? In thunder, lightning, or in rain?*' he murmured.

She finished the quote from *Macbeth*. '*When the hurly-burly's done. When the battle's lost and won.*' Hopefully long before that, she added silently.

The inspector rose to his feet, and once again she was struck by how tall he was. He held out his hand. She placed her hand in his warm, strong one, and he drew her up.

'And so, my lady, will we work on another case together, I wonder?' he asked, looking down at her.

'Wonder no longer, Inspector,' she replied with an impish smile. 'I have no doubt that we will.'

He raised an eyebrow. 'You won't be able to stay out of trouble?'

'I wouldn't have thought so,' she said proudly.

'Is that the famous female intuition?' The inspector sounded amused.

'If you'd like to think of it that way,' she teased. Poppy suddenly felt very sober, and she couldn't bear to see him go. 'You have no time to play something for me?' she asked softly.

'Another time, my lady. That's a promise.' He seemed to realise he still held her hand and he took a step closer.

She thought she must burst with pleasure at the closeness of his tall, splendid body.

'Will I see you at the Gathering Hall dance tonight?' he asked.

'Better than that,' she managed to reply in a careless voice, 'you may take me to the dance.'

Poppy could almost hear the fiddle and the accordion playing, see the candlelight flickering as the dancers spun and clapped and laughed, feel the beat of the music echoing in her heart; she imagined her fingers in the inspector's tousled black curls, the tender look in his eyes, the taste of his warm lips on hers.

She would wear the pale pink backless evening dress with crystals around its dropped waist that cascaded down the skirt. That should do the job nicely.

He bowed, took her hand and kissed it. She laughed at his deliberate formality, but she felt a warm glow inside.

'There's a hint of red in your hair when the sun shines,' he said in wonder, gazing at her.

The warm glow spread.

'I will pick you up from your hotel at half past eight, my lady.' He smiled.

'Absolutely, Inspector!'

A LETTER FROM LYDIA

Dear reader,

I want to say a huge thank you for choosing to read *Murder on a Scottish Island*. If you did enjoy it, and want to keep up to date with all my latest releases, just sign up at the following link. Your email address will never be shared and you can unsubscribe at any time.

www.bookouture.com/lydia-travers

I'd be really grateful if you would leave a review on Amazon and Goodreads. I love to hear from readers, so please keep in touch through Facebook or Instagram.

Thank you!

Love,

Lydia x

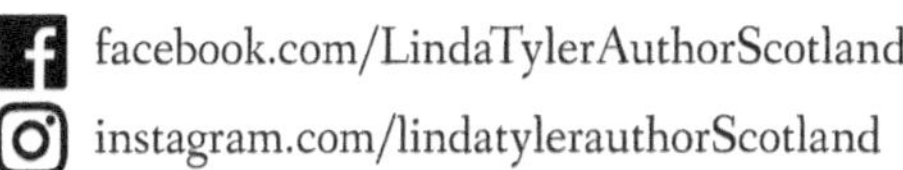

facebook.com/LindaTylerAuthorScotland

instagram.com/lindatylerauthorScotland

ACKNOWLEDGEMENTS

Thanks as always to two particular friends: Joan Cameron for her plotline wizardry and support, and Julie Perkins for her eagle eye and so much more.

Thanks also to my friends Sheila Gray, Jon Tyler, Beth Keshishian, Rachel Stewart, Wilma Nicolson, Margaret Owen, Vicki Singleton, Trina Iley, Ella Egan, Deb Goodman and Lynda Leslie, who've all helped in some way with the writing of this book.

Special thanks to the Plockton Library, and to the Skye and Lochalsh Archive Centre in Portree on the Isle of Skye.

A vote of thanks to the team at Bookouture.

Last but not least, thank you to my readers!

Influences on my writing include the work of comic geniuses P.G. Wodehouse and Compton Mackenzie (no relation, as far as I am aware, to Inspector MacKenzie).

A liberty has been taken with the train times (although not the length of the journeys), the telephone system in Plockton and on Skye (Button A and Button B kiosks weren't introduced until the year after Poppy uses one, and the island had no telephone exchange until the year after that), and with holding the Isle of Skye Highland Games on a Tuesday (today the Gathering takes place on a Wednesday).

Any mistakes are my own.

Copyeditor

Gabbie Chant

Proofreader

Lynne Walker

Marketing

Alex Crow
Melanie Price
Occy Carr
Cíara Rosney
Martyna Młynarska

Operations and distribution

Marina Valles
Stephanie Straub
Joe Morris

Production

Hannah Snetsinger
Mandy Kullar
Ria Clare
Nadia Michael

Publicity

Kim Nash
Noelle Holten
Jess Readett
Sarah Hardy

Rights and contracts

Peta Nightingale
Richard King
Saidah Graham

Dear Reader,

We'd love your attention for one more page to tell you about the crisis in children's reading, and what we can all do.

Studies have shown that reading for fun is the **single biggest predictor of a child's future life chances** – more than family circumstance, parents' educational background or income. It improves academic results, mental health, wealth, communication skills, ambition and happiness.

The number of children reading for fun is in rapid decline. Young people have a lot of competition for their time, and a worryingly high number do not have a single book at home.

Hachette works extensively with schools, libraries and literacy charities, but here are some ways we can all raise more readers:

- Reading to children for just 10 minutes a day makes a difference
- Don't give up if children aren't regular readers – there will be books for them!

- Visit bookshops and libraries to get recommendations
- Encourage them to listen to audiobooks
- Support school libraries
- Give books as gifts

There's a lot more information about how to encourage children to read on our websites: **www.RaisingReaders.co.uk** and **www.JoinRaisingReaders.com**.

Thank you for reading.

www.ingramcontent.com/pod-product-compliance
Lightning Source LLC
Chambersburg PA
CBHW030533190726
48283CB00006B/1891

9 781836 184652